Also by Katie Golding

T0022834

WRECKLESS

KATIE GOLDING

sourcebooks
casablanca

Published by Sourcebooks Casablanca, an imprint of Sourcebooks
P.O. Box 4410, Naperville, Illinois 60567-4410
(630) 961-3900
sourcebooks.com

Printed and bound in the United States of America.
POD

For my husband—I remain your biggest fan.
Wanna battle?

Chapter 1

Lorelai Hargrove—March; Doha, Qatar

THIRD GEAR.

The cool night air screams past me as I downshift in my approach to turn fourteen, a hard right corner on the Losail International track. A smile rushes across my lips as my Dabria lies deep into the tighter-than-tight turn, my knee scraping the Qatar track rippling past my helmet.

I tuck in my elbow and control my breathing, harnessing all my anticipation into crisp, unbridled focus. Twenty-one laps down, two turns to go, and then I will fly over the finish line: the first woman in history to win a race in Moto Grand Prix. The first woman ever to race in MotoPro. And all I have to do is what I've done for ten years: beat Massimo to the finish line.

Fourth gear. I tilt my bike vertical and charge toward the sharp left of fifteen. Fifth gear. Sixth. Golden dust flashes on my right, black pavement and gray bailout gravel rushing by my left. The stars of Doha are sparkling above me, but the stadium lights of Losail lead the way—a lit path on the dark track guiding me home to the checkered flag, riding the glory rained down on me from the thousands of screaming fans I can't hear over my engine.

They want it—for me to win—and I can't wait to give it to them. *Time to deal with Massimo.*

I fade left, forcing my oldest rival farther inside the lane than he wants to be. As far as I'm concerned, that's what he gets. Massimo peeks at me over his shoulder, and I don't care how sexy his stubble is. Today is the day I'm going to make history.

Fifth gear. Fourth. Third, and lean.

My body lies flat, my bike flexing under ruthless speed and gravity pulling it further down. It takes everything I have to stifle the primal fear that wants to creep in, screaming how I'm going to crash and die because I'm going too fast to hold it. There's too much speed, too much weight, and the laws of physics don't mean crap, because they don't exist.

I swallow the lies and bury them under the truth: even though looming death is on my left, my body is caught in the middle of a love-and-war affair between gravity and centrifugal force, and it's the only place I want to be. But when I lean harder into the turn, Massimo's blue chassis and front tire are all I can see around the curve, blocking my view of the finish line. And I'm *sick* of him taking my finish line.

His right knee is closer to my helmet than my own gloves, the space between us growing dangerously closer. When I check, I'm clear to move: there's at least a four-second gap between us and the rest of the field.

See ya, sucker...

With the first hint of victory swirling through me, I let off the accelerator so I can duck around behind Massimo. He should push dangerously right, but the jerk slows down with me. I curse in my helmet and speed up, over the games and ready to secure my win. He stays with me, then starts to drift outside and directly into my left knee and elbow. He's out of the apex and taking me with him.

I'm already calculating my options, none of them good. Once again, he's risking my win, my bike, and my life. It's crap like this that made me realize it doesn't matter how intoxicating his smile is. The cold truth is we both need to win more than anything else, and if he's going for the kill every chance he gets, so am I.

I can't afford to downshift into second gear and lose any more speed to get around him. Hard way it is. Gritting my teeth, I hold the turn, my arms and abs bellowing in anguish from the G forces, but I refuse to cower. I won't drift farther right and toward the gravel bailout. I know I can hold it...

My heartbeat thuds in my ears, my breathing fast and increasing. Blue paint and black tires are inching closer to my bright red fairings, and survival instincts tell me that if I don't move over in the next half second, he's going to hit me and crash me out, and... *Shit!*

I let off the accelerator or risk losing it all, my engine slowing as I careen right, my tires bumping on the curbstone and the bike wobbling in the gravel. My breath cascades into my lungs as I grapple for control, my reflexes throwing a glance to my left to make sure I won't run over Massimo and kill him. He should be sliding on the ground in front of me. Maybe tumbling down the dark pavement. There's no way he held that turn at that speed when he was so far out of the apex. Except when I look, Massimo's gone.

He's just freaking *gone*.

A roar rises from the stands as my head whips forward, and blue paint is meters ahead. He didn't crash, somehow pulling off that screwed-up apex without hitting the gravel.

I swerve back onto the racetrack, my determination screaming as I shift up fast from third gear to fourth. Massimo's transmission roars deep in sixth, and his helmet peeks over his shoulder. When he sees the space between us on the last straightaway, the asshole pops a freaking wheelie as he takes the win.

The stands explode, booming his name as green, white, and red flags billow from every direction. Television cameras rise on cranes as fireworks light up the night sky, and I curse where no one but me can hear it, soaring across the finish line behind him two seconds too late.

Bye-bye, history. And first place.

―――ᴠᴠ―――

I step down off the podium, squinting from the lights and my cheeks hurting from smiling as I pump my silver trophy in one hand and a bottle of champagne in the other. A new wall of screams erupts from the fans in the stadium, all shouting every translation of congratulations while waving signs with my name and picture and #77.

The whole place is a massive party waiting to explode. It always is after the night race in Qatar: the first Grand Prix of the nineteen-race circuit that takes us all over the world from March to November. There's also nothing quite like the capital city of Doha—spicy desert air, the hum of Arabic tickling your veins as you sit in traffic, staring up at a skyline that beats New York any freaking day of the week. Especially at night, when the buildings are lit up so the world is a neon rainbow reflected in the Persian Gulf.

It's a hell of an upgrade from my family's ranch in Memphis, where the horses are treated like kings and farmhands come and go like seasonal allergies. But partying in Doha isn't an option for me when my diet is on lockdown, I've got a plane to catch for the next race, and really, I'm counting the minutes till the cameras are off me so I can cry in private over my first MotoPro loss.

Everyone expected me to win this one. Which I know because they didn't have a problem telling me beforehand—my mom, my dad, even Billy King. The reigning World Champion's ankle is still healing from his brush with a bull, and he whispered to me on our flight from Memphis that I need to enjoy every minute of Qatar. Because after that, he would be fine and was coming for me. But taking advantage of Billy being slow didn't even matter when Massimo was still too fast.

After one last wave, a smile and flirty wink to the crowd, I head toward the door that leads to the pit boxes where our crews will meet us. I tuck my trophy under my arm to haul it open. But I get knocked aside when Santos Saucedo brushes past me, whistling his way down the hall with his third-place trophy propped on his shoulder. Jerk.

I follow him into the hall, the sounds of the crowd and the stadium disappearing behind the door. Even though I shouldn't, I drink deeply from my bottle of champagne. I knew it wouldn't be easy to be a woman in the racing world. I certainly didn't expect the guys to take turns braiding my hair between practice and qualifying sessions. But I never expected the ostracizing to last all the way from the Rookie Cups to MotoPro.

"Lulu," an Italian accent drawls behind me, and I lengthen my strides away from the worst of them. It doesn't do me any good. Two seconds later, I have Massimo in my face. Then he drops to his knees.

My patience is already nil and quickly creeping into the negative as Massimo smiles up at me with his arms outstretched, the champagne we sprayed on the podium still sparkling in his black hair: shaved brutally short on the sides, long and thick on top, and all slicked back in that weird Italian bouffant thing.

He's been wearing the same bad haircut since we were fifteen, and I refuse to tell him. It's the best running joke I can think of. Although it'd probably be a lot funnier if he didn't pull the look off so well, balanced against the controlled stubble darkening his cheeks and nearly black around the line of his jaw.

Taryn swears I called him "damn hot" one night when she and I went swimming in a bottle of tequila. But I have no memory of saying that, and I'm betting she made it up just to mess with me. She knows that is not—and never will be—an option.

"Marry me, Lorina," Massimo says in his thick Italian accent. I roll my eyes, so not in the mood for his crap right now. This is no less than the fifth time he's done this. Usually, he's drunk, but sometimes, his wins pull out his proposals. Like beating me to the flag is the way to get me to the altar. Yeah, okay. "Today is the best day of my life. Marry me."

I shrug, wondering if there's a path of least resistance here that I haven't tried before. "Yeah, all right."

His smile stretches wider. "Sì?"

"No!"

I walk around him, but he's back in an instant. Guess that didn't work. "Why are you always so difficult, Tigrotta?" He leans closer, whispering, "You know you love me."

I elbow him out of my personal space, tucking my trophy under my arm and turning to face him. He's still freaking smiling as I jam my finger into the front of his leathers. The plate underneath protecting his lungs and ribs is like a block of cement, and I wonder if his heart beneath is made out of the same stuff. "How could you do that to me today? I don't care what the win is. We aren't supposed to try to hurt each other."

His dark eyes flash and burn a little more fiercely, a dangerous smile curving his lips. Like that's supposed to scare me. "No?"

I push my finger harder into his chest even though it makes my knuckle ache and he probably can't even feel it. "No." Of all the people I figured would wager a win against my life and still dive for the flag, I never expected it from him. He knows what it's cost me to be here, how hard I've had to fight to be on the grid beside him. "You crossed the line, Massimo."

He swallows, but he doesn't apologize. He never has, whether I deserved to hear his "Mi dispiace" or not. I grit out a frustrated huff and storm around him. I'm barely past his shoulder when he snatches my hand, tugging me back into his chest.

My eyes fly wide, adrenaline from the race still pumping strongly in my veins and surging even faster at the regret sinking the corner of his mouth. I check around for anyone else in the hallway who could report to the world that one of Moto Grand Prix's most talked about rivalries filters a little differently behind closed doors. But luckily, or maybe not, we're completely alone.

Massimo's grip on my hand loosens to just a gentle press of his palm covering mine, keeping the back of my hand flat against his leathers. It's too much—how close he is, how his eyes seem to peer straight through me and see it's not the loss making my eyes want to prickle with betrayal. It's the fact that he thought five points were worth me possibly ending up broken in the hospital, never able to race again.

Stay focused, Hargrove.

"Well?" I do my best to keep my voice steady under the intensity of his stare, his bottle of champagne dangling forgotten in his other hand and his trophy gone, possibly on the floor. "Are you going to apologize to me or not?"

"You want me to apologize for crossing a line? Sì, it is true. I did, Lorina, and I will not lie to you and say I did not."

His grip on my hand tightens, and my eyes drop to where he has them secured against his chest. His personally crafted version of my first name isn't new, nor is the softness in my chest when he says it. But when he leans forward to whisper in my ear, his lips are so close that I can almost feel his stubble scrape my cheek, and I'm no longer the fearless moto racer from fifteen minutes ago. I am now completely frozen.

Talking is one thing. Whispering, alone, while he's holding my hand, is another.

"I crossed the line," he breathes, and a shiver I'm not proud of trembles through me. "I crossed the finish line, first."

I reel back, my gaze narrowed as Massimo puckers a kiss at me. I snatch my hand away from him, Massimo throwing his head back in laughter as he turns, striding down the rest of the hallway. Once he's a few steps away, I pick up the tattered shreds of my dignity and stuff them back into my racing boots, carrying me down the hall behind him.

I should be used to it by now: his jokes that aren't funny, his pranks that only serve to piss me off. But it still hurts.

As soon as we're in pit lane, Massimo's manager and crew rush over to hug him while screaming victory accolades in Italian. Basically treating him like the God's gift to racing he thinks he is. So he won here at Qatar—big deal. There are eighteen races left in the circuit, and the competition is far from over.

Heading into my garage, I leave Massimo for where my own crew is waiting by my bike. It helps a lot that Billy and his younger brother, Mason—my Dabria teammate—have left their own pit boxes and are waiting to congratulate me. We may be competitors on Sundays, but Billy and Mason stumbled into their racing careers as farmhands on my mom's ranch. So it's kinda nice to have their country accents around when we're traveling in Europe so much.

"Lori, gimme some sugar, girl!" our manager, Frank, bellows before he runs over to wrap me in a hug, even though I probably smell like pure Pennzoil.

When I pull back, I give him a sweet smile as I hand him my trophy. "You know your old gut can't handle no sugar."

Frank bursts out laughing as he drops a kiss to my forehead. He turns to the King brothers and my other crew members, already busy passing around my trophy.

"Hell of a race, Lorelai," Billy says in a drawl that's thicker than my leathers. He tips his Yaalon-covered cowboy hat at me before he ducks off to a corner of my pit box, his cell phone permanently pressed to his ear. He's been that way ever since he and Taryn got back together, but at least she seems happier. For now.

"He isn't kidding," Mason adds, holding out his hand. I clasp it in mine, my teammate's crystal-blue eyes still alive from the battle on the track that landed him in fifth place to my second. He pulls me in for a bro hug, the only one who ever does, reeking of sweat and cologne over the faintest trace of whiskey. "Hope no one breaks the news to Massimo that we're still getting the kinks worked out of the engines."

I laugh, loving the way he thinks, and I lean back to point at him. "I won't say a word if you don't."

Mason scrunches up his face at me under his cowboy hat, the picture of innocence. "A word about what?" He winks and lets me go, probably to go bug his brother. Fine by me. There's one other hug I need before we head home to Memphis for the two long weeks before we race in Argentina.

Nudging my way past my constructor and crew, I head for my bike and our customary postrace ritual. I squeeze her tight, petting her fairings and thanking her for keeping me safe until an unmistakable whistle catches my attention.

I rise and turn to find Massimo leaning against the open door of my garage, the strangest look on his face like he wants to try to smile, to talk to me again, but can't decide whether he should. I'd *almost* bet my bike it's because even though he just messed with me, the truth is, he's not-so-secretly worried about the damage the near hit caused to our *already* strained relationship.

He'd never admit it, but he really can't seem to stay away from me. Which wouldn't be the worst thing in the world except that he also doesn't know how to apologize for the crap he does. He's probably never apologized for anything in his life.

The part that kills me is that as angry as I get, I can't really claim any innocence in this situation. I've gone after him too. Attacked him too. Even though there have been so many times when I thought there could be something more between us than just rivalry. At the very least, I wondered if somehow, someday, we could be friends.

"All right, Lori," Frank says, shaking hands with my crew. "You about ready to hit the road, girl? I need to get you and Billy and Mason to the airport. Oh," he adds, "Taryn called to say, and I quote, 'Way to go, bitch.'"

I snort at my best friend's message, wondering when she hung up with Billy long enough to leave it for me. But I can't seem to muster more of a response than that. Because without saying anything, Massimo sets down a clean, white towel at the entrance to my garage. When he straightens, dark eyes locked with mine, I cross my arms and stand a little taller. It's not the apology I want, not by a long shot, but it'll do for now.

The smile he was restraining breaks free, and with nothing more, he turns and heads the other direction, leaving me to wonder what words would have come from him if we were alone instead of surrounded by the watchful eyes of hundreds of thousands of fans, on top of the ever-nosy press.

Mostly because the younger, naive part of me wants to hold close the idea that this silent, private ritual—the clean white cotton, soft, carefully folded, and laid at my door—is the safest language in which he can communicate that he'd never try to hurt me. However, the twenty-five-year-old professional racer me says I also don't need him to tell me to brush myself off and keep going. Not to get discouraged just because today, he beat me to the checkered flag.

I've been doing this as long as he has, and I don't need his help.

Frank's massive barbecue-filled frame knocks into me, shaking me into awareness. I chuckle as his arm comes around my shoulders, squeezing tight. "You okay?"

I nod absently. But really, I'm still wondering if Massimo's white towel of truce would carry the scent of him. That familiar spicy sweetness of exhaust and that stuff he puts in his hair. The aroma that's never been far and I'm drawn to breathe more deeply than I should... It's as comforting as a promise from my crew, as familiar as a scolding from my conscience.

"Yep," I tell Frank. "Just thinking about that apex in sixteen." And whether Massimo would've had nightmares about me dying on the way to the hospital if he'd crashed me out. The way I did when he wrecked in the Netherlands last year.

"Aw, don't sweat it, Lori. You'll get it next time." Frank winks, then hollers over my shoulder, "Boys, hit the showers." He gives me another pardoning smile, steering us out of the garages and toward our respective RVs so we can at least shower and change before we leave for the airport.

"Yeah, honey," Billy rumbles a few feet behind me. "Should be home soon, in plenty of time to make your dad's work thing. Oh yeah? What'd he do—Taryn! Stop letting Dax do that. I don't care. It's my horse, Dax is a hired hand, and I made it very clear that Gidget—*carrots*?"

"Uh-oh," Mason mutters, snickering.

As Billy keeps whining on the phone about his beloved stallion, I glance over my shoulder at my bike, like I always do when I have to leave her between cities. At that towel, left where Massimo laid it.

It was only six weeks after the Netherlands that Massimo came back to the circuit following his biggest wreck to date, and the nightmares eventually stopped. I've come back after my own crashes, and I'm sure I would've even if I had crashed today. The extra weight of my chest and back plates on my body, the restriction of my elbow and knee sliders, and the imprint on my chin from the strap of my helmet say so.

But after all the races, all the close calls, and all the times I've challenged him…

After all the almosts and all the fights, all the times when I've wondered and hoped and had those dreams come crashing down…

After ten years of racing against Massimo, I have to accept the truth: it's too late for anything to change.

GRAND PRIX OF QATAR
Doha, Sunday, March 10

Pos	Pts	Rider	Time	World Rank
1	25	Massimo VITOLO	42'36.634	25
2	20	Lorelai HARGROVE	+2.169	20
3	16	Santos SAUCEDO	+4.976	16
4	13	Billy KING	+5.865	13
5	11	Mason KING	+7.138	11
6	10	Cristiano ARELLANO	+9.653	10
7	9	Giovanni MARCHESA	+11.223	9
8	8	Elliston LAMBIRTH	+11.598	8
9	7	Harleigh ELIN	+12.214	7
10	6	Deven HORSLEY	+13.365	6
11	5	Gregorio PAREDES	+14.732	5
12	4	Aurelio LOGGIA	+17.998	4
13	3	Fredek SULZBACH	+18.244	3
14	2	Donato MALDONADO	+21.685	2
15	1	Diarmaid DEAN	+23.463	1
16		Galeno GIRÓN	+28.258	
17		Timo GONZALES	+30.511	
18		Rainier HERRE	+42.113	
19		Gustavo LIMÓN	+45.769	
20		Cesaro SOTO	+53.886	

Chapter 2

Massimo Vitolo—March; Ravenna, Italy

I DRUMROLL MY HANDS ON THE KITCHEN TABLE, SO WOUND UP you'd think I was at a friend's stag party instead of a fourteen-year-old's birthday. But I can't wait for Dario to open his present from me. He's gonna love it, and I've been dying for this moment since the minute I crossed the finish line in Qatar. Snaking Lorina's first MotoPro win just made it all the sweeter—a glorious payback for her winning our teenaged debut at the Blue Gator Rookie Cups.

"Open mine next," I rattle off to my little brother in Italian, jerking my chin in the direction of the box I wrapped myself, Chiara's help not included. The rest of our table is a mess of playing cards, board games, half-drunk drinks, and dirty plates that I was supposed to clear but haven't yet. Don't really plan on it either.

"You are so bossy," my mom scolds. I wave her off as she tucks her silver-streaked hair behind her ear, then begins the process of checking on all the food she's got simmering on the stove and baking in the oven.

She's a symphony conductor in the way she lifts lids and stirs and smells and sprinkles in random herbs. I nearly groan out loud at the heavenly aroma of baccalà alla vesuviana, linguine with mussels, crab cioppino, and lasagna with anchovies—my absolute favorite. My brother's too. Pretty sure I also saw some chilled oysters in the fridge when I grabbed a bottle of water earlier, and I'm *starving*. No way is Vinicio gonna let me eat half of what I want, though.

"It's Dario's birthday." My mom straightens and closes the oven, looking at me like she's ready to stuff me in there next to the lasagna if I don't watch it. "Let him open the presents he wants."

But my little brother is already reaching his whole upper body out of his wheelchair and across the kitchen table for the box I happily knock closer into his hands. "What did you get me? New PS5? A Nintendo Switch?"

"It's socks, I swear to God." I start helping him unwrap his present with as much enthusiasm as him, my mother incessantly yelling at me to let him do it himself.

"No way!" Dario yells when we finally get the paper off. He holds up the box containing the VR headset he's been watching endless reviews for. According to his YouTube history anyway.

"This was the one, yeah?"

He nods quickly, his eyes as big as his smile as I proudly pop the tab and take out the headset I made sure to charge before I wrapped it.

"Check this out, man." I hand it to him and reach over to tap the screen, but nothing happens. "It's already got the new Moto Grand Prix game app downloaded, so you can ride with me on the track. Even battle me if you want."

Dario carefully turns over the VR in his hands, his smile going from genuine to forced before he clears his throat. "Massimo, this is really cool but…it doesn't work like that. You have to download the game app onto a phone that you hook in. And mine…it's too old. It won't work for this."

"Oh yeah, that's right." I frown at Dario like I screwed this all up.

My best friend, Chiara, snorts behind him, propped against the windows and eternally driving my mom nuts by wearing a Starfleet

Academy T-shirt, black suspenders, and a pair of my old jeans that she decorated with nail polish and then attacked with a straight razor.

She shakes her head at me, fighting a smile behind her pursed lips. She's been giving me that look since we were six and she'd bust me sneaking extra communion crackers when the priest wasn't looking. But I've never been able to keep secrets from her. Or behave in church.

"What?" I say to her, then slip the new phone from my shirt pocket and *gently* toss it down in front of my brother. "Happy birthday."

He scrambles to pick up the new mobile phone. "Is this the—"

"Yep."

"Thanks, man!" he shouts, reaching toward me. I laugh and get up to hug him, soaking up the way he still leans his head on my shoulder and clings to my shirt before he pushes me off, his fingers already busy flying over the massive screen.

"Massimo," Chiara quietly chides, but I don't care what I spent on my brother. He deserves it, and as far as he's concerned, our family can afford it. Me, the successful moto star, most of all.

Dario doesn't remember the third-floor shoebox flat that my mom and my dad and I lived in before here. My father bought this house when I was about five, and Dario has only ever known a world on the first floor—four bedrooms, decent kitchen, basement, garage, a small balcony into the garden, and all of it on a quiet street where neighbors know each other.

He remembers that Dad had a moto shop but never asks why we don't own it anymore. He knows Mom works too many shifts at the hospital as a nurse, is probably about to trade in her car soon, and our stepfather, Vinicio, draws a healthy manager's salary from my racing career.

Dario has everything he needs, whenever he needs it, and that's all he needs to know.

"Now open Vinicio's," Chiara says, Dario already reaching toward a long wrapped tube that better not contain what I think it does. Our stepfather looks over from where he's busy flirting with our mother in the kitchen, both of them still swooning over each other like they're teenagers every minute that Vinicio and I are home.

Could be worse. The guys she dated before him were complete dicks—some after her money, some after my fame. But Vinicio has known my family's secrets since before he was helping cover them up, and he's always been good to Dario. More patient than he is with me. But it was easier to take his racing advice when he wasn't sleeping here.

At least Dad liked him, trusted him. But Dad liked everyone.

"Hope you like it, buddy," Vinicio says to Dario. He winks, raising his wineglass from where he's standing next to my mother, his arm around her waist. Then he looks at me, chuckling as he takes a deep pull.

The hell is that about?

I look to my mom, but she just arches an eyebrow, the sharp angles of her jaw and cheekbones challenging me to say anything. Then she downshifts into peppy and energetic. "What did you get, baby?" She slips away from Vinicio, grabbing her phone from the counter and preparing to take probably a hundred pictures. Dario starts ripping open the paper on his present with enough force that the paper shreds get tangled in the cords of his oxygen concentrator.

"Easy, man." I chuckle, reaching over to clear the mess as Chiara picks up the rest behind him. But Dario's still going after the tube with the same focus I have on the track.

"Yes!" he shouts when he's got the wrapper off, thrusting the poster in the air. When he unravels it, his face explodes in even more excitement as he screams, "Thank you, Vinicio!"

"What the fuck!" I shout right after him, gesturing to the giant poster of Lorina in her Dabria leathers posing like she's Rosie the Riveter.

Her leathers are so sinfully *red*. Her brand name down her arm so irritatingly sexy, all with that look in her eyes like she can't wait to kick my ass on the track and we both know she can. I am never gonna get this image unburned from my eyes, for a bunch of good reasons and a whole bunch of bad ones.

"Massimo," my mother scolds, still snapping pictures of Dario's ecstatic face. Chiara cracks up laughing, and this *cannot* be happening.

"This is the brand-new one that just came out," Dario says, his eyes gorging on every pixel of the image before him. It's only from her hips up, but with the way she's twisting and holding her flexed bicep, she takes up the whole damn paper. "No one is gonna have this one yet and—it's signed! Oh my God, it's signed!" He lets out a noise I didn't think the men in my family were capable of. I wince, wiggling my finger in my ear. "She actually freaking signed it!"

I glare at Vinicio, cracking up in my kitchen. "You're welcome, buddy. I'm glad you like it." He crosses over and leans down to hug Dario, my brother bouncing with joy as my mother captures the moment to remember for all time, and I hate my life. Bunch of traitors.

"Open mine next." Chiara points at the suspiciously red box in front of my brother.

"I swear to God," I say under my breath, but she still read my lips and bursts out laughing even harder, doing a little victory dance that all but confirms whatever is in there is Dabria themed. Not Yaalon.

"Can't." Dario pushes Vinicio away, lays the poster on his lap, then shoves his chair back from the table and flies across the kitchen, down the ramp, and zooms down the hallway toward his bedroom, cutting the apex perfectly. "I gotta hang this up!"

I shake my head, looking over the VR headset and brand new mobile phone forgotten on the table. Chiara mockingly pouts at me, collecting the rest of the trash and balling it up before she throws it away. "Oh, suck it up, star. Did you really expect any different? She's been his favorite racer for years, and that's not changing."

"Wish it would." My mom swipes through the pictures she just took before she locks her phone, her jaw, and then her arms across her chest.

"It's fine." I wave her off instantly, despite half of me still being irritated about it. It's not a new fascination, but it makes things infinitely more frustrating when her face is all over his bedroom. "He can like her."

"Well, I don't." She goes into the kitchen like that's the end of the conversation.

Vinicio sets down his wineglass, reaching out a hand toward her shoulder. "Maria."

She shakes him off at the same time as Chiara warns, "Massimo…" but I'm already up from the table, halfway there.

"Why not?" I ask my mother's back, not buying her sudden need to organize the folded hand towels in the drawer next to the stove. "What's she done that's so terrible?"

Mom slams the drawer shut, no one in the kitchen breathing. Her bedside manner has won her awards, but when she pivots to face me, all I see in her eyes is the same iron will I have. Fighting the fatigue I'm sure she's feeling after working a double—though she never, ever complains about being tired. "She dives for you. And I don't have to like anyone who endangers my son."

"It's what we do." Every word is slow, strangled as I fight to keep from snapping at my mother. "Everyone dives for everyone. That's racing."

She doesn't budge, doesn't blink, and she and I both know that isn't the real reason she has a problem with Lorina. But we can't fight about the truth until I give her a reason, and I'm not going to. Not yet.

My phone dings loudly in my pocket, and my mom throws her hand up like that's my fault, turning away and grabbing Vinicio's wineglass. I sigh and pull my phone out to read the text message from the number I was half expecting but still detest with every bone in my body.

You're late.

My eyes meet Chiara's over my shoulder, and she already knows what's happening, why I'm shoving my phone into my pocket with more irritation than should be able to fit inside my body. I walk away from my scowling mother and head to the opposite kitchen counter where Chiara's purse is set.

"Seriously," she says, not bothering to stop me when she comes up to my side. I'm already digging through the pockets, trying to find her car keys. "Now?"

"Yes. Now."

"Massimo," my mom complains behind me, "we haven't even eaten yet. You know how much your brother looks forward to you being here for—"

"I'm already late, and if I'm any later, I'm going to have to—"

"Okay, okay!" she concedes, but only because she can't hear me say it. We allude to it, but we don't outright discuss it, because I don't think she likes the fact that she agreed. But it was my idea to sacrifice myself so that she and Dario were safe, and I'm not debating it with her anymore. It's done.

Chiara is another battle.

"You know, it's a really, *really* bad day when I have to pretend to be the responsible one," she whispers. At least we're out of range of my mother, currently frowning at her husband as Vinicio rubs her arms and shoulders, quietly saying something to her I can't make out. "But I know what you're doing, Massimo, and you're paying him off too fast. Like you're counting on win bonuses from races you haven't even run yet."

"Where are your keys?" I've been through every pocket, every nook, and I can't find them anywhere. No way could she have lost them already.

Chiara reaches behind her and holds them up with a derisive smirk, dangling them in front of me. "What I really can't believe is that it was your terrible idea instead of mine for once." I reach for the keys, and she yanks them back, her voice going sharp. "You do realize you're doing exactly what he did, and you're risking us now?"

"You're fine." I turn toward my stepfather, my mother avoiding my presence as she opens the oven and checks inside again. Vinicio digs in his pocket and tosses me a set of keys, and I'm out of here. He knows I have to do this, that every single person in this house is at risk if I don't. We already lost the shop over this. There won't *be* a house for them if I don't go right now.

It's three short steps to the door to the garage, to Vinicio's moto, and three different voices saying my name behind me: "Massimo..."

The third one stops me in place, so much regret slamming through my veins that I'm nearly sick with it. I look back at my little brother, disappointment painting his face until it hardens in an icy stare. "Bye."

His voice is deeper than it was the last time I was home, and it kills me that I'm hurting the person who least deserves it. But I can't bring myself to tell him why I have to go. If everything goes according to plan, he'll never have to worry about this kind of stuff. He'll never know how close he was to it his whole childhood.

"Happy birthday, Brother." I offer him a smile, but he doesn't return it.

With one angry push of his arm, he propels his wheelchair out of the room. Probably to go break the phone I got him. But I can still give him this. I head out into the garage, resigning myself to what this is gonna cost me, in all the different ways that keep adding up.

Grabbing my helmet and my jacket from the pegboard on the wall, I thread my arms through the sleeves before I take out my phone and hook in my earbuds. Cue up my Tedua playlist, then slide on my helmet and swing my leg over Vinicio's moto. The engine starts with a throaty growl that matches my mood, and it's only another few seconds before I'm pulling out of the garage and onto the street where I first learned how to ride a moto. And how much it hurts when you wreck one.

Our oldest neighbor waves at me from where he's watering his garden, the rest of the area quiet but still lined with parked cars. I dodge a few opening doors as I merge out of my mother's neighborhood and onto the highway that curves around my city, and it won't be long now.

Trying to stay calm, I ride the beats and rhythm of the music playing through my earbuds, and I relax into the come and go of the lazy Ravenna traffic. Flip up my face shield, but the nearby sea is barely more than a taste of salt on the wind. I sit back, steering with my knees and reaching my hands out toward the buildings stretching above me: old pizzerias and new nail salons, petrol stations and bookshops. But they're not as tall as the stadiums of Argentina, of Austin, of Jerez. The world is too quiet, too—the endless homes packed into the circular echoes of the heart of the city eerily silent.

Soon, though, the houses and businesses will carry something else between them. Baptisteries. Opera houses. Basilicas. Mausoleums. More echoes, but of another time—like my father's moto shop, coming up on my left, and now a high-end furniture store.

I avert my eyes as I pull off into an alley, slowing for the foot traffic as I approach the piazza. People are strolling, some riding bicycles, most unwinding at the restaurant tables lining half of the cobblestone side street. I'm not really supposed to ride my moto through here, but it's faster.

"Hey, look! Go, Massimo!" someone calls from one of the tables, followed by a few whistles and a spattering of claps—a quiet purr of the beast that only really comes to life in grand stadiums. Still, I pump my fist as I cruise by to a growing cheer from my hometown fans.

They're on their feet by the time I hit the end of the alley, drawing the attention of not just the whole piazza but also the cops walking around. *Shit.* The local police love me for all the wrong reasons, and if they stop me, they're searching me. And I can't get searched with what's in my back pocket.

I flip down my face shield and pop my clutch through the turn, easily doubling the speed limit as I cut through one alley, then another, checking to make sure I lost the cops and the trail of fans before I slow down, circling back. I'm a couple of blocks away from the piazza but not far enough with the way it's already bristling with life, not that it ever really stops.

A few businesses down from where I'm headed, I finally find a spot to park. Across from a brand-new Maserati GranCabrio that's practically got my name on it, and the ride here was not long enough to prepare me for this. But it never is. I cut off my moto's engine, the sound sucking out of the world. Kill my playlist, too, reminding myself to stay in control. But *fuck* this guy.

My helmet is heavy in my hand the whole walk across the street and into the building for my accountant, his receptionist looking up at me from her desk—all smooth dark-brown skin and a warm, inviting smile because she hasn't worked for her dick of a boss long enough to realize she should've quit already. "He's waiting for you, Mr. Vitolo."

I nod politely, not trusting my voice to say more than a stuttered, "Thanks." His receptionists are the only ones who ever call me that. And it feels so freaking weird when my father is the whole reason I'm even here, but she doesn't know that.

I don't bother knocking. I blow through the closed office door, hoping to startle the hell out of Gabriele. But the prick is the picture of peace: stretched casually back in the tufted leather chair behind his desk, his arms laced behind his graying head, and not a single wrinkle in his custom-made suit. "Massimo," he oozes out, his hands extending toward me and cuff links sparkling under the light of vintage lamps. "My favorite client."

I shut the door, my temper threatening to get the best of me as I sit across from him. But I blow out a long stream of air through my nose, trying to harness the calm focus instilled in me by years of moto training—the mental game separating the simply fast from the professionals.

Gabriele leans forward at an antique desk that looks like he swiped it from Buckingham Palace. Then he starts moving his hand over a fancy mouse to an even fancier computer, and I hate him. So much.

"Let's see where we're at, yeah?" He nods at me like he doesn't already know exactly how much of my father's debts are still overdue and how much I owe Gabriele just for the simple, *illegal* act of moving the estate from my mother's name into my own.

But after everything I'd done to try to save the shop—failing in the end—I couldn't stand it when they tried to take the house. I couldn't look at my brother and tell him the only home he's ever known was no longer his. And it wasn't fair to my mom; what did she do besides trust my father and then lose him?

I still can't bring myself to blame him for the mess of his estate: the debts, the taxes, how far behind it got, and so fast. I know it wasn't all his fault. But it wasn't my mother's fault either. And it wasn't fair to Dario.

So I bribed Gabriele to move the estate and all the debt to me, and he's been bleeding me dry under the table for the privilege ever since.

"Okay, so with the garnishment from your last race—congratulations, by the way—plus the additional amount you just put toward the principle, this is what you still owe." He turns the screen toward me, and I scoff heartily. I hoped that moving up to MotoPro would help, but I barely moved the needle at all. "Interest," he says with a smirk, like it's a joke. "But keep winning races, and we probably won't be seeing that much more of each other. Could be done by the end of this season maybe."

"That's my plan."

He stiffens a little, the mortgage on his wife's vacation villa in Lake Como and the payment on the sports car outside probably feeling a lot heavier than they did a moment ago. "Well, I'm rooting for you, buddy." He grins and points at me, but the movements are all jerky, and it makes me feel a fucking ton better that he's already sweating over what he's gonna do when the money I risk my life for is no longer his discretionary fund.

"Thanks," I bite out, a sharp smile right behind it. I slam my helmet down on his desk, and Gabriele jumps this time. I slowly rise, pulling a folded envelope from my back pocket and tossing it onto his desk.

He glances toward the wall where his receptionist sits on the other side, young and beautiful and painfully unaware. He takes the envelope, peeking inside and thumbing through the thick stack of bills. When he's finished counting, he slides the envelope into his top desk drawer before looking up at me with a grin. "Was glad to hear from my nephew the other day. Says he's really enjoying the circuit so far."

I tilt my head at the taunt. Getting his nephew a job on my pit crew is only the latest perk he's squeezed out of my career. Payback for his discovery that I have Chiara on my payroll as my social media manager slash personal stylist.

The garnishment was taking nearly everything I had, and with Gabriele taking all that was left, I needed a way to hide *some* money or we were gonna end up on the freaking streets. Gabriele was furious. He can't touch anything in Chiara's name, and he spooked hard at the idea of being caught by the authorities. But Chiara isn't going to report him, and at least his nephew knows his way around a moto, which I made sure of before I officially requested him.

"Remember," Gabriele warns, his voice dropping. "This stays between us. Not a word to him or anyone else from here on about our arrangement, or I'm considering you in default."

Default. His private word for invalidating the forged estate rejection my mother signed years after legally allowed, and he filed to declare me the sole beneficiary. If that paper disappears, all the debts transfer back into my mother's name, and all her assets become subject to seizure: her car, her house, and my brother's whole sense of security.

"What's the matter, man?" I smirk at him. "It's not like you're doing anything wrong." I slide my helmet off his desk, directly into the picture of him and his wife on a yacht. The frame falls and crashes on the tile floor, and I throw open his office door and leave it gaping behind me, only slightly enjoying the mumbled curses flowing out of the room and the clatter of glass hitting a waste bin.

"Have a good night, Mr. Vitolo." The receptionist smiles, and I smile and nod back but forget her face as soon as I leave the building.

There's only one that matters at the end of all this.

I check around once I'm outside, but no one's close by or seemed to recognize me yet on the dark street. I walk down and spit on the door handle to Gabriele's car, then cross the street and slide on my helmet before I swing my leg over Vinicio's moto, everything in me ready to *go*.

As long as I keep playing this smart, there's no reason I shouldn't be finished with Gabriele by the time I take the checkered flag in Valencia. So Lorina better watch herself in Argentina, because I'm done fucking around.

GRAN PREMIO DE LA REPÚBLICA ARGENTINA
Termas de Río Hondo, Sunday, March 31

Pos	Pts	Rider	Time	World Rank
1	25	Billy KING	41'48.448	38
2	20	Lorelai HARGROVE	+1.013	40
3	16	Santos SAUCEDO	+1.853	32
4	13	Massimo VITOLO	+6.471	38
5	11	Cristiano ARELLANO	+8.652	21
6	10	Mason KING	+9.336	21
7	9	Deven HORSLEY	+12.710	15
8	8	Gregorio PAREDES	+15.916	13
9	7	Elliston LAMBIRTH	+17.068	15
10	6	Giovanni MARCHESA	+23.942	15
11	5	Aurelio LOGGIA	+26.381	9
12	4	Fredek SULZBACH	+29.883	7
13	3	Donato MALDONADO	+34.456	5
14	2	Harleigh ELIN	+39.262	9
15	1	Timo GONZALES	+44.198	1
16		Rainier HERRE	+48.349	0
17		Diarmaid DEAN	+52.489	1
Not Classified				
		Galeno GIRÓN	3 Laps	0
		Gustavo LIMÓN	15 Laps	0
		Cesaro SOTO	16 Laps	0

Chapter 3

"So get this," Taryn says from two stalls down, cleaning Gidget's while I do her mare's. Which really isn't fair, because Aston Magic is a way messier horse than Gidget, but everyone always assumes I don't like Billy's stallion. More like the Akhal-Teke has something against me—probably because Gidget can tell that the ranch life has never fit me as well as it was supposed to. Not like it fits Taryn. "Miette tried to convince me we were supposed to race on Bridgestone tires instead of Dunlop, and when I didn't go for it, she tried to pander some story to the press about how my parents were first cousins."

I crack half a smile, even though my heart and soul are locked away with my Dabria. She and Miette have been warring for as long as Taryn's been on the Superbike circuit, it seems. "Yeah?" I pull out the ultimate one-upper. "My toothpaste exploded in my suitcase on the way home and got all over my new Alice + Olivia sundress."

Taryn laughs and groans as I throw all my weight into the dig, my hands sweating in my gloves and my shoulders aching, abs straining. I keep my groan to myself as I heave the soiled straw into a wheelbarrow. The Memphis breeze kicks half of it back, sticking to my sweaty neck and tangling in my hair. I bat it away with a curse, only making things worse.

I *hate* doing ranch chores—cleaning horse stalls most of all. But Taryn asked me to hang out with her, and I really wanted to see all she's done with the ranch she and Billy just bought. Except my version of "hang out" looked a lot more like sitting on her porch with some curse word coloring books and maybe shopping online for new furniture. Or clothes. Not sifting through straw in search of horse manure.

"So how's MotoPro been?" Taryn calls down. "Seems like you're liking the cc jump. Mason definitely won't shut up about it every minute he's here and eating his way through my fridge."

"Pro's freaking awesome," I call back, taking a moment to lean on my muck rake and wipe the sweat from my brow. It's hot as hell in their barn, but at least there's a breeze through it. Does a doozy of mixing the smells, though, pushing them so far up your nostrils, it smells like your whole head is up a horse's ass. "I almost had Massimo in Qatar—like, I freaking had him—and I kicked his ass in Argentina."

I don't know what his problem was in Termas de Río Hondo. It was like he was possessed or something. Anytime a reporter asked him a question, they had to ask him twice, he was so focused on studying the track telemetry that was practically glued to his hand. Didn't really matter, though. Five laps to the flag, Billy checked him in turn seven; Massimo went wide, I cut through, and he never caught us after.

"Can't wait for COTA next week," I tell Taryn, my whole body wound tight with anticipation over our next showdown. "He has no idea what's coming for him."

Taryn laughs from her boyfriend's stallion's stall. "You realize I asked you about the power jump and you went straight to bitching about Massimo?"

"Shut up," I singsong, going back to work with more fervor.

There's not much more to do before I can wheelbarrow out the dirty straw and lay down some fresh. "Anyway, his style is totally different, so the Yaalon isn't working for him like it did for Francesco. But sucks for Massimo, because my style isn't that far from what Luca's was, so it's not that big of a deal to tweak the Dabria to work for me. We've almost got it perfect already too."

My new constructor is a genius and is somehow able to understand exactly what I need when I need it: more front end feel, more bite on the back end, when she's tight on the right turns and jelly in the lefts, *anything*. Every practice, every qualifying, every race, we get closer to finding that synergy between me and her, and it's so hard to be away.

After shoveling the last of the dirty straw into the wheelbarrow, I take a second to catch my breath, propping my muck rake against the side of the stall. It's not far to the dump pile behind their barn, but it feels a lot farther when you're barely tall enough to see over the pile. Guess it's a good thing Frank's been okay with me incorporating body building into my workout routine. He is still worried about the muscle weight gain, though.

I try to mentally silence the ten-year debate over my ideal diet and physique as I haul out the dirty straw, dump it, then bring in fresh and start to spread it out, avoiding the puddles of horse piss. And once more, I can't stop wondering what Taryn sees in all this. How it was worth it to turn down a condo in Munich paid for by MMW, instead dropping 2.5 *million dollars* on an eighty-acre ranch for her and Billy.

She swears she made the right choice for her in the end, though— staying in Superbike even while living in the States, kicking ass and taking trophies on badass production bikes instead of our purpose-built prototypes. And I love to give her crap that she wouldn't be able to handle my Dabria compared to her stock MMW, but the power gap isn't really all that different. There's also less of a glass ceiling for women in Superbike, as opposed to the one I spent years smashing my head on in Moto Grand Prix.

"Any word from Etienne?" Taryn asks from behind me, and I stop shoveling straw to face her. She's as sweaty as I am, but with her long legs, blond hair, and blue eyes, she looks like a western deodorant commercial. "We're done. This is fine," she says, indicating the stall.

I take another glance at it, and my mom definitely wouldn't call this fine. She'd call this fired. But it's Taryn's ranch, and I didn't wanna do this anyway, so I go ahead and follow her out.

"No," I admit, propping up my muck rake next to hers. "Haven't heard from him, and I don't expect to."

Taryn gives me a look like I'm the one being stubborn about this, but I don't want to hear her opinions on my perennial lack of a love life. I definitely don't want to think about it.

Etienne was *gorgeous*: a six-foot-one dark angel of dirty sex, with soft skin, hard abs, and double degrees in sixteenth-century poetry and organic chemistry. But our "relationship" was one physically blazing weekend while I was in France for Le Mans, and then six months on the phone while I was everywhere else. Thanks to the time difference between France and Malaysia, he ended up dumping me on my voicemail—I was asleep when he called.

"Well, then," Taryn starts all innocently like I don't know exactly what she's about to suggest. "Why not consider—"

"No."

"But—"

"*No.*"

She rolls her eyes, not saying anything else about the subject we do not speak of, since thankfully, Billy and Mason are walking up from where they've been working with Dax and Bryan all day. It's a lot easier to agree to come over and help when the ranch hands they hired are both super freaking hot. Dax has that whole tall-and-shaggy John Krasinski thing going on, and Bryan could win a World's Sexiest Smile contest, *no* contest. He's practically Michael B. Jordan's hotter fraternal twin. Too bad they're also one of the sweetest couples I've ever met, so no luck for me there either.

"Hey, honey," Billy drawls to Taryn when they stroll up. He touches his hat in my direction before he bends down to brush a kiss across Taryn's lips. I look away, something in my chest pulling tight across where something else is empty. My eyes settle on Mason. Leaning against the barn entrance, his black Stetson is dangling in one hand, his other using the open lapels of his pearl-snap shirt to wipe the sweat from his face.

His abs are better defined than my eyeliner ever is, his dark hair a little long and rustling into his baby-blue eyes. A gust of wind slams me with manly sweat and Italian cologne, and I grind my teeth together, finding something else to focus on.

Taryn's right. I need a boyfriend before I end up sleeping with freaking *Mason*. And Mason has slept with everyone. His reputation among the sponsor models and umbrella girls is almost too big to be believed.

"How's Aston's meadow?" Taryn asks, her palms flat on Billy's chest as she looks up at him like he lit the stars just for her.

"Bryan's got it under control. Ants are finally out, Aston's on her way back in, and Gidget's pouting up a storm because she won't let him come in there with her." He steals another kiss off Taryn's smiling lips, then glances around. "Y'all are done cleaning out the stalls already?"

"Yeah." Taryn shrugs, planting her hands backward on her waist.

Billy's head slowly tilts on his neck, Taryn only standing straighter. Until Billy wanders down and looks into both the stalls, then flatly calls out, "Mason."

I'm not surprised—Billy worked for my mom for years, and his high standards when it comes to cleaning horse stalls are almost worse than hers.

"Man," his brother whines, picking up the muck rakes Taryn and I abandoned. "Why is it that when you buy a ranch, I gotta do all the damn chores?"

I look at Taryn, my eyebrow arched in a silent *Right?*

She sticks her tongue out at me.

"Because." Billy comes back to take one muck rake from his brother before he gently shoves him into Aston Magic's stall. "When it's your ranch, you're gonna be calling me every five minutes for help. So consider this a bunch of favors you can call in later."

Mason hooks his hat on his head, then makes a face my way, grumbling, "Never buying a ranch. Too much work."

I nod along in silent agreement. *Try knowing you're gonna inherit one—twenty times this size.*

"Billy," Taryn complains, following her boyfriend down the barn and into his stallion's stall. That she already cleaned. Kinda. "It's fine, honey. You've done enough. Go take a shower and rest your ankle."

"Ankle's fine," he calls out loudly. Followed by a bunch of harsh whispers and...*oh no.*

My pulse spikes into fat-burn territory, and I sneak into Aston Magic's stall, where Mason is busy finishing the job I half-assed. "Hey," I whisper, waiting until he pauses to look at me. "His ankle is still bothering him?"

Mason doesn't say anything. But his eyes flicker toward the stall where his brother is, then back to me, the corner of his mouth slightly pulling down in acknowledgment. He goes back to shoveling straw, and I can't believe this.

"Does Frank know he's still hurting?"

Mason nods, and he never shops shoveling, but he breathes back, "Frank says we can't say nothing. That he doesn't know how much longer his Yaalon rep's gonna let him keep riding with the way he's falling apart. First his knee, and now his ankle."

"Jesus," I mutter. That has to suck so freaking much.

It's not Billy's fault that he needed knee surgery after that fluke cold tire wreck. His ankle injury *was* his fault, but it shouldn't cost the guy his whole career. I also don't know what he and Taryn are going to do if the sponsors push Billy out now and force him to retire.

"Yep," Mason says, making quick work of the job I reneged on. He stabs and pokes at the straw, fluffing it the rest of the way and spreading it around, then straightens and faces me. "Speaking of: you start prepping for COTA yet?"

"Yeah." I nod, mentally going over the list of things Frank has me working on—better torque control and rear wheel steering. "Kinda ready to get there, to be honest. Coming off turn one is a bitch, and I want as many passes at turn two as I can get before Sunday."

Mason shifts his weight, shaking his head. "Hate that track. Leave it to Austin to build something like that."

I grin. It's a downhill acceleration off turn one, your speed tripling, all while you try to control the wheelie, shift twice, and then bank for turn two. "I live for that shit."

Mason laughs, his personal brand of gentle sarcasm thick in his words. "Yeah, we know, Lori."

"You just gotta...let it go, man. You hold onto your bike like it's a bull trying to buck you, and you're strangling it."

He wipes the sweat off his face with his shirt again before he rests his elbow on his muck rake, his voice in a different accent as he playfully says, "Damn it, Jim. I'm a bull rider, not a doctor."

I roll my eyes at his Bones impression—ever the Trekkie. "Yeah? Well, try being a bull rider on a bull and a motorcycle racer on a motorcycle." I wink at him before I go in for the kill. As nicely as possible—Taryn must be rubbing off on me. "Stop being so scared of it. Let the bike do what it wants to do, and you'll be fine. She's not a bull, and she doesn't want to hurt you. She wants to win. So stop choking the throttle."

His mouth twists to the side because he knows I'm right. Frank's told him too. But I think the truth is Mason still gets scared of the battling sometimes.

He's a hell of a bull rider, but that's just him versus the bull. There's twenty of us on that race track, and as daunting as it is to ride at the speed we do, it's a million times harder once you start playing chicken with people at 200 miles per hour in a negative slope.

"So I'm still choking it," Mason repeats.

"Yeah." I reach out to clap his shoulder. "But you'll be okay. Let her loose in Austin and see if I don't know what I'm talking about."

"What *are* y'all talking about?"

I jump at the sharpness in Billy's voice. He's about as aggressive as a comatose kitten most days.

"Nothin'." Mason tugs on his cowboy hat, switching his muck rake to his other hand. Taryn's eyes dart between the three of us, subtly shaking her head at me from where she's standing next to Billy, and I am a terrible, sucky friend.

If she's waving me off, I'm going right for it. I'm not frightened of her Ferdinand boyfriend. She shouldn't be either.

"COTA," I say clearly. "We're talking about COTA. That a problem?"

"Yeah, it is," he barks, and my eyes widen as Billy Freaking King starts storming my way.

"Billy!" Taryn shouts, but her normal jerk on his self-imposed leash falls flat, my best friend looking at me with huge, freaked-out eyes as her boyfriend stops nearly on my toes.

"You two need to get something straight." He looks between me and Mason like we're both his younger siblings instead of just the one of us. "You're not in the baby brackets anymore, and this isn't a fucking game."

I suck in a breath. I don't think I've ever heard Billy curse before. Taryn winces behind him, turning away and wrapping her arms around her head.

"You want to help each other? Go ahead. Do it. See what happens."

"You've helped me plenty of times before." Mason squints at his brother like he's seeing someone completely new in his place. "You always give me tips before we get to the track…"

"And it's gonna stop right now," Billy growls. "I helped you when you were in another category. But we're all in MotoPro now. Y'all ride for Dabria, and I ride for Yaalon. And if you think I'm gonna lie over and let the two of you threaten my livelihood, you're dead wrong."

"We weren't plotting against you," I tell him. "I swear. We were just talking."

"Talking about the race we're racing against one another in a week." He shakes his head at me, disdain plain in his eyes. "Figure it out, Lorelai. Y'all are at the top now. The only place left to go is out, and you have no idea how hard these guys will fight to stay in. They have a lot more to lose than a rancher's daughter does."

My temper snarls in my chest. I didn't choose the name I was born into any more than he did. "No one wants to win more than me."

He stares me down from under his big black cowboy hat. "You sure about that?"

"All right, that's enough," Taryn announces.

Billy glowers at his brother, then marches out of the stalls and the barn, and I nearly collapse from the shock of squaring off with him. We aren't exactly besties, but we've never been enemies. Never.

I look at Mason, and he's a statue. His jaw is locked, blue eyes blinking at the place his brother's boots just were, and his skin a little paler than a moment ago.

"I'm sorry," Taryn says to us with a sigh. "He's not really mad at y'all. He's just under a lot of pressure right now. With his…"

His ankle. Or his knee. Maybe both, or something new.

"It's okay," I tell Taryn, offering her a smile. It's the only thing I can think to do when their whole future is in jeopardy. She makes good money racing Superbike, but not as much as Billy makes with MotoPro. And they're also supporting Dax and Bryan now.

She half returns the smile, then turns and jogs out of the barn. "Billy, wait!"

I lay my hand on Mason's arm, and he shudders back to life. Together, my teammate and I wander out of the horse stall, my eyes lifting a bit to spy on Taryn as she stops Billy on the way back to their house.

His hands move animatedly as he rants and raves, gesturing toward the barn and the house and her and himself. Taryn just stands there, her head patiently tilted as he goes on and on. Until she stretches up and hugs him.

Billy's hands go still. The wind even seems to die down. Then he curves forward, his black hat dropping onto her shoulder as he hugs her, the two of them finding their strength in each other.

She holds him for a long time under the shining golden sun and clear blue skies, as long as he needs. And when they pull apart, walking toward their house, their arms are so woven across each other's backs, it's hard to know who is who.

Loneliness bubbles in my throat, and I force myself to swallow it down, starting the short walk back to their house behind them.

God, I need a freaking boyfriend. But a win at COTA will more than suffice.

CIRCUIT OF THE AMERICAS
Austin, Sunday, April 14

Pos	Pts	Rider	Time	World Rank
1	25	Lorelai HARGROVE	43'52.437	65
2	20	Cristiano ARELLANO	+1.368	41
3	16	Billy KING	+2.499	54
4	13	Santos SAUCEDO	+6.126	45
5	11	Mason KING	+7.842	32
6	10	Gregorio PAREDES	+9.796	23
7	9	Giovanni MARCHESA	+12.536	24
8	8	Elliston LAMBIRTH	+16.884	23
9	7	Deven HORSLEY	+19.642	22
10	6	Harleigh ELIN	+23.531	15
11	5	Fredek SULZBACH	+27.379	12
12	4	Donato MALDONADO	+31.942	9
13	3	Aurelio LOGGIA	+35.557	12
14	2	Galeno GIRÓN	+42.389	2
15	1	Diarmaid DEAN	+48.419	2
Not Classified				
		Rainier HERRE	3 Laps	0
		Timo GONZALES	7 Laps	1
		Gustavo LIMÓN	8 Laps	0
		Massimo VITOLO	16 Laps	38
Not Finished 1st Lap				
		Cesaro SOTO	0 Lap	0

Chapter 4

Massimo Vitolo—April; Austin, United States

ALL HAIL PRINCESS LORINA, VICTOR OF COTA.

My knee is killing me more with every step past the double doors into the gaudy Austin hotel ballroom, and even though it's Lorina's fault, I glare at Vinicio.

"Massimo," my manager warns, but I don't want to hear it. I shouldn't have to bow and scrape at Lorina's feet in a tux just because she won a race in MotoPro. Especially when that win—and its cash bonus—should've been mine.

Forty-five minutes, then I'm out of here. I won't look at her, talk to her, or even think about her. I'm gonna be good this time.

Maybe thirty minutes.

"You want a water?" Vinicio asks in Italian when we get inside. All I can do is scoff and gesture toward the banner draped across the ballroom, congratulating Lorina on her victory.

I don't know why everyone is so shocked that she finally did it. I always knew it was only a matter of time once they let her on the moto. But dozens of people are swooning over her victory as waiters sweep by with trays of hors d'oeuvres. I've clocked at least two fountains of champagne, a string quartet just started playing in the corner, and *Christ*, what did they spend on this thing? Pretty sure all I got in Qatar was a pat on the back, followed by a stern "Don't fuck it up in Argentina."

I look at Vinicio, my voice as cold as my mood as I point at the banner. "You think I'm drinking water under this? You're out of your mind."

"You can't drink." There's a warning in my manager's words that we both know extends further than this party. "You're on painkillers."

I almost chuckle at the cruelty of it all, a ruthless smile curling my lips as I turn fully toward him, clapping him on the shoulder. "Whatever you say, boss." Then I walk off, swiping a glass of something dark off a waitress's tray and throwing it back. Vinicio curses from somewhere behind me as the liquid burns happily down my throat, but I smile at a group of sponsor reps like a good little puppet, weaving through the crowd and trading my empty glass for a fresh one along the way. Twenty-eight minutes.

"Hey, Massimo," more than a few of the sponsor models purr in a spattering of languages, their bodies draped in black lace, black silk, black chiffon, like they're all going to a funeral after. I only wink at their smiles and keep moving, not in the mood for company tonight after the nightmare of today. I should've expected it after I beat Lorina for pole position.

Not the first time it's happened. But considering she's still pissed about Qatar, she most graciously accepted her second-place starting pole by pressing me toward the bailout in lap sixteen until I crashed today. When she came back around the track, I threw her a gesture from the dirt that no man should ever do to a woman, and she looked forward, shifting up a gear.

My knee is strained, I've got a hairline crack in my rib, and bruises cover half my lower body. But most of that was because I fucked up the roll after she forced me down, and we're straight. Square. Even, for now. But it doesn't change the fact that I'm stuck in an over-crowded room listening to everyone babble about how *amazing* she is, all while my knee has a pain in it that I need to go the hell away. My Yaalon teammate, Billy King, has spent the last few years in and out of surgery proving exactly why.

It doesn't take long before I find a corner tucked in the back of the ballroom, one a little darker, a little shadier than the rest, where at least I can lean against the wall to try to take the weight off my knee. It should absolutely keep me away from the line of fire, and I need to get through this thing unnoticed as much as possible.

We're all here for her, which means they're all gonna be watching me. And I'm not in the mood to play nice when the fact that they're wrong about us sleeping together is a slap in the face.

"Hey, man," someone says in Spanish, and I barely resist a groan when Santos Saucedo strolls in my direction.

He moved up to MotoPro three years ago, but we raced together in the lower levels before that, and he's such a dick. I don't know what Giovanni sees in him besides a ranking.

Santos takes a swig of champagne, then hooks his thumb over his shoulder toward the party. "Believe this?"

"Not really that surprising." I do my best to ignore his cringe at my accent, my Spanish more than passable, but not perfect enough for Santos, apparently.

"Waste of money if you ask me. She's never going to last the full circuit, and she should've kept her perky little tits in Superbike along with the rest of 'em."

My eyes narrow in his direction, wondering if he's ever dared to say that to Billy, whose girlfriend rides Superbike. But Santos doesn't notice my reaction. He's already back to scanning the crowd.

So I shove the hell out of his shoulder, making sure he gets it.

Santos stumbles, surprise darkening his face as champagne sloshes over the rim of his glass. I chuck mine over my shoulder as bystanders start to whisper and scoot back, and I don't give a shit what they fine me. Tonight is not the night, and he's way over the line.

"What the hell is your problem, man?" Santos straightens, fluffing the lapel on his jacket before he lowers his voice. "Not that everyone doesn't already know. Worst kept secret in the whole fucking sport."

I storm forward until I'm in his face, forcing him to back up more with every word. "The fuck are you so afraid of? Is it because she's faster than you? Or because she'll still be here winning races long after you're forgotten?"

His eyes flare, the glass shattering when he drops his drink the only warning I need.

I sidestep out of his swing, my palm landing square on his chest as I shove him into the wall. His head snaps back, his teeth knocking together from the force of it. My fist is primed for his rebound when someone fishhooks my collar and yanks me out of reach.

Vinicio appears in front of me, his arm an iron bar across my chest as he drives me away from where Santos is sagging against the wall.

"Anything else?" I spit at him.

Santos shoves himself vertical, pointing at me as microphone feedback crackles through the room. "Watch your back, Vitolo. Your girlfriend too."

I ram my weight against Vinicio to get past him, but he's got sixty pounds on me, and I'm screwed when his hands clamp on my shoulders, whipping me around. "Enough!" he hisses in Italian.

"Hi, everyone." Lorina's nervous chuckle floods the ballroom as Vinicio marches me away, my pulse pounding and every inch of me desperate to finish the fight he stopped. "I'll try to keep this short," she says in country-twanged English, "but I just want to thank y'all so much for being here with me tonight to celebrate the future of women in Moto Grand Prix. And especially to the other riders," Lorina adds, her voice a little sharper before she smooths it out again. "Just, thanks, guys, for always saving a place for me on the grid."

Everyone claps while still managing to throw me scandalized scowls on our way past, Vinicio's grip on my shoulder tightening as a couple of guys call out friendly taunts in heavily accented English. I grit my teeth, Lorina giggling like they're all best friends. She has no idea they have a running pool over whether she's going to cross the finish line or leave the track in an ambulance. Every. Single. Race.

I look over my shoulder at Santos, who started the whole thing and is now busy arguing with Giovanni.

That prick's not gonna see anything above fifth place in Jerez.

As though he can read my thoughts, Vinicio smacks my head and elbows me into a corner. I round on him but he blocks me, his eyes furious when he raises a single finger in a warning.

Lorina starts thanking everyone again, going down the list of all the people who sign her paychecks. The ones she's contractually obligated to mention in that Memphis twang of hers every time she opens her mouth in public, and I'm calming down, but still.

"Thank y'all so much again," Lorina finishes, "and I hope y'all have a great rest of your evening."

The room erupts into polite applause, and Vinicio leans toward me. "What the hell were you thinking back there?" he says in Italian, his voice low. "Do I really need to remind you what's at stake if you blow this?"

I don't answer, looking away and tugging my tie loose.

"Get it together," he growls. "She doesn't need you to fight her fights, and you need to stay focused before—"

"I am focused."

"Yeah? On what? Because it sure isn't on your knee, your family, or—hell, I don't know—not getting suspended for fighting when the ink isn't even dry on your contract with Yaalon."

I lock my jaw, taking it because he's right. I know better than to let Santos bait me. His entire strategy has always been to piss people off into screwing up on the track when it matters. But he doesn't usually go for the Lorina button, and I'm the moron who let him know exactly how well it works.

Vinicio sighs, looking at me for a long time before he gives up, waving me off. I take full advantage of the reprieve and head for the open bar, keeping my head down and my eyes trained on the patterned carpet, my back firmly to the rest of the room.

Fifteen minutes.

"Grappa morbida," I order when I get there, but the Texan bartender just stares blankly back at me. "Bourbon." This he understands.

I take a deep pull the moment he sets it down, even though I'm gonna pay for it later. I always do—pay for the stuff I say, the mistakes I make, the fights I start. For the things I've stolen, that were stolen from me before I even realized I had them to lose.

"Hi, if it's not too much trouble, can I have sparkling water in a champagne glass? And can you put a raspberry in it if you have one?"

Shit.

"Sure thing, honey," the bartender drawls. "Anything for the first woman motorcycle racer."

I roll my eyes—*Americans*. That's not even right. She's not the first woman motorcycle racer, just the first to advance all the way to MotoPro. And if I were a better man, I'd already be halfway through the emergency exit. But I wasn't born to play the good guy, and Lorina knows that. After ten years of racing against her, I've made sure of it.

My fiercest rival delicately clears her throat next to me, the air now glistening with hints of lemon chiffon, and the last of my self-control caves to the demon whispering on my shoulder—the one that lets my dick make all the rules. And despite the pain still throbbing in my knee—the pain that's only there because I pissed her off—I finally let myself look at what I'm up against, and I instantly start to smile.

She never looks anything less than incredible, whether she's in dirty red leathers with *Wreckless* scrawled above her ass or in a dress barely covering it. Tonight, she's pink and sparkly: her rose-gold sequined top stopping short at her waist, the back open in a graceful drape, and paired with a creamy tulle miniskirt that slips the whole thing from stunning to sweet without bothering to cancel out the sexy. It's ridiculously unfair...and exactly how she races.

Lorina glances at me, her earrings sparkling from where her hair is twisted up even though she always wears it down. Except for Sundays, when she French braids it. "I'm just waiting for my drink, then I'm going. So please, don't feel the need to say anything." She looks forward, mumbling, "Or make another scene I'll have to distract people from."

I take a sip of bourbon to curb the guilt swirling in my stomach, just waiting. I know from experience, my Tigrotta's not done yelling at me yet. It only screws my head up more that arguing with her always translates to my dick as foreplay, but never, ever do we make it across the finish line into the bedroom. Might help our chances if she'd crack a book on Italian, or if I took the time to better my English. Not likely when beating her on the track takes up the majority of my priority list. I know winning is the only thing Lorina cares about.

True to form, her head whips in my direction. "You realize I wasn't even supposed to have to talk tonight? Is your ego really that out of control that you had to get into a fight with Santos because you can't share the attention for two freaking hours?"

I tilt my head, unable to resist baiting her with the truth when it freaks her out so much. "Why are you so angry tonight, Lulu? Is it because your boyfriend did not want to come to your party?"

"Don't ask about my sex life."

My cock twitches, a grin teasing the corner of my mouth. "I said boyfriend. You said sex."

Her eyes drop to my lips before bouncing up to my eyes. It's fast— everything with her is fast—but not so fast I didn't see. Since I like the way my face is arranged, I don't do more than arch my eyebrow to let her know she's busted.

"Ass," she mutters.

I can't help but laugh, especially when the bartender sets down her drink: the sparkly sweet appearance of danger that's secretly innocent. Because unlike me, Lorina actually *is* the good little girl her sponsors love to parade around. Paparazzi never bust her slipping from the back doors of clubs in the hours we're supposed to be asleep. She doesn't drink, always prays before she races, and she's usually glued to the gym every minute she's not on the track.

I gesture dismissively in her direction. "Non è possibile for you to have a boyfriend anyway."

Lorina flashes me a fake grin, raising her drink to me in a mock toast. "Whatever you need to tell yourself." She takes a deep swig of her raspberry-tinted water like that's gonna do anything for her.

"Bene. You tell your boyfriend you are going to travel to other countries nine months of the year so you can ride moto." I lean over, waving at no one. "Bye, boyfriend! See you in dicembre! Non ti pre-occupare about the other sexy Italian men in moto."

She looks at me, but when I don't back down, she snatches my bourbon from my hand. My eyes widen with every higher tilt of the glass, Lorina drinking the whole thing in no less than six little swallows.

She winces and coughs when she's done, her hand splayed on her chest. So it's what I heard, then. That French prick she was dating broke up with her. What a dumbass.

Lorina glares at me, her voice strained, but we both know it's not from the bourbon alone. "You're such an asshole."

I nod, as though I'm satisfied. I'm supposed to be, but it's hard to remember why when she sounds like that. "It is good to have something you can count on. Like being a man and knowing that whatever happens during sex, it is not over until we are finished. For women?" I shake my hand in a maybe. "Depends how much your man likes you."

She gapes at me, then bursts out laughing. "God, I hate you so much."

I take the laugh and forget the rest. It's not the first time she's said it to me, and it won't be the last. This always ends the same—her walking away, more determined than ever to beat me on the track. None the wiser of the truth. It's exactly how it's supposed to be. Except for the part where I should've bailed out of this five minutes ago.

Her little temper tantrum and crashing me out cost me a lot of money today. And like Vinicio said, I need to stay focused on beating her in Jerez and making it up as much as I can. I can't risk falling behind on my payments to Gabriele.

"So what about you, Massimo?" Lorina takes a sexy little sip from the rim of her champagne glass, and I will not think about all the other things I want to see her glossy pink lips wrapped around. "Girlfriend?"

My pulse kicks up a gear, but I only shrug, throwing a quick glance over the rest of the gala. Her manager is busy wrangling our teammates: Billy on the phone, probably with his girlfriend, Taryn, and Mason flirting with a sponsor model. The manufacturer reps are still giggling under the crystal chandeliers, congratulating themselves over the money Lorina brought in, and none of them have noticed she's over here with me instead of safe with them. Good. "I have a... friend," I tell Lorina. "A good friend. We have known each other for a long time."

"Ooh. Sounds serious."

I shake my head. "Not in that way. But it can be difficult."

Lorina chuckles to herself, turning back toward the bar and setting down her water. "Well, whoever Miss Difficult is, I feel sorry for her."

I grin, more than a little encouraged about the direction this conversation is going. "Perché you are jealous."

"You travel a lot, and you're a known club rat." Lorina shrugs. "Men stray when they're not getting laid. Meaning you probably cheat on her constantly while you're on the circuit."

The words smash my mood and break all my momentum, and my pulse thuds hard and angry from the character assassination I should've been expecting but foolishly wasn't. I pluck the raspberry from her glass, throwing it at her.

Lorina leaps back, stunned as droplets of clear liquid sparkle on her dress. But she can afford to buy a thousand more like it, and no matter what she's heard, I'm *very* careful about when I take my clothes off.

"You cheat," I say before I can stop myself. "Rules mean nothing to you—"

"If you're about to accuse me of cheating today—"

"Who cares about almost hitting people in straightaways—"

"You crashed because you were being a coward," she says, pointing at me.

I lean closer, irritated to the point that I can't find the words in English, and let them come fast and sharp off my tongue in Italian.

"You're the coward, Lorina, and you only race like you want to die because you're too afraid to live."

She blinks her thick black eyelashes at me, amber eyes searching mine and calculating her next move, and then she scowls. "It's cheating to speak in Italian when you know I don't understand what the hell you're saying."

Right. Because why should she learn my language, even though I learned hers?

She arches a smug eyebrow like she's decided she won the argument, and I storm away, ignoring the terse whispers as I make my way out of the room, down the corridor, and out the back entrance of the hotel.

I don't know why I ever fucking try with her. Nothing is ever going to change.

The hot Austin air slaps into me once outside, but even the downtown lights and music flowing from Sixth Street bars aren't enough to calm my temper as I raise my hand for a cab. If there is a God, one of the dozens in the crowded street will pull over before Vinicio comes outside to rip me apart with a bunch of crap I already know. How pissed my sponsors probably are. How reckless it is to risk my career when the estate taxes balloon with interest faster than I can cross the finish line. How pointless it is to let her twist me when it's been ten damn years, and she still doesn't get it.

"Massimo…"

Christ, I just can't catch a break. I hold my arm farther out into the street like that'll speed up my ability to get the hell away from her. But the bitter smells of barbecue and traffic exhaust are already bowing to the soft grace of southern citrus, and the harshest part of the truth is it's me that can never stay away.

I blame my father. It's his fault for putting the idea in my head in the first place. And I've done every screwed-up thing he told me to do, but none of it has made a difference when Lorina's so fucking difficult.

Maybe my mother was right. Maybe he was backward, with all his rules and all his theories. Maybe I am ruined. But I have to believe he knew what he was talking about when he told me how to be worthy of her heart, because she is exactly what he said she'd be: infuriating.

Lorina's high heels click on the pavement, then stop a few feet behind me, and I let out a sharp whistle in a prayer for just one cab to pull over before she says it again. I took it fine the first time, but I can't handle a second "I hate you" right now. I'm not even close to drunk enough.

"Do you think it's possible," Lorina says, her voice soft over the traffic, "that we could ever, just once, have a conversation for longer than three minutes without fighting?"

The words unnerve me so much that even though I shouldn't, I look at her, my brow furrowed. Fighting is what we *do*. It's the only thing I allow us to do, for a very important reason.

But her bare arms are hugged across her chest, a curly strand of brown hair starting to fall from where she pinned it back, and this would be so much easier if I didn't know how exhausted she probably is. Especially after racing today, then having to dress up as Princess Moto for all these assholes. The only thing keeping me going is pharmaceuticals and frustration, and just as the sponsors shouldn't have made me go to this thing, they shouldn't have thrown it for her in the first place. Not tonight at least.

They should've allowed her to rest, to recover. To have fun if she wanted.

She deserves that.

"Sì, Lorina. I do."

A breath rushes from her lungs that sounds like pure hope, and if we were anyone else, this would be simple, my next move as clear as the red lights that set us free on the track. But I stay where I am. Because I am me, and she is her, and every time she looks my way, I have to shrug off the itch in my shoulders that wants to hunch in her presence.

I don't know if she can tell that under the expert cut of expensive clothes, I'm still very much the kid in the alley boosting motos to save my father's mechanic shop. But whether or not she sees it, I still know it, and it's reason number I-lost-count of why I'm going to tell her good night, then walk away. Exactly like I should've done after she followed me to the bar just so she could yell at me, rightfully, for getting into it with Santos.

"Però..." I clear my throat when my voice nearly gives me away, and I can't let it give me away. Not until Valencia, when the last cent will be paid. "I think you would miss the fighting, Tigrotta."

Something flashes in her expression like she wants to fight me on that too. But it would only prove my point, and Lorina still hasn't learned how to lose. The pain in my knee, in my ribs, says so.

A cab pulls up beside me on the curb, and I throw her a wink as I slide into the back seat, shutting the door. After a quick question, the driver nods and pulls away, steering me toward the basement bars where I already know I'm going to spend the rest of the night—drinking, dancing, trying to forget under the hands of strangers the truth that's burned in my veins since the first time I met her and she left me in the dust.

None of it's going to make a difference, but somewhere in me, I hear my father's voice whispering it's fine. It's good. That Lorina is safely back in the hotel, because she went back to racing, and this is exactly how it's supposed to be.

It's bullshit.

Chapter 5

Lorelai Hargrove—May; Jerez, Spain

SPEEDING DOWN THE STRAIGHT BETWEEN TURNS FIVE AND SIX AT Jerez, the world is a stadium roaring in unison, swaying in bright reds and greens. I bend lower over my bike, trying to gain every inch on the leaders I can. It shouldn't be a problem here in Spain. I kicked ass at COTA, earning myself a special award party to boot. Too bad my head has been a complete wreck since then.

I still have no idea what Massimo and Santos were fighting about, but I heard the whispers afterward that it revolved around me. I don't need to know more—what they said or who said it first. They've all taken their shots through the years. But I can't help wondering if it had something to do with the way Massimo was looking at me at the bar...

And there was something about the way his voice sounded outside in that thickly sweet Austin air. Like maybe, one day, we'd be able to talk about something other than who finished first and who won what. About things that are real, that matter, away from the circuit.

A glare from the bright Andalusian sun reflects off my face shield, taking me back to plotting gear shifts and apexes for the Jerez track. *Stay focused, Hargrove.* I refuse to let a man distract me from going after my dreams. I promised myself a long time ago I never would. Not after what happened to my mom.

The Spanish crowd rages as I fly past, and I lose myself in their chants, rising and falling to the rhythm of my engine and calling me home. My true home.

Fifth gear. Fourth. Third, and lean.

I grit my teeth through the right turn closer to 180 degrees than 140, my knee sliding on the ground and gravity beckoning for my life. Gray track curves in my peripheral vision, then straightens. I pull my bike vertical, resitting more to the left as I push into a higher gear, preparing for the smoother left of turn seven.

Santos Saucedo from Hotaru Racing pops up and steals the apex, and I curse as I glide through the turn behind him. I'm slipstreaming his Hotaru, but I'm stuck staring at his tailpipe through the left of turn eight, the right of nine, and another in ten. From there, it's sixth gear all the way: gaining inch after inch as I come up on his right side, level as we barely lean through the smooth slide of eleven.

Coming out of it, I check behind me. Three-second gap between me and the next pack, Massimo in front, Billy right behind him, and both of them gaining. Worry about that later.

Looking forward, I duck a little lower through turn twelve: another right curve that's more straight than turn. Then I pinpoint my focus on turn thirteen ahead of us—a switchback that's practically another 180, and it's the one that matters. Come out of turn thirteen ahead, and you take the finish line. Every single time.

Hotaru orange takes over my vision in my left eye as the turn approaches, sand and gravel creeping in on my right. Panic rises in my throat. I'm on the edge of overshooting the apex, but I can't go anywhere. Santos is still inching closer and closer... *Damn it.* It's too late to get behind him, and he's not backing off.

He looks at me, unbridled hate in his eyes, and *screw this dude.* I'm not backing off. We're going to have to do this side by side.

I downshift once, then twice, starting the lean as my abs tighten and—

His right knee jerks upward into my left elbow.

My balance buckles, gravity wins, my left hip and the rest of my side slamming into the ground. A collective gasp from the crowd sounds like someone sucked the air out of the top of the stadium. Pain blasts through my leathers and deep into my bones, my helmet banging the track. The world darkens, time spinning, even as I know I'm careening off the track at nearly 100 miles per hour with no hope for control. My eyes open, and curses scream in my mind.

I'm high side.

The tire wall grows into a tsunami of encroaching death, my left leg coming free as my bike shirks away. But my left hand hasn't unclenched the handlebar yet, and *oh shit*.

My bike hits the curbstone and swings for me, a violent beast with a taste for blood. It pulls my hand and arm backward. Something snaps, and I scream.

At the jarring change from track to gravel, my fingers release the handlebar when lethal speed windmills my body. Tumbling without end, the ground punches and kicks me, splintering bones shrieking through my hand and ankle.

In flashes, my eyes search for my bike.

I see her. I scream again.

She's coming for me. Flipping end over end and breaking. Dabria-red fairings are flying off, hurtling toward me for hurting her.

I lurch to a stop on my stomach and glance over my shoulder, horrified.

Oh God. She's right—

Chapter 6

Massimo Vitolo—May; Jerez, Spain

I CAN'T BELIEVE WHAT'S HAPPENING.

My boots squeak shakily down one of the side corridors in the hospital, nurses and doctors rushing by with rapid Spanish spilling from their mouths. And even though I just promised a thousand things to my little brother—her biggest fan—none of it erases the truth still screaming behind my eyes.

How her moto broke apart as she tumbled out of control. How her helmet lifted up once she came to a stop because she tried to move out of the way. But the wheel hit her in the head like a boxer throwing an uppercut, knocking her back and flipping her over, the 130 kg moto rebounding off the tire wall and landing directly on top of her 50 kg body.

I come to a wobbly stop outside her room, and I only give myself one second to scrub my hand over my face and suck it up. I need to check on her. I need to make sure press didn't sneak into her room. And I need to get the hell out of this hospital before anyone realizes I'm here and not on a plane back to Italy. It's the only thing I'm allowed to give her.

My hand is still shaking as I open the door as quietly as I can and check inside. She's still asleep, her brown curls hiding the ugly pattern of the hospital gown at the top of her shoulders because I undid her braid. I wouldn't have done it if she were awake, but at least she'll never know it was me. Probably won't even think to ask when she's going to be begging for painkillers when she wakes up.

My eyes steal a long glance down the gentle slope of her cheek—bruised and swollen, parallel bars of bandages trying to put her back together. I swallow, leaning against the wall by the door, hidden from her view. Someone knocks for the room next to us, and my fingers itch for my sunglasses, but I don't have them with me. God only knows how long it'll be before I stop seeing her crash behind my eyes. Doesn't help that it's playing on every TV in every waiting room, and I can hear it through the walls.

"Frank?" Lorina faintly coughs, her voice soft and broken. "Is that you?"

My head falls back against the wall. Of course, she doesn't expect it to be me. I never follow her to the hospital. She doesn't come for me either. But of all the times I've seen her go down, today is the first time I honestly didn't think she would walk away.

I should feel better that she's alive. That she's awake. Except it doesn't change the fact that I'm still pissed as all hell that she couldn't back down, just once, and choose to live instead of win. But that's not who she is.

"Frank?" she asks again. Then, more scared, "Hello?"

I pivot around the corner so she can see me, my jaw locked taut. Her eyes widen. "Massimo?"

"Rest, Lorina." My voice sounds weird—too soft. But all of this is weird considering it's us. "You will not be alone. I will stay."

Her eyes brighten, but it's quickly lost, her expression fading into shame and fear, confusion. She glances around, her bottom lip trembling. Faster than I can blink, she tries to sit up in the bed, but I don't need scrubs and a stethoscope to know she has no strength in her left shoulder, and her right hand is broken.

I'm there before she can ask for help, Lorina flinching at my fingers gently cradling her upper right arm. My other hand slips between her back and the bed, supporting her weight, and I am not going to think about—

She glances up at me next to her, and my eyes find hers.

Shit. I look to the pillow behind her, pushing it down so it can take the place of my hand. When I'm done, I step away and clear my throat, crossing my arms.

I don't touch her. Ever.

Lorina swipes her fingertips under her eyes. "What are you doing here?"

I don't answer. She wouldn't believe me anyway.

"Come to gloat?"

Gloat. I search my mind for the meaning but come up blank. The only thing in there is the sound of the crowd gasping in horror. The flashing lights of her ambulance peeling out from the track on the way to the hospital. "What does 'gloat' mean?"

She glares at me. "To be happy in front of me because I'm hurt. That I crashed."

I bear the force of the verbal slap and use it to propel me toward the door. "I will go."

"Massimo, wait—" Her words rush past her lips before I can even cross the end of her bed, and it's a sharp yank on the string that has me tied helplessly to her. I'd cut that thing in a heartbeat if I could, but I *can't*. I can only pause, looking over at her.

Her eyes sweep over my leathers, still covered with dust and exhaust. She's probably pissed I didn't have the decency to shower before coming to see her when she likes everything clean and tidy and overly organized. She can get over it. I had to watch her crash.

"Um..." she starts, wincing. "Have you seen Frank?"

I face her fully, a little concerned that's what she asked first. She's not usually one for avoiding a tough subject. "He is downstairs, talking to the press. I was not supposed to leave your room while he was gone, but my brother called me, and I had to answer. So I left and went into the corridor, and the nurse told me she would stay until I returned." I clear my throat to see if that'll somehow stop me from babbling more. Doubtful. But she threw me off with the Frank question. "So it is my fault you woke up alone."

"Oh."

Oh.

I should probably leave before she asks why her manager was cool with me standing guard when normally, I'm the one they guard her against. But I don't get much further than that in my mental debate when she takes a deep breath, then asks, "Massimo, am I okay?"

Yank, yank, yank. And still avoiding. If I didn't think she'd call security, I'd already be pushing her buttons until she'd be too busy roaring at me to remember she's hurt. But my Tigrotta *is* hurt, and today, it's left me with no other choice than to be the version of myself I keep safely away from her.

I walk over and take the seat on her left, leaning forward with my elbow sliders resting on my knees. I keep my eyes trained on my hands because I can't look at her when I say it. I'm still telling it to myself, over and over, and even with her awake and beside me, it's nearly impossible to believe when I was so convinced she was gone. Everyone was. "Lorina, you are okay."

She lets out a long, quiet breath.

"Your shoulder, it was—"

"I remember."

My eyes flash up to hers, but she's staring at the blanket, and I don't force it. "Bene."

The last thing I want to bring up is how she screamed when they reset it. Knowing Lorina, she'd probably be embarrassed to the point that she'd hurt herself worse trying to prove to me what a badass she is. The woman is as tough as they come, brave to the point of absurdity, and she screamed like she was being murdered. No one should have to know that pain. No one.

She clears her throat. "Is that it? Just my shoulder?"

"You also have a bump on your head, but it is very small." I shrug, but it's the understatement of the century.

Her helmet cracked. Like it was struck by lightning from the bottom of her chin to her forehead, and all the way across the American flag on top, straight to the back of her crown. The faceplate was also shattered, but she must have pinched her eyes shut tighter than anything against the blast. The shards cut her cheeks and forehead, but by some miracle, she wasn't blinded.

Her helmet is now in a plastic bag, inside my room in my locked RV, parked behind gates on the paddock. It's gonna be a massive pain to smuggle it into Italy when Dabria is probably tearing apart all of Spain looking for it, but I've moved stuff before, and Ravenna is the last place anyone will look. I never want Lorina to see it. Her manager agreed, and he's the one who slipped the bag into my hand when the officials weren't looking, too busy doing media damage control and talking about how the safety measures worked and the sport is safe, blah blah blah.

"You have some broken bones in your right hand," I continue, "and these..." I lay my palm flat against my own left rib cage, forgetting the word in English for the body part. I'm on a roll today. "But nothing is broken in your ankle, only twisted. They said you are still okay to race at Le Mans in two weeks, if you are ready."

Her brow furrows, that temper of hers already poking its head out. "Why wouldn't I be ready?"

Of course. I tell her she nearly died, her body is broken, and all she wants to know is when she can race again. I should've told her she was paralyzed so she'd consider taking the next race off to recover, but it's more likely I'm gonna be the one unable to walk when I tell her what I did.

"I told your manager...it may be difficult."

Her whole body jerks, her voice blasting out, "You told Frank to sit me out of the race?"

"Five turns to the left, Lorina!" I take a second, getting myself back under control. "Which is good for your shoulder, since it is not too many. But the left turns are bad for..." I touch my palm to my side again.

"Ribs," she grumbles.

"Bad for your ribs. Also, there are nine turns to the right, which is too much pain for your hand and ankle. Molto dolore."

She glowers at me, her chin tilting up. "I'll be fine, and it's not your place to make Frank worry."

My eyes narrow. Her little I-have-it-under-control look may work on everyone else, her manager included, but it doesn't fool me. "Sì, you already did this enough on your own. Playing a dangerous game on the racetrack that makes you crash while he is forced to watch from the garage."

She only lasts a second longer before her bottom lip trembles, and she breaks eye contact.

Damn it, I'm going to have to hit a church on my way out of here, because I just bought a first-class ticket to hell for making her cry right now.

"Have you seen my bike?" she whispers.

There it is. The one question I've been waiting for and dreading the most. I can only bring myself to nod once.

"Is it...?"

Christ, I can't do this. I always give it to her straight, and she knows that. But I can't be the "suck it up" guy I usually am with her. Not with the tears making her eyes sparkle in a way I *never* want to see again.

She promised me a long time ago that I would never see her cry, and I was counting on that. It's what keeps me fast on the track behind her, able to cut around in front of her.

She sniffles, and I can barely get my swallow to go down. "She is gone, Lorina."

She chokes on a raspy sob, tears streaming down her face as she looks toward the light coming through the window. I need to go. She probably doesn't want me here when she's this upset. I definitely don't want to see it. But I still can't bring myself to leave her alone in this cold, unfamiliar room.

Damn string. She has one of those too, but hers isn't tied to me. It's tied to the moto I just pronounced dead. And I'm the biggest hypocrite in the world, because even though I'd probably feel the exact same, I need to make her stop crying. Five minutes ago.

"It is okay, Lorina," I say like it's no big deal. "They will make you a new moto."

It's the truth. She knows it, but still, she shakes her head. "It's not the same."

I drop the act. Wasn't like it was working anyway. "I know."

She glances over at me, those tears still caught in her eyelashes, and that string is now a cable slicing my chest in half until I can't stop my brow from creasing in strain. She hurriedly wipes at her eyes, and the wound isn't healed, but at least it isn't gushing my entrails anymore.

I sit up, grasping for a change of subject but not landing far. "I watched the replay of the race very close."

Her eyes widen. "Did you see it?"

I shake my head, disappointing her as always. "None of the

cameras see. Not even your OnBoard; you were leaned over too far. It only shows you and Santos in the turn, and then you crashed."

"But you know, don't you?"

Slowly, I nod.

Santos Saucedo is becoming more of a problem every day. Picking fights during press conferences after having close calls in nearly every turn, and I don't care what his side of the story is. The only thing that matters is that every version ends with Lorina in here.

"What happened after?"

The muscles in my jaw flex as I glance at my folded hands. I barely remember the rest of the race, apart from trying to get through everything as fast as possible so I could get here. "He won first, took the podium, gave his interviews with the press."

She shakes her head, her voice low with anger. "That asshole. He hit me, Massimo. And not accidentally. On purpose."

"Sì, I know."

I also know it might be my fault. Because after I shoved him into that wall in Austin, he warned me to watch my back—to watch hers—and I didn't. I didn't warn her about the fight I'd started, and I didn't protect her. I just let her go after him, alone.

"Are they even going to do anything about it?"

I shake my head. "The stewards already reviewed it. They said there was nothing wrong."

Filing for an investigation won't help her cause either. The most she's gonna get is Santos earning a long lap penalty in Le Mans, and she doesn't need to spend weeks reliving the wreck to a bunch of investigators who'll probably try to blame it on her. She should've backed down long before he was close enough to do what he did.

"But—"

"Quel ch'è fatto è fatto. What is done is done. You need to look forward now, Lorina."

"Look forward to what? To someone else trying this crap again in two weeks at Le Mans? They're all out for themselves!"

"Sì, and if you let fear in your heart"—I snap my fingers—"you die."

"I am not afraid!" She winces from raising her voice, her head probably pounding, and I still can't make myself leave. Now more than ever.

"No?" I lean forward, my voice just between us. "I think you are very afraid. I think you are scared to lose. I think you fear the other riders."

She glares at me. "They're dangerous."

"So are you, Tigrotta."

She jerks back, blinking at me like she can't believe I actually admitted it. But I'm not taking it back, and I'm not above switching tactics when necessary.

"When we were at Qatar, you pushed me, and you pushed me hard inside turn sixteen. You did this even knowing I was probably going to crash. You did the same thing in Argentina, only that time, I *did* crash."

"No," she breathes, shaking her head as her eyes grow horrified. "I never meant to make you—"

"You scare me, Lorina. I was never going to tell you this. But you have no fear of me on moto, and you push hard." I narrow my eyes, daring her in the way she's never been able to resist. "You need to push everyone else the same way. So when you see yellow and red and Santos orange, and you feel fear? You think Massimo blue. Then…" I wave my hand. "You will have no more fear, and you win."

I sit back in my chair, propping my boot on my knee. I don't actually think some crap about color association will work, but it's something to get her head out of the wreck. Out of this hospital room flooded with so much antiseptic cleaner, it's burning my nostrils. It's exactly how my mother always smells at the end of her shifts.

But I don't want to think about her or how she feels about Lorina right now. And Lorina needs to start thinking about Le Mans if she's not going to sit out. She needs to crave revenge. The win. It's the only thing stronger than fear.

She stays quiet for a while, probably riding the track in her mind. Visualizing turns and already deciding what gear recommendations she's going to ignore, what braking suggestions she's going to fly past. How satisfying it's going to be when her heel drops and wrist twitches, launching from the starting line.

It's what I should be doing. Reconciling myself to the fact that when she gives me an opening on that day, I'm going to have to take advantage of it. Swerve and steal, probably scare the shit out of her. I don't have a choice if I'm ever going to get out from under Gabriele's thumb, and it's exactly why I shouldn't be in this hospital room.

"It's weird, isn't it?" Lorina asks, and I tilt my head, no idea what turn sequence she's talking about. "Ten years we've been racing against each other, and it's only now that we're able to talk like this."

I shift in my seat a little. So much for visualizing Le Mans. "Hai rimpianti? Do you...have regrets?"

"Like regret racing against each other?"

"No, that is not what I asked." I run a hand over my hair, trying to find the guts to say all the words of the question I'm really wondering. "Do you have regrets about what happens *when* we race? Together?"

It takes her more than a few deep breaths before she whispers, "Yes."

Holy shit.

I nod once, like the simple act of her saying that hasn't almost convinced me to forgive all the times we've nearly killed each other out there, but it helps. "Bene."

A small laugh slips out of her, quickly followed by a grimace. I need to go, let her rest. She closes her eyes and breathes through it, then reopens her eyes and asks, "How is that good?"

Five more minutes, then I'm out of here. Before whatever drugs they gave her wear off, and we start fighting when she remembers she hates me.

"If you had said no, I would think you a liar." I risk a grin that's a little more suggestive than I should dare, considering we're alone. "Everyone has regrets. Even you, Lulu."

She levels a look at me, indifferent to me noticeably flirting with her and not even acknowledging her least-favorite nickname. "Fine. If we're playing this game, then what are your regrets?"

"Not today," I tell her. "Maybe domani. Maybe tomorrow, I will tell you."

No chance in hell.

"Sounds like you're the one who's afraid."

The simple taunt is too much to endure. I sit forward, my hands folded calmly, but tension ripples off me. I'm not afraid of telling her the truth. It just won't change anything when all she cares about is winning, and my bank statement says I need to keep seeing her as a competitor. Not a woman who braids her hair only for races and lets it live free the rest of the time. Who never fails to break my sentences in half when she walks into a sponsor party wearing a gown that would look right at home on any red carpet.

The problem is, as much as she can't back down from a race or a fight, I can't back down from her.

She swallows, and I wouldn't be surprised if she were to hit me with all I'm letting sneak past my eyes. I know to stop it. I can't. Today, I saw her die, and I didn't stop to help her.

I jerk my chin toward her, my personal rulebook firmly and completely disappeared. "Close your eyes."

She doesn't close them; they only widen. Can't really blame her. "Why?"

There's no way I'm answering that, so I just wait. She swallows again at my silence, but then surprisingly, she does as I ask. Definitely finding a priest on my way out of here. There's got to be one roaming the corridors.

As quietly as I can, I grab the stuffed tiger I bought while staring blankly at the shelves in the gift shop, taking it out of the bag I left in here earlier. Then I set it next to her on the bed.

"Massimo," she whispers, nervous because her eyes are closed and I'm alone with her in the room. I deserve it—I've spent years making sure she doesn't get close enough to trust me. What I can't remember was whether that was for Lorina or for me.

I look at the bandage on her hand, the one on her temple, and I remember. So with all the parts of me that are good, the ones I don't let her see, I silently rise, then press a kiss to her cheek. In it, I leave the longing I've never dared voice. The pride I have for her. The love that has ruined me for anyone else.

She trembles, and I pull back and turn to leave the room.

Christ, I shouldn't have done that. We're rivals, and she will always love racing more than anything else.

"Massimo?" she says, and because I am hers, I stop.

She pauses, and I tell myself to suck it up. The sure to follow "Don't do that again." The "That's nice, but I don't feel that way." I've heard worse from her, and I've lived through it.

Her voice is quiet and unsure when she finally mumbles, "See you in France?"

I pivot, the corner of my mouth turning up as I respond with something low in Italian. Something she can't accept but I've known since we were fifteen.

She rolls her eyes. "In English?"

"Ciao."

I disappear around the corner, ignoring as she calls after me, "That wasn't English!"

Damn right it wasn't. And it never will be.

GRAN PREMIO DE ESPAÑA
Jerez de la Frontera, Sunday, May 05

Pos	Pts	Rider	Time	World Rank
1	25	Santos SAUCEDO	41'08.685	70
2	20	Billy KING	+1.654	74
3	16	Giovanni MARCHESA	+2.443	40
4	13	Donato MALDONADO	+2.804	22
5	11	Massimo VITOLO	+4.748	49
6	10	Harleigh ELIN	+7.547	25
7	9	Rainier HERRE	+8.228	9
8	8	Mason KING	+10.052	40
9	7	Cristiano ARELLANO	+10.274	48
10	6	Galeno GIRÓN	+13.402	8
11	5	Cesaro SOTO	+15.431	5
12	4	Timo GONZALES	+18.473	5
13	3	Aurelio LOGGIA	+20.156	15
14	2	Deven HORSLEY	+26.706	24
15	1	Fredek SULZBACH	+28.513	13
16		Elliston LAMBIRTH	+36.858	23
Not Classified				
		Gregorio PAREDES	3 Laps	23
		Gustavo LIMÓN	5 Laps	0
		Diarmaid DEAN	12 Laps	2
		Lorelai HARGROVE	19 Laps	65

Chapter 7

Lorelai Hargrove—May; Le Mans, France

"HOW'S SHE FEEL?" FRANK ASKS AS I PULL INTO MY GARAGE, MY crew propping up the back tire for me once I come to a stop.

"Gimme a second to breathe." I haven't even gotten my helmet off. As soon as I do, I limp toward the folding chair set up for me in the corner, grabbing my phone and earbuds. The week and a half since Jerez was not as long as it normally was. And even with how much I slept, I'm still not as healed as I expected to be by now. Which royally freaking sucks.

Frank doesn't even try to argue about me needing to do a debriefing. He just brings me two aspirin and ice packs for my shoulder and ankle. "You sure you don't wanna—"

"Nope."

I hook in my earbuds and Frank walks off, my crew already prepping the bike to make adjustments based off the endless statistics the computer feeds back about gearshifts, RPMs, and a thousand other things that can't *actually* explain why my practice time was nowhere close to where it should've been.

But it's fine. I'll be fine on Sunday. I just need to rest.

Sitting back in my chair, I close my eyes, letting the music bleed through me and calming the adrenaline still coursing through my body. I'm not going to think about how Massimo was right and I'm in so much pain from my practice, I don't know how I'm going to race tomorrow. I'm absolutely not going to think about how last year, I spent all of Le Mans in a daze and barely at the track.

I was too busy letting Etienne whisk me from wine bar to wine bar, making out with him under the arches of Gothic cathedrals before falling into bed at his family's château. Those rolling green parks where we picnicked and I busted my diet on rillettes and baguettes while he waxed poetic in liquid French? Those places no longer exist.

An engine screams over my music from Billy and the Q2 group tearing up their final practice laps, and I adjust the ice pack on my shoulder, resisting the urge to peek at my crew. I hope whatever they do to my bike, it helps. After losing out on any and all points at Jerez, I need a top three finish here at Le Mans more than ever.

My earbuds are tugged harshly out of my ears, my eyes popping open in shock at the murder of my postpractice soundtrack. "What the hell?"

I half expect it to be Mason, wound up with nerves about the coming race and looking to avoid the inevitable by losing to me in poker. But it's *Massimo*.

He grins, swiping a hand through his sweat-soaked hair. He should be doing his own debriefing, far, far away from my pit box. Yet here he stands, in the same pose—facial expression included—he uses for his more risqué press shoots.

It's disgusting. And horribly sexy. And the fact that it's both and not just the former does *not* help the acid gurgling in my stomach.

"God, what now?" I take off my ice packs and toss them aside. I should keep them on, but I refuse to look any shade of weak after he saw me all busted up in that awful hospital gown.

"Relax, Lulu. I only came to say hi to my friend. After my friend finished her practice."

The last sentence earns me a whole new look. The kind that

usually comes from my inner critic. I know my practices haven't been great—I don't need him to tell me that. And I don't have to answer to him. We don't...we're not...

"We're not friends," I tell him, because technically, that's the truth. Ask anyone, and they'll testify to it. There are even pictures and videos and a couple of magazine articles that could be admitted into evidence.

Except I don't know if that is still true after what happened in the hospital. He only kissed my cheek, but I felt it *everywhere*. I'm still feeling it. Everywhere.

Massimo arches an eyebrow, nodding a little like he's considering my answer. If my heart was racing before, it's probably registering on the Richter scale by now.

What is wrong with me that I'm always such a bitch to him, even when he's trying to be nice? I *hate* the idea that we're always going to be enemies, but it also can't just come from him. I have to try too.

He crouches in front of my chair, his gloved hand landing on my knee. I jump back out of instinct and glance toward my crew, but they're too busy to notice: rushing around to get my bike ready for tomorrow.

"Ah, Tigrotta," Massimo drawls. "We could be friends."

He winks and puckers a kiss at me, and—

Oh yeah. That's why.

I knock his hand off my leg, storming to my feet so abruptly that he falls backward on his ass. "Don't touch me. Ever."

He rolls his eyes but stands calmly, his boots squeaking against the floor as he brushes off the backs of his leathers. But there's also something in his expression that looks...almost like he's happy I'm mad at him? Like it was exactly what he wanted.

God, he's such a dick.

"Bene, Lulu. I only came to say that it is supposed to rain tonight and the track will be fast domani. The second turn—the Dunlop—you need to brake a little sooner than you like. And same in ten and eleven."

My head jerks back. "I know the track, ass."

"Not like this. And now is not the time to be taking risks, Lorina. Now is the time to let your body heal. If you want to get better, you need to think about being safe."

My eyes narrow. I know Massimo, and with as many times as he's gone after me, trusting my life to the pads and plates I wear, I know this isn't about me being safe. It's about him taking advantage of me being vulnerable, planting doubts, and making sure he wins.

It's always about who wins.

"You'd like that, wouldn't you? For me to doubt myself. Well, guess what? I made it through practice and qualifying without your help."

He shakes his head. "Per poco. Only by a little."

My back stiffens. I may be starting in tenth place, but it's better than twentieth. I only wobbled twice, and I didn't crash.

"You need to leave," I tell him. "I have a race to prepare for, and somehow, I don't think your little freak-out is part of what *my* premier manufacturer would consider a suitable pep talk." Not to mention that Billy would officially lose it if he knew his teammate was giving me pointers before a race.

Massimo grits his teeth, taking another step closer. "If you are afraid, they will know, Lorina. And they will use it against you. So I am asking you, as your friend, to think about something other than a trophy for once in your life."

My heart slams in my chest for a whole new reason, and it has everything to do with how stone-cold serious he is. At the concern in his eyes, searching every facet of my features as if this may be the last time he sees me.

I can't afford to catch his fear when I have enough of my own.

I lift my chin. "I'm not scared of them. And I'm not quitting."

"Lori," Frank calls over. When I look at him, he waves me toward him.

"Do me a favor," I say to Massimo, waiting until he steps back. "Don't ever come in my garage again. I don't need you spoiling my victory tomorrow with your rider beware bullshit."

I push past him, joining Frank and Gianni huddled around a new readout. When I check over my shoulder, Massimo is thankfully on his way out, his shoulders taut and his hand raking harshly through his hair.

So much for not being afraid of anything.

—⁓—

Locked in place by the red lights, I stare straight ahead at the coming turns of Le Mans, the world tinted through my face shield and my bike rumbling beneath me. My hands tighten into fists, and I knock them together, fighting through the ache of my broken bones.

I refuse to sink. I will defy those who question my loyalty to the sport I love. I will work harder, train longer, give the middle finger to the fear vibrating in my veins. Once my hands stop shaking.

I did fine during the warm-up lap. Not great, but not awful. Now, I've got seventy-three miles of tight first gear corners, conquered by braking just a little too late and then barreling out of the turn, my future hanging on how much traction my rear tire can claim.

Rolling out my neck and my left shoulder, I blow out a long, smooth breath. I already know, just like Massimo warned my manager—this is going to hurt. Everywhere.

The crowd rages, my eyes surveying the grandstands and the sun too bright for the day. Cameras pan and rise on cranes, the world full of disjointed colors on rippling flags and signs, some with my name on them, most not.

I wonder if it was the same for Alberto Puig before he crashed so badly that Le Mans was taken out of the circuit after being declared unsafe. It took five years before the track was back in play, following a behemoth of safety improvements. Too bad nothing is safe enough when you spend your life on a tight wire, bridging wildly fun and terribly dangerous.

People still crash here. They still get hurt, and some die. All while one hundred thousand spectators look down upon us, some worried over whether we will make it back in one piece, some foaming at the mouth for the opposite. And those who are eager to see the blood spill, like Romans rooting on soon-to-be-buried gladiators, are not all in the stands.

Santos looks back at me from the fourth pole, and it's a sight I can't stand: not just him but the endless tailpipes in front of me. That I'm staring down the backs of nine other men instead of having a clear path ahead.

Even from the distance between us, I can tell Santos's shoulders are shaking in laughter when he looks forward. I haven't spoken to him since the crash, and I won't. If I get close to him, I'll do something incredibly rash and risk my career even more than he did. The only chance I have at any sort of revenge is to make sure that when we cross the finish line, I'm first.

Winning is the only thing that matters. The only thing that's ever mattered.

I focus on the clock tower. Bile rises in my throat. The red lights look like sirens on an ambulance. Like blood, my blood, spilt and thickly dripping, staining the steel gray of the track that seems more like a morgue slab than a trampoline to immortality.

The red lights disappear. I flinch, pushing off seconds late.

My left side slams hard into the ground, ungodly pain surging through my already-broken body.

I cry out in my helmet from the white heat of it burning me everywhere, straining to keep my head off the track as momentum slingshots me toward the curbstone. Blue sky laughs above, clouds tinted the color of lead fleeing in the opposite direction with a speed too fast to be real. My arms cover my head, terrified of the tires of the four men who were behind me. For the one who warned me to go slow, but I didn't listen, because all I cared about was winning.

My eyes squeeze shut, listening to them coming around the corner, and for the longest half second of my life, I pray for gravel. When I find it, I pray for death.

The curbstone is a launch pad, spiraling me toward the sky. When my shoulder and hip crash back onto the ground, the pain rips me apart all over again.

A yelp tears from my lips as I tuck my hands into my body, protecting them as I roll without end. My helmet bangs the earth, and I squeeze my eyes shut against the torture of tumbling over leagues of rocks, trying to center myself through the dizziness.

Somewhere in the middle, the cold hands of physics reach up and grab me, and my roll morphs into a long skid on my back. My heart pounds as the tire wall encroaches, my eyes searching in desperate flings for my bike. She's tearing up the bailout four feet away, gouging a line of failure with her right side fairings. But she's not flipping, not coming for me.

I plant my feet, my body catapulting up until I'm running through the gravel. My ankle shrieks and tries to roll as people burst from behind the gate: safety officials and medics running toward me. They're gonna have to get over it.

I turn and bolt toward my bike.

I'm three feet away from her when vertigo takes me.

My knees hit first, the world tilting sideways as blurred people rush closer from my right. I tip farther and finally fall, my screwed left shoulder catching the brunt of my weight. I shout in agony, squirming onto my back and still cradling my hand to my chest as medics swarm in, the crowd growing silent.

I was there. I was right there.

"Mademoiselle Hargrove, stay still until the ambulance can arrive," someone says in a French accent. "You are going to be okay."

"No." My voice is thick with tears as I roll onto my stomach. "I can keep going."

"We need to check you first... Your health is more important."

I bat away the medics. "I'm fine! Just get her up!"

This is my job, and no matter how much I want to quit right now, I can't.

A scream tears out of my throat when my wrist gives, my chest slamming back to earth. Dusty gravel becomes a cloud of lonely horror, and I bite back another sob as I pull my wrist under my chin, trying to stand once more. Encouraging applause from the French spectators finds me when I get to my feet, stumbling toward my bike.

Why didn't I listen to him?

"Mademoiselle Hargrove!"

"Get her up!" I scream at the medics. I grab hold of the handlebars and pull with everything I have, using all the muscles in my back and legs. Something sharp bites through my lower spine, the pain in my shoulder and ribs nearly buckling me. I try again, but at 300 lbs. and my body barely held together with ACE bandages and aspirin, she's too heavy for me to lift on my own.

I'm not strong enough to do this.

It takes four of us to get her vertical, setting her on her thankfully still-inflated tires. I swing my leg over, praying she's rideable. Her right fairings are fucked, the front forks scuffed, but they don't look bent. I can't tell if the swingarm is damaged. I start the engine, and it stalls.

"Come on!" I yell, starting her again. Her engine barks and then snarls to life, loud and angry. I freeze. This new bike hates me. I can feel it in my bones.

The blast of motorcycles rushes past on the turn behind me, sounding faster than ever, their engines a demonic snarl that used to be a symphony. Fury and shame clench my throat as I watch them fly past: orange and red and yellow and blue. Freaking blue.

They all see me, here, in the dirt. That alone should be enough to have me peeling out behind them, but all I can do is close my eyes, trying to stifle the noose of fear around my neck.

I don't know if I can do this.

"Mademoiselle," a medic says. "Please, let us check you. You can race another day."

His hand lies on my arm, and I flinch away from his touch, my eyes flying open. Nausea swarms me from the recollection of having my shoulder snapped back into place without the doctors waiting until I was unconscious or at least under the influence of numbing painkillers.

"Get back," I warn, then push off the dirt with the toes of my boot. My wrist twitches to open the throttle, the drop of my heel shifting from first gear into second as I charge from one hell toward another.

Once I'm on the track, I duck low over my handlebars, leaning left into the turn. My breath is shaky in and out of my lungs, and everything in me sobs in anguish when my kneepad scrapes the track.

Please, don't let me die.

GRAND PRIX DE FRANCE
Le Mans, Sunday, May 19

Pos	Pts	Rider	Time	World Rank
1	25	Santos SAUCEDO	43'49.762	95
2	20	Billy KING	+3.508	94
3	16	Massimo VITOLO	+6.126	65
4	13	Giovanni MARCHESA	+7.745	53
5	11	Cristiano ARELLANO	+9.499	59
6	10	Mason KING	+12.365	50
7	9	Deven HORSLEY	+17.136	33
8	8	Fredek SULZBACH	+22.385	21
9	7	Aurelio LOGGIA	+29.388	22
10	6	Elliston LAMBIRTH	+32.684	29
11	5	Galeno GIRÓN	+36.713	13
12	4	Lorelai HARGROVE	+41.575	69
13	3	Harleigh ELIN	+45.992	28
14	2	Gregorio PAREDES	+53.357	25
15	1	Rainier HERRE	+1'04.534	10
16		Cesaro SOTO	+1'07.091	5
17		Gustavo LIMÓN	1 Lap	0
18		Diarmaid DEAN	1 Lap	2
Not Classified				
		Donato MALDONADO	17 Laps	22
Not Finished 1st Lap				
		Timo GONZALES	0 Lap	5

Chapter 8

Massimo Vitolo—June; Mugello, Italy

I CRUISE TO A STOP INSIDE MY MUGELLO PIT BOX, ALWAYS MY BEST on Italian soil and my entire body still vibrating with *fuck yeah* energy. Mason King set a blistering practice pace for us yesterday. Billy and Giovanni are barely keeping up, and I know Santos has got to be sweating his balls off. It's not a problem for me, though. I've been moving at warp speed ever since Le Mans.

We're only five races into the circuit, but with the high rankings I'm pulling down, my financial breakup with Gabriele is not only becoming a touchable reality, but the end date is moving up. Valencia is starting to look like Malaysia. Possibly Australia. Could be even sooner depending on how I race this Sunday and whether anyone important crashes out.

I mentally curse myself for the jinx as soon as I think it. As much as I love watching Gabriele squirm every time I step foot in that asshole's office, I really wish those envelopes weren't heavy because Lorina is wrecking. Beating her in a battle is one thing. Passing her by when she's in the dirt is another. But she'll bounce back soon. She always does.

As soon as I take off my helmet and tug out my earplugs, my crew and Vinicio greet me with their standard postpractice applause, Gabriele's nephew included. Right on cue, Chiara leaps up from her chair, running over to me with a squeal and wrapping her arms around my neck in a hug that chokes the hell out of me.

"I hate you so much for this," my best friend whispers in Italian. "I'm so freaking bored."

I chuckle guiltily as I pat her back and untangle myself, getting off my moto. Chiara switches back into groupie mode, batting her eyes and fidgeting with her hair, and she's laying it on way too thick. Lucio is never going to believe the act, and I really, really need him to buy this.

Somehow, word got out that I followed Lorina to the hospital in Jerez. Ever since, my crew chief has yet to stop asking about my relationship with her. But it's not him wondering whether Lorina's sleeping in my bed. It's Angelo Maggiore—the person Lucio reports to at Yaalon.

Technically, Angelo can't bar me from talking to Lorina. From visiting her in the hospital or being friends. Fine print is a bitch to dig through, but for once, it's coming out in my favor instead of detailing how much my fine is for popping wheelies in front of her garage.

What it also didn't say—but I already know—is that with her riding for Dabria, Angelo can question my loyalty. Whether I want to see my team's blue colors cross the finish line first or her team's red ones. With my luck, that insinuation could downgrade into a threat, and it could happen fast.

Her, or them.

Too bad hindsight doesn't help dick, so it's useless to long for the days when they only saw us as rivals and didn't think to look any closer. I should have kept it that way. I don't know how I'll ever choose between Lorina and the paycheck that protects my family if they try to make me, so I can't let those assholes make me.

I sling my arm around Chiara's shoulders and bring her with me to the edge of the garage, Lucio and the rest of my crew already starting to break down the stats readouts and prep the moto for adjustments. "They say anything while I was out there?" I ask quietly.

"Nope. Just that you should definitely beat her for pole position tomorrow." Chiara pivots to face me, smiling like the sun shines out of my ass. She hands me a bottle of water, petting and poking at my leathers, and it's annoying as hell. But Lucio glances over and smiles at me, then goes back to what he's doing, so I let it go. Chiara drops her voice to a whisper. "I thought you said she was getting better?"

"I said she was going to get better. And she will."

Chiara scowls at me like this is somehow my fault. "You need to help her, Massimo. You picked the fight that started this, which means you need to set it straight."

I gape at her, hating how much she's right. "I didn't tell you that just so you could throw it in my face."

She grips my jaw like a grandmother adoring a child. "Where did you expect me to throw it?" she says in a baby voice. I bat her hand away, Chiara snickering.

"Look, what do you expect me to do? She doesn't need my help, and she wouldn't listen even if I tried. The only reason she ever talks to me is to yell at me."

Chiara shrugs. "Have you done anything lately she should yell at you for?"

I think for a second, but I've been good at press conferences and keeping my mouth shut during riders' meetings. "No. I haven't even gone near her since her practice at Le Mans. When giving her advice didn't make a single bit of difference, like I told you it wouldn't."

Chiara's whole expression slips into a mischievous smirk that makes me want to check for my wallet. She jerks her chin at something behind me. "It made a difference."

I glance behind me, and *holy shit*. Dabria leathers are heading my way. I whip back toward Chiara, my pulse racing even faster than before.

"Be nice," Chiara says patronizingly. Then, for real, "And don't say a single word about her practice time. I mean it. She needs a friend, not another man telling her what she's doing wrong." Chiara glances at Lucio and my crew, then pecks my cheek and spins around, breathing, "Smack my ass."

I can barely keep up with her absurdity at this point. "What?"

"Smack my ass!" I give her a little pat, and she jumps and squeaks loud enough to draw the attention of my entire crew. "Oh! Massimo, you're so bad!"

Vinicio groans and covers his face with his hand. But Lucio is drooling as Chiara jogs her "Keep Calm and Klingon" tank top and yoga pants out of my garage. I turn toward pit lane to see if Lorina's going to stride past me on her way to the paddock and her RV.

Wonders will never cease. She stops in front of me, cloaking me in sharp lemon and sweet moto exhaust. "Hey," she says, a quiet smile to match her voice. "Do you have a second?"

Yes, I have a second. I have all the seconds. Something she would know if she had ever willfully sought me out before, but usually, she just runs the other way. "Forse," I tease her, shaking my hand in a maybe as I switch to English. "Depends on what you want, Lorina."

"I..." Her hands and entire body start to fidget as her smile and gaze drop to the garage floor. "I just wanted to say hi to my friend. After my friend finished his practice."

I can't help but chuckle at my own words coming back to me, Lorina peeking up from under her eyelashes: all rich amber eyes searching mine, the Tuscan sun sparkling over her curls and cascading over her red leather shoulders, and I have no idea what racetrack we're at anymore.

Maybe that talk in her hospital room did more good than I thought. Maybe, finally, we're really becoming friends.

At least until Lorina wrinkles her nose in confusion at something over my shoulder, then tentatively waves. I turn in time to see Chiara waving enthusiastically at Lorina, and I whip forward, even more tongue-tied than before.

"Is that…your cousin or something?" Lorina leans past me to get a better look, and I quickly block her view.

Explaining my and Chiara's history is gonna be more than a little complicated, and it's not something I'm looking to share with Lorina yet when we're barely starting to talk. Not fight, but *talk*.

Lorina looks back to me, her eyes narrowed. "Just forget it."

Not likely. She's starting to trust me, possibly even like me—if I can get out of this—and that's better than any qualifying time. Fine or no fine. "Why should I forget?"

"Well, considering you have some mystery guest you're refusing to explain…" Lorina gestures behind me.

My smile grows impossibly wider. If she wants to go there, let's go there. "I am not hiding anything."

"Then who is she?"

I take a step closer, whispering, "First, admit you are jealous."

Lorina shakes her head, like that'll keep her from getting more pissed off. "Whatever. Keep your secrets. It's not my business anyway."

"Lorina, it is not a secret. It is just—"

"Massimo," Vinicio says behind me. I glance at him, and his eyebrow arches, every word heavy with importance as he continues in Italian. "She cannot be here right now."

My gaze follows his toward my crew. Who have stopped what they're doing. Lucio is standing in front of them, his arms crossed, as though just the sight of them having tools in their hands is giving Lorina some kind of advantage for the coming race. Yeah, okay.

Still, I don't have a choice but to turn to back to Lorina, concentrating hard on what's most important—what has to come first anyway. "Speaking of secrets, if you want to spy on me, maybe next time you should wear something more sexy than leathers. It would work better."

Her eyes widen. "What do you mean 'spy'?"

"They are working on my moto for the race, and—"

"Oh." She backs up, embarrassment coloring her features as she looks at Vinicio. "Sorry, I'll go." She turns on her heel and starts heading back the way she came, but at twice the speed as before.

Since when does she back down that fast?

I take a drink of water, steeling myself. I should get back to working with my crew in case they have any questions about the changes I need them to make. To make sure Lucio sends a favorable report to Angelo about my loyalty.

Lorina dodges Santos walking past her, and she hugs her arms around herself. *Yank.*

"Ehi! Lulu," I call out before I can care about the kind of trouble this stuff has caused in the past, and I find myself jogging out of my garage, ignoring Vinicio calling my name.

Lorina looks at me once I'm caught up to her, and under the scent of sharp citrus layered with hints of deathly speed, I'm already struggling to keep my thoughts straight. But something in her eyes reminds me of her crying in the hospital, and I'm completely screwed. I glance around, but there's nowhere we can go to talk privately. Definitely don't want to think about the fact that my *very empty* apartment is only a couple of hours from here. I should probably count my blessings for that, but I never did find that priest.

"I am going to get something to eat," I lie. "Come sit with me, and you can tell me all your dirty Tigrotta secrets. I will not even judge you for them." I lean a little closer. "Much."

Hope brightens the corner of her lips, turning up into a smile. "Okay."

I nod, and together, we head off pit lane and into the open paddock, where there are plenty of people. So far, so good. Most of their eyes widen a little when they see us; they've all been witnesses to our arguments over the past years. At least by being in public, they can all report to anyone who asks that nothing is happening that shouldn't be.

Once we're outside the cooking station set up for me and Billy and our team, Lorina takes a seat across from me at a table. But instead of merrily glaring at me under the perfect Tuscan weather, she's staring at her hands in her lap, dark circles under her eyes like she hasn't been sleeping enough. She's also shrinking inside her leathers instead of wearing them like a superhero costume as she normally does. I practically have to bite my tongue to keep from asking her what the hell happened at Le Mans.

I'm telling myself it was just the soreness. I told her those broken ribs were gonna hurt. But Lorina is also Centauro—a true racer, in heart, in spirit—and I never really expected her to sit out. I'm also expecting her to mount a comeback challenge this Sunday, which means I can't rule out that *all* of this—the surprise garage appearance and the quiet sullenness—could be a ploy to get me to drop my guard.

Kinda doubting it, but with Lorina, anything is possible.

"So, um, how was your break?" she asks the table, and I nearly choke from pure shock. I didn't know Lorina was aware there was life outside the circuit. Apart from that disastrous conversation surrounding her last boyfriend, we've never discussed our home life.

"It was okay," I tell her carefully. Expensive would be more truthful, but that's a lot to unpack. "Um…" *What do I say?* Nothing about racing or her practice time, Chiara said. What else is there?

"Your family in Memphis, you raise horses, yes?" Billy never shuts up about his stallion, Gadget or Gidget or something, during our team meetings.

Lorina nods, something a little sweet playing in her voice. "Carthusian-Andalusians."

I had a joke teed up about whips and saddles, but for the life of me, I can't remember what it was. "So...beautiful horses," I say instead.

She nods again, but the movements are all skittish and impatient. Same with the sigh she lets out before she glances around, then demands, "What do you do when you're not racing, Massimo? Or what would you do if you...couldn't race?"

I repeat her words in my head multiple times, hoping I'm getting one of them wrong, but *nope*. Why is she talking about retiring? We just made MotoPro, and barring any more big wrecks, she has ten years to go before her age becomes a factor. Must be Billy freaking her out while they're home in Memphis. Especially with how everyone is constantly on his ass to hang it up.

"Why would I tell you?" I taunt. "You probably think all Italian men do is drink vino and eat pasta, ride moto, and make passionate love to beautiful women."

Her eyes spark to life, earning me the shadow of a smile. "Prove me wrong, then."

I grin. "Cannot. This is what we do."

She chuckles, but it fades fast, Lorina dissolving back into the pale version of herself like someone dumped a bucket of sand on all her fire. "What do you really do when you're not racing? No bullshit. I mean, I'm sure you have a family, but you don't talk about them much, and apart from your...cousin, I've never seen them at any of our races."

I twist the water bottle in my hands, forever debating how much

I'm willing to tell her against what I think she probably needs to hear. Another racer walks by, making a gesture behind Lorina's back, and I flip him off. "I have Vinicio."

"He's your manager. Not exactly the same."

I look back to Lorina, realizing what I just said. "He is also il mio patrigno. Um, stepfather. Mio papà, he died many years ago."

"Oh." She sits up as her shoulders drop, and *why* did I tell her that? I should've told her something nice about kittens. "I'm sorry. I didn't know."

I wave her off, starting to regret not grabbing my sunglasses before I walked out of my garage. It's bright as hell out here. "He was old, and he died happy, with his wife and family. So it is okay."

Lorina props her chin in her palm like she's settling in for a story, her eyes thankfully empty of any trace of pity. "How did he meet your mom?"

I shake my head, grinning, and I can't believe just her smile is enough to get me to babble like some prepubescent altar boy at his first confession, but whatever. At least she doesn't seem as upset anymore. "My papà was traveling, on his way to the wedding of a friend, and he crashed his moto. Not too bad, but bad enough, and she was a nurse at the hospital where they took him."

Lorina gasps, but her voice is all swoony. "No way."

"Sì," I say with a nod. "She was very young and very beautiful, and I do not know why she married him, because he was very old and very poor."

Lorina laughs, sounding a lot more like she usually does when she's strutting around the paddock, waiting for her next chance to prove us all slow.

"But l'amore è cieco," I add, and her brow furrows.

"Love is…blind?"

I point at her, wondering if she realizes that over the years, she's gone from not being able to understand a single word I speak to getting about 98 percent of it, no matter what language I'm dabbling in. "Sì. Molto bene, Tigrotta. So they married and had me, and many years went by, and then they had mio fratello." I debate whether even to tell her, then decide to do it anyway. Can't hurt. "My brother, Dario? He spends molto time watching moto, and he thinks you are a perfect Centauro." I feign insult at the whole thing. But it gets Lorina's smile to deepen, and if she keeps looking at me like that, I'm never going to shut up.

"Sounds like I need to meet your brother."

I narrow my eyes jokingly. "No. He probably would hug you and kiss you until he had a heart attack, and he is too young for...some things." I lean a little closer, my eyes dropping to her lips. "But I am older."

Lorina's eyes widen, but they're also instantly hungry and dark with desire. I can't resist laughing that I busted her so easily, and I get up from the table.

She's fine, and I'm getting out of here before I get myself in deeper trouble, fun as it is.

"You're such a jerk," she mutters.

I swipe my water bottle from the table. "Why you are surprised, Lorina, I will never know." I take another sip of water as I head toward the safety of my garage, but I don't get far.

"Massimo?"

Shit. I wonder if she practices saying my name that way just so she can wield it over me whenever she chooses. She's killing me.

I pivot toward her, drawling, "Sì?"

"Thank you, for Tigrotta."

I don't understand why she's thanking me for herself. And then it clicks.

When I check, no one important is in earshot. "You named the toy Tigrotta?"

Lorina nods, and I feel myself start to smile. She wouldn't have named it that if she truly hated the nickname, and I really, really need to get my debts paid off and my life in order. Yesterday.

"Okay."

She tucks a loose hair behind her ear, having a hard time finding my eyes. Once she does, it seems impossible for her to look away. "Is it?"

No. It's not okay. Not when I have to be the bad guy on the track, which means I can't be the good guy away from it.

She swallows, looking down at my silence, and *damn it*. Blood pounds thickly through my veins, my steps heavy with it as I ignore every single reason why I should focus on protecting my career and head over to her anyway. I crouch down, and she shifts a little on the table bench, but not away from me like she did in her garage in Le Mans.

I drop my voice, drop the jokes. Drop all of it. Right now. "We have to be careful, cara."

Her brow furrows because she doesn't understand the nickname. But I'm not ready to tell her what this one means. Not yet.

"Careful like, people watching us?" she asks. I nod, and her chin lifts. "It doesn't matter to me what they say. And if it's your 'cousin' that has the problem, then—"

"It is not her that has the problem. And is not what people say. It is...to who it will be said."

Her shoulders drop, realization flooding her eyes as she glances at the garages and then back at me. But still, she nods.

"At least we are still racing together." I try to smile at the compromise I've been clinging to for years, but it's weak. It's all so *weak*. "It is something, Lorina."

She laughs, but it sounds anything except relieved. Probably because she always gets what she wants. When she stays quiet instead of spouting off a retort, I nudge her leg with my water bottle. Her head pops up, and my breath locks in my throat at how scared she looks.

Something's going on.

Maybe Chiara was right: Jerez wasn't just another wreck for Lorina, and even though she walked away, it messed her head up more than I realized. More than I ever wanted to admit was possible. Especially since I picked the fight that started it all.

"It's just, sometimes," Lorina whispers, "I wish it were just you and me on that track, you know?" She shakes her head as though that isn't a huge red flag in itself, and I can't believe she's admitting this to me—the last person who should know she's struggling. The last person she would ever *want* to know. If she weren't so shaken up. "I know it sounds ridiculous, but it would make things so much easier right now."

Her eyes lock with mine, vulnerable and filled with so much need that it cuts me to my core, and God help me, this woman is going to rule my entire life and never let me kiss her. But I don't know how I'm supposed to do anything about it when Angelo is already suspicious, and I've got Gabriele bleeding my bank account dry every time I touch down in Ravenna.

I can't be everything Lorina needs me to be. Not yet. But I can't do *nothing*.

I rise, holding up a finger for her to wait when she stares at me. It's two seconds over to the cooking station, then I'm back, sitting across from her. "Give me your hand." With wary movements, she stretches her left hand out across the table. "Make a fist," I tell her, doing the same as an example.

With half a smile on the verge of being complete, she tucks her fingers into her palm so her skin draws tight. I pull her hand closer, ducking over it so no one else sees what I'm doing. Not even Lorina.

"I never realized you were left-handed," she murmurs.

"Mm-hmm." She is too.

She doesn't say anything else as I quietly, secretly, in the flat part between her thumb and forefinger, draw two numbers inside a small shape in blue pen, then color it in. She giggles a little like it tickles, and when I'm finished and let her go, her eyes triple in size when she sees what I drew. I sit back and take a sip of water, aware of all the eyes watching me on the bright, sunny paddock.

Her fault. All her fault.

"Thank you." Lorina's voice is a little strained, but she clears her throat, glancing around. When she looks to me, she narrows her eyes, but it seems forced—like it's more for our spectators than for me. I know it for sure when the volume of her voice rises to a public level. "Well, it's been more than a pain in the ass speaking with you, considering you are nothing more than a narcissistic jerk who... smells. Now, if you'll excuse me, I am going back to my garage."

The corners of my lips pull up. Just a little. Then I shut it down.

Lorina rises, flipping me off with her left hand—showing me the colored-in blue heart, my number 32 left clear in the middle. "Get ready to get your ass kicked on Sunday, Massimo."

I fake a scowl. "Not if I kick yours first, Lorina."

She stomps away, her shoulders square and her braid fierce down her back, and it would be great if the fact that I made her feel better made *me* feel better. It doesn't. Not when I'm dying to go after her and sick to death of everything that's holding me back. Mostly my own fear that it wouldn't matter anyway because she'll never see me as anything but someone who has hurt her, too many times.

GRAN PREMIO D'ITALIA
Mugello, Sunday, June 02

Pos	Pts	Rider	Time	World Rank
1	25	Massimo VITOLO	41'37.152	90
2	20	Billy KING	+2.531	114
3	16	Santos SAUCEDO	+5.691	111
4	13	Mason KING	+8.342	63
5	11	Harleigh ELIN	+12.578	39
6	10	Giovanni MARCHESA	+16.226	63
7	9	Gustavo LIMÓN	+17.720	9
8	8	Aurelio LOGGIA	+22.423	30
9	7	Rainier HERRE	+27.096	17
10	6	Galeno GIRÓN	+33.573	19
11	5	Gregorio PAREDES	+39.496	30
12	4	Diarmaid DEAN	+42.979	6
13	3	Cesaro SOTO	+45.372	8
14	2	Deven HORSLEY	+52.841	35
15	1	Elliston LAMBIRTH	+56.725	30
16		Timo GONZALES	+59.654	5
Not Classified				
		Cristiano ARELLANO	2 Laps	59
		Fredek SULZBACH	5 Laps	21
		Lorelai HARGROVE	17 Laps	69
		Donato MALDONADO	19 Laps	22

GRAN PREMI DE CATALUNYA
Barcelona, Sunday, June 16

Pos	Pts	Rider	Time	World Rank
1	25	Billy KING	42'38.897	139
2	20	Santos SAUCEDO	+4.032	131
3	16	Massimo VITOLO	+12.577	106
4	13	Mason KING	+17.371	76
5	11	Cristiano ARELLANO	+21.433	70
6	10	Fredek SULZBACH	+26.802	31
7	9	Galeno GIRÓN	+30.581	28
8	8	Giovanni MARCHESA	+33.194	71
9	7	Rainier HERRE	+35.672	24
10	6	Gregorio PAREDES	+41.153	36
11	5	Cesaro SOTO	+43.731	13
12	4	Donato MALDONADO	+48.825	26
13	3	Diarmaid DEAN	+52.493	9
14	2	Timo GONZALES	+1'07.942	7
15	1	Deven HORSLEY	+1'09.710	36
16		Harleigh ELIN	1 Lap	39
17		Lorelai HARGROVE	1 Lap	69
Not Classified				
		Elliston LAMBIRTH	10 Laps	30
		Aurelio LOGGIA	17 Laps	30
		Gustavo LIMÓN	22 Laps	9

MOTUL TT ASSEN
Assen, Sunday, June 30

Pos	Pts	Rider	Time	World Rank
1	25	Billy KING	40'51.968	164
2	20	Santos SAUCEDO	+1.582	151
3	16	Mason KING	+4.376	92
4	13	Massimo VITOLO	+6.449	119
5	11	Fredek SULZBACH	+7.510	42
6	10	Timo GONZALES	+9.103	17
7	9	Deven HORSLEY	+14.946	45
8	8	Donato MALDONADO	+17.591	34
9	7	Aurelio LOGGIA	+23.753	37
10	6	Rainier HERRE	+29.164	30
11	5	Cesaro SOTO	+34.834	18
12	4	Gregorio PAREDES	+42.089	40
13	3	Diarmaid DEAN	+46.277	12
14	2	Elliston LAMBIRTH	+51.596	32
15	1	Gustavo LIMÓN	+1'02.636	10
16		Lorelai HARGROVE	+1'09.710	69
Not Classified				
		Galeno GIRÓN	1 Lap	28
		Giovanni MARCHESA	6 Laps	71
		Cristiano ARELLANO	7 Laps	70
		Harleigh ELIN	21 Laps	39

MOTORRAD GRAND PRIX DEUTSCHLAND
Sachsenring, Sunday, July 07

Pos	Pts	Rider	Time	World Rank
1	25	Santos SAUCEDO	41'05.019	176
2	20	Billy KING	+2.196	184
3	16	Giovanni MARCHESA	+2.776	87
4	13	Deven HORSLEY	+3.376	58
5	11	Aurelio LOGGIA	+5.183	48
6	10	Cristiano ARELLANO	+5.780	80
7	9	Galeno GIRÓN	+7.941	37
8	8	Fredek SULZBACH	+12.711	50
9	7	Rainier HERRE	+14.428	37
10	6	Elliston LAMBIRTH	+21.474	38
11	5	Gregorio PAREDES	+25.809	45
12	4	Diarmaid DEAN	+25.963	16
13	3	Donato MALDONADO	+29.040	37
14	2	Cesaro SOTO	+29.325	20
15	1	Harleigh ELIN	+34.123	40
Not Classified				
		Timo GONZALES	3 Laps	17
		Gustavo LIMÓN	7 Laps	10
		Mason KING	8 Laps	92
		Massimo VITOLO	11 Laps	119
Not Finished 1st Lap				
		Lorelai HARGROVE	0 Lap	69

Chapter 9

Lorelai Hargrove—July; Chemnitz, Germany

"HOW COME THERE ARE NEVER ANY MINIBARS IN THESE HOITY-TOITY suites?" Mason pulls out another drawer on the single writing desk in Billy's hotel room, like that'll have a surprise stash of the Tennessee whiskey he's craving.

I shift again on the couch, sore and impatient. It should start any minute now.

"Thought Germans loved to drink?" Mason adds.

"And you don't need to," Billy rumbles, sprawled out in the patterned accent chair with one boot across his knee. His temple is propped against his fingers, his eyes closed, and I wonder if he's hurting again. If he ever stops hurting. With all my crashes lately, I can't seem to stop either, no matter how many Epsom salt baths I take. I'm also going to have a big-ass bruise on my side and shoulder tomorrow, but that's becoming standard too.

"You don't need to," Mason mocks, making a face behind his brother's back. He wanders his Wranglers over to the curtains, pulling them wider open to reveal the night sky. He lets out a low whistle. "Y'all know we can see the Sachsenring from here? Hey, baby!" he shouts at the window. "You may have won me today, but me and my Dabria will see you next year!"

He flips off the racetrack, and I lean over, slyly picking up the remote that Mason abandoned on the sofa before he went on his whiskey hunt. Frank just went downstairs to take a phone call, but the three of us are stuck here instead of being on a red-eye back to Memphis because of a pilot strike. I can't really blame them, but I also can't bring myself to care about Frank booking us rooms at Hotel Drei Schwanen as a consolation prize.

I couldn't give a flip about private messages, crystal chandeliers, or terraces that open to the Ore Mountains when almost every view also includes the Sachsenring stadium that owned my ass each minute from Thursday to Sunday.

I just... I don't know what's happening to me. I can't find the speed I need, can't find the rhythm. My dreams are all nightmares of me wandering in an empty desert, a fractured helmet in my hand and no bike anywhere to ride, no matter how long I search. Frank says it's just me wanting to get back to normal, but I think it has more to do with whatever's going on with my equipment.

My chest plate looked like it had a crack in it when I checked it before Mugello, and my helmet felt too light before Catalunya. Frank told me it was fine both times, but in the Netherlands, it was all still wrong: the speed tasted like ash, every turn a death sentence I wobbled through, until today, when the Sachsenring won the fairings of my now-battered bike. Even my new injuries aren't bad enough to keep me from racing after the break, but still. Another crash logged, and more bruises rising where others have yet to heal.

"Mason." Billy's voice is a sharp tug on his brother's name. My eyes flick to the eldest King, his gaze pinned on his brother's back.

Mason turns away from the curtains and the view, drawling an annoyed, "What?" But then he looks to me. He swallows, glancing back to his brother before he clears his throat. "Sorry, Lori."

"It's fine." I glare at Billy. "And don't do that."

Billy doesn't respond other than to pull out his cell phone as

Mason comes over and collapses on the couch next to me, bumping my shoulder with his. "Hey, it'll be okay, man. You'll come back. You just need some time at home to get your boots back under ya."

I offer him a smile, checking the time on my phone before my eyes dart to the TV screen. "Thanks, Mason." He means well. He always does.

"Aww, man!" He gestures toward the television. "What happened to the Michael Dorn biography I was watching?" He starts looking around for the remote. That I hid.

"Ended." My heart starts pumping faster and faster as a commercial plays, and I wonder when I started having anxiety attacks about absolutely everything. It's only a nightly sports news recap. But it's gonna have interviews with the other riders about the big story of the day. Mainly their hot take on me locking up and crashing out. Again.

"Hey, honey," Billy says, followed by an extensive yawn. I look over, and his phone is pressed to his ear like always. "How was your day?"

A jealous twist pulls at my lips. Maybe *I* needed to talk to Taryn. She may be his girlfriend, but she's my best friend. Except, come to think of it, I don't even know what track she's preparing to race on. The Superbike circuit is completely different from Moto Grand Prix, and I haven't been paying close enough attention. Too wrapped up in my fledgling career to remember there's another world outside the circuit gates.

I've really sucked as a friend lately.

The commercial ends, morphing into a banner with the standard anchor photos and name of the program. It fades again to the anchor desk, a dark-haired guy smiling at his gorgeous coanchor before they start speaking German.

"Crap," I mutter, pulling out the remote.

"Fibber," Mason says. "Should've known you stole it."

It takes a second to find the button, but every time I check, they're still showing pictures of guys in soccer uniforms and haven't started Moto Grand Prix yet. One more click, and then English words start scrolling across the bottom of the screen. It should make me feel better. It doesn't. I debate whether to turn them off.

"Hey, hold on." Billy pulls his phone away from his ear. "Lorelai, what are y'all watching?"

I glance at Mason, who isn't saying anything, but his smile is pure guilt. "Movie."

We're not supposed to watch this stuff, according to Frank's rules. He says it only does more harm than good, and I get that. I do. But…

"Think they'll have an interview with Santos?" Mason says.

"Hey, one of you turn that off before Frank gets back!" Billy jumps up from the chair like his ass caught on fire. "I'll call you back." He ditches his cell phone, practically running over to the flat-screen TV mounted on the wall. He feels around the side and squints at the bottom, then tries to see the back. "Where're the buttons on this thing?"

"Get outta the way, Billy!" Mason barks. "I wanna see if they show my crash today."

The picture in the corner of a guy making a soccer goal disappears, and I peer past Billy's pearl-snap shirt blocking the TV as the camera focuses on just the two anchors. When I get a glimpse at the subtitles, I only have to see the word Sachsenring to know I'm up next.

"Five minutes," I barter as he keeps searching for the power button. "Billy, come on!"

"Aw, hell." Billy gives up with a defeated fling of his hands, going back to his chair. He picks up his phone as he sits, sticking it up to his ear. "Hey. Yeah, you're not gonna believe what these two yahoos are doing while Frank isn't here. *Jesus*, Taryn, they aren't doing that! What's wrong with you?"

"Hey, I heard that!" I call out loud enough for her to hear me through his receiver. The TV screen changes to a clip of me going down today. Like clockwork, a cold sweat breaks out over my skin. I squeeze my eyes shut, but I still hear them play it. Three times. I'm guessing from different angles. Great.

Mason bumps my elbow with his. "Tough luck, Lori."

I bump him back. Gently, considering my newest injuries. Couldn't have asked for a better teammate, really. Mason doesn't care about rivalries or sabotaging anyone. Just sucks that I'm bringing him down. That I'm bringing *all* of Dabria Corse down.

Rapid German takes over, and since it's safe to look, I do. Except Santos Saucedo is now on my screen, looking more thrilled with himself than ever.

"Screw you, asshole!" I yell at the TV, flipping it off.

"Boo!" Mason yells in solidarity, tossing a throw pillow at the screen.

We share a high five as Billy groans and props his boot carefully on his opposite knee. I don't care what he thinks either. This is all Santos's fault. If he hadn't hit me, I wouldn't have crashed. I would be winning and happy and... *Goddamn it!*

The screen cuts to a clip of Santos finishing in sixth place, and then I hear it: Massimo Vitolo.

"Uh-oh." Mason's body stiffens beside me. "Hey, um, Lori, you find that clicker yet? I think I saw the last Bourne movie playing a couple channels back..."

I don't respond. I'm too busy sending up a prayer that Massimo didn't totally rip me apart with criticism like he's done in the past, always more than happy to tell the world they moved me up in divisions too soon, that I should be fined for reckless behavior, that he doesn't know what place I finished because he doesn't worry about the riders who aren't a threat to him.

But that's what you get from a guy with the nickname "No Mercy."

"Hey, Billy," Mason says loudly. "Where's your deck of cards at? Why don't we play some poker or something while we're waiting for Frank to get back?"

"That is a great idea," Billy says loudly, tilting the receiver away from his mouth. "Go find them."

"You go find them."

"You're closer to the bag..."

"It's your bag, and I'm not supposed to touch your stuff..."

I ignore the bickering King brothers, my brow furrowing when another crash plays on the screen. I suck in a breath when I realize: it's Massimo. He went down today too.

It's more of a slide than anything—he came around a corner in lap seventeen, and she just slipped out from under him. Easy, controlled slide into the dirt, and then he was up, jogging to a stop. He and a crew of people mess with the bike for a minute, Massimo eventually walking away and ripping off his helmet, clearly pissed.

I glance down, realizing my hand is clenched in a fist over my heart, and I recross my arms. He's fine. It doesn't stop the ice crystalizing down my back when Massimo appears on my screen, a microphone in his face.

"I am verbally giving you express permission this one time—"

"Both of you shut up!" I snap.

Something-something in Italian, the guy on the TV says, then my name, and that's when Massimo's eyes change. But it's not just his eyes. His *whole face* changes from frustrated to feral, defensive to predatory, and the guy interviewing him goes dead freaking silent. Massimo walks off.

"Wha..." I sputter, but when I check the subtitles, I barely get a chance to mutter, "Oh no" before the image on the screen changes to the photo from last year. "Shit!"

"See?" Billy says. "This is why we don't watch this crap. Mason, turn it off."

"You turn it off! And stop telling me what to do all the time!"

I claw my hands through my hair, but the damage is done. Has been for a while. And it was just another simple little crash, except that time, we crashed together.

He claims I hit him. I distinctly recall the opposite. But considering we both received a pit lane start penalty and walked away, no one cares about that. What they still can't shut up about was the picture of us squaring off in the dirt, which, if it hadn't caused such a PR nightmare, I might have appreciated for the artistry.

But screw that.

The day is gorgeous in the background, the colors vivid and bright, and it's an expertly framed shot of Massimo leaning toward me, full tilt, screaming in my face. His arm is outstretched over my shoulder because he was telling me to get out of said face, and sport, and country, and life, and I...

I am perfectly opposite him. Black MotoA leathers to his white ones. Also screaming. My braid blowing gloriously in the wind. Flipping him off with both my middle fingers.

The photo graced the cover of every Italian newspaper, motorcycle magazine, sports show, and even a couple of late nights in the United States with the caption "No Mercy for Wreckless."

They'll probably still be showing it at my funeral.

The anchors on the sportscast share a presumptuous look that does nothing for my mood, but thankfully, they cut to a clip of Giovanni Marchesa celebrating his win.

"Hey, they didn't show me," Mason complains. "How come I never get any love from the sports shows?"

The hotel door unlocks, and I rush to grab the remote and change the channel, but I barely get it clicked to an action movie before

Frank booms behind us, "Okay, so that's done. International flights are still cancelled. Breakfast is downstairs in the morning. Billy and Mason, get out."

Mason flinches and looks at me, but my eyes are darting past him to gauge Billy's reaction. "I'll call you back." He lowers his phone and slowly rises. Sometimes, I forget how tall he is until he unfolds all the way like that. "Everything okay?"

"Yeah, of course," Frank says, smiling and fidgety and waving him off. "You and Mason just…go to Mason's room and hang out for a minute. Play cards or something. I need to talk to Lori. About a, uh, birthday gift. For her mom."

Liar. Her birthday was three weeks ago, and Frank sent her a bottle of Dalmore 25.

Mason looks between us. "So…go talk to Lori in her room. Why we gotta move to mine? I already took my boots off."

Frank doesn't react as Billy rolls his eyes, then grabs his brother by the scruff of his neck and hauls him up, marching him toward the door. "We'll be next door," he says to Frank, glancing back at me with a pitying look just before he shuts it behind himself and Mason.

Billy sent my mom flowers for her birthday. Like he's done every year since he first worked for her. He knows this isn't about her.

I turn back to the TV. It's nearly impossible to look at Frank. He's always so upbeat and more confident in me than I am in myself. It's exactly why I can't stand to see the disappointment on his face. I'm falling apart just when I finally made it. And the fact that it's even happening…it feels like someone's playing a bad joke.

This wasn't supposed to happen to *me*. The most focused, most dedicated. Racing has been the only thing I've thought of for as long as I can remember. I don't even rodeo anymore, unlike *some* people.

"So we can do this in a funny accent…" Frank rubs his hands together as he comes around to stand in front of me. "Or we can make up some rule like we're not allowed to use the letter *T*—your choice of letter banishment, of course—but either way, we're talking about this."

I shake my head, changing to another channel. Some cooking show. Lots of butter. "We're not. Go deal with Mason or Billy. His ankle is bothering him again."

Frank sighs. "Ignoring what's happening isn't going to help you or anyone. You have to face it sooner or later, and I'm not above printing it on a billboard. I'll even use that picture from your eleventh birthday with your cake smashed in your face, and you've played poker with me, girlie. You know I suck at bluffing."

I turn off the TV, then look at him, furious. "I don't have to face anything, because everything is going to be fine!"

Frank's eyes flare, his jaw locked tight. I swallow, shrinking into the tufted sofa. I never talk to him like that. Mason does sometimes when the pressure gets to him, but Billy and I don't.

"Now is not the time to turn on me." Frank's voice is deep with a lack of humor that shrinks me to about six inches. "This is the time for us to pull together and figure out what we're going to do. Because I can't...I can't keep making promises I don't know if we can keep."

My heart seizes, everything in me going cold as I look up at him. "What promises?"

My manager swallows, his eyes softening along with his voice. "I just got off the phone with Dabria. After three crashes and with no sign of improvement in your practices or qualifying, along with the fact that the constructor is technically right in telling them it's not a tire issue or anything mechanical that's causing the problem—"

"But my gear—"

"Has been cleared by Dabria and your sponsors and everyone else repeatedly, and now...your contract is coming into question."

I clench my hands into fists to keep them from flying to my mouth in horror. It's happening. I always knew it was there, and at my worst, I told myself it could happen. That it would happen. But self-deprecating internal threats and someone actually taking your bike away are two entirely different things.

My gaze drifts from Frank to the open curtains, the lights of the city shining just outside. Stars twinkle as my entire future flashes and blinks out before me: packed stadiums flicker into empty fields, podiums melting into suffocating horse stalls. It takes everything I have to keep my voice steady. "What's the condition? How close are we to being in breach?"

Moving slowly, as if his movements ache, Frank slumps into the overstuffed chair Billy was just in. Guilt owns me. He must be exhausted after days of watching me fumble during practice and qualifying, then crashing again at the Sachsenring. "It's not a breach per se. But the only way to ward off replacement by a wild card rider is for your point tallies to be higher and to climb faster. They want to be on the podium for World Champion."

My eyes close. Holy hell. Before, I would've laughed. It would've seemed so simple. Too simple. Now? I may as well have to lug my bike up the Himalayas. "Can that even happen?"

Frank clears his throat.

I open my eyes and look at him, my voice cracking when I repeat, "Is it even mathematically possible for me to make the podium?"

He nods, his hands folded in his lap. "It's possible. But it's going to take everything, absolutely everything, plus a miracle or two that I don't want to wish happening to anyone else." He leans forward, resting his elbows on his knees as he stares me down. "There is no room for mistakes anymore, Lorelai."

My jaw drops. "I'm not making them on purpose! I'm doing the best I can, and I don't care what everyone says. I know what's right, and there's still a problem with my safety equipment, and you know it too, Frank."

I've never felt unsafe on my bike. I've taken too many safety seminars to count, and I've even promised little kids there's nothing to be afraid of as long as you're wearing the right gear. But when I saw my bike coming for my face, I knew it wouldn't make a difference. That nothing would keep my skull from crushing, my neck from snapping.

It did—keep my skull intact, my neck safe. I don't know how. No one knows how. No one seems to know what happened to my helmet either, seeing as it disappeared from Jerez before the officials could get their hands on it. But they said not to worry. Just keep trusting in the equipment, since it obviously works.

It doesn't feel like it to me.

Sure, I've always walked away. Yes, I walked away this time. But every crash, my equipment gets weaker. Cracks. Splinters. Stress. And I'm checking it constantly, but no one sees the wear in it that I do. No one will replace it when I say the plates are too thin, that my helmet doesn't feel right. They just keep putting me back on the bike, and it's not my fault I can't find the speed I need when I'm gauging how many Gs my chest plate can take before it shatters and pierces my sternum like buckshot.

"The fact that you believe that…" Frank shakes his head, then rises, heading toward the door of the hotel room. "We may as well go home tomorrow and not come back."

The door slams behind him, and I flinch. How the hell is that supposed to make me feel any better?

—⁓—

Back in my own hotel room, I repack my suitcase for the sixth time in the last ten minutes. I tug and curse once more at my jeans sticking out of the side of my carry-on, needing to be ready to board the plane home to Memphis the very minute I can. But the hem is caught in the zipper, and it won't come free.

"That's *it*!" I give up, completely melting down by the time I sit on the edge of the bed. My stiff and aching shoulders curl in on a choked sob that I don't let reach the geometric carpet or the silk striped wallpaper.

Nine races down, ten to go, and that's it. These could be the last ten races of my career.

My head hangs at the thought, a cold emptiness spreading through me. It feels like the dark desert in my nightmares, and I shiver under the chains of failure, the desolate nothingness when I try to imagine what else my life could be. But it's impossible. There was only ever winning. Only ever racing.

The worst part is that it's not just my bike I'm losing. It's not just the life or the speed. It's the people. My crew who I'll never see again. Frank will be busy managing Billy and Mason and no longer with me every day, nine months of the year. I'm going to lose whatever weird, broken, and backward relationship Massimo and I have been piecing together.

Pull it together, Hargrove.

I lift my head and wipe the tears off my face, making myself breathe and trying to dislodge the thoughts before they stick. I can't break yet. I can't think this way. I have time to figure this out. Three weeks of home. Of horses and my closet and my mom. Of Taryn and Billy bickering every minute they're not sneaking off to have sex, and Mason following them around like a lost dog because he doesn't know what to do if someone's not telling him what *not* to do.

Closing my eyes, I push away the smell of circulated air and imagine the smell of the barn and the color of the dirt, the weight of reins in my hand, and the hard seat of my saddle on my mare's back. I know that life, that world. It may not be my favorite, but I know it, and Mason was right. It's exactly what I need.

Then my phone rings.

I don't even look at it, just unfurling on my bed and pulling one of the spare pillows over my face. My mind bleats how it could be my mom with news of the foals, or maybe it's Taryn, finally off the phone with Billy and ready to regale me with a curse-filled retelling of her latest catfight with Miette. But I already know who is calling me.

It happens after every race now, and there's nothing he can say I want to hear. But there's also something weirdly comforting in the fact that he lets it ring until it goes to voicemail. He doesn't know how to give up.

I wonder if that'll change once I lose my contract and he no longer respects me as a racer—if he ever did. He may have been right not to.

My phone chimes with a new message. I groan, my masochistic tendencies out to play when I toss the pillow to the side, then check the voicemail.

"Lorina, you cannot hide from me forever. Answer your phone, or I will come to your room."

Empty threat. He doesn't know where I am.

Then again, he'll probably have Vinicio call Frank and find out (which is how he got my phone number), and then Massimo will burst through the door, because subtlety is not his style.

My phone rings again, and I roll my eyes, answering. "What?"

"You went too big on turn thirteen—"

I hang up. I wasn't the only person who crashed today, and the hypocrite needs to focus on his own recovery—if he even has any injuries—rather than blowing up my phone. It's not like I ever have answers to the facts he shoves down my throat every Sunday night: the endless list of mistakes I'm making.

I study the telemetry readouts, and I memorize them and plan like I'm supposed to. But when I'm on the track, I can barely remember how to shift gears, much less how to push them to the limits.

I don't know how I ever did half the stuff I did.

A few minutes go by, then my phone rings again. God only knows why, but I accept the call. Maybe it has to do with the fact that Taryn has been impossible to reach lately, completely caught up in her and Billy's new chapter of ranch ownership. So it sometimes feels like Massimo is all I have in the world. Him and Tigrotta.

I hold the phone to my ear, covering the receiver so he won't hear me when I take a shaky breath, trying to hold it together.

"Lorina," he says, his voice calm. "You are Wreckless. You are Centauro. So be Wreckless. Be Centauro."

I nod, even though he can't see me through the phone.

"Today was difficult. It is okay, Lorina. Domani, we will do better."

"Okay," I breathe, wiping at my face and sniffling.

He pauses for a moment, and his voice is so soft that I barely hear him. "Per favore, cara, non piangere."

My eyes close, my shoulders shaking in exhausted laughter. I'm monumentally drained, incredibly sore, and so confused as to why it's comforting that he never cares I don't speak Italian. "I don't understand what you said."

But the only answer I get from Massimo is, "Not today. Maybe domani. Maybe tomorrow, I will tell you."

I let out a quiet laugh. "Fine. Be like that."

Massimo clears his throat, apparently not in the hurry to hang up that he usually is. At least there's no muffled club music in the background; half the time he calls, I can barely hear a word he says. But it's an easy way to tell it's him, especially when it's super late and he doesn't say anything after I answer. Probably pocket dialing me.

I get up and wander over to my bag—which now unzips no problem—then I take out Tigrotta and carry her back to my bed, sitting up against the pillows.

"You have been crying, even before I called you," he says.

"It's fine," I lie, smoothing my hand over Tigrotta's orange and black stripes.

"Dabria...did they stop your contract?"

He says it so easily. Like it's not the worst possible thing that could ever, ever happen. The very words make my stomach lurch into my throat, and I know, *I know*, I shouldn't answer. My contract isn't his business, especially when he rides for a competing manufacturer. Billy would completely lose what's left of his shit if he knew Massimo and I were even talking about this stuff.

Still, it's *Massimo*. And technically, I've known him longer than I've known Billy. It's the excuse I cling to as I hear myself mutter, "They're thinking about it. I have to place on the podium for World Champion. But after this weekend, I don't even know if they're gonna bring me back after the break." My heart aches at the possibility I have no idea how to face, how close I am to having nothing to do with my days, my life. No purpose, no place. "Frank said we were gonna prep for Czech Republic like normal but to be ready for them to call up a wild card."

Silence.

Massimo blows out a breath. "Okay." His voice is stronger the second time. "Okay."

"Okay? That's easy for you to say. When was the last time you finished lower than—"

"Basta. Enough," he interrupts. "You...this...this is not Lorina. Not the Tigrotta who fought for her place in moto when people said there was no place for you."

My mouth twists, memories flooding me that feel like they belong to someone else. "Is that what I did?"

"This fear you are letting control you, it is death, Lorina. And now..." He hesitates, then grits out, "You are dying."

"I don't know how to fix it," I whisper, ashamed. "The more I try, the worse it gets. And there's…something's wrong with my safety gear like it's—"

"Cosa? Has your constructor said this? Is this with your helmet, Lorina, or your plates or…?"

"All of it. It feels like it's all just gonna…shatter. And they keep telling me nothing's wrong with it, but I don't know, Massimo. It doesn't feel right. And they don't believe me."

He blows out another breath, then starts muttering to himself in Italian, and my whole heart is in my chest over what he's going to say when he switches back to English. Whether he's going to be on my side or theirs. "Lorina, you should come sit with me."

My hope bursts, my voice blasting out right behind it. "Why? So you can tell me how it's all in my head and—"

"No. If you think there is a problem, I will not say you are wrong when I do not know this without seeing these things for myself. And I cannot see them. But…I think you should still come sit with me. Stanotte. Tonight."

My hand stutters over Tigrotta's stripes. A thousand responses trill through my mind, like how he said we needed to be careful—although I'm not sure why, if it's a gossip thing with the other racers or what—along with just a resounding, instinctual no.

It could be a trick or a trap.

But when I think about all the times just being close to him has centered me and how close I am to possibly never seeing him again, I find myself looking toward my bag and my clothes as I hear myself answer, "Where?"

Chapter 10

HE ANSWERS MY KNOCK ON HIS DOOR QUICKLY—IN THE SAME hotel, but two floors down—Massimo checking down the hallway when I cross inside.

"Watching for assassins?"

He doesn't answer, just shutting the door and walking around me into the suite. Rolling my eyes, I turn to follow after him, but stop short when I find he's now sitting on the bed with his back against the pillows: an exact replica of the room I just left, except the accent colors are different.

It hits me all at once, and I can't believe I didn't...

We're in a *hotel room.*

Why the hell did I say yes to this? He could think...

I might...

I swallow, trying to assess how much danger I'm in on a temptation scale.

He's still just chilling. The collar of his hoodie is smoothly rumpled around his neck and jawline, his dark stubble a little longer, his mustache a little thicker than he normally lets it grow before he shaves it again. The hem of his sleeve is almost meeting the remote he has lazily cradled in his hand, his arm draped over his bent knee and his fingertip just barely grazing the top of the pause button but not pushing it.

Yep, I'm screwed.

He is ridiculously sexy when he's comfortable. And he's comfortable on a bed with me in the room like it'd be totally normal for me to slip into the sheets beside him, curl up on his shoulder, and fall asleep to whatever he's watching. Except I doubt there'd be any sleeping in Massimo's version of…whatever this is.

I cross my arms and lift my chin. He can never know how badly I'm handling this. Not with how well he appears to be. "If you called me down here to watch some twisted Italian porn, I'm leaving."

A smile tugs at the corner of his lips, and damn him for that, because it makes him even hotter and, at the same time, lures me farther into the room.

With every step toward him, it feels like a decision I don't want to name. The conclusion of where this ends that I can't wrap my mind around yet because we don't…do *that*.

But here I am. In his room. And he's on a bed. Waiting for me.

My pulse throbs in my chest, and I pull my eyes from his dark jaw, looking anywhere that will stop me from racing down the road toward the unthinkable.

I glance toward the safety of the TV.

My back stiffens, and I whirl toward the door. "Yeah, good night."

"Lorina," he says, and it stops me dead in my tracks. It doesn't stop the cruel hand of fear inching toward my throat.

Of all the things that could be playing on his television set, it's the crash at Jerez that has threatened to ruin my entire career. Betrayal bites at me, and I can't stop wondering why it feels like I found another woman in his bed.

"I don't want to watch this, Massimo. I lived through it, and that was more than enough."

"Come sit with me," he says again, softer. "It is easier to watch if I can see you, so I can remember you are okay."

His words lock me in place, breaking me in half. He isn't supposed to say those things to me. He isn't supposed to sound like he really means them. Like it really does hurt him to watch the crash, and he really does want me next to him, just so *he* can feel better.

I should go. I shouldn't even be here in the first place. I can't be in his hotel room. What would people say if they knew? Mason and his never-stopping mouth would say we were sleeping together, and we're not.

I don't care if Massimo is sexy. I don't care if it would feel good. I'm not doing it.

"Per favore, cara…"

Damn it. Not that name. That's the new one. The secret one. The one I'm afraid to translate online because I want to hear it from him first. Why he's calling me that. Why now.

I take a deep breath, squaring my shoulders. I can control my actions, thoughts, and feelings. And I can hang out with a guy without it meaning anything more. I work out with Billy and Mason all the time when we're home, and I can watch TV with Massimo. It doesn't have to end in nudity and orgasms and awkward "Where do we go from here?" conversations. We can just spend time together. As friends. While we can.

Keeping my back to the screen, I walk toward the bed and sit next to him. It's a little weird, trying to find a way to sit where I'm comfortable. But that's basically impossible with the small amount of space between us strangling me. How easy it would be for it to become less. How cold the air is on my skin, and how warm he looks in that hoodie.

Maybe that's what he had in mind all along.

If it was, he doesn't act on it. He doesn't do or say *anything*, just rewinding the video to restart the sequence of events. My fingers pick distractedly at the down comforter, waiting for the sound of the crash. Massimo's hand lies on my calf.

I startle at his touch, my eyes flying to his and pleading with him not to go there. I can't take it right now on top of everything else. He doesn't move his hand, only slightly arches his eyebrow, and I swallow. He waits.

I wish I'd worn something more modest than shorts and a T-shirt. I wish I'd worn nothing but lacy lingerie under a trench coat, a scarf and set of handcuffs in the pocket.

God, what is wrong with me?

Whatever it is, it doesn't matter now. Because with just the tiniest bit of pressure that tingles over every other part of my body, he begins gently massaging my leg, and I can't bring myself to do anything except look at the bedding and let him keep touching me.

What the hell is happening? How and when did we get *here*?

"Your technique in turn nine is magnifico," he murmurs. Like that's something he would ever admit to me under normal circumstances.

I prop my chin in my hand and remind myself I am in control, even as my heart races faster with every graze of his fingertips on my skin. I am not acting on anything; we're just hanging out. At least until Massimo's fingers increase the pressure, slowly climbing higher up my leg, and my knees open wider before I can stop myself because I want *more*.

"But, in turns two and three…" He whistles. "You *fly*, Tigrotta."

My eyes fall shut. I love the beginning of the track in Jerez, the sensual swing from right to left—it's all hips. It's not as much of a rush as the chicane at Laguna Seca, but it's still a blast.

Massimo's fingertips dare toward the inside of my knee, goose bumps betraying me with their encouragement. I don't open my eyes, but I can almost feel his smile. I absolutely feel the pad of his thumb, lightly sweeping across the border into my inner thigh.

A shiver tingles down my back, my hips aching to shift closer and closer—it feels so good to be touched. Doesn't help that I haven't been with anyone since Etienne. Wincing off the memory of eloquent French hands and a breakup voicemail, I shift my head in my palm, listening to Massimo breathe quietly next to me over the muffled sounds of the crowd on the video.

It's impossible not to soak in the silent whisper of his fingertips on my body and my own secrets of how I want them higher, deeper, in the private places of me I swore he'd never touch. But with Massimo, nothing is simple.

We're enemies by trade, forever competitors. Except it's together that we're secluded from the world behind chains around the paddock, living in airports and train stations. He's a sign of home on foreign continents; a stranger I shouldn't trust, but I do.

At the same time, I will see him *always*. Every track, every press conference. And the reminder of what's coming, the races and the watchful eyes of Dabria on my point tallies, puts a stopper in this more than any other consideration.

Despite how easy it would be to give in and take what my body is obviously craving—what he appears to be silently offering—and despite how easily I could shift and pin him, strip him down, and sink deep and ride... I have more important things to think about than sex. And the absolute, *very* last thing I need to do is fall down another slope that might have no bottom.

My eyes open, and I bat his hand away from my leg. "Stop touching me."

He huffs, his hand tossed up in exasperation. "Why do you always have to be difficult?"

"Because. This is the last thing I need right now, especially from you."

He shakes his head, but at least he's not going aggro on me. "Life does not let you choose simple, Lorina."

"I don't need simple," I tell him, my temper twisting the more he stays calm. "What I need is to figure out how to get back to winning on the track, and sleeping with you doesn't help me fix that, does it?"

He arches a haughty eyebrow. "I never said I was going to help fix you."

I sputter, though I don't know why I'm even surprised. He's probably thrilled I'm tanking right now. "Well, that's just great," I deadpan. "And since I'm apparently on my own, let me make this clear: I don't have time for whatever romantic crap you're trying to pull."

"That is okay." He shrugs, relaxing back into his pillows and twirling the remote in his hand. "I have plenty of time."

"What is that supposed to mean?"

"You think you need to wait to have fun until you are no longer afraid? You will wait forever, and trust me, Lorina, I know. I made the same mistake."

I know that was English, but that couldn't possibly have meant what I think it did.

He sits up a little more, pausing the video. "Always when we race together, I have to choose between you and moto. I know that if I want to win, I will have to make you angry, scare you, maybe even make you crash. And I cannot be afraid for you because of the bad choices you make." He pauses, his eyes dark with the competitive fire I've known for years. But with nothing more than a blink of his thick eyelashes, his expression softens, a new shade of him coming into view. "But if I want you to smile," he says, something velvety teasing the corner of his voice, "if I want you to be happy, to win, then I will have to lose." He blinks again, and my blood chills as it all falls away, a cold determination the only thing left in his expression. "I choose to win."

I look away, my hands clamping into fists so tight, my nails cut my palms. Nothing about what he said should shock me, and yet it hurts like hell to hear him say it. Especially after the last few months, when he's been so...so *close* to me. "You are such an asshole."

"Sì. So are you."

My eyes flare, but a knock on his door turns both our heads before I can respond. My pulse surges wildly at the prospect of being caught in his room, Massimo getting off the bed and heading toward the door, gesturing for me to stay put.

He cracks it open, Vinicio's voice sneaking past. "È tardi. Vai a dormire."

Massimo rattles off something to his manager, then he closes the door, locks it. He turns and starts striding toward me. I get up and meet him halfway there. I can read anger in his gait from a mile away, I've known it so many years, and I'm not about to let him tower over me when he starts yelling.

His steps come to a harsh halt, his voice even more so when he points at me. "I am not the only one who chose to put moto first. You just told me that you have to find a way to win before you can think about love. And I understand why you did this when we were young and still trying to make MotoPro, but we are here now, and it is *enough*, Lorina. I am tired of choosing between winning or losing, between friends or enemies. I have what I want in moto, but I want a life after too. And I am tired of waiting to have both."

My eyes search his, stunned.

The sexual tension between us lately...that's one thing. Understandable, even, when he's been drawing cute hearts on my hand and whispering, "Buonanotte" to me on the phone at night. But he can't seriously tell me he's been waiting *ten years* for this, because everyone knows: you can't compete against the person you care about.

He sighs like he's crumbling apart under the agony of hesitating, then he continues shocking the holy hell out of me. His hands come up and cradle my jaw, his thumbs sweeping over my cheeks. My heart races, my mind trying to decide whether to register him as friend or foe. It should feel strange, to be touched so sweetly by this man I've hated. But so many times in my dreams, I've felt the calluses on his fingertips, the warmth of his palms. I don't know if I like it. All I know is that in real life, it's different.

Instead of the roughness I expected, his fingers are smooth, long cared for by his racing gloves. He's warm but cooler than I thought he'd be. His touch is more gentle. His eyes are more stark. And I know: that's exactly what he's saying. For ten years, he pissed me off to keep me at a distance. We were cruel to each other because we couldn't afford to be anything less.

His hands slip down to my neck, over my shoulders, and down my arms. My palms catch his forearms, wrapped in the soft cotton of his hoodie and bruisingly solid underneath. We're locked together but far enough apart that I can still breathe as my mind speeds, trying to remember who started it. Trying to determine if there could have been another way.

I look at Massimo a little more closely—his jaw tight and eyes more vulnerable than I've ever known—and I hate what I see. He's right. We were trapped. I had to hate him if I was going to resist him. I couldn't worry about his life on the track; I had to worry about mine. And I couldn't risk feeling guilty for winning when it meant he'd lose.

He brings me a little closer, his warmth soaking into my skin when he drops his forehead to mine. My eyes fall closed, my heart throbbing in my chest as my hands dare to slide higher up his arms, feeling the swell of his biceps until I land on his shoulders. There's no reason why we can't try to be together now that we've made it past the finish line of advancing to MotoPro. My eyes pinch tighter shut. Except we're still racing against each other, and I'm losing, bad.

Massimo shifts a little, hooking a finger under my chin and tilting my face up to his. It would be so easy to let him kiss me. So easy to melt into him and forget that right now, I can't find my way back to the biggest love of my life. That adding a relationship with Massimo into the mix isn't going to make anything clearer.

He could make it go away, though. All the confusion and the pain and the frustration. He could make me forget until he's all that's left. I know he could.

Stay focused, Hargrove.

I can't let him.

Me first. Career first.

I cover his hand with mine, then pull it away. When he looks at me, the frustration that was in his voice is now anger popping his jaw, hurt burning in his eyes. It kills me, seeing it there when I never meant for this to happen. But there's no going back now.

"What are you doing, Lorina?"

I shake my head, running a hand through my hair. "This, us… It's not that simple."

"It is simple," he rushes out. "For the first time since we met, the first time in ten years, it is now simple. But you want to wait? Fine," he sneers. "Do as you like, Lorina. You always do. I am not waiting anymore."

I take a step back from him, my hand held out between us. "What does that mean?"

He looks at my hand like its very presence offends him. "Why do you think I follow you to the hospital? That I call you? That I asked you to come here?"

"I thought…" My mouth is a desert. "I thought you were doing it because you wanted to help me."

"Wrong." Everything about him gets infinitely darker—his eyes, his voice, even his words. "I cannot fix you. I do not even think you are broken. You are just a spoiled little girl, crying so someone will pat you on the head, tell you it is not your fault, and then give you a new doll as a prize. Or new plates."

My eyes bulge. "What?"

"Wah," he mocks. "A boy made me crash. I am so scared now."

"Screw you!"

"The only person who thinks you are broken is you. You need to stop crying and accept that you crashed not from me or Santos or anyone else. You crashed perché you are dangerous, Lorina, and you still have not learned how to lose. And not only to lose a race"—he barks out a pitiless scoff—"but to lose everything! You are holding on too tight to the things that do not matter, and you have so much of them that you forget nothing is promised to you. Not even moto."

Infuriatingly, my eyes start stinging with tears. "I cannot believe you're saying this to me right now."

He nods. "I choose. I choose to tell you the truth. I do not care if you are sad. I do not care if it makes you cry." He steps forward, barely an inch away. "I do not care."

My bottom lip trembles, and I bite it. Hard.

His eyes follow every movement.

"The problem," he continues, "is that you think I say this because I am an asshole. But I say these things because you ask this of me!"

"I didn't—"

"You asked me to be your enemy when I would rather be your friend." His voice cracks on the last word, Massimo wiping a hand over his mouth like that'll erase that it happened, and it shatters me. Totally and completely. "This is not what I want, the way I want for us to be. You think because I make jokes, I do not feel these things you say? 'I hate you, you are an asshole,'" he mocks. "But this is what you want, so fine. I do this for you."

I swallow, heartbroken at the pain in his eyes. Even worse, he's right. Every time he's tried to fix things, I've pushed him away, doubted him, focused only on my own finish line.

"Since I gave you this favor, I thought, maybe it was safe to ask one for me. This was the only thing I ever asked of you, Lorina—to let me love you, my way, while we still have the chance."

I have no air left in my body, my eyes wide in shock.

"And you could not even give to me this one simple thing," he continues, his voice growing louder with every word, "perché you must have everything your way, your time, so you can win, and fuck anybody who wants different." His eyes narrow, everything about him sharpening back into the fiercest rival I've ever known. "Vaffanculo, you and your waiting," he says, gesturing harshly. "You are not the princess you think you are."

Massimo turns away, walking around the end of the bed, his hands bluntly still after how animated they were only a minute ago.

My mind stutters, disbelief turning my veins cold.

He loves me? He's never even said that he liked me. He flirts with me sometimes, but I always thought it was a joke.

How can he love me when all we do is fight?

Massimo rips back the covers on his bed, shaking his head in frustration. "Go," he says, sitting against the pillows once more and kicking at the comforter until it's bunched by the footboard. "You need to go back to your room. I want to sleep now. You make me esausto."

I hug my arms around myself, more than a few tears slipping down my cheeks. I don't even know if it's because we're fighting—again—or because he's sending me away after saying he loves me.

It's terrifying: the mess I've stumbled into. I also don't know whether I created it in the first place. I don't think I've led him on. Maybe I did. Is it leading someone on when you don't know if you like the fact that he loves you?

"Lorina," he says sharply, and my eyes snap to his. Hope flutters in my chest that he used his own private name for me, even now. "You go, or you stay. But if you stay, no more talking. And this time, you watch the crash."

I sniffle and nod, wiping at my eyes before I walk to his bed, sitting beside him with my back to his pillows. He rewinds the last few minutes of the video, and my eyes stray to him as he presses play and focuses intently on the race. My shoulders instantly soften.

Honestly, I don't know how I didn't see it. Massimo has always shone a little brighter, his words cutting a little deeper than all the other guys I've spent my life battling against. Because he's the kind of guy who will watch a video of my crash but not laugh at it like Santos would. The kind of man who defends your right to race to the peers who cut you down behind your back, but you hear about his tirade on gender equality from Billy and Mason. Not from Massimo.

My eyes drop to his lips, and I don't regret a lot of things, but I'm starting to regret the last ten minutes. Because he's the kind of man whose eyes appear to know every curve of my body, but his hands never have. And that is absolutely my doing, for better or for worse.

Massimo looks at me, and my pulse takes off. The breaths I'm pulling in give no satisfaction, and if he tries to kiss me right now... I'm not going to stop him. Not this time.

"Close your eyes, cara," Massimo tells me, and I swallow, then do exactly as he says.

The air crackles against my skin as I wait for whatever he's going to do, but I'm still not prepared when his arm comes around me, his palm settling on my far hip, and his other hand lying gently over my bicep between us. His intoxicating warmth caresses every part of me when he scoots a little closer, his body clicking into place around mine.

"This time," he breathes, "we ride it together."

I nod, comfort melting through my veins as I lean into him.
I think, maybe, we were always supposed to.

"Turn six," he says, then tilts our bodies deep to the right.

Chapter 11

Massimo Vitolo—July; Chemnitz, Germany

SHE FELL ASLEEP HALFWAY THROUGH *LIVE AND LET DIE*. I SERIOUSLY never expected that Lorina and I would spend our first night together watching moto and old Bond movies and *not* having sex—she turns me on way too much, and with the way I catch her looking at me sometimes... Yeah, no way. But with all she's going through right now, I think this was better. Actually, I know it was.

After drawing the clippers over the side of my hair, I glance out of the suite's bathroom toward Lorina, still asleep in my bed. Like I should even know what this looks like. I still don't know how I got lucky enough that she agreed to come over here in the first place, but she did, and I can't screw this up.

I knew the sponsors would only take the losses for so long, and her manager's warnings were the same ones I'd give her: if Dabria makes a change, it could happen with little to no notice. And I didn't want to start down this road with her until I was free from Gabriele's shadow, but with the risk of her going home to Memphis and never coming back...

I'm close enough to my payoff date to pull the trigger. I've been placing well and sweetening my garnishments with extra drops toward the principle. It's a gamble against getting injured, which would pretty much send me into instant default, but I'm holding up okay for now.

With Lorina, I may not get another chance.

I reluctantly shave the next line of hair, then eye my shirt on the counter. I should probably put it on before I wake her. In ten more minutes. Maybe twenty. She probably has a flight to catch. I do, but flights can be changed.

There's a rustle of sheets behind me before I can make up my mind, and I set down the clippers, blowing out a breath as I stare at myself in the mirror.

I told her I loved her last night, and she cried.

But she also stayed, and I meant what I said. I'm done hiding— what I feel, what I want, who I am.

I grab the cross on my necklace and press a kiss to it for good luck, preparing myself for any and all reactions. Then I step into the doorway. Lorina's eyes go wide as she spots me from beside the bed, where she's halfway through making it like she's trying to hide the evidence of her stay. The white sheets and plush down comforter drop thoughtlessly from her hands, and I hook my thumbs into the pockets of my jeans, letting her look.

Like my heart's not pounding faster the longer her eyes spend cataloging the span of my tattoos: rotting and dead faces snarling from my shoulders and all the way down my arms, blood and torn flesh dripping from their twisted mouths. A scythe curving around my ribs, a stack of dates down the other side. She swallows, and I gesture to the elaborate script over my heart. "La paura è la morte. Fear is death," I translate for her.

She clears her throat, but her voice is still raw when she asks, "Is there more?"

There's so much more. But none of it is perfect or pretty in the way she deserves, or even close to what she's used to—her family's loaded, and she's never known hunger or real fear. I'm really not thrilled about the day I'll have to confess my arrest record, but I can take her judgment. I just can't take the easy road. She deserves to know the truth, screwed up as it is.

I turn around, my hand on the edge of the sink, letting her take in the Catholic Madonna that's most of my back and centered over my spine, the words in the ribbon below her feet.

"La velocità ti salva," Lorina mumbles, and I bite down a grin at her country accent, somehow even more distinct when she's speaking my country's language. "Speed is savior," she breathes, and I turn to face her—my angel of speed, faster than death. But still so afraid of me.

"Did you sleep okay, Lorina?"

She kept reaching for me in the dark, her unconscious self determined to snuggle into my side no matter how many times I scooted back. I eventually let her have her way. I also kept my hands to myself and got up this morning before she realized what she was doing.

"Um…"

Her eyes are glued to my chest, my abs, dropping down to the front of my jeans.

"Lorina," I try again, and a shiver races through her that makes my mouth water for her skin. She needs to cut that out. Especially when she's wearing those shorts and we're in a bedroom. With the door locked. "Maybe if I put on my shirt, you will remember."

Heat rises in her cheeks, and *God*, she's cute when she blushes. "I, um, I slept fine. Sorry if I made you late for a train or something. You could've woken me sooner if you needed to go."

We could be stuck in this German hotel room for the next three weeks and I wouldn't give a shit. "And miss out on my chance to take a video of you snoring in my bed?" I wink. "Silly Tigrotta."

Something like relief floods her features, and she tries her best to glare at me. "I don't snore."

"As you say," I drawl, holding up my hands. "Video says different." I turn away from Lorina's growing smile, facing the mirror and picking up my hair clippers. But I can't help watching from my peripheral vision as she walks around the unmade bed, past the door, and keeps coming my way.

I half assumed she would've bolted by now—this is more reality than she usually likes to confront where I'm concerned. But I also want her to know what this looks like. To start our jet-lagged days in foreign hotels, together. It doesn't have to be so scary for her to be with me, and I'm fully capable of being nice. Romantic even. And it's time she knew that.

Like usual, she throws all my plans out the window. She stops next to me and barely runs a knuckle down the bruise starting to darken my side. Every nerve in my body goes haywire from her touch, and I suck in a breath from the electricity surging through my veins and congregating behind my zipper.

"Does that hurt?"

I shake my head, grateful for the Tylenol I took earlier so I don't have to lie. "No." I also eye her shoulder, which I know she landed hard on yesterday. "Are you hurt?"

"I'm okay," she says softly, but I'm not entirely convinced she's telling the truth. I don't get the chance to question her, though. She snatches the clippers from me without warning, lightly pushing my shoulder so I face the mirror again. "Look forward, or you're gonna have to downgrade to a crew cut."

"Lorina," I ask warily, "you have done this before?"

The woman is a force to be reckoned with on a moto, yes, but this is my *hair*.

Without answering, she tilts my head down and threads the razor's teeth from the base of my neck up toward my crown. A shiver of pleasure surges through me, Lorina thankfully pulling the clippers away with a grin just before she gets to the edge of the longer strands. "Nope."

"Fantastico." My chuckle is pure nerves, but it's seriously fantastic when she scoots closer and settles her left hand on the side of my neck. I wonder if I can get away with adjusting my erection without her noticing. Probably not.

"If you needed a haircut…" She happily winces as she glides the razor up the back of my head. "Why didn't you just go to a barber?"

There it is. I tell myself to stay calm. To take the opening and do what I promised myself I would: make my move, be honest, and tell her everything. Except telling her everything means telling her about everyone, and this is so dangerous, but I know we can get through this.

My father said we could. If it was right. And he was right about everything else.

"I cannot go to a barber."

"Can too." She blows a burst of air so the freshly cut hairs fly away, and goose bumps rise on my neck. Because that's not embarrassing or anything. At least it's not as bad as when I was seventeen and had finally grown a full mustache, and she laughed me straight out of the paddock. "Italy isn't the end-all-be-all of the world, you know."

"No." I smile at her in the mirror like I'm not about to royally piss her off. And that's so messed up, but I need her calm before I pull the rug out from under her. It's my only chance for survival. "I cannot go to a barber, because Chiara would be angry. She handles all my clothes, my hair, as my…" What's the word in English? "… stylist. So she is the only one who gets to cut my hair according to her backward mind."

Lorina looks at me in the mirror, and there's no doubt about it: she's pissed just hearing another woman's name come from my mouth. But there's no way around the fact that Chiara and I have been inseparable since we were kids. We talk every day, she's practically a part of my family, and that isn't changing anytime soon. I also technically told Lorina about her before, way back in Austin—that it's complicated, and we aren't together, but we do sleep together sometimes—though I doubt Lorina remembers or even cares at this point. I'm definitely not bringing it up like a selling point to my innocence.

"And Chiara is...your cousin, who was at Mugello?" Lorina says slowly, testing me.

I fail with flying colors. "Not a cousin. Friend. As you called, Miss Difficult."

Lorina's glare sharpens, and there's an angry strength in her hand when she shoves my head down. But at least she doesn't stab me with the clippers. She also doesn't lay her hand against my neck when she shaves the next line of my hair. But she stayed.

She fucking *stayed*.

"I, um, I didn't realize you guys were still..."

"Sì." I clear my throat. "Not always. But sometimes, yes."

She strengthens her jaw, cutting the next line. "Well..." She forces a smile as she continues around to the other side. "I hope I'm not getting you into trouble by helping."

I wonder if she realizes she just hesitated to pop from fourth gear to fifth.

"It is okay," I tell her. "Chiara will not care if you do this."

"Because she knows there's nothing going on between us?"

I scoff. "No. Chiara and I have known each other a long time, long before you, and she knows how I feel for my Tigrotta." I reach back and tickle Lorina's side, and she barely even reacts.

"I'm lost," she mutters, tilting my head to the side to check for missed pieces. "How can you...be with someone and tell them you care about someone else?"

"That is easy." My eyes close as she carefully trims around my ear. God, it really should not feel this good just to have her cut my hair.

"Chiara and I are always friends first. We grew up together, and there are no secrets between us. But people also need affection, sex, someone to welcome you home when you are gone for months and months. And Chiara…" I wave dismissively. "She needs to have someone when I am gone. Though many times, she still has someone even when I am home, but that is fine too. We have not been serious together for a long time, and after so many years, we both have accepted the truth."

Lorina brushes away some loose hairs, then walks around to my other side, trimming behind my other ear. "And what's this truth you've accepted?"

I catch Lorina's eyes in the mirror, waiting until I know she's really listening. "Chiara and I will always be in each other's lives. As friends. But she is not mine, cara. I am not hers."

Lorina pulls away the clippers, brushing off some stray hairs from my neck. "You know, I thought you were a good guy, but I guess I should have trusted my instincts." She sets the clippers on the counter, scowling at me. "You always were a cheater."

I turn around, irritated enough that I have to remind myself to stay in English for her. "What do you think, Lorina? You think because you are important to me I was going to sit around, waiting for you to think of me as something other than your enemy? No. I am a man, and I was to see the women I like. I was to get from them things I cannot ask from you."

She sucks in a breath, her eyes incensed. "You never asked!"

"Because you are afraid," I say before I can stop myself. "You cannot separate one from the other. You even said to me that you have no time for love because you need to fix you as Centauro first. So do not look at me like I am a terrible man when I say I have a friend who I care about, who cares about me, and so yes, I have sex with her. You want this to change? Then tell me things are going to change, show me you are no longer afraid, and then it will be done."

She looks away, her jaw shaking, and *Christ*, I shouldn't have said that. But she pisses me off to no end when she never gives me the benefit of the doubt, especially when I'm murdering myself with the truth.

Lorina takes a deep breath, and I hold mine, waiting for her to strike. To fight back in the way she does, that I've always relied on. That now, I'm dreading.

"Chiara," she says quietly, looking down at the floor and not at me. "Is she nice to you?"

I almost recoil in shock. But I'm not so dense I don't also see the trap for what it is. "Lorina—"

"Is she nice to you?" Her eyes snap up to mine, and that's when I realize: it's not a trap. She feels guilty, and it only makes me feel worse.

I sigh, half wishing I'd never brought it up and wondering how long it's gonna take me to recover from this. A year? Six? "Sì. She is a good friend."

"I'm glad," Lorina mutters, nodding. "Glad you have her."

I level a look at her. No woman I've ever dated has been okay with Chiara's presence in my life. Quite the opposite, in fact.

"Okay, fine," Lorina says, exasperated. "Look, I know I'm probably redlining on your awful bitch meter because I can't give you what you want right now, and to be honest, yeah, I hate the idea that there's another woman in your life. But if she's your best friend, then…okay. At the end of the day, I still want you to be happy."

There's no stopping my smile after I mentally translate all that. And because I can't help but live my life on the edge, very tentatively, I reach out and sweep her hair over her shoulder, the very tip of my finger grazing her neck. Lorina shivers at my touch but doesn't seem alarmed at me touching her or even opposed to it, and I may come out of this alive just yet.

"I am happy, cara. I am here, with you, and we are finally talking about the truth. I have what I want. Maybe not everything, but enough." I duck my head, catching her eyes. "And what do you have?"

"A headache," she says flatly.

I chuckle, but it's not really funny. "You need to take something? I have, um…" I look toward my toiletry bag, but she waves me off, sounding wholly defeated.

"No, it's fine, really. I just… I wish I knew what I needed."

I lock my jaw before I serve up a couple of options that could get her feeling a whole lot better, multiple times. But I can't be the solution to her problems on the track, and I won't try to be. She'd probably kick my ass for even thinking I could. But it doesn't mean it's not impossible for me to watch her struggle like this. She's always the first to punch off the grid, no matter what pole she's starting in.

Lorina tosses her hair, but she stops halfway, her eyes deadlocked with the clippers on the counter. Her gaze flicks in my direction, the start of a wicked smile curling her lips. My pulse ticks up as my dick hardens and my hands start itching for a throttle because I *know* this look. But I haven't seen it since before Jerez, and I've *missed* it.

She picks up the clippers, toying with them in her hand. Everything in me is cheering her on when she drawls, "Massimo, how good are you with these?"

Somehow, I get myself to keep a straight face as I swipe them back from her. "I am good at everything, Tigrotta."

—⁓—

I can't believe she talked me into this. Actually, yes, I can.

Lorina never trembles as she leans her cheek deeper into my palm, my eyes following the flat-edged thread of the clippers moving up toward one of the deep side parts I lined. I don't know what the hell the press is going to think when they discover Princess Moto with an undercut, and I am definitely not looking forward to a run-in with her manager. But this was her brilliant idea, and it's not like I was about to turn down having a little extra time with her, especially when she's still wearing those sexy-as-sin shorts. So I said okay.

I glance at her, almost unable to believe how completely calm she looks in my hands. "Afraid, Tigrotta?"

She smiles, her eyes still closed and long eyelashes resting on her cheeks. "Nope."

I chuckle, then slower instead of faster—because I am an evil, selfish, bad, bad man—I go over everything one more time. Debate whether to take off the guard and carve 77 into one side. Decide against it—baby steps.

Once I'm finished, my hand moves to just a single fingertip under her chin, tilting her face up to let the light reveal any imperfections. The only one I see is that her lips are dangerously close to mine, and I'm not kissing her. I set down the clippers, Lorina giggling and squirming when I rub my palms over the shaved sides of her hair until she's full out laughing. "Can I see yet?"

I shut down my grin, pretending to be outraged. "No."

She laughs harder as I grab my bottle of hair product, then start working it into what's left of her long curly hair, both of us chuckling while I'm ruffling and tossing it. I'm probably grinning like a complete dork, but I don't care. Because more than just getting to be alone with her, she seems completely cool with my arms on either side of her—comfortable enough that she picks up the cross on my necklace, inspecting it. "This is beautiful," she says, her voice soft with the same reverence I feel about it.

I clear my throat, nodding. "My mamma, she gave it to my papà on the day they were married." I smile at Lorina, then return my focus to her hair, twisting some strands and smoothing others. "Before he died, he gave it to me. Maybe one day, I will do the same."

"Really?" Her voice is strained like she's seconds away from laughing. "Would've taken your club-hopping ass for more of the terminal bachelor type."

I tug on her hair a bit, just hard enough to make her barely wince. Try not to notice that based on the flare of fire in her eyes, she also seems to like it. "You forget, I am Italian. We are very romantic men, Lorina. We love our women, and we like to practice to make babies. That way, we are very good at this when it is time to do seriamente."

She gapes at me, then cracks up laughing. I have to pull my hands from her hair from the force of it. "Oh my God, I am never gonna get you saying that out of my head."

"Why is this so funny?" I tease her. But I'm not exactly joking. "You do not think about these things? You do not want a family one day?"

"I..." She shakes her head once she collects herself, looking everywhere but at me.

"You only think about moto."

"Yeah," she mutters, looking down.

I nod, going back to her hair, because I knew that already.

It takes her a minute before she finds the guts to peek up at me, her eyes calculating where I'm at while she worries her bottom lip. I wink. I really did suspect that. It may not be what I want, but it's fine. My mother will never understand, but there are a lot of fights that have to happen before that one, and I'm not stressing about it now. "Pronta?"

Lorina lets out a relieved breath. "Whatever you said. Yep."

Stepping back, I turn her around to face the mirror, and everything about her lights up.

"Oh *hell yeah*." She leans forward to toss and play with it.

I chuckle as I wipe my hands off on a towel. I have to admit, I'm kind of impressed at what I just pulled off—her long curls are deliciously feminine against the shaved undercut, and the whole look is unjustly sexy.

"That's gorgeous," she tells me, turning to check out the full view. I nod to myself—like that's something I haven't known for years. Lorina turns to face me, an enigmatic twist to her lips. "You gonna do this for me every day?"

"No. And you buy your own." I pick up the bottle of hair product, flip it in the air, then tuck it into my back pocket.

She bites her lip against a smile, only growing more dangerous as her mood climbs. But waiting for her claws to come out has always been the best kind of terrifying. "You know, you don't have to cover up your tattoos all the time. With the hoodies and sweaters and the endless string of dress shirts."

I instinctively cross my arms, rolling my eyes like I haven't systematically kept this from her over the years. I even had a clause put in my contract that forbids my sponsors from photographing me shirtless—Vinicio told them it was against my religion. No one realizes I say my rosary to Lorina alone. "I get cold."

She levels a look at me, her voice a soft reproach. "Massimo…"

Fuck. There is no resisting that. "I, um…" I shrug, long resigned to the truth. "I thought maybe you would not like to see them. You like sweet, soft. Owls and horses, and furry tigrottas."

Her shoulders fall, a disappointed sigh right behind it. I'm always disappointing her.

"It is not a bad thing, Lorina," I say quickly. "I know you are invincible on moto, but I like that you are also…"

Delicate. And beautiful. And everything that is good in this messed-up world, but I can't say that to her. Not yet. Even though with the way I can feel myself looking at her, it should be entirely obvious.

"Massimo?" She shifts her weight, biting her lip again, and I wish I could tell her that she doesn't have to be nervous. Not with me. Not like this. Whatever she wants to know, I'll tell her. "What does cara mean?"

My grin widens, even though I'm suddenly very aware of the fact that I'm not wearing a shirt and she can probably see my heart beating straight out of my chest. But my Tigrotta doesn't back down from anyone or anything, and she never looks away as she waits for the answer I'm happy to give.

"'Darling,'" I confess. "It means 'darling.'"

All the air in her lungs rushes out, her hands falling to her sides, and I wouldn't be surprised if she's going down a mental checklist of all the times I've called her that. Times when I knew what I was saying and she didn't, but now she does, and she looks *pissed*.

"Goddamn it, Massimo," she says, and I'm the asshole who smiles. Because she's not mad. Not really. She just loves the way she hates me and hates that she might love me. But she *might*.

I jerk my chin at her, waving toward myself. "Let's go, Tigrotta."

She bites out a curse I don't catch, then storms forward and shoves at my chest. She's an explosion of strength that knocks me back into the counter, but her palms catch my jaw on the rebound, Lorina crashing her mouth to mine. I scramble to lock her against me before she vanishes like she does in my dreams. But she's *real*, and it's happening: her nails scraping down my jaw as her tongue sweeps hungrily into my mouth, a moan crawling from my stomach and vibrating raw through my throat. I have no idea how she manages to kiss like she races, like it's win or death, but it's fucking *fantastic*, and I'd be happy to die right here and let her win, always.

I have her hips before I can think I should've gone for something higher. My palms flatten on the small of her back, sneaking under her shirt, and *God*, she's so soft. She pushes herself closer against me, kissing me harder, deeper, and my hands obey, plunging down over the back of those shorts until I know every curve my eyes have spent years worshipping. A moan rips through her that I want burned in my memory, so I squeeze her ass again and score another.

"Massimo," she whispers, her knee hitching on the outside of my jeans. There's nowhere for her to go with the counter behind me, and time to move.

I shove us off the counter but keep her body pulled against me, her teeth scraping my lip, and I nearly buckle. She undoes mine, on my belt. That's it—gotta get her up. Gotta get her naked. I can do the love stuff with her later.

Downshift into carnal instinct—hitch thigh around waist. Bend and lock arm under ass. Lift, turn, set down on counter. Check for braking markers.

Lorina shakes back her hair as her legs tighten around me, her hands on my belt tugging me closer. Kiss her. Deep. Keep hands on her waist. Wait for opening. Fuck, she tastes good. She squirms, her leg drawing higher up my side because she wants it, and the red lights are out. Go.

I thrust against her so hard, her head throws back in a gasp, covering my hiss because zippers freaking hurt. Take her neck with my tongue, her hands scraping up the back of my head to hold me to her, and hard left of my hand to her soft inner thigh.

She moans. I crave. Don't back off the throttle.

My fingertips dare farther up toward the hem of her shorts, my name a moan and a prayer on her lips, and I am never letting us out of this bath—

Her ass vibrates against the counter, a harsh grating noise that reminds me of grinding gears on a transmission. It's the worst sound I have ever heard. Even crueler, Lorina slams the brakes: a frustrated curse taking the place where my name was only a breath ago, her hands already loosening and letting me go, and that's it. Race called on account of thunder and lightning.

I drop my forehead to her shoulder, breathing heavily and desperate for another taste of southern lemons. But her fingertips are sweet on my neck like she's not ready to let go either. It should make me feel better. Except there's no explaining that to my dick. Fucking mobile phones.

Jesus, my hand is under the hem of her shorts. I force myself to move it so it's flat on the counter beside her. Her leg drops from where it was hugged around my side, and I hate the English language when she says, "That's probably Frank. I'm supposed to be going home to Memphis this morning. For the break."

I nod. "Me too. To Ravenna."

With the last bit of my willpower, I straighten, nearly having to push myself away from her. Lorina blows out a breath, then slides off the counter. But she blushes fantastically when I have to tug at my jeans or risk passing out from the pressure against my swollen cock. She's a whole other shade of red when I rehook the buckle on my belt. That she...broke. Cool.

"I, uh," she starts, grinning as her eyes close, then shaking her head. Her eyelashes finally flutter open, and she giggles. "I totally have no idea what to say to you right now."

I rack my brain for something cool. Smooth. Debonair. "Um…"

I bet her panties are crystal white. Cotton. And a thong.

Fuck my life.

Lorina's hands fly to her mouth to cover another giggle at my apparent inability to even freaking speak, and any other day, I'd be pissed that she straight up just laughed at me. Especially when I'm so hard, my dick could probably cut a diamond. But her giggle is possibly my new favorite sound in the universe, so I don't really care.

She pulls her hands away, doing her best to sound serious. "Sorry."

I shrug it off, and it helps a little—a lot actually—that she doesn't back away, doesn't glare, doesn't hit me or tell me she hates me as I get my shit together and take a step closer to her to close the deal. She only smiles and looks up at me, patiently waiting to hear whatever I wanted to say and couldn't get out the first time.

I wish I had the guts to tell her how serious this is to me. That I'm ready to commit to her, only to her, even though she's still struggling with it: how to be my biggest rival on the track and the most important thing in my life away from it. But I don't know how to say those things to her, no matter what language we're fumbling to communicate in.

I do the only thing I can think of: I slip my bottle of hair product from my back pocket, holding it up between my fingers. Lorina's eyes search mine, her smile sweet but her voice still a little nervous when she whispers, "Yeah?"

I nod. "Done."

Lorina beams and snatches the bottle from me, and I can't resist my own smile at the words she doesn't know how to say either.

She's ready to try to trust me.

I just can't screw it up.

Chapter 12

Lorelai Hargrove—July; Memphis, United States

With the sunny heat of Memphis filling me up, I ride my mare like I stole her as she bounds past the training pen and leaps over a stick like it's a fence.

"Damn it, Lori! Slow down!" a cowboy yells, but the colt he's training in the pen is fine, and he can take it up with my mom. He probably will, but she can deal with it too.

She's been constantly on my ass since I got home three days ago—asking me a thousand times what happened to my hair and if there's anything she can do to help me deal with my "problems." I don't need her help, just some freaking space. Because I'm definitely not thinking about the fact that I haven't heard from Massimo since leaving Germany. But it's fine.

This time is different, and he's not going to screw me over. Not like in the past. I have nothing to worry about. Yep. Gonna be fiiiine.

"*Ya!*" Betty hits her next gear, churning dirt under her hooves as she breaks away from the massive barn and heads straight past the barracks for the farmhands, barreling right into the grazing fields. The fierce drug of freedom fills my veins as we fly past foraging horses, even though a nudge from my conscience says I should probably be riding my bike—the Dabria I keep in my dad's gearhead garage. But I haven't gone near it since I've been back.

I'd hoped Mason was right and coming home would make me feel better. That I would feel like myself again. But it didn't, and I don't. My bedroom is a montage to the ranch life I was supposed to embrace, but barrel racing never did it for me like moto did. Worse, I don't know what's left of me without a contract; who I am once you take away the sponsorships and the leaderboards, the single focus to win. I thought I knew, but maybe I was wrong.

Maybe that was never me to begin with.

At least I know who I am out here, where the sun is threatening either a righteous burn or a glorious tan as the rays sink deep into my arms. Where I can let go of everything that comes with battling on the track and not even care about tight right turns or sharp left corners. Until Betty White starts taking us toward the creek and not turning for the bridge.

"Don't you dare," I warn with a laugh. But she crashes through the bank with abandon anyway, a delighted squeal bursting out of my lungs from the splash of water licking up my legs and hers.

It's cool and refreshing, adrenaline pumping through me as she barrels up the other side of the bank. She lunges forward to the crest, my body catching the ripple of momentum. When her hooves find flat ground, she doesn't hesitate to launch into a full-out run as I duck a little lower over the saddle.

"Go, girl, go…" I urge her on, a smile breaking across my face from the wind in her white mane and the loose strands of my pony-tail slinging onto my back.

Trees blur past us, fluffy clouds streaking by in the clear blue sky as Betty cuts across the field like she's never tasted freedom. When we enter the grove, she slows to dart around trees, dancing over roots and ducking under branches. It's a pure rush, giving her room to decide our course based on her instincts. Just to ride, without questioning brake times and gearshifts. But not being in control is fantastic until she comes to a harsh halt when the grove stops at the line of my driveway.

She plants her front hooves, my body lurching forward.

"What the hell?" I sit back, unsure why she didn't just cross the driveway or turn toward the house. Leaning down, I pet her neck soothingly. "What's wrong?"

She shakes her head, tossing her mane.

"Well, we're not staying here for the rest of the day." I click my tongue and urge her forward. She takes a step but then halts and squirms back into the tree line, stomping her right front foot. "What the—"

The sound of a car cuts me off, white dust from my caliche driveway billowing up from my left. In another blink, a yellow taxi comes around the bend and drives past us. Betty White bristles at the car, stepping farther into the tree line. A branch scratches my arm, but I hardly notice. No way did I just see…

"*Ya!*" I command, Betty bursting from the grove and heading down the driveway.

When we come to the opening, where the driveway circles around in front of my house, the back seat door is already opening.

"Whoa," I tell Betty, keeping her back from the cab.

A brown loafer steps out from behind the door, finding the driveway. Followed by dark-wash skinny jeans, a cocoa-colored button-down, sunlight glimmering off black sunglasses and even blacker slicked-back hair. Betty shifts restlessly beneath me, my heart pounding in my chest as my grip tightens on the reins.

He's here. The one guy in my life who has always been The Guy, whether he was playing angel or demon, or both.

Please, let this mean what I think it does.

I can't resist beaming at him as I swing a leg over, getting down from the saddle. "Your flight home take an unexpected detour?"

Massimo chuckles after dismissing his ride, his smile wide as he pushes his sunglasses up into his hair. "One truth is always the same, Tigrotta. You are difficult no matter what country we are in or what day of the week it is."

Heat rushes into my cheeks as I stop in front of him, shifting Betty's reins into a lead. "Where's your luggage?" My eyes rake down the length of him and back up, Massimo bristling when Betty snorts at him. He eyes her warily, and I have to remind myself that he probably doesn't know horses like everyone else around here. "Somehow, I'm thinking you weren't just in the neighborhood."

"Ah, cara." Massimo grins at me, apparently deciding it's worth it to risk the wrath of my mare. He hooks a finger below my oversized belt buckle, then pulls me forward until my chest brushes his. "I could have been."

A soft laugh tickles my throat, but it quiets as Massimo tentatively leans in, then kisses me, and I can't *believe* this is happening.

We're doing this. We're giving us a shot.

I let myself sink into the delicious depth of his lips, instantly back in that German hotel bathroom. No man has ever dared to kiss me with that much confidence, with that much drive, but also slow enough to relish it. And I was more than ready to relish him: the mental image of his shirtless body burned behind my eyes like a dirty picture I only caught a fleeting glimpse of.

I nearly murdered Frank when I got back to my room that morning. But now, it's almost hard to remember why I was upset when Massimo slowly pulls back from my lips. His thumb trails lovingly down the edge of my jaw as his eyes search mine, and instead of a background of a foreign circuit or a random hotel, it's my home, my family's land, and it's so surreal that all I can do is smile. "I...I can't believe you're here."

His grin grows even brighter, a burst of wind swirling his cologne into my lungs. I inhale it like a salve for all the rest of me that still dares to hurt.

"I cannot believe you are wearing this belt and not falling over."

I burst out laughing for what feels like the first time in forever, and Massimo shrugs.

"You look good, though. Like you found...Lorina."

Everything in me softens, and even more so when I look more closely at his face, taking in the darkness under his eyes and how his hair is still a little wet. He must have showered just minutes ago.

"You look exhausted," I say, and Massimo chuckles. "No, like really exhausted."

He shrugs, his fingers still toying with my belt. "I have been in Heathrow for a day and a half, maybe two days now, because of a storm in London. Delay, delay, cancel, standby. I only just got off the plane, stopped by my hotel to take a shower, then I came to see you."

Oh my God, he did not just say that. But based on how he looks? I totally believe it.

Massimo winks, touching a fingertip under my chin and bringing my lips back to his, and I have no idea who this guy is that just flew halfway across the world to see me and didn't even presume to bring his luggage to my house. But I'm wrapped in his arms, and everything about him feels so good that I can't think of a single reason why I should ever, ever move.

"Did I hear someone drive up?"

I startle, pulling back from Massimo to see my dad coming out of the house, my mom right behind him. I also don't recall dropping the reins, but I have to scramble to collect Betty from where she wandered off to graze a few feet away.

Massimo clears his throat next to me once I'm back beside him, apparently not registering the big ol' smile lighting up my dad's face as he shakes a finger. "You must be the famous Massimo Vitolo we hear so much about."

Infamous, more like. Massimo dips his head, a smile curving his mouth. Embarrassment floods my cheeks as my mother stares me down from the porch, a satisfied arch to her eyebrow because I already know exactly what she's thinking, and it *sucks.*

My dad practically jogs down the stairs to shake Massimo's hand. "It's good to finally meet you. Probably should've extended the invitation sooner, considering how long we've been watching you race. How was your flight? 'Cause by my count…" My dad looks at his wrist for a watch he's not wearing. "You're a couple days late."

I gape at my dad, but the direction quickly flits to Massimo as the conspirators reveal themselves. "It was not bad, grazie."

"You little…" I mutter. Then I look to my mom. "He's been stuck in the airport for days, and he needs to sleep."

My mother reopens the front door, waving Massimo toward her. "Why don't you come inside, and James will get you settled?"

"Actually," Massimo says, "I have a room at—"

"Nonsense," my dad interrupts. "We have plenty of room, and I insist."

Massimo turns to me, sneaking me a smug wink before he turns back to my dad. "Grazie, Signor Hargrove. That is very kind."

I snort. "Smooth. And his last name is Mattison, not Hargrove. That's just me and Mom."

Massimo's brow furrows, but I'm not sure if it's because I mumbled that too quickly or he's just surprised. I jerk my head toward my dad, who is friendly as can be but doesn't like to be kept waiting.

"Tell you what," he says when Massimo starts walking toward him, my father clapping him on the back and steering him toward the garage. As though this is all a totally normal thing. "We'll go grab your luggage first. Gives me an excuse to take out the Lambo."

Massimo flinches, peeking back at me but still walking next to my father. "You have a Lamborghini?"

Dad laughs. "That ain't all I got. Come on."

The pair of them head toward the separate warehouse garage, disappearing inside, and I kinda hate that I'm missing Massimo's face right now. My mom, however, beelines it straight for me.

I swing up into the saddle, gaining the high ground. "So you knew he was coming and you didn't tell me?"

She comes to a sharp stop beside Betty, her curly brown hair a mess in the wind and already waving me off like she expects us to bolt. "Oh no... First, you get to explain how long you and Massimo have been seeing each other. Because last I heard, you hated him. The next thing I know, you come home looking like a punk rocker, and some Vinny guy is calling from Italy in the middle of the night asking for our address and whether it's okay if Massimo 'swings by.'"

I shift in the saddle, getting as comfortable as I can in such an uncomfortable situation. "We're just friends."

"Mm-hmm." Her gaze narrows into the look that makes hard-worn farmhands bow to her every command. "Funny how your friends always live in other countries."

"Mom," I warn, but she just keeps right on going: starting the same old argument about me self-isolating. Which isn't true. I'm just not interested in dating cowboys who are all belt buckle and no buck, and she keeps trying to set me up with them.

"Kinda like how that first guy you were all hot and heavy with conveniently lived in Spain..."

"I was seventeen, and he barely spoke English," I pop back. "How serious did you think that was going to be?"

"Then what about the Australian? And the guy from Britain? They spoke English just fine, and you were in your twenties."

I roll my eyes, Betty getting restless under me. "And one by one, they dumped me when I wouldn't ditch a race to go see them. Bravo to the most selfish generation in existence."

My mom shakes her head, stubborn as always, but it was different for her. Easier. Well, maybe not easy, because she was still fighting off the debt collectors when she met James.

Thanks to the mismanagement of my asshole of a bio dad, the ranch had been teetering on the edge of going under. I know she never wanted him to have control of it in the first place, but Massimo called it: love blinds you to the greed and ruthless selfishness of certain people. But after their marriage whittled down to her choosing him or the ranch and they divorced, in walked this accountant with a hat as big as his smile, and he didn't try to save her.

There was no swooping in with a magic calculator that fixed the numbers. Instead, he hung out with two-year-old me so she could work the problem. She ended up building one of the biggest and most respected ranches in the southern states, all by keeping her eyes on the prize. It was James who introduced me to motorcycles, and by that point, I was already calling him Daddy. She was calling him Husband. We never looked back.

All I've known is James, forever calling me Peanut and telling awful jokes with each breath he takes. But I *also* know that my mom getting a happily ever after with my adoptive father is the exception. And every guy I've dated has only further convinced me that my bio dad—the person asking you to give up your dreams because when you have two competing sets of them, only one can win—that is the damn rule.

"Lorelai, commitment isn't horrible," my mom says, her arms crossed and her boots locked in the dirt. "You can't live your life alone. One day, you're going to want more than racing."

"Like what? A Jet Ski? And I don't recall you being like this when Taryn and Billy were moving in together. You gave him such a guilt trip that he is still praying it off. And Billy doesn't even pray."

I get the look. "Taryn is not my daughter, and don't think I don't see what you're doing." Mom steps closer. "You'll date these guys, sure, but you keep an ocean between you and them. You're just afraid of—"

"I am not afraid!"

A couple of farmhands picking mud off their boots outside the barn stop what they're doing, looking over at us. I take a breath, trying to calm down. My mom is my mom, but she's also their boss, and I try not to disrespect her in front of the men who work—and live—under her authority.

"Look, Massimo can be nice," I tell her. "And yeah, I'm attracted to him. But I won't let any man take what is mine. Nobody, absolutely nobody, is going to make me choose."

My mom sighs, probably as sick of having this argument as I am. "Honey, no one is asking you to choose. And the right one, he won't."

"Yeah, well…we'll see."

She reaches out and pets Betty, presses a kiss to her nose, then turns and heads toward the house. "I guess we will."

———

"More! Harder!"

Massimo pants out a raspy groan that brings me endless satisfaction, his sharply defined arm muscles glistening with sweat. My back arches at the next hit, my hips bowing to pure power, and I cry out with all the air in my lungs, harnessing my stamina and endurance and focusing only on the sweet release of victory.

"More!"

"Basta! Enough, Lorina!"

Frank chuckles from where he's standing guard over us in my

home gym, placing another sandbag on each of our lower backs—the fifth since we've started doing weighted planks. Massimo's roar on the gym floor next to me grows louder, fire burning through my abs and singeing its way through my arms and legs.

"Come on, Peanut!" my dad cheers me on. "You almost got him. He's shaking! He's about to drop!"

"Get those hips up, Lori," Frank counters. "Good job, Massimo. Nice form."

I grit my teeth through the growl tearing its way up my throat, glancing at Massimo next to me. His hands are fisted so tight, his knuckles are white, the bump of his bicep and triceps and deltoids trembling above his elbows. The scythe on his ribs bleeds a fresh drop of sweat as he strains to keep his hips up from the floor, a stack of sandbags covering the Madonna on his back.

I look away from temptation incarnate, focusing on the row of my promo posters hung on the gym wall. Massive images of me in all my different leathers over the years, flags and banners strung from the ceiling. I duck my head under another groan, determined to remember I'm home to heal and get better.

Me first. Career first. Just like Mama taught me.

Even if she no longer agrees.

"More!" I shout.

Massimo barks out something in Italian as my father puts another bag on his back, looking a little too happy about the painful noise Massimo is making. My mother, however, totally tried to set him up to stay in my room, which he super awkwardly had to decline because no, we're not sleeping together.

Yet.

The weighted bag I called for hits my back, my core screaming as my hips sink, and I am an idiot for pushing us this far. But he's been acting like a child all day: exercise after exercise, circuit after circuit, he won't stop daring me into seeing who is stronger. And even though I've kicked his ass the whole way through, he still won't give up.

"More," Massimo growls, sneering at me while Frank places another bag on my spine.

A strained yell pours from my lungs. "Dick!"

"Lorelai," my father rumbles, placing another bag on Massimo's back.

"No more," Frank announces. "Y'all are gonna end up hurting each other before—"

Massimo collapses almost the moment I do, but he gave out first. Sucker.

"Good job, Lori," Frank says, already sweeping the bags off my back. A pocket of air rushes into my lungs, and *holy hell*, those were heavy. I am so going to regret this tomorrow. "Way to tough it out."

"That was ridiculous," Massimo pants out, rolling over to catch his breath. My father extends his hand, helping him to his feet.

"You're just saying that 'cause you lost." I push myself to standing, sweat trickling down my back and flooding the bottom of my sports bra and the waist of my leggings. I take a towel from Frank, wiping off my face and the back of my neck. I finish in time to see Massimo squirting a stream of water into his mouth, his whole upper body swelling and sinking with every breath, and it only exaggerates how freaking cut his hips are.

God, I'm totally going to end up sleeping with him. If I don't, it'll be a miracle.

"I did not lose." He shakes out his hair before running his hand through it. "I made the decision that it was not worth it to keep going. I put *me* first."

I scoff, taking a drink from my own water bottle. "Says the loser."

My dad chuckles from where he's finished helping Frank clean up the sandbags, bumping his shoulder. "Is it weird that I want to put them in a boxing ring and let them go at each other?"

Frank stares down my father. "Yes." Then he looks to me and Massimo, clapping his hands in the signal for more torture to come. "Okay, tough guys. Since you're still more concerned with outdoing each other than focusing on your workouts, time for jump ropes."

"Ugh," Massimo complains, toweling off his chest. "I am not the one distracted. Lorina can hop. She is the one who cannot—"

"Tell you what," Frank interrupts in his I-am-so-over-this-shit voice he uses on Mason. I take another sip of water, waiting for the smackdown. "Considering I am under specific instructions from Vinicio to run your ass into the ground and keep you focused on Brno while you're here? Five miles, now, or it becomes ten."

Massimo glares at my manager, then points at me. "See what you have done?"

I shrug innocently with a grin so big, my face feels cracked in half. "Nope."

I'm on Frank's side. Three weeks can turn you into mush before you know it, and Massimo ate way too much of my mom's carb-loaded cooking last night, my dad and him singing her culinary praises with every bite, and my mom's proud grin practically daring me from across the table to reverse the room arrangements.

I swear, it really kinda sucks she's so happy with James, because it makes me wonder if she's right. If maybe I could have it all, but I've been subconsciously avoiding it by dating guys who live overseas, knowing there's an assured breakup around the bend. If maybe I have sacrificed too much of my life for one thing, and if it abandons me, I'll be left empty.

Massimo starts muttering under his breath in Italian, walking over to his bag and pulling out a hoodie. My eyes can't help but lick his ripped body with every movement as he tugs on the gray cotton fabric, hiding the view I've had way too much fun admiring all morning.

He looks over and busts me, the corner of his mouth twitching up before his eyes drop to my lips, and I have *got* to get this under control. I've already had to recharge the batteries on my vibrator twice since I've been home.

"Outside, now!" Frank commands. "I want the full loop, Lori."

Massimo chuckles, looking away and taking another sip of water as I head out of the gym, letting the door close loudly behind me. I gulp in the fresh air, free of cologne and male deodorant, then start running on the path my feet have been beating since I was a kid, putting some sobering distance between us.

The second we get back to the house, I'm going to my room, taking the coldest shower *ever*, and then I'm getting out my laptop. I need to study the Automotodrom Brno. I need to replay videos of my races from the past and remember, plan, and strategize. I need to stay ready so I can head back to the circuit and win until there's no question of making the final podium for World Champion and keeping my contract with Dabria. I need...

To go to his room and see what's hiding behind those jeans, because I felt it in the bathroom when we were making out, and I'm pretty sure he's rocking at least—

I shake my head at myself, pushing more power through my legs and concentrating on the taste of the hot air streaming into my lungs.

Moto. Not Massimo.

God, what the hell is wrong with me?

I clear my mind and focus on the sight of tall trees and open sky, the wide cut of grass with plenty of space to run. And yet Massimo is soon caught up and riding my ass, close enough that I start to hope one of my shoes catches him in the shin. It never does, and he keeps right on pushing us, faster and faster.

I inch to the right so he'll just go around me and do whatever it is he wants. He moves to the right with me. I fade left a few minutes later, but again, no budge from him. I don't know if he's staring at my ass or just trying to screw with my head by pretending to slipstream, but all it's doing is pissing me off. I get enough of the battle crap on the racetrack. I don't need it while I'm running.

The sound of his shoes hitting the ground gets a little louder like he's closing in behind me. I push more power through my legs to regain my distance from him, but Massimo's speed only picks up more until I'm nearly sprinting with how hard he's pushing me. We start across the wooden bridge over the creek, and I glance back over my shoulder to curse him out for whatever childish game he's playing. He darts past me.

Orange Hotaru paint flashes in my vision, the groan of crashing metal tumbling down pavement ringing in my ears. His elbow brushes mine. My body flinches away, and I stumble, falling into the water.

It gulps me down as my shoulder burns with the memory of pain, and I scream underwater. That's all that rushes into my lungs.

I'm going to die.

Right now.

Muddy spots blot my vision, and my weightless body is no longer at home in Memphis but strapped down in the back of the ambulance in Jerez. Gone are the cheers of fans, the heat of the sun, the growl of my bike. The world is only muffled Spanish voices and my hot breath slapping into my face under the plastic nebulizer.

Frank's face appears above me as he smooths his hand over my forehead, pushing away my hair. "Breathe, Lori. Just breathe," he repeats. His hand runs down my arm while my back bows in pain at a bump in the road, followed by a sharp turn. The G forces roll me into the strap belted over my chest, and it's a hammering ax to my ribs, puncturing my lungs. "Everything is going to be okay," he tells me, a strained smile on his face.

I burst into sobs. It hurts too much to see, the lie scaring the absolute shit out of me.

"Frank..." My words catch in my throat, but I manage to squeak out, "I'm sorry."

"Oh, honey," he breathes, his eyes misting as he forces another smile. "It's not your fault."

He's wrong. It's all my fault.

One of my shoes scrapes the sodden bottom of the river, striking me back to reality. Panicking, I claw my way toward the sun as my lungs continue to flood. When my head breaks the surface, all the water I just swallowed comes right back out.

I stumble toward the bridge, hooking my elbows onto it for support. Icy fear and water lap at me from every angle, my breaths shaky as I try my hardest not to cry. It's just...it's so hard not to when I can't stop seeing the crash behind my eyes. When I can't stop hearing my bike's engine, but it's no longer a hum telling me I'm home. It's a threat. A warning. And that is so, so wrong.

A finger tucks a loose, wet hair behind my ear, and my head lifts. Massimo is crouching in front of me, concern in his eyes that doesn't match any other part of his expression. He blinks and it's gone, his normal cocky gaze in place and his hand held out to me. "Andiamo."

I knock his hand away. The corner of his mouth twitches, like he wants to smile. Jerk.

He straightens and steps back as I push out of the river, water pooling in my shoes.

"Are you hurt, from the fall?" he asks.

"No." I squeeze out my hair. "I'm just royally pissed at you for pushing me in the freaking water!"

He shakes his head, but it's barely a reaction. "I did not push you. You were afraid, and you jumped."

"Bullshit."

He mumbles to himself in Italian before he switches to English, sounding annoyed in both languages. "Why am I surprised that because you are in denial, you think I know nothing? Hmm?"

I don't respond. And he's the one who's in denial.

"Fine. I will tell you a secret. Then, maybe you will believe me." He grins, his voice dropping as though someone may hear us. But we're deep into my property, and I haven't seen a horse or farmhand for a while. "You like to win, Tigrotta. But more, you like to chase."

I cross my arms, staring him down. "Do you make sense in Italian? Because you fail at it in English."

Massimo doesn't take the bait. "When I am in first, you race better. You lose your fear."

My back straightens, pushing me a little taller. It's not enough to bridge the gap between our heights, but I feel bigger. Stronger. "I am not afraid of anything."

"That is a lie." Massimo shakes his head. "When you are in second, you look forward. No fear. When you are first, you always look over your shoulder. Afraid. And now..." He checks over his shoulder again, his voice dropping further. "Your fear is even worse since your crash at Jerez."

My hands tighten into fists. "You don't know what the hell you're talking about."

He nods like he's placating me, then he steps forward again. But this time, we're closer than dancing close, making love close. And very gently, he runs a fingertip down the scar on my forearm, goose bumps streaking instantly across my skin.

"You still have not learned how to lose, Lorina," he whispers. "You think if you lose a race, lose your contract, then you will not be Tigrotta anymore. But you have forgotten, cara: you were already Tigrotta when we met at the Rookies Cup. And you were Tigrotta when we raced MotoB and MotoA. Because Tigrotta is not about what you ride or who you ride for. Tigrotta is *here*," he says, gently poking at my heart. "So let go of Dabria. Let go of the contract. Be ready to lose. You will still be you. I promise, Lorina."

I swallow thickly, no idea how to rise to his challenge. To be me and also back down.

I've never backed down from anything.

Massimo dips his head, touching his forehead to mine. But just for a moment before he steps back, his eyes and voice back to normal. "We run again. This time, I will be in front. When you are ready, you take first."

Embarrassment is rife through me. "I don't need you to do me any favors."

"Then I will not give you any." He grins. "Maybe I like it when you take it from me."

I gesture for him to lead the way before I think too much about that.

Massimo starts an easy pace on the path. I walk it, watching as he follows it into the woods. When he's no longer visible, I start to jog, my feet squishing in my shoes and my thighs rubbing awkwardly from the wet spandex. But I find my rhythm until I'm breathing the right way, my arms bent at the elbows in a natural swing.

Learn to lose, Massimo says. More like Frank would lose his shit if he heard him say that.

I do my best to ignore the conflicting words echoing in my head, and I let the smell of trees soak through me instead, drowning in the whisper of animal feet scurrying in the brush. But after turning a corner, my peaceful run through the woods is interrupted by the sight of Massimo dead ahead. He's running, but not nearly at the speed he was earlier.

I push harder, my eyes homing in on the back of his hoodie. I'm three feet behind him when his pace shifts into a higher gear, and I adjust to overtake him.

It's nothing I haven't done countless times before: proving I'm faster than he is. And I know, *I know*, there's a part of him that hates me for it—for wanting the win more than he does. It's why he's always yelled at me, accused me, embarrassed me every chance he gets.

And he thinks *I'm* the one who needs to learn how to back down?

I'm less than a foot away when his eyes stay forward, but his hand reaches back.

Everything in me says to ignore him. That it's all a ploy. Massimo has perfect timing when it comes to finding me vulnerable, convincing me that this time, he's changed. But then out of nowhere, I'm left reeling in pain, stunned by whatever insult came out of his mouth while he saunters away, laughing. So him holding out his hand? He's probably going to push me into the trees in his attempt to teach me some pointless lesson about trusting your competitors.

I should push *him* into the woods. Teach him a lesson about screwing with me, that I'm not as weak as he thinks. I should take his hand, then use it to slingshot around him and get back to the house long before he does. If he falls in the process, he falls.

I take his hand. Our steps never falter as we continue to run, me slightly behind him and the sound of our shoes hitting the path falling into sync. I get ready to overtake him, but my plan goes out the window when he settles my palm on his shoulder.

My eyes prickle in shock as he holds me there for a second, letting me feel every shift in his muscles from the relaxed swing of his arms. Then he squeezes my hand and lets me go, keeping me with him but pushing our pace a little bit faster.

Something warm tingles through my veins until it's all I feel, and it's something I only ever feel when I'm with him. Because I still can't lose, and neither can he. But he can't let me fall behind either.

For the rest of the run, I never move my hand.

Chapter 13

Massimo Vitolo—July; Memphis, United States

"HEY, BUDDY? YOU DOING ALL RIGHT THERE?"

Christ, not another one. I do my best not to roll my eyes at the cowboy. Her house is crawling with men. But I don't need one of the ranch hands giving away my position. "I am okay," I tell the third one who's asked me that, giving him an American thumbs-up and a smile so fake, it hurts my face.

He tips his cowboy hat at me, then keeps meandering past the garage and toward the barn. I check my watch again—she's late. She usually rides her horse after she's done kicking my ass in the gym all afternoon. But little does she know: I'm not reading in her father's library while she rides today.

Five more minutes, then I'm going looking for her.

My watch vibrates and lights up, and I wonder if I'm busted and Lorina's calling to find out where I am. But nope. It's a third call from Vinicio.

Unable to ignore him any longer, I dig my phone out of my pocket, having to swipe a couple of times before the screen accepts the press through my gloves. "What?" I answer in Italian, backing into the garage a little, just in case.

"What do you mean 'what'? What the hell are you still doing in Memphis? You were supposed to be back here yesterday for prep."

I turn away from the sunny world outside in favor of the parked McLaren closest to me—the one my father would have lost his mind over and probably serenaded with a love song before presenting it with linguine. There's no reason for me to fly back to Italy this early, especially when I know Lorina wouldn't take it well. I just got here barely a week ago. "No one cares where I am. It's fine."

"Massimo, everyone is wondering where you are. Including Angelo."

"What? How does he know I'm not at home?" I dare to run my finger down the length of Lorina's father's Lamborghini. "He spying on me?"

"Doesn't have to. Some fan posted a picture of you on Twitter: asleep on a bench in Heathrow airport with a departure board full of cancelled U.S. flights in the background."

Great. What do I need, a disguise now? "What did you tell him?"

"What do you think I told him?" Vinicio snaps. My mind comes up with a billion shitty possibilities as he pauses, letting the threat sink all the way in before he sighs. "I lied and said you went to see some friends in California, and I assured him you would be back in time for the next Grand Prix. Which you will be."

Is he—? I gesture, flabbergasted, to the last model of the Lotus Esprit they ever put into production. "When have I ever missed a race?"

"Never. But we also made a deal when you left that you'd be back here by yesterday to start prepping for Brno, and you're still screwing around in Memphis. So I'm having a hard time trusting what you say you're going to do." He lowers his voice, but his words only sharpen. "Not to mention, how the hell do you expect to handle Gabriele from over there?"

I glance over my shoulder, but the view is clear of any cowboys or otherwise. "I have it under control."

"You're really gonna make her—"

"She can handle the drop. And I'm not missing the race." I hang up, then turn off my phone, heading back to the edge of the garage. This is such bullshit.

No one gets to tell me how to live my life, where I go, or who I see. Not Vinicio. Not Gabriele. Certainly not Angelo Maggiore. Besides, I'm not doing anything outside the boundaries of my contract. I'm not that reckless.

Racing is the blood in my veins, what wakes me up in the morning, and what puts me back together when everything breaks. No way in hell am I walking away from that. Especially when I can't risk losing that kind of income when I have people who are counting on me.

I'm pushing the line, but I'm not crossing it. So Angelo can learn to deal with it.

I check the time on my watch once more, doing my best to shake off the argument, and then I wait. Again. It's not much longer until I finally spot Lorina walking toward the stables, her boots sinking into the damp grass. *Perfect.*

Ducking back inside, I sneak through the shadows and past the rows of her father's cars that he refuses to even let me sit in, much less take for a spin. But he happily tossed over the keys to her Dabria when I asked, and the Atrani 1299S is nearly invisible in the darkness. The fairings must have been custom-painted—instead of red, the whole beast is a geometric mix of sleek obsidian and matte titanium, and I cannot wait to ride this thing. More, I need to get Lorina on it, yesterday.

I tug on my helmet, flipping down my face shield and securing the chin strap. The part that really irritates me is that I didn't actually come here to help Lorina get her head straightened out when it comes to her moto. She's a big girl, a professional, and she knows how to handle this stuff. I *came here* because I've been in love with this woman since before I knew how to give one an orgasm, and with Gabriele's money-sucking presence nearly out of my life, I'm ready to get the next phase together.

But Lorina's also earned the right to retire on her terms, and I can't do nothing when she's hurting this much.

Swinging my leg over, I wait until she crosses in front of the garage, pulling the rim of her cowgirl hat a little lower. Adrenaline and something a little kinkier floods the base of my skull when my thumb flicks and wrist twitches, the engine roaring to life.

She jumps and looks toward me, her hand clasped over her heart, and I grin, everything in me impatient to go. On the road, as fast as I can. Up to her room, with her laid out bare on the bed. I want it all, five seconds ago. Ten years ago. Now.

It takes her a second to recover, her eyes traveling up from my boots to my jeans, past my black leather jacket and my blacker helmet. With the dark smoke face shield dropped down, I can read every shift of her expression, and she can't see a single aspect of mine.

"Get off my bike, Massimo," she says, but her attempt to make her voice stern is a bust. I smile wider as my gloved hand lifts from the handlebar, daring her to come closer with every inward curl of my finger. She straightens her shoulders, being difficult as always. "That's too much engine for you to handle, and you're not used to the clutch or the brakes."

I barely keep from laughing. Her Atrani is basically a jet plane on pavement, but it still doesn't come close to what we race with on the Pro level. Should be enough to ease the twitchiness that's been setting in, though. I can only be away from that kind of speed for so long before I want to burst out of my skin. Sex helps, but we're not having it. So it's either this or another shower, and I'm sick of showering.

Just to remind her how much she likes it, I rev the engine low, slow, letting it build until it comes to a screaming climax, and then I drop it into no-satisfaction blankness. Her chest expands like she sucked in a breath because she *wants*, and she knows I want to give it to her.

Lorina shifts her weight, glancing at the house, then at me. Finally, she deflates. "I have to get my jacket."

I point to the table in the garage, where I set out her leather jacket, her gloves, and her helmet. I checked them all, very carefully, and they're totally safe and completely fine. I almost want her to give me an excuse about tears, cracks, or splinters, because I'm happy to set the record straight.

All she says is, "You suck."

I grin behind the safety of my face shield when she walks into the garage, then picks up her jacket and threads her arms through her sleeves. I fidget, restless to go as she trades her cowgirl hat for her helmet, and her nose wrinkles as she slides it on. Probably at the thought of riding as a passenger on her own moto. Good. That's the whole point.

There's no telling this woman anything, whether it's to slow down or suck it up, so until she's ready to own speed, all I can do is satisfy my own cravings. There's also a fair chance it'll make her jealous enough that tomorrow, she'll steal back the keys to her Dabria while tossing over the ones for her older Sasebo—currently parked in the back with a cover draped over it.

Lorina flips down her face shield, and almost immediately, the rise of her chest goes triple the speed. She doesn't move to grab her gloves.

I'm off the moto and in front of her in half a breath, and she never even glances my way. I don't have to be able to see through her face shield to know her eyes are closed, completely frozen in panic.

She startles when the gloved fingertips of my left hand tease her right one. Not really slipping between them and not taking her hand, just lightly grazing mine against hers, tip to tip. The tightness in her shoulders relaxes, and I reach around her side and pick up her gloves, handing them to her. She has to ride. Today.

I head to her Atrani and swing a leg over. It takes a minute, but she takes the spot behind me. As soon as I sit, all the things about riding that turn me on get doused in lighter fluid as Lorina drops the match, and I have no idea how I'm going to be able to concentrate. Her inner thighs are hugging my hips, and I can feel every shift of her body against mine. Still, my left foot instinctually kicks up the stand, my right leg taking the weight to support us.

I want to touch her everywhere.

She's not holding onto me.

I peek over my shoulder, and her hands are clinging to the passenger seat in a death grip. I pull her arm forward, wrapping it around my side. Heat pools in my spine as she gives up and lets her other arm join, and maybe this was a bad idea.

Somehow, I manage to keep the throttle easy as I pull out of the garage, determined to keep myself in check no matter how badly I want to open it—her back slammed into the wall, her legs draped over my arms, driving into her until I can't do anything else. But I cruise slowly down her long driveway, and when we get to the end of it, I pause, waiting for nonexistent traffic.

My mouth is watering, every muscle in my body drawn tight at the promise of nothing to slow me down. My hand comes off the handlebar with a questioning thumbs-up, and fate smiles on me. Lorina returns it, her thumb hitched toward the sky.

I rev the engine once.

She hugs my back.

We peel out onto the highway, and her body ducks down with mine over the handlebars as I open the throttle and let her RPMs scream as I shift up through the gears. We're zero to sixty in fewer than three seconds, and I tease the throttle like peaked nipples over the endless gray road and blue skies above, the heel and toe of my boot kissing her gears in front of trees lining the road, dotted with the occasional farmhouse.

Lorina never balks, and I drive harder, faster, mentally counting the minutes until I can get back to my Yaalon waiting for me in Brno, because I need *more*. Sharper turns and checkered flags, leaning deep and pushing the limits until the world is deliciously tilted.

I push it now, gambling with the promise of police over the crest of every hill but swearing to myself I could outrun them if I had to. I've done it plenty of times before, and I can't get her arrested when I need to take her riding with me every day for the rest of my life. Nothing feels as good as the world blurring by with her on the seat behind me: leaning into turns, ducking for more speed, chuckling when I have to swerve for an errant chicken. She doesn't even care when I take my hands off the handlebars and steer with nothing more than the strength in my legs. She hugs me a little tighter at first, but she's with me every step of the way when I intertwine our gloved fingers and stretch them out toward the open air roaring past us, and I can't believe I didn't do this the first day I got here.

After an hour or maybe longer—the sun fully set and the world black except for the gleam of the headlight—Lorina points to the right at an intersection. I follow her directions away from the ranch lands until the highway bleeds into downtown traffic. It's the best idea I wish I would've thought of on my own.

I take the first exit from the highway that looks promising. It doesn't take much to sniff out the Memphis bar scene—blues music pouring from clubs as people dance and sway on the sidewalks, some in the street, and unlike the crowds I have to duck through in Europe, no one here has a clue who we are.

Lorina is quick to get off the moto once I pull into an open spot on Beale Street and walk it back, taking off her gloves and her white carbon fiber helmet. She shakes out her hair and tosses it, her face lit up with an easy smile, and I am a happy, happy guy. It nearly makes up for the fact that I'm starving to get her undressed and into a bed, right now.

Actually, screw the bed. Give me a wall. Give me a tree. Give me nothing but air, and I'm good to go.

Lorina chuckles, flicking my helmet at my stalling. I ditch my gloves, dumping them into the interior of her helmet before taking off mine. "It is not a bad moto, Lorina," I tell her, grinning. Her hands aren't even shaking. "Brakes maybe a little too tight, but it is not bad."

"Apart from the clutch, yeah."

Her clutch is a bitch, but the more she rides, the better it'll get, and I know she knows that. She waits as I get off the moto, and I glance around at the neon lights, feeling the music, the tipsy laughter, the smell of beer and sweat and piss a little more boorish than I'd prefer, but it'll do.

I look back to Lorina, and she smiles, shrugging. "Figured your inner club rat was probably going stir-crazy, cooped up at the house all the time."

I was, but I wasn't gonna say anything about it. At least she hasn't tried to make me ride a horse again, because that did *not* go well, and we agreed to forget it ever happened and tell no one. "I could have made it another day before I started doing a striptease at breakfast."

Lorina laughs. "Trust me, no one in my house wants to see that. Plus, my dad's likely to join in."

I grimace. "Then maybe I will be good."

She laughs again as I grab her hand, bringing her along with me until without warning, Lorina swings us into a bar. I chuckle, happy to follow her through the cloud of smoke and the blaring country music, and when she spins toward me on the dance floor, smiling as she wraps her arms around my neck, I almost can't trust it's real.

We're finally, finally free.

———

There are certain perks to knowing someone for ten years before trying to date them. For instance, I know Lorina gets off on crowds but doesn't like them close enough to touch her. She's a sucker for tulips, avoids chocolate like the plague, and her earbuds blare dubstep before she races, but the rest of the time, it's country love songs all the way.

What I didn't know is that Lorina can *dance*, and like everything else she does, she's damn good at it when she finally lets herself have a little fun. She's having a blast tonight. She hasn't stopped smiling since we parked the moto well over three hours ago, and I haven't either.

She's so easy to be with, and I shouldn't be surprised that this part works too. Everything else since I've been here…it's like it just makes sense. Teasing her at breakfast. Lorina getting her revenge during our workouts in her warehouse gym. I'm still not sure why she'll only kiss me good night, then ban me to my room, but I guess it could be worse.

She whistles and claps when the couple butchering a song on the karaoke stage finishes, Lorina leaning toward me to whisper over the scattered applause, "Oh my God, that was so awful!"

I chuckle as she sits back in her chair, taking another sip of her beer. A new guy on the stage starts *uh*-ing and snapping to a beat, and as she cracks up, my eyes trace my favorite scar on her forearm: the first one I ever watched bleed. It wasn't big, but it was deep, and

I couldn't believe how furious she was that she had to stop for the day because she needed stitches. She never cried, though. Just argued and yelled until she finished her teenaged fit with a kicked-over chair.

Lorina glances at me, a hint of a smile on her lips. "What?"

I lean forward to rest my temple against my fist, knowing there are so many more of those scars to be found on her body. I also know where every single one of them should be. Ten years' worth of wrecks she always bounced back from, until she couldn't anymore.

I am so in love with this woman, it's embarrassing, and I'm buzzed just enough to let the words slip from my mouth. "Marry me, Tigrotta."

She cracks up laughing before she points at me. "Not funny, and now, more than ever, you need to stop doing that."

I let it slide—she's reacted worse. "Perché?"

"That's, like, the sixth time."

"Undici. Eleven." Lorina stares at me, and I clear my throat, the truth a little thicker than I expected. "I asked you twice this year. This is eleven." Her cheeks darken under the dim lights, but there's a smile brewing in her lips that spells nothing but trouble. I reach over and cover her hand with mine, my voice more serious than she's ever heard when I take a breath, then look deep into her eyes. "Lorina…"

The blood drains from her face as her eyes widen. "Oh my God, I—"

"Lorina," I interrupt, barely able to keep a straight face. "Braking markers are not suggestions."

She blinks at me. And blinks at me. Then she groans, pulling her hand from mine and taking a deep pull from her beer. "I really hate you for that."

My eyebrow twitches, but I do my best not to react any more than that. I probably deserve it. Actually, I know I do.

She toys with the label on her beer bottle, but she's not paying attention to the singer on the stage anymore, and I probably need to get her home. She never stays up this late, and I doubt it's going to stop her from knocking on my door at the crack of dawn to make me go running.

"You ready to go, cara?"

She shrugs. "Yeah."

But we haven't even started to move when a blur of blond hair appears from freaking *nowhere*, practically tackling Lorina in her seat. "Oh my God, what are you doing here? I saw your Instagram post. Do you know it's a week night?"

Fight or flight? Fight or flight?

Lorina resembles a squished fish before the blond woman pulls back, and then Lorina is right there with her—squealing like all her dreams came true as she leaps up from her seat to better hug...whoever that is. "Holy crap! When did you get home?"

"Like two days ago! Billy told me about your hair, but I didn't believe him. Now I gotta pay the jerk ten bucks!"

They pull apart, laughing, and start messing with what's left of Lorina's curls, a tall presence taking up the space to my left. I catch a whiff of Old Spice, and the pieces start clicking into place before I ever look up. When I do, sure as anything, there's my Yaalon teammate and the reigning World Champion: Billy King.

I clear my throat and rise, my heart pounding in my chest and no idea what he's going to say. We've been cool so far, but that's all I'd call it: cool. He very much knows he's on the way out, and I very much know it's people like me threatening his career. But mostly, we've been fine. Guy's a hell of a card player.

"Massimo," he drawls, a twang to his voice that's thankfully more smug than sinister. "Weren't aware you were in town."

Yeah, and I would've rather kept it that way. He reports to Angelo, same as I do.

"Hi, I'm Taryn Ledell," the blond woman says, reaching her hand out toward me.

I shake it firmly, a little surprised once I get a better look at her. Would've considered her way out of Billy's league, but good for him, I guess.

"Massimo Vitolo."

"Oh yeah. I know."

I flinch at the implication in her words, unsure who has been talking about me: Billy or Lorina. My eyes dart to Lorina. Who is completely avoiding my gaze.

"Anyway...have y'all been here long? How's the karaoke been?"

"Awful," Lorina says with a chuckle. "It's been...yeah. Anyway, I think we were probably about to head out?" She looks at me with half a shrug, and I nod, not really in the mood to socialize more than this.

"Well, y'all will have to come have dinner at the house soon." Taryn's grin drifts from me to Lorina, the latter elbowing the former. "What?"

"Taryn's right," Billy says. "Y'all should come have dinner before we go back. Massimo." He extends his hand to me with that same haughty smile. Until his grip tightens a little as he leans closer, breathing, "Be careful, buddy."

The hell is that supposed to mean?

He lets me go and claps me on the back, then walks over to Taryn and gently steers her away from Lorina and toward the bar. "Let's go, honey. I need a drink."

"Lor, you really do gotta come to the house, though. I have to tell you something. Text me!" Taryn waves, Lorina waving back until Taryn whips around to Billy. "Wait, you need a what? Why?"

I blow out a breath for Billy's sake, glad I'm not the one getting Taryn's blue-eyed glare. She's scary. But it makes perfect sense to me why Billy likes her. No woman on the planet scares me more than Lorina.

I drop some cash on the table before I look to her. "Now are you ready to go, cara?"

She chuckles, but it doesn't last as long as it should, and I already know what's happening. Where her head is. And it's not in this karaoke bar with me. "Yeah."

We're not far from her parked moto—we bar crawled for a bit before stopping at the last place to eat. But it doesn't matter that the rest of Memphis didn't get the memo and is gearing up for the night: couples flirting down the sidewalks as the laughter from the bars grows louder with the music. Lorina's steps start to drag the closer we get to her Dabria.

Once we're finally beside it, she goes stiff, her heels dug into the ground and her arms crossed over her chest. I groan, pivoting toward her and turning my back on the moto she won't look at. "Cosa, Lorina?" She shakes her head, looking down, and I tell myself that no matter what, I need to stay calm and patient. It's what she needs. "This is how we get home, cara. We do not have another way."

She nods, swiping at her cheek with the back of her hand before she looks up at me, shrugging a shoulder against the busy street like everything's fine. "I know. Let's go."

Christ.

I need to get her on the moto. I need to break all the speed limits with her on the seat behind me until she's smiling like she did earlier. But I don't move. I can never seem to make myself do the right thing when she's crying, and I'm sick and tired of her crying.

She's not the only one who's worried about what's going to happen, but at least I'm trying to move forward, trying to stay positive. But I can't do all this by myself, and I need some kind of sign from her that there's at least a little bit of hope *somewhere*. That any part of this is going to get better.

It doesn't have to be everything, but I'm starving on nothing, and

I don't know why she can't seem to remember that just because I have a dick in my pants, it doesn't mean I don't have a heart in my chest too.

She's not going through any of this alone. She never was.

"Lorina…" I scrub a hand over my face, downshifting past avoidance and steering right into the truth. "Why am I here?"

"I don't know." She sniffles. "You wanted to go for a ride?"

"No. Why am I in America, Lorina? Not at home, with my brother. Why?"

She bites her shaking lip, but she can't even say it—the simplest answer to all the fucking questions.

I gesture absently in her direction. "Fantastico."

She looks away, wiping at her eyes again, and this is probably all going to blow up in my face, but she has completely forgotten who she is, and she won't speak up for what she wants.

I head over to her and take her face in my hands. A stunned breath pops from her lips, but it's late and I'm tired, and I don't care about pretending anymore. "Lorina, I am right here. Your moto is right here. You have always taken what you want, and you can take these things now. Take your win, Lorina. No one is going to stop you."

She shakes her head at me, tears running down her cheeks. "I don't feel like that person anymore, Massimo. I just… I can't."

The frustration bursts from me in a gritted yell. I walk away from her, tearing my hands through my hair when she sobs brokenly behind me.

I'm losing her. Everything we've worked for, the whole reason I put our careers ahead of what I felt for ten goddamn years, and she's letting it all slip through her fingers instead of fighting for any of it. And that's not the woman I fell in love with.

She sniffles behind me, her voice cracked and raw. "So what now? You leave? Go back to Italy? Give up on me like everyone else?"

I grit my teeth, looking up at the stars over her city, and I breathe in slow. Deep.

She still doesn't get it, no matter how many times I've tried to tell her.

I look back at her, and it shatters me. How alone she looks, how small and scared, and that's not my Tigrotta. But whether she's in jeans or leathers, crying or smiling, in love with me or unrequited hate, she will always be my Lorina. And I will never, ever give up on her.

I walk over and pull her into me, hugging my arms around her. It takes her a second before she hugs me back, but she does: her hands settling tentatively on my back, then slowly sliding higher until she's gripping the hell out of my shoulders, tucking her face into my neck.

Everything about her shivers and shakes as she quietly cries where no one but me knows the truth, and it's ripping me apart with every single one of her tears that slips down my neck and dips below the collar of my shirt. But I hold her tighter instead of pulling back and yelling at her, and I bite back every piece of advice, every sliver of proof from wrecks past that says she'll come back again.

I run my hand down her hair and press a kiss to her temple, and I let her cry on my shoulder for as long as she needs. Nothing else is working, and I'm still not giving up. But I don't how much longer I can keep her from giving up on herself.

Chapter 14

Lorelai Hargrove—July; Memphis, United States

MOONLIGHT TRICKLES THROUGH THE GROVE LINING THE DRIVEWAY, Massimo slowing so the engine quiets the closer we get to the house. Riding with him…it's become almost routine over the last week.

Work out in the morning, and once the afternoon rain stops, we head to the garage and my Dabria. We cruise on the back roads for about an hour until we head into the city, exploring museums, art galleries, the Memphis Walk of Fame, and sampling the blues bars on Beale Street.

It's been fun: visiting all the places I never bothered to see before, too wrapped up in my career to enjoy my hometown. When he first got here, it didn't even cross my mind that he'd be interested in any of the touristy stuff. I'm glad he makes us go, though, and I've spent more than one afternoon laughing as he dances with street performers, gazes wide-eyed at paintings, or makes me take pictures with him in front of landmarks. He's *always* taking pictures of us.

But still, despite knowing what will happen when we get to our destination each day—how the pressures of sponsors will disappear under his relaxed "We'll figure it out when we get there and everything will be fine" attitude—I still have a panic attack half the time he starts the engine in the garage. And sometimes when he takes a turn a little too fast.

Somewhere in the middle of our journey, though, I always realize I'm okay.

I'm not thinking about the plates I'm not wearing, the pads missing from my knees and elbows. I'm not trying to remember the specifications of my helmet and exactly how thick it is.

All I think about is him, and wondering why I haven't stopped him yet.

From tempting me with nothing more than a knock on my bedroom door, my helmet in his hands. From reaching back when we're at a stoplight and very gently cupping the back of my thigh. Like he wants me to know it's okay to be afraid, but he won't let anything hurt me.

Maybe it's because I haven't stopped myself.

Since the first time he took my hands away from the passenger seat, I've wrapped my arms around his waist. I lean into the hard muscles of his back, closing my eyes and simply trusting him to get us there and home safely.

I've spent hours with my body tucked into his—my thighs around his hips, my legs bent into a shadow of his own—and throughout it all, I smile. The world is easier, simpler, a little quieter with the engine roaring beneath us.

The world is quiet now, my parents' house dark as we pull past it into the garage and stop in the designated space for my Dabria. I swing my leg over the bike, pulling off my helmet and setting it on the table. When I glance over my shoulder, Massimo is off the bike and taking off his own helmet, hooking it onto the handlebar.

He runs a hand through his hair, his dark eyes licking the curve of my lips. My nipples peak under my leather jacket at the memory of only minutes ago, his fingers feasting on my jeans and squeezing me to the rhythm of the motor vibrating between my legs. Tonight, he held me more than on any of our other rides, and we rode forever. I didn't even want to come home, but it's nearly midnight, and we had to come back eventually.

I'm still reduced to just staring at him, enraptured, when his fingers curl around the snap-buttoned flap of his jacket, pulling it open with one swift twitch of his wrist and revealing the black T-shirt molded to his body underneath. "Continua a guardarmi così, sarò costretto a fare qualcosa al riguardo."

Heat pools in my belly at the slick words, the speed at which he spoons them out and how everything in Italian sounds unmistakably dirty. Especially when wrapped in his voice: deep and thick in the summer heat and the dim light of the garage.

My secret Rosetta Stone lessons are coming along, but I'm nowhere near far enough in my understanding of his language that I caught what he said. So I tick my chin up, drawling with a smile, "And that's supposed to mean?"

He shrugs out of his jacket, tossing it onto the table behind me. When he steps forward until I'm a single sucked-in breath from my chest grazing his, I'm lost, completely drowning in the smell of clean sweat and the product he puts in his hair. There's also something that's just him. Spicy and a little bit dangerous, but also warm and unmistakably familiar.

His hips nudge mine as he dips his head another inch like he's going to kiss me, and everything in me is screaming for it. For the richness of his lips, but mostly for the strike of his tongue. More than anything, I want him to bite me. I want to bite him. I want to scratch my nails up the Madonna on his back and claim the holy hell out of his cock, and he knows it. Because instead of brushing his mouth against mine, he smiles.

My pulse screams, heart thundering as he shifts so the space between his lips flirts with the edge of my ear. My eyes roll back at the quick flick of his tongue over my hooped earring, the lock bowing to his tongue and my earring slipping right out. Massimo chuckles darkly as his fingers retrieve it from his lips, then he tucks it deeply into the back pocket of my jeans, and I am so screwed.

It's taking all my willpower not to sneak into his room every single night. To do nothing more than kiss him and watch his bedroom door close, leaving us on opposite sides of it.

I'm trying to stay focused. Focused on what, I can't even remember when he pushes a little closer toward me, his erection testing the hollow space between my thighs.

A raw moan slips out of my throat, soft black cotton on his shoulder kissing my lips. My teeth scrape the seam of his shirt before I can help it, and his hand snatches my hip, holding me commandingly tight.

"What are you waiting for, Tigrotta?"

Somewhere deep inside me, something roars.

I don't know if it's more animalistic or machine. Just like I don't have an answer to his question—why I can't let go and just take him when I want him this much. My eyes travel over his skin, the tight tendons of his neck and the brutal shortness of the sides of his hair, his chest solid against my own. My knee hitches, and the roar grows louder.

I know what it is now.

It's 1000 ccs. It's 211 miles an hour. Pure speed and pure sex, and my eyes close as I bask in it, the noise and the adrenaline and the heat. The vibration. The need to win. For the first time in a long time, it feels like it's supposed to.

I feel like I'm supposed to.

But at the same time, the fear is crawling closer, the same one that's been choking me on the track. It's the taunting whisper that my tires are cold. That the setup is wrong. That when I least expect it, it's all going to crumble beneath me, sending me tumbling through biting gravel and toward the fatal stop of a wall that chomps bones.

"Tsk-tsk." Massimo clicks his tongue, and my eyes fly open when he leans back, his eyes garter-belt black. "So much fear."

Shame sinks in my stomach as he turns away, walking toward the exit of the garage. My left foot props itself on the table leg behind me. I know what I have to do. I know what I want to do. I just…

It's *Massimo*, I tell myself. His gears shift cleanly, his form nearly perfect. He leans into turns with confidence, and he never wobbles. He knows how to ride, to control being out of control.

Screw it. I want what I want, and I'm *tired* of being afraid.

My left foot taps the table leg like it's the shifter on my bike, and I push off.

Fourth gear.

I stride forward and grab Massimo by the arm, whipping him around with the confidence that carried me from the Rookie Cups to MotoB, then MotoA, and all the way to MotoPro.

"I am not afraid of anything." Then I push him.

He stumbles back, dropping with surprise into a chair behind him. The weight of his muscle-cut body scrapes the chair legs over concrete, the seat tilting back in a freefall. I stomp down on the bar between the legs, and all four feet slam to the floor.

Thick black eyelashes blink once, then twice as I flip off every promise I ever made that I wouldn't do this, and I straddle his lap. He's breathing hard, growing thick in his jeans when I grab the hem of his shirt and tug it up and off, allowing myself just one second to drink in the decorated ink on his body. The mask and threat he wears every day of his life to intimidate those who see him.

But then his hands settle on my jaw, his thumbs gently sweeping over my cheeks and urging my mouth down to his, breathing, "Lorina…"

And he's right: I *am* afraid.

But I won't let the fear take me like it has at the circuit. So I drop my heel on the leg of the chair and shift to fifth, pushing his arms away.

I quickly unbuckle his belt, then rip the leather free from denim loops. It comes out in a blur and snaps the air like a crack of thunder, his cock swelling beneath me. The predator in him bows to mine when I grab his hands, pinning them low behind his back. He hisses and hardens, nipping brutally at my jaw. It nearly ruins me, the grace of his lips and the knowledge that he'd probably do this sweetly if I let him. But I can't let him have this win.

I pull the belt tight around his wrists and hook through the metal clasp. "The word is 'gearshift' if you want me to stop." He nods in acknowledgment, but the truth is, neither he nor I care about being safe. We get off on danger, and Massimo keeps his mouth shut.

As soon as he's secure, I stand, ditching my boots and my jeans. I leave my shirt and jacket on, a last defense against him. Massimo's eyes are fully black as they devour the lower half of my body, his breathing picking up even further when my fingers undo the button and zipper on his jeans—tugging them down over his hips and leaving them at his knees.

Damn it, he's so beautiful: cut muscle stained with ink, a hard cock punching up into the night air. I tremble as I look him over, hesitating at the rich color and silkiness of his skin, the mouth-watering size of him.

The corner of his mouth turns up. "Afraid, Tigrotta?"

Afraid? No. I'm *terrified* this is going to change everything, and not for the better. It won't fix what's wrong inside me, won't promise me that I'll start winning and somehow keep my contract, and it can't be undone.

If I do this...at best, I'll never be able to stop. At worst, after tonight, he'll walk away, because pretending to care about me was the key to reaching his true finish line. But as dangerous as I know this is and despite the fact that there's nothing to save me when this all comes crashing down, I can't deny that he's what I want. He's the win, his body the trophy, so I lift my chin, and I answer, "No."

My knee bends and straightens, my heel tapping the floor.

Sixth gear.

I straddle his lap again, his eyes locked on mine as I pull my panties to the side. I should tell him I'm on birth control. I should ask when he was last tested. He doesn't ask me either of those questions.

In one smooth motion that scares the holy shit out of me, I sink down on him. My breath squeezes in my throat at the first thick stretch of him filling me, my body warm and soft enough that it gives way to how punishingly hard he is. Massimo's head falls back, a moan ripping out of his throat, and I rise, drinking in his heavy gulps for air. I lower all the way down once more, slipping around him more easily as he grows impossibly thicker inside me.

"Porca vacca…" he groans.

I cover his mouth with my palm. I don't want to hear his voice when I can't risk kissing him right now. Not like this. He was never supposed to be mine, even though it feels like he always has been, and if it hurts this much to lose racing…

I leave room for him to breathe under my palm but not much more, draping my other arm around the back of his neck so it won't hurt on the edge of the chair. Then with one swivel of my hips, I start to ride.

I fuck him with no fear, because according to the ink on his chest, fear is death.

And I don't move slowly, because according to his back, speed is savior.

Hard and fast, I take every ounce of pleasure from every inch of his cock, losing myself in the fact that his eyes are sharp but his lips are soft, teasing my palm with strokes of his tongue and scrapes of his teeth. All it does is spur me on more.

The fantasy of kissing him as I recall the taste of his tongue in scorching detail but won't let myself submit to focuses every nerve of my existence on one thing and one thing only. It's not the burning in my thighs or even the strength of his beneath me. It's the fire in my heart and stomach, stoked from the moaned growls rumbling from his chest and up into my hand.

I arch back and rock harder at a different angle, searching for that spot as my legs lock around the chair. My thighs hug his hips, and I love that the monsters on his arms are cradling my calves, my crossed ankles resting above his bound hands. The leather of his belt flirts with my skin, the buckle a sharp bite of pleasure, and when he curls his hips up into me, he finds what I've been searching for before I can get there myself.

Fire licks up my spine, my stomach tight with white light bursting from my breasts to my toes at every swollen flex of his head. I hold onto it for as long as I can, but as soon as it starts to back off, my body cries for more.

I lean forward, and Massimo's eyes are midnight fire and somehow still soft. I can't resist uncovering his mouth so my thumb can sweep over his bottom lip, tasting it for me. He kisses it, and my eyes squeeze shut.

I'm not supposed to love riding him more than my motorcycle. Racing was always supposed to come first.

"Lorina?"

My eyes fly open, and I cover his mouth with my palm once more. Before he can call me another one of his pet names. Before he tells me he loves me again. Before he can say *anything* that'll make me forget that for the last ten years, all I've cared about was beating him.

His words are poison. They sink too deep, and there's no way to get them back out. Just like the regret, because his brow furrows at me silencing him once again. So I rest my forehead to his temple where I can't see. I can only feel.

My body starts to roll and ride him again, but something feels different. The kisses he presses to my palm. The way his head leans into mine. How it feels like every measured thrust of his hips is a promise he's somehow capable of making, even when I have him bound and captured beneath me.

The rhythm between us slows, but it only intensifies what's really happening. It's not just the culmination of ten years of sexual tension that, once satisfied, will fade into nothing. If this were nothing, the aroma of his skin wouldn't be seeping deep into me. Calling to me. Commanding me to tilt his chin up, my mouth touching his jaw. He trembles, the muscles popping and flexing beneath my kiss. It beckons my hands to move, fisting in his hair and bending his neck back so he's trapped and I'm safe.

His eyelashes flutter with each swivel of my hips, and I dip my head. Just close enough that I can feel the heat of his breath. My tongue tests the air between us, tasting his bottom lip. Massimo jolts, his own body locking taut beneath me.

A sound crawls from his throat I've never heard another man make, blistering heat pumping into me, and I crave all of it I can get— riding him harder until his eyes squeeze shut, making sure Massimo's well past his breaking point. Only then, after one final thrust of my power, do I downshift all the way to first gear and release him.

My body unfurls, my forehead finding his shoulder where I'm sure my eyes are hidden from seeing the truth in his, and I wait for it. The high from being first. The peace from knowing it was me. Just me. At least Massimo doesn't say anything as I catch my breath and he searches for his own, our bodies still locked together and his hands bound behind his back. But then he dips his head so his cheek smooths against mine, and the feeling of pride, of power...it never, ever comes.

My chest starts shaking, and I bite my lip, blinking rapidly. *It didn't work*. Massimo still hasn't moved or even uttered a single complaint, and I don't get why he's so patient with me when I'm always such a bitch to him, tonight more than any other time in our history.

He was so sweet to me all day, working out and talking, and then going for our customary sunset ride on my Dabria. Then we came back here, I tied him up, fucked him in the garage, and I wouldn't even kiss him. And I accuse him of hurting me when I least expect it?

Massimo exhales, and his voice is so soft, I barely hear him when he breathes, "Let me be free, cara."

I shake my head, still refusing to look at him. "No." He sighs, frustrated, and my mouth moves over the words, "You'll touch me or kiss me, and then I'll cry because I screwed this up. You deserved better than this, and I..."

I never care about the consequences until it's too late.

Because I only ever think about winning, about myself.

I take a deep breath, telling myself to let him go so he can run. Back to the other woman who lets him kiss her when they're together, who doesn't tell him she hates him when it's the last thing she feels. Who appreciates the way he tries to help and doesn't yell at him.

I raise my head, trying to find the words to apologize for all the ways I've failed him, but I never find a single syllable. He's still him, the same man I've always known. Dangerously sexy jawline, a mouth that melts panties as easily as it spurs off insults that strike me straight in my soul. And even though I deserve those right now, his eyes are...different. Fully delved into that rare gentleness that's been sneaking out of his voice the last couple of months and only when he thinks I'm not paying attention.

I'm paying attention now, and just like that, Massimo's not my oldest rival, the guy to beat and the one I'm always chasing. He's just a twenty-five-year-old guy, trying to find his way through the confusing foreign lanes of love and lust and friendship. He's a man who works hard at his job, has dreams, a home, a mother and a brother, and...and me.

Me, who is difficult.

Little Tiger, he calls me. Afraid to be tamed yet yearns to be petted. Approach at the wrong moment, the wrong speed, and I'll rip you apart. But for all the times I've attacked him, he keeps coming back, rattling my cage when I need to remember I am deadly, because the truth is, I'm hurt.

Like now. When he said goodbye to his friends and family and flew halfway across the world to support me in the only way he knows how: by pissing me off and letting me take it out on him because he's strong enough to withstand it. It doesn't mean he doesn't feel my claws, though. That he doesn't hurt. That he doesn't love. If anything, it means he does all those things more. Selflessly.

In the darkness of the garage, I see him more clearly than I ever have. I see myself and the ways I've used him. The millions of ways I've hurt us both because I've been stubborn, so stubborn, and the aching truth is that I don't want to do any of this alone. Not anymore. And I don't want anyone else but him. I never have.

My hand cautiously moves from his deadly shoulder to the purity of his cheek, and the final gear shifts, locking into place. Right where it was always supposed to be.

As though he could feel it—the shattering of the last of my resistance—he grins, then winks. I can't help but smile, my forehead falling against his. It's the first bounce: when you land on your back, sliding until your feet catch and you're up and running again.

I should have known he wouldn't have been like the rest of the men I've met. That putting an ocean between us didn't keep him away, and neither did wearing my shirt and my jacket while I stripped him bare.

Running from my fears has gotten me nowhere except alone in the dirt, and it's past time for my guard to come down and my clothes to come off. To stay close enough to see what he'll do when I give him all of me.

I'm scared, but I'm ready. So ready.

"You finished being difficult yet?" he asks. "I know this is a lot to ask. For you."

A choked laugh bubbles from my chest, everything in me feeling lighter, stronger already. "Gimme a break," I tease, leaning forward to unclasp the belt from around his wrists. "It's taken me ten years to get here."

Massimo clears his throat. "That is a long time."

"Mm-hmm. Ten years of wanting you, and hating you..." The leather hits the concrete, the buckle pinging on the floor. I sit back as Massimo rolls out his shoulders, my palms cradling his jaw as his hands settle on my waist. "Ten years of trying to resist you."

He grins. "I think you did very good at this."

I lift a soft kiss from his lips, and then, very controlled, I lower the zipper on my jacket, letting the sleeves slide down my arms until it falls on the floor of the garage. When I grab the hem of my shirt and pull it off, taking my sports bra with it, his eyes widen, focused on the last parts of me I've been keeping from him.

"Every good memory I have," I say, waiting until I'm sure I have his eyes, "every best moment in my life, you were there."

He nods. "As it is for me."

"But you're also in every single one of my worst moments, and I can't just pretend they didn't happen."

Massimo swallows, the fear in his eyes the same as that flowing through me. But he's the one who said I have to be willing to risk it all, to lose, if I ever want to win again. And I trust him. He wouldn't steer me wrong.

"So promise me, Massimo. Promise me you won't break my heart, and you can have it."

A breath rushes out of him that's all the answer I need, and I kiss him deep and full. Massimo's arms come around me, holding me to him, and I don't want to think about fast or slow, right or wrong, enemies or contracts or complications.

I only want to melt into the sweet promise of his tongue against mine and the uncrackable protection of his hands plated on my body, refusing to let me go.

If I'm lucky, he never will.

But only if I'm lucky.

Chapter 15

Massimo Vitolo—July; Memphis, United States

PRAYING THE HINGES DON'T SQUEAK AS LOUDLY THIS TIME, I OPEN the door to Lorina's room and slip inside. Then I nearly collapse from death by lingerie.

I was prepared for her to be in bed—cheeks flush and hair a mess, clutching a sheet to her bare chest. I half expected her to be asleep. I was *not* ready for her to walk out of her closet in a navy-blue bra and panty set that crisscrosses its way down her stomach from her breasts to the bow and looks like it should come with a set of instructions.

It instantly pulls a low groan from my throat, and she stops short, her eyes wide and darting to the closed door behind me. "What?"

I can't do more than stand here and shake my head in admiration. Screw every person who told me you're not supposed to meet your heroes and you're not supposed to sleep with the girl of your dreams. Fuck 'em all for saying she'd never live up to the fantasy, because she *does*. Every single one.

"Seriously," she says. "What?"

I finally get it together and find my smile, then kiss my fingertips before I fling them away, trilling, "Brava."

She laughs, giving me a cute little curtsy. "Thanks." Then she heads toward the bathroom, finger combing her hair before she separates it into three sections and starts to braid it. My eyebrow arches, but I keep it to myself, following behind her. *Christ*, the back of that thing is ten times more torturous than the front.

I lean against the doorway to her connected bathroom, unable to resist picking a little bit at the strings and straps, searching for a clasp that has yet to reveal itself.

Lorina only giggles and continues braiding her hair, her eyes catching mine in the mirror. "Did my dad bust you?"

She red-flagged me midstroke this morning with the realization that we'd left her panties in the garage last night. Cut to her kicking me out of the bed while yelling at me to get dressed, me sneaking downstairs, and thanking Christ I didn't meet her dad on my way back up to her room.

I pull her panties from my back pocket, twirling them around the hook of my fingertip. "No."

She giggles again, and I fling them behind me without paying attention to where they land on her white carpet, somewhere between her white western furniture and under the watchful eyes of all the horse paintings in ornate frames on her long, white walls.

Lorina whips open a drawer and dips in her hand, nudging it shut with her hip in one quick movement I barely caught. Her fingers deftly tie off the end of her braided deathhawk, and when she turns toward me, she's pure, uncorrupted skin peeking out from naughty straps and a genuinely sincere smile with only the faintest hint of a blush. "Thanks for doing that."

I steal a kiss because I just can't help it. "In return? I want you to ask him."

"No," she says, laughing as she holds up a finger. "That is not a fair trade."

"Come on, Lorina. He will not tell you no."

"Because I'm not gonna ask him," she says, walking past me out of the bathroom. "First, no way in hell do you get to drive it before me, and second, he's never gonna say yes."

"Why?" I whine, heading over to her bed and collapsing on it. Lorina heads into the closet again, and I'd rather have her taking off clothes than putting them on, but if she's doing what I think she is, I'm not gonna complain. Probably will work out better in my favor to wait anyway. "It is unnatural that an American man should own an Italian car and not let an Italian man drive it."

"Massimo," Lorina says from the closet. "That Lamborghini is his baby. He loves that car more than me."

"Bullshit," I mutter in Italian.

Lorina chuckles as hangers clink and zippers pull. "If you want one so bad, go buy one yourself."

I gesture in her direction, even though she can't see me. "The American woman's answer to everything," I respond in English. "Go buy it."

I'm not really surprised. I've seen the way she lives. The way her family lives. The cars, the furniture, the rugs, and the books. And the more I see of her closet, the more I'm thinking her credit card statement probably resembles a phone number. Out of country.

"If that's what you want, then yeah," she says. "Besides, it's not like you have bills to pay. Don't you live at home in Ravenna with your mom and your brother?"

I walked straight into that.

When I double-check, Lorina is still safely in her closet, and I bite my thumbnail, debating what to tell her. Her situation is no different from nearly every other racer on the circuit—we're all gone the majority of the year, so except for the married guys, everyone forgoes the rent and mortgage and just crashes with their family in the downtime. But living at home just wasn't a long-term option for me, and even with Gabriele's bank account–draining antics, it's gotten a little more complicated than that.

I bite out a curse under my breath, then give her the truth. "I have un appartamento."

Lorina pokes her head out of the closet, still shirtless and a wicked smirk on her lips. "Really?"

I pillow my head with my hand and somehow chuckle, even though I'm internally cringing like all hell at the hope in her voice, at the light in her eyes at the chance for privacy when we're always surrounded by our managers, our crews, the fans, and the press. And, apparently, her parents. "Sì. But...I have a roommate, Lorina."

She groans, disappearing back into the closet. "We're never going to be able to have sex in peace, are we?"

I scrub a hand over my face, listening to the clink of more hangers. Does it always take her this long to get dressed in the morning?

"It is okay," I tell her. "Very soon, I will buy us a house. Then, no one will care what we do, where we do it, or how loud you scream. Okay?"

She laughs from the closet. "Sidestepping the part where you literally were just bitching about spending money... It hasn't even been twenty-four hours since you've seen me naked, and you're ready to start looking into real estate?"

It takes me a second to make sure I got all that, then I nod. "Sì."

Lorina laughs again because she thinks I'm joking. "All right, I'll bite. Where we gonna live, Massimo?"

Since she can't see me, I go ahead and smile. Because about an hour from my mom's, in the Emilia-Romagna countryside, there's a three-bedroom villa that's big enough for her, not too big for me, with a separate guesthouse, plenty of land for a stable and a couple of horses, and no neighbors anywhere close. I ride past it every time I'm home, but it's always just been there. Vacant. Torturing me with how very close I was to having it all and how very far away.

"In Italia."

Lorina comes out of the closet, and I sit up, a grin tugging at the corners of my lips at her black leather jacket over her white T-shirt and dark blue jeans, the sleek motorcycle boots that probably cost more than my rent. She smiles as her hands settle on my shoulders, despite all the times I've hurt her and directly in the face of all the times she promised me this would never, ever happen because she hated me so much. "Of course we are."

I grin, happy to let her kiss me like she actually meant that and knowing I deserve every one of the monsters scarred into my body when I don't stop her and bring up my roommate again. But there's no such thing as a roommate when Lorina's breaths go shallow, her hands grasping at my shirt and pulling it off me.

She flings it away, her hands fierce on my jaw as she kisses me deeper. I thought she was leaving, but I can't remember where I thought she was going or why I was fine with it when she's this freaking sexy.

Lorina pulls back, a fire in her eyes that I'm dying to feel in the way she rides me, but I'm red-flagged *again*. "I fully expect you to be naked when I get back."

I blink, barely able to think about anything except *where is the clasp on her lingerie?* Then I remember—why I'm not going to fight her. Why I'm going to let her go. Why I'm always letting her go.

"I may not wait for you."

Lorina kisses me again until I'm wrecked, but she's never been scared to wreck me. Just love me. "Your loss."

She leaves me with a wink and a smug little laugh that rises and falls to the sway of her hips, her bedroom door swinging shut behind her. I blow out a breath, trying to calm my racing heart. Then I wait.

Down the hallway, past my empty room.

The first flight of stairs, turn at the landing, down to the first floor.

Across the living room, past the kitchen, through the foyer, out the front door. Flower beds, flower beds, flower beds. Garage.

Go.

I half run from her room, coming out and slamming straight into her fucking *father*. Currently standing outside my door with his fist raised to knock. Now staring at me coming from Lorina's room. Not wearing a shirt.

His eyes widen and his jaw hardens, and my stomach chokes my throat, but I don't have time for this. I vault over the railing, landing on the stairs below the turn.

"Massimo!" her mom shrieks from the kitchen, but I'm fine and I stumble down the rest, catching myself with a wobbled slide on the living room rug. I skid to a stop, then turn and bolt the other way, past her gaping mom as I hurdle the coffee table and land on the runner in the foyer, controlling a slide toward the front door. "What the hell is going on?"

"Ricky Ricardo's got some splaining to do, that's what," her dad snaps from upstairs.

I don't respond, just looking out the window beside the front door and waiting, listening.

Any second. She can do this.

"James," her mom starts. "Give him a break, okay. It's not like we didn't know this was—"

The Dabria roars to life in the garage, and her parents go quiet behind me, everything in me wound tight and vibrating as I urge her on under my breath.

She took what she wanted last night and all this morning, and she can take this win too.

Heavy steps come up behind me, but I don't look when her father stops on the other side of the front door, looking out the window toward the garage.

"James," her mom starts again, but she stops when he raises his hand. I don't know if he's holding his breath, but I am.

Three seconds.

Four.

Come on, Lorina.

The engine barks and she flies out of the garage, dark and ducked low as she barrels way too fast down the driveway, and I can't resist a shout at seeing her. Her dad does it too, and I laugh as she disappears behind a cloud of white dust—she's wearing my helmet instead of her own, but that's okay, and she'll get there.

She went. By herself. Because she wanted to. That's all that matters.

"Was that really Lorelai?" her mom asks, so much relief in her voice that I can't help but let it fill me up too.

Best night and best morning of my whole life. No contest.

And then her dad looks at me.

"Yes, that was really her," James says. Then he faces me fully, crossing his arms. I swallow, still watching where Lorina disappeared and the dust has yet to settle. The last thing I need is her parents hating me when I need them to be okay with us staying here in the breaks. And they've been cool with me so far, but I know to her father, it might not matter how old we are or how long this has been building.

She's always been his, but I want her to be mine, and he doesn't have to say yes.

If he kicks me out right now, I'm totally screwed. Lorina is never going to buck her parents' disapproval, and even if she did, I can't take her back to Ravenna with me yet. She won't understand, and I need more time with her first. Time like this, away from the track when she's actually willing to give me a chance to prove that I might do messed-up stuff sometimes, but I do it for a reason, and it's never to hurt her.

Her father leans toward me, and I lean back a little, but I don't look down, and I don't blink. "You still can't drive the Lambo," he growls, then he turns and walks away.

I let out a breath, then loudly groan. "Oh, come on, James. It is my birthright as an Italian." He waves me off, heading to his office. I peek at her mom to see how I'm faring there. Lynn's in the living room with one hip slightly jutted out, a scowl on her face she purposely put there to make me sweat. I know it for sure because her daughter gives me the same one. Regularly. "Per favore, Lynn. I would never hurt his car."

When she stays silent, I twist my lips into a pout, shoving my hands in my pockets and slowly walking toward her, my head hung. Halfway there, I throw a single skip into my step.

She laughs like a champ. I have a sneaking suspicion Lynn knew what was going on between me and Lorina long before her daughter did.

"Don't try and charm me," she says with a smile, then nods upstairs. "Go take a shower, and I'll make you some breakfast."

"Grazie, Signora."

"Don't smooth talk me either."

I make a serious face. "Sì, Signora."

She rolls her eyes, but she lets me drop a kiss to her cheek before I whistle my way up the stairs, happy to wait for Lorina to come back and make good on her promise. I'm definitely keeping mine.

The second I pay off Gabriele, I'm buying that house.

I'm just praying I can do it before she gets anywhere near my apartment and the shaky ground I'm strolling on completely crumbles apart under me.

—◦◦◦—

"You got him! You got that sombitch!" Mason yells at the bull rider on the TV. He's been yelling that for over the last hour to *all* the bull riders on the TV.

Billy and Bryan are on the edges of their seats in Billy's farmhouse living room, Mason and Dax already on their feet, their boots matting the faded shag carpet. I survey the four of them cautiously from my spot against the wall. Under a pair of mounted antlers that smells…fresh.

"Don't let go!" Billy perks up. "Keep spurring him!"

I glance at the screen. The bull rider looks like he's gonna have the worst neck ache of his life when he wakes up tomorrow morning, and the bull looks *furious*. This is fun? Where is the elegance of teamwork, the glory of a perfectly struck goal?

I look into the kitchen behind me—which Billy must have just repainted, because the crisp white cabinets and yellow walls don't match the rest of the aging house—to see what Lorina is doing. My brow furrows into a scowl when I find her and Taryn leaning against the kitchen counter, talking.

I push off the wall, dropping my empty beer in the waste bin on the way there.

"No, it's totally not like th—Yes?" Lorina drawls, smirking up at me when I stop next to her.

I keep scowling, pointing to the cutting board by her hip. The one with a clean knife and a whole head of garlic. Unpeeled. "I thought you said you were helping to cook dinner."

"I am."

I groan, my entire body running on nothing after she spent all day draining me dry. Not that I'm complaining. "Lorina, I am hungry. I told you earlier: you have to feed me and let me rest, or I break. Most importante: food, cara."

Taryn cracks up laughing, tossing her long blond hair before she recrosses her cowgirl boots the other way. "God, you're just as bad as Billy. The spaghetti will be ready in a few minutes."

I glance around at that interesting announcement, and water is boiling in a pot that I pray doesn't have pasta in it yet, tomato sauce simmering in a skillet. But the smells are all wrong.

"Anyway, back to MMW possibly coming to MotoPro..." Taryn says.

The girls are already back to talking as I go over to the stove, turning off the burner under the water and lowering the one under the sauce.

"I can't believe MMW is really considering crossing over after all this time," Lorina says. "I thought that would never happen."

Pull out a wooden spoon from a utensil canister on the counter to taste it and—

Don't react. I very slowly put down the spoon. Start thinking. Fast.

What would Nonna do? *Throw it away*, my mind whispers.

"Get him, get him, get him!" the men's voices swell in the living room. Followed by a cheer that reminds me of my uncles whenever Francesco Totti made a goal. A sad twist pulls at my lips—can't believe Il Capitano retired.

God, I miss Italy.

"Werner said they've played with the idea before," Taryn says as I head over to the cupboards and start looking for the salt, maybe some oregano. I'm not counting on finding anise. "But that it was way too expensive with the engineering it would take to get their bikes competitive in the MotoPro arena. Not to mention the—hold on. Um, excuse me? Hi, you with the tattoos. What are you doing?"

I check over my shoulder, and yes, the beauty queen is addressing me. "Cooking. I would like to eat before we fly to Brno *domani*."

Lorina snorts into her hand, Taryn drawling, "By all means, Massimo. Because when Billy and I invited you over for dinner, it was so you could cook it yourself."

"Grazie. That was very kind." I nod at her and keep searching, coming up with stacks of mint-green ceramic plates and flower-print bowls, at least a dozen flour-free cookbooks, and an endless arrangement of coffee mugs.

"Jesus Christ," Taryn mutters with a laugh.

I finally find the spice cabinet, taking out what I need. Fresh herbs are better, but dried is better than nothing. And I mean *nothing*.

"See? Now do you understand what I'm dealing with?" Lorina says.

Just for that, I smack her ass on my way back to the stove. "Sì, but you love it."

A low growl rumbles from my Tigrotta on the other side of the kitchen. "No, I don't."

"Uh, yeah you do," Taryn tells her. "Ow! Don't pinch me..."

"Ow! Don't pinch me either."

I chuckle to myself as I let the flavors fall from their plastic tubes with automatic flicks of my wrist, leaning closer and wafting the smell up to gauge the balance. Better.

"So if MMW comes to MotoPro, are you going to try to move with them?" Lorina asks her friend. "I mean, wouldn't that make everything a million times easier on you and Billy so you're not racing on opposite weekends?"

"Girl, you have no idea. Look at our schedule this year."

I glance over, the pair of them looking at Taryn's phone.

"What do the yellow boxes mean?"

"We're home at the same time."

"But there's, like, none."

"Yeah," Taryn says with a humorless chuckle. "Most months, we get maybe one or two days. Some months are worse. Right now, I'm counting down the days to Valencia."

Jesus. I don't know how Billy does it—being apart that much. I knew it was bad with the way he's always on his phone, but I didn't think it was *that* bad. Except with the way the Superbike and Moto circuits overlap so there's almost no downtime for the fans...yeah, it would be.

Heading over to the sink, I wash my hands, then head back to Lorina, sliding her two inches to the left. "What are you..." she sputters when I slip my arms around her waist, then get to work on the garlic she was supposed to be chopping but didn't. "I can move, you know."

"This is okay." I scoot a little closer, stealing a kiss to her neck before I begin watching what I'm doing over her shoulder. For all her protesting, she leans back against me, and I love the way she feels in all the places I want to feel her most. It almost makes me want to take my time, but the garlic should've gone in long ago.

"Okay, so you are...really good at that," Taryn says with a chuckle.

I shrug. "I have done this once before. Maybe twice."

The girls laugh, Taryn going back to looking at her phone. "Anyway, so...since we have a few more minutes while the guys are distracted, and since Massimo has decided to recook my dinner, I'm gonna go ahead and show you something. But, Lor? You can't freak out."

"Since when do I freak out?"

I lift my head, looking at Taryn.

"I mean it." Then she turns the screen to Lorina.

"Screw you too, Miette," Lorina mutters. Then she scrabbles to pull the phone closer, blocking my view of the cutting board. I drop the knife on instinct before I accidentally cut one of us. "That's my bike!"

The words are like a jagged rod of dry ice getting jammed down my spine—and it's not even *my* moto. I lean closer to check, Taryn showing both of us the screen. Some blond chick is blowing a kiss in red Dabria leathers, captioned with the words, "Having a nice break, loser?" But she's not standing next to the production model they race in Superbike. That's the MotoPro prototype Lorina rides, except for the different number on the front.

My eyes flick to Lorina, waiting for the explosion when the realization hits her: Dabria isn't just thinking about dropping her. They're already courting replacements, and if she doesn't ride well in Brno, it won't even matter what her final World Champion standing is. She'll be gone long before then.

Damn it, she didn't need this right now. Her confidence is shaky as it is, and now more than ever, she needs to own all our asses in the Czech Republic and prove everyone wrong.

"You think that's real?" Lorina asks Taryn, her voice at a quarter of its previous strength.

"Scusa." I slide Lorina out of the way with an easy smile, grabbing the cutting board and the minced garlic and carrying it to the stove. They could probably debate the minutiae of this for hours, but Lorina doesn't need to dwell on it. She needs to keep riding, keep focused on what she can control, and let go of all the crap she can't.

Taryn shrugs, putting her phone back in her pocket. "I don't know but...let me know if you need me to talk to anyone about a sponsorship for you."

My knife stops midscrape into the pan, my heart seizing in my chest, and I can't believe I didn't...

Of course she would go Superbike if Dabria backs out. It's the next logical step. She'll take a loss with the power gap, but she'll still get to ride, and she'll be with her best friend.

But it also means when I'll be racing in the United States, she'll be in the Netherlands. When I'm in Australia, she'll be in Qatar. When I'm at home in Ravenna during a break, she'll be in Thailand. Portugal. France. It's like that through the whole circuit.

I go back to scraping garlic into the sauce I'm not sure I can save, trying to keep calm.

"But even as I say that," Taryn goes on, oblivious to the shock-wave she just sent through my universe, "I also feel like I should mention that a couple days ago, Miette was saying something about the 'powers that be' maybe creating a women's division. And considering it was Miette and that this was translated by yours truly because said conversation was originally in French, I wouldn't put much—"

"Later." Lorina's eyes dart to mine from across the kitchen, but it's fast. Too fast. "We'll talk about it later." Then she clears her throat. "I really like what you've done with the cabinets."

Fuck, she's totally going Superbike.

———

The night air is thick and sweet as I rock slowly in one of the chairs on Taryn and Billy's big back porch, taking a pull from the cigarette Dax offered me: a very nice, very tall cowboy who speaks a little high school Italian as it turns out. He and Bryan already went back to the second house on the property I can't see from here anymore but could kind of make out earlier. Mason and Billy are inside. Watching more bull riding.

I take another drag, looking at constellations I don't recognize as strange bugs make strange sounds. But I can't stomach the stars for long before I close my eyes, trying to push from my mind the last call I had with my mom: how pissed she is that I'm here, proving all her worst fears into reality. Mostly how hurt Dario is that I've been gone for all of my longest break of the circuit.

The back door creaks, and I scuff the cigarette on the underside of the rocking chair and drop the butt into my beer bottle, all without acting like I'm doing anything. "Tigrotta," I casually drawl when Lorina busts me a second later. Her arms are hugging a blanket she's got wrapped around her shoulders, along with a pretentious arch to her eyebrow.

"That's disgusting."

I give her that. "It is not a habit. Just a pleasure." No budge. "That I am apparently quitting." I score half a smile, and she takes my outstretched hand and comes around my side, settling her ripped little body on my lap. The woman has more individually sculpted back muscles than I'm able to name, in any language. "Ugh," I groan, adjusting her so my dick isn't breaking in half. "You are a heavy Tigrotta tonight."

She sticks her nose in the air, then continues getting comfortable. "Not my fault you're a really good cook."

"I told you once already, cara: I am good at everything."

Lorina gives me a whole smile this time, but it comes with a devious curve to her lips. "Except for riding horses."

I gasp, pretending to be shocked. "That was supposed to be a secret," I growl at her, Lorina cracking up as I go for the spot where she's most ticklish. I'm also the biggest hypocrite in the world, because despite all my preaching, I don't know how I'm supposed to be okay with losing her if she doesn't make it all the way back in Brno and the worst happens.

I didn't come this far, wait this long, to lose her this fast.

Lorina drops her forehead to mine, her smile brighter than the moon when she lifts a soft kiss from my lips, and I can't resist a low moan at how delicious she is, always. "I love when you taste like pasta."

Lorina giggles, her hand cradling my cheek and holding me to her as I nuzzle my way into her neck, breathing in lemons and moto exhaust from our ride over here. It feels like a lifetime ago that we were competing in Germany. When she was dodging my calls in her hotel room, not realizing I was calling from right outside her door. But it's only been a few short weeks. And even with as much as I miss home and my brother and some real freaking espresso, I'm *still* not ready to go back.

I need another week. Another month with her. I just need...*more*. Worse, I already know the very second we cross the circuit gates, everyone is going to be keeping us apart: Frank, Vinicio, Angelo, everyone. And there's not a damn thing I can do.

"I love you," I whisper in Italian, because I can't help it when I'm already missing her this much. Lorina captures my lips with hers and kisses the hell out of me, but she doesn't say it back. She never does.

"I want to ask you something," she whispers instead, her bottom lip nervously bit.

My heart slams in my chest, and I mentally scream at myself that if she asks if I'm okay with her going Superbike, I will say yes. I will support her dreams, no matter what, because for Lorina, racing comes first. Always has, always will, and I swore to myself that I would accept being second place in her life as long as I got to have her in mine.

But *fuck*, I don't want her to go.

"How come," she says, her cheeks darkening, "when you say 'I love you' in Italian, it translates as 'I want good things for you'?" She peeks up at me, shrugging. "I thought you were supposed to say ti amo."

I cough out a laugh from the shock of the question I was absolutely not expecting, and honestly, I don't know which one I'd rather *not* answer more.

"Don't laugh at me," she mumbles, and I am *such* a jerk.

"Oh, Lulu," I drawl with a pout, shaking my head. I press an apologetic kiss to her forehead; at least she lets me. "I will explain. In Italia, there are two ways we say it. Ti amo is more for...for Billy and Taryn. They live together, and they will probably be married soon. For friends? We say ti voglio bene."

Lorina stiffens on my lap, the wind beginning to bend the trees behind her. "Did you seriously just tell me that you think Billy loves Taryn more than you love me, which is why you're using the friends-only version?"

I roll my eyes. "No." Though I doubt me explaining this more is going to make a difference when she only ever hears what she wants to. "I said they are committed to each other. Both of them. You have trouble admitting to your friends we are even together. So to you? I say ti voglio bene. It does not change how I feel. Only what I tell you I feel."

Lorina looks away, a guilty tug to her mouth. I gesture at the fields and fishing pond, because I'm an idiot. It really doesn't bother me that much when I didn't expect any different. You have to trust before you can love, and she's still learning to trust me. But she's trying. I know she is.

"Look," she says quietly, but she's staring at the porch and won't meet my eyes. "Saying that to someone...it's the one thing in my life I do slow. As in I have never said that to anyone. And when I do, I want it to really mean something. I want it to be real."

I nod, sweeping her hair back from her face. "And I want you to take your time, cara. I am not in a hurry. I have waited for you before. I will wait again."

She blushes fantastically at the moon and the fields. "I don't understand you, Massimo. You keep saying I need to let go, to be ready to lose everything. 'A car is a car. A moto is a moto. A contract is just a job, Lorina,'" she mocks. "But then how do you explain your attachment to me? A girlfriend is a girlfriend?"

I scoff, hating how well she just busted me on the very problem that brought me out here to start with. "It is not the same. I did not buy you."

She does a double take in my direction, then glowers at me. "Damn straight you didn't."

A smug curve takes the corner of my mouth, because I can't resist going for it. "I would not have paid as much as you probably think you are worth."

She pushes my shoulder, tuning away from me as much as she can. "Ass."

"Lorina," I groan, adjusting her on my lap. My leg is dead asleep. "A car is a car. A moto is a moto. You are...you are a part of me."

She peeks at me from the corners of her eyes, because she can't resist either. I know she can't. "What, like your heart?"

"No, not my heart."

She gives up on acting mad and turns back to me, snuggling up on my chest. "Your lungs, then? Am I the very air you breathe, Massimo Vitolo?"

"Now who is the ass?" I shake my head as Lorina laughs, hugging my arms around her again and rocking us slowly in the oversize chair. "No, cara, you are not my lungs. You are like...you are like my dick."

She guffaws, full-out giggling when I start tickling her side again.

"What is wrong with this?" I ask. "You make me a man, make me feel strong."

"Aww," she teases, batting her eyelashes at me.

"Ti voglio bene," I tell her, not a single tremor in my voice as I meet her eyes and say the truest words I've ever said, in the first language I ever learned. "And I will do what it takes to make you happy, keep you satisfied, and protect you."

"Mas..." Lorina melts into me, because at some point in the last couple of weeks, she's started understanding Italian. I have no idea when she's sneaking in her study sessions, but as long as I go slow and enunciate, she gets it. I did have to start taking my mother's calls in another room, though.

"But," I say, switching back to English. I brush a kiss to her hair before I shift back, catching her eyes. "I also know if someone cuts off my dick, I will not die. I will not be happy, but I will live. At the same time, if someone were to say to me, 'I can kill you, or I can cut off your dick,' I would probably say, 'Kill me and leave my dick alone.'"

Lorina smiles at me like that was the most romantic thing she's ever heard. "You'd probably say that?"

"Sì, probably," I confirm. "I like my dick. It is my favorite part of me."

Lorina laughs, but I'm not kidding.

I *love* her, and like Taryn and Billy, we've got a real shot at making this work if we can keep working through our baggage. Something there is no shortage of after ten years of diving for each other on the track. But we can't fix that stuff if we're constantly apart. And if she loses her contract? It won't even matter whether she decides to go Superbike or just retires to Memphis to hide out. I'm going to be so lost without her beside me every day—as she's always been—that I doubt I'll be able to stay away from her for long. And I don't trust that I won't do something really dangerous to get back to her.

Lorina yawns and shifts a little closer, her head going right to its place on my shoulder. The wind blowing through the trees starts to pick up, and I tuck the blanket a little tighter around her, wishing time would stop, just for once, instead of speeding up.

Starting tomorrow, I have to win the next ten races. I have to find a way to pay off Gabriele faster than I ever thought possible and somehow, at the same time, make sure Lorina makes the podium for World Champion and keeps her contract with Dabria.

I *have* to.

All the other options, they're just not good enough.

Chapter 16

Massimo Vitolo—August; Brno, Czech Republic

I'VE HAD LORINA LAUGHING FROM MEMPHIS TO MADRID, MADRID to London, and London to Brno, which is good. Great, even, considering she's staring down her first race back since tanking in Germany. She didn't sleep much our last night in her bedroom, tossing and turning until she left and went for a ride on her Dabria. But she's not acting nearly as nervous as she was in Le Mans or Mugello. And despite that fact that I'm 95 percent sure she's going to be fine on Sunday—especially considering our recent inauguration into the mile high club that took place somewhere over the Northern Atlantic—I'm 100 percent sure I'm in big fucking trouble.

I'm barely across the gate into the timbered Automotodrom paddock when I see them waiting for me: Vinicio about nine levels past pissed off under baby-blue skies and white fluffy clouds, and Angelo practically salivating behind him, appearing to grow as tall as the thick woods surrounding the circuit. Because I just served up proof of exactly where I *wasn't* supposed to be over the break.

"Wanna get something to eat?" Lorina hooks the security badge around her neck like no one would recognize her after her freshly shaved undercut, but whatever. "Mas?"

I don't answer. I don't shake my head. I just keep walking, blending into the herd of people closest to me and trying to make it look like it was a coincidence that we got here at the same time and not that we shared the cab pulling away from the curb. That Billy and Mason and Frank also just poured out of...

Screw it. I'll take the lecture, say I'm sorry and I won't do it again, and then...done.

Back to moto. Back to Lorina. Simple.

"Okay...I guess not, then," I hear called out behind me. Some of the people nearby stop and glance around to see who she was talking to, but I keep my head down and keep moving. I'll deal with the fallout later. She's forgiven me for worse. Like being a jerk for ten years running specifically to keep us apart because *I knew* it was dangerous, and we had things to focus on. Like making it *here.*

Vinicio waves me toward him as if I weren't already headed that way. But neither my manager nor sponsor rep says anything as I approach—no excitement about the coming race or animatedly running me through my press and practice schedule. They only turn and lead me toward the historic green-and-white grandstands, then inside it and down a long hallway until Angelo pulls open a door to a conference room. He waits as Vinicio crosses inside, then me, gesturing for us to take a seat at the solid teak table big enough for forty rotund capitalists that only see me as a profit margin. But there's no one else here.

No witnesses.

Everything in me is freaking the hell out as I drop my bags that still smell like Lorina's bedroom in Memphis: vanilla sweet and sensual lemon, and nothing like the salty air of Italy. Vinicio is paling next to me as we both pull out rolling desk chairs, his deodorant overtaking his cologne because he's probably sweating through his shirt under his jacket. He's always hated confrontation.

"Massimo," Angelo growls in Italian the moment my ass hits the seat. He glares at us from in front of a big blank whiteboard that shows a faint trace of the track with arrows pointing at the corners even though it was recently wiped off, the adjacent wall of video screens completely dark, and the silence in the soundproof room is nauseating. "I'm just gonna cut to the chase here."

Bile rises in my throat. He still hasn't sat down.

I tell myself that no matter what happens, not to let myself puke from the stress until after it's over. All I've gotta do is ride it out. Get to the finish. This can't be as bad as he's making it seem. I've read my contract very carefully, and he can't dictate who I'm with or who I love. It's none of their damned business.

At the very *most*, he can fine me for unbecoming conduct or disobedience. But this still isn't even close to some of the other stunts I've pulled in the past. He's just trying to scare me.

Fuck him.

Angelo starts pacing back and forth behind his side of the table. "I shouldn't have to tell you that we're more than a little disappointed to have discovered that during the break, you accompanied Lorelai Hargrove to her home in the United States. Even after we made it clear we had concerns over the nature of your relationship with her. And while we are always proud of the camaraderie of riders..." Angelo stops and faces me, a sadistic smirk on his face. "We need you to understand that you are contracted to see Yaalon place on the podium for World Champion. Not Dabria Corse."

My feet are flat on the floor, my palms on my thighs, and I just started pouring sweat like I'm running for my life. The fact that Angelo thinks I need to hear him say that says it all: he didn't like the relationship. Fine. But I pissed him off, and now, he's accusing me of throwing races we haven't even run, of rolling out a red carpet for Lorina to take my spot on the podium.

The hell I am. I would *never* do that, whether we're sleeping together or not, and we haven't done a thing to deserve this. The insinuation alone is insulting.

Angelo leans forward, bracing his weight on his fists. The table creaks. "The fact that there is no precedent for this kind of relationship between riders makes this even more complicated. So I'm going to see if I can make the situation a little clearer."

His face tightens, and I barely keep my eyes from narrowing. No precedent? Wait till he finds out about Santos and Giovanni. That's been going on for just as long as me and Lorina. Except they've *actually* been sleeping together for years, whereas everyone just assumed wrongly about us.

"While at present, there is nothing in your contract that prohibits you from having a relationship with her, be advised," Angelo snarls. "Any evidence you are sharing confidential information about your strategy to win races—including the disclosure of any changes and/or modifications made to your motorcycle after practice and qualifying—will be viewed as subversion. Furthermore, Lorelai Hargrove is not to be in your garage, pit box, or Yaalon-provided RV at any time from this day forward. Equally, you are not to be in her garage, pit box, or Dabria-provided RV. And because we are all aware she is under pressure from her own manufacturer, if at any time it is discovered that you are assisting her in winning races or manipulating the point system, you will be excused from the remainder of your contract with Yaalon Moto, indefinitely."

The air conditioner kicks on overhead, chilling the room ever further, and I can't breathe.

Angelo just wrote himself a blank check on how to fire me.

I expected threats. Restrictions? Sure. Maybe a fine. But I already know that staying out of her garage won't matter in the end. The very minute I don't place where Angelo wants, he'll say I did it to help her, and there will be no way to argue. No way to prove I didn't back off or tell her anything about my moto when we're away from the track.

I can't see a way out of this...

I could go to the press. Maybe I could convince Lorina to do some kind of photo shoot with me that I fundamentally disagree with but know would work to get the fans on our side. They've already been speculating about us for years. If we give them their happily ever after fantasy, maybe their roars against the manufacturers will be enough to give us immunity.

He can't do this. This can't happen.

"Finally," Angelo says, straightening. He adjusts his shirt sleeves under his jacket, checking his cuff links. "I would advise you to cease whatever relationship you have with her immediately. Because if"— massive emphasis on the if—"you continue to ride for Yaalon in the coming years, you should expect modifications to be in your contract that will clarify this…issue, so we can all remain confident we share the same goals."

He smiles at me. For a long, long time. Letting the words echo in the soundless room. I glance at Vinicio—this just went from bad to apocalyptic.

Angelo unbuttons his jacket, then finally pulls out a chair and sits at the table, his chin high and hands clasped in front of him. My temper is raging, but I already know if I speak right now, I'm fired. It doesn't erase the fact that everything in me is ready to fight, to protect her, protect us, and let the rest of the bullshit come crashing down, because she'd be worth it.

She's the future. My only future if it comes down to it. I know what I want. I won't let him make me forget.

"Massimo," Angelo says like he's on my side. But all he cares about is cashing his bonus check, the one he gets if the team he recruited lands on the podium. I know what he drives and how much that watch on his wrist costs. "We signed you because you are one of the most promising riders we have seen in many years. You showed focus and talent while competing in MotoB and MotoA, and we expect that same focus to be applied to seeing Yaalon Moto on the podium for World Champion. For that to be your only focus. Are we clear?"

The fuck we are.

I place my palms flat on the table, more than ready to grab my stuff and go—back to Lorina, back to my RV, and let Angelo follow through on his threats.

I'd love to see that asshole try it.

But Vinicio's hand shoots out, closing around my wrist. My eyes dart to his, and I'm sledgehammered by the terror in his face. The fury and the helplessness. "Mio figlio," he mouths.

My son.

He lets me go. I sit down. I sink in my chair.

I lose. Just like that.

Because it doesn't matter that I won't let anyone take Lorina away from me. This isn't just about us. It's about Vinicio too: my mother's husband, the stepfather of my little brother. The other provider for my family. It's about Gabriele and the money I need to pay him in a week or watch everything we own get seized overnight. A recurring amount so egregious I have no other way of earning it fast enough to keep up, through legal channels or otherwise.

I nearly gag at the noose Angelo unknowingly looped around my neck.

I won't give her up—*I can't*—but I can't risk their future either.

It's for that reason, and that reason alone, everything in me splits apart as I hear myself yield: "I understand."

Chapter 17

Lorelai Hargrove—August; Brno, Czech Republic

BREATHING HARD ON THE SUNLIT TRACK, I CHECK OVER MY RIGHT shoulder. Four men directly behind me. I look forward, debating whether to shift gears. The grassy knoll against the edge of the fence is blurry in my peripheral vision, going by too fast for me to see clearly. Two more laps, and I'm in twelfth place: seven men in front of me in the pack. Another four in front of them, leading the first group.

Panic threatens at the edge of my mind, telling me this is it. If I don't make at least sixth place, there's no way for me to numerically make the podium for World Champion, and I'll lose my ride. I'll lose him. And I still don't know how to accept either of those possibilities.

Fifth gear. Fourth. Third, and lean.

My body lies left into the sharp corner of turn six. My kneepad scrapes the track, my eyes trained on the rear tire in front of me, but I can't stop thinking about yesterday. When Massimo broke the track record during practice.

Pull vertical, lean left into turn seven. Cut inside, steal apex. Eleventh place. How proud I was of him, not threatened. Swing left for turn eight. Steal apex again. Tenth place. Screw it. Bump down to second gear to steal RPMs. Right to turn nine, open throttle.

Third gear, fourth, fifth. Sixth gear.

Ninth place.

A grin breaks across my face as I barrel down the straightaway, daring to let hope touch me. But over the sound of the crowd, raging in the green-and-white grandstands while waving endless red, white, and blue American flags for me, Massimo's voice is echoing in my head:

"You like to win, Tigrotta. But more, you like to chase."

Ignoring the fear in my stomach, I watch the four bikes in front of me. We're approaching the hard right of turn ten. It's a third gear turn if you're an idiot. Second gear if you're smart. When I took the record here last year, I was practically suicidal. Massimo screamed and screamed at me afterward because he knows how I did it. Just like he did yesterday, when he broke said record.

Hypocrite.

"When you are in second, you look forward. No fear. When you are first, you always look over your shoulder. Afraid."

I glance toward the braking marker, somehow clearer than my vision has been offering. I want my record back. I won't get a chance until next year, if I'm still here, but I can give him a run for his money today.

My breathing slows, and I listen to them downshift ahead of me. Fifth gear. Fourth. Third gear. Second.

I downshift to fourth, cutting to the inside and flying past them as I pray. My leg hangs to cut the momentum before my knee and elbow scrape the track, my abs screaming at the G forces and my fairings flexing like they want to shatter. But she holds together, and one bike, then two, three, then four move seemingly backward on my right side. Fifth place.

I yank her vertical, and the crowd explodes, homemade signs and massive flags pumping high into the clear blue sky. Grinning in my helmet, I downshift to second gear, pulling hard to the left for turn eleven even though I already know: I am going to get so much crap from him later for doing that. Still, I'm practically giggling as I swing to the right for the chicane of turn twelve, coming into the straightaway.

Santos is dead ahead, practically even with Massimo a third of the way through the last straight. The moment I've been waiting for.

Massimo told me during our last night in Memphis about what really went down between him and Santos in Austin. That Massimo thinks my crash was half his fault, because he picked the fight that started it, and how badly he's felt about it since. I told him there was no reason to feel guilty. Fight or no fight, Santos chose to hit me, and it was my fault for not backing off in the first place. A lot of mistakes were made, but they weren't Massimo's.

Santos and I still ended up having it out in a press conference yesterday—the look on his face was nearly priceless when I smiled and said I hoped he'd enjoyed his time on the podium. Because it was over. And yeah, it was a cheap shot to take, but I can't escape the jerk's constant presence on the circuit, and I'm not going to be afraid. I'm not going to flinch. I *am* going to beat him so badly that he never dares come near me again.

Mas glances over his shoulder, first at Santos and then at me, and I grin wickedly. His transmission only roars louder as he looks forward, and I know he smells the blood in the water, just as I do.

The fans ripple in a wave as I fly past, and I let it feed my soul, ducking low over my handlebars. My speedometer creeps past 150, 160, 170 miles per hour, and I am gaining on them faster than Santos can cope with. He downshifts to second gear for the sharp left of turn thirteen. Mas and I drop to third.

We're right on his ass as we come out of it, shifting up into fourth. Santos looks over his shoulder at us again, and Mas and I lean right. Santos looks forward too late, jerking harshly into the lean in an attempt to recover, but it's over. His bike falls, orange fairings crashing onto gray track and shooting him to the left barrier.

He's sliding safely on his back, his bike far enough away that I don't worry about it, and Massimo and I continue through the turn, leaving him behind. *See ya, asshole.*

Fourth place.

Pulling vertical, I smile at Massimo next to me on the straight as we cross the finish line together with one lap to go. We push into fifth gear, sixth, then back all the way down for turn one. But he hesitates to take the line in time, and I cut past on the inside, stealing the apex.

I'm directly in front of him through turn two and turn three. He takes back the lead from me in the straight in the approach to turn four. But in turn five, I downshift and dart past him, then swerve around Billy and Giovanni to take the lead in six, and after that, I'm gone. Just fucking *gone*, flying so fast through the last lap, I can't even hear Massimo's Yaalon behind me anymore.

The announcers are too loud shouting my name and hailing my call sign, chanting me home long before I even cross the finish line. But coming out of turn fourteen, there it is: the most beautiful black-and-white checkered flag I've ever seen, ready and waiting just for me.

Pride and relief and vindication and wrath burst through my veins and pull joyous tears from my eyes, and I yell out in victory as I pop a wheelie and take my win: my name a forever chant echoing through the tops of medieval trees, my front wheel chewing Bohemian air, right through the doubts and slander of all the freaking naysayers.

My front tire slams back to the earth, but my fist stays in the air, pumping to the roar of glory that I'll never be able to quit, no matter what he says. And by the time Massimo crosses the finish line for second place—a full three seconds after me—I know with every glittery fiber of my soul that life is going to be absolutely, perfectly okay for me from here on out.

—⁓—

"Lorelai!" Frank yells from outside my room in my RV, and I stifle a laugh at the fake fury in his voice, not even pausing in finishing my lipstick. There's no way anything is wrong, especially when I just freaking won.

I steal a last glance at my makeup in the mirror before I hook my purse over my chest, then blow a kiss to Tigrotta on my bed. But Frank loves to play this game when he's happy, so I tentatively come out of my room, crossing my arms nervously over my comfiest gray cashmere sweater, paired with my lucky black leggings and favorite chunky ankle boots. "Yeah?"

Frank is scowling like I broke his favorite cereal bowl into a million pieces, his own arms crossed. Then he bursts into laughter, nearly doubling over with the force of it. "God, you're gullible."

Oh yeah, he got me. Still, I gape at him like he doesn't do this every time I win. "You're such a jerk." I shake my head as I stride past him on my way out of the RV, but I don't make it far.

Frank bear-hugs me from behind and spins me around, still riding the adrenaline of my comeback. Both of us are chuckling when he sets me down and turns me to face him. Until he puts on his manager face again. "I need you to do me one favor tonight when you're out celebrating with all these yahoos."

I groan, impatient to go. "No promises. Especially to someone who uses the word 'yahoos' in everyday conversation."

He gently takes me by the shoulders, bending down to better catch my eyes and beaming like I was his own daughter. "Have fun, Lori. As much as you possibly can. You deserve it."

Everything in me melts. "Thanks, Frank. And don't worry. I plan on it."

He drops a kiss to my hair, then waves me on. I practically bound out of my RV and onto the paddock, flooded with half-drunk racers and tipsy sponsor models, sponsors, and VIPs all talking and laughing, some singing. I tip back my head and drink in the perfect night air, the stars shining and twinkling above, and with the thick forest surrounding us on every side, it almost feels like Memphis. But *better*.

"Congratulations, Lorelai," people tell me in a spattering of accents as I make my way through the paddock, and I smile and wave and thank every single one, my steps so light with the high of winning and being home at the circuit that I'm almost skipping by the time I get to Massimo's RV and knock on his door.

"Way to go, Wreckless!" someone calls.

I turn to smile at them, but Vinicio answers the door first, pushing it open so abruptly that I startle and stumble back a step. He blinks at me and blinks at me, then checks around like he was expecting someone else. When he looks back to me, he swallows, then pastes on a tight smile. It dawns on me that I'm interacting with Massimo's stepfather. "One moment," he says in a thick accent, holding up a finger.

I've barely opened my mouth to speak when he slams the door in my face. *Okay...?*

It reopens a second later, Vinicio coming back out with Massimo right behind him, the former locking the door and then walking away, head down and not another word said.

"Tigrotta," Mas rumbles the second his feet touch pavement, and I'm already dizzy under the mixture of his shampoo and cologne swirling with a hint of my fabric softener. My mom must have washed that shirt for him when he was at my house.

Stay focused, Hargrove.

"Want to share a victory beer?" My mouth is bone-dry with how sexy he looks when his hair is wet, and I can't believe it's been four freaking days since I've felt his hands on my body. But I figured Dabria probably wouldn't take too kindly to seeing Massimo leave in the morning when he rides for a competing manufacturer. As of tonight, though, we are done with our duties and officially off the clock. "Mason said the Budweiser guys have a game of pong set up by the cooking stations. Or if you were up to being a little bad, I thought maybe we could sneak off track and go grab dinner downtown. And maybe a hotel room. My treat."

He scrubs at the back of his neck and tries to smile, but it doesn't hold—his eyes flicking everywhere else like he's waiting for the same ambush Vinicio was. "I, um, I would love to, Tigrotta, but I cannot. I have to go. To Ravenna."

It takes me a second to make sure I heard him right, because... he's *what*?

It's now that my eyes notice the black strap of the bag on his shoulder, blending perfectly into his shirt.

"Tonight?" I look up at him, trying to find in his eyes the piece of the puzzle I'm not grasping when we're supposed to be celebrating our freaking asses off. Together. Naked. With the really expensive bottle of champagne chilling in the suite I just booked online at the Grandezza Hotel Luxury Palace. Then my eyes pop. "Oh my God, is Dario okay? Is he—"

"No, no, he is fine," Massimo rushes out, then smiles real enough that I believe him. He'd never lie about that. "Però other things have come up, and I..." He shakes his head, rolling his eyes like it's all stuff out of his control.

My brow crinkles as my pulse spikes to where it was when I crossed the finish line. Massimo and I may have been born in different countries, but we were cut from the exact same stock, and he only ever does what he wants, when he wants to. If something is pulling him in a direction he doesn't want to go, something is wrong. Very, very wrong. "What things?"

He adjusts his bag on his shoulder. His eyes go back to darting over the party on the paddock, then he clears his throat and looks back to me. "Niente," he lies, then winks since I think his smile might be broken. "I will see you in Austria. In realtà," he drawls, "I am going to kick your ass in Austria."

The taunt is a last-ditch effort. A Hail Mary to distract me from the way he's breathing faster than he should and can't stop fidgeting. A bitter fear starts to solidify in my spine, because everything about this feels like a fumbled escape—but not quite from me, and not from us.

I cling to that amendment *hard*. Hold it tight in my chest, feel its warmth, and remind myself a dozen times over that Massimo isn't like the other men who have always left me. It's the only thing that allows me to force my brow to smooth, then playfully shove at his chest like everything's cool. "Dick. Pretty sure I smoked you today."

He sighs with all the relief I wish I could feel. But that's impossible when he's leaving, and he won't tell me why. But I trust him. I'm trying to anyway.

"Massimo!" Vinicio calls out, and I startle at the urgency in his voice, finding him over by the exit gate with a cab ready and the trunk open.

I look back to Massimo, but he's eying the hem of my sleeve, his jaw locked like he's in physical pain. With a gruff clear of his throat, he opens his mouth to speak, his eyes searching mine as a thousand things rush behind them, and I prepare myself for the inevitable: *Come to Ravenna with me, cara. Right now, with no notice, and spend the rest of the night dealing with airport security and signing autographs from fans in the terminal instead of privately celebrating in a five-star suite.*

Except I don't have the first freaking clue how to answer that question.

It's not like I have a problem with Ravenna—even though I'm

pretty sure his mom has a problem with me. I *do* have a problem with setting that kind of precedent when I'm already terrified about the fact that if I lose my contract and he keeps his, I'm going to get a choice. How much I'm willing to travel, how much of my own free time I'm willing to give up in order to be with him.

The worst part is, even though everything in me screams that I shouldn't have to—that if he wants to see me, he can get on a plane, because no way in hell am I letting a man pressure me into being anywhere I don't want to be, to go places I don't want to go—it's *Massimo*. Meaning there's also a very convincing whisper in my heart that swears he'd be worth it. The exception. Just him. Whatever he needs. No matter what I have to give up.

Tonight, the question never comes.

"I will call you later," he tells me in Italian instead, trusting I know what he said without ever bothering to check.

With a pain-filled smile, he steps around my side and walks toward Vinicio, slipping his bag off his shoulder and passing it to his manager before disappearing inside the cab. I hug my arms around myself, already missing him so much it hurts. The rest of the paddock keeps on celebrating my win without realizing I'm watching his cab pull away, and once I turn and start heading back to my RV, to Tigrotta waiting for me on my bed, I can't stop thinking that this is exactly the problem with him.

That it would be so much easier if he were making impossible demands on me, because then I wouldn't want to break the one rule I swore I never would.

GRAND PRIX ČESKÉ REPUBLIKY
Brno, Sunday, August 04

Pos	Pts	Rider	Time	World Rank
1	25	Lorelai HARGROVE	42'53.042	94
2	20	Massimo VITOLO	+3.462	139
3	16	Billy KING	+10.397	200
4	13	Giovanni MARCHESA	+13.071	100
5	11	Rainier HERRE	+15.650	48
6	10	Galeno GIRÓN	+15.725	47
7	9	Deven HORSLEY	+21.821	67
8	8	Aurelio LOGGIA	+23.240	56
9	7	Gustavo LIMÓN	+43.784	17
10	6	Cristiano ARELLANO	+45.261	86
11	5	Mason KING	+49.973	97
12	4	Fredek SULZBACH	+50.174	54
13	3	Gregorio PAREDES	+54.437	48
14	2	Elliston LAMBIRTH	+54.624	40
15	1	Harleigh ELIN	+1'00.316	41
16		Donato MALDONADO	+1'01.595	37
17		Diarmaid DEAN	+1'02.388	16
18		Timo GONZALES	+1'05.944	17
19		Cesaro SOTO	+1'11.407	20
Not Classified				
20		Santos SAUCEDO	21 Laps	176

Chapter 18

Lorelai Hargrove—August; Ravenna, Italy

SEVENTEEN LONG, IMPOSSIBLE HOURS OF TRAVELING TO RAVENNA, and I'm finally in front of a door. I just hope it's the right one. I don't have time to keep crawling all over this city of a thousand alleys looking for him. Frank, Billy, and Mason are already in Austria, and I've got barely forty-eight hours before I'll have to backtrack to Spielberg for the next race. But despite Frank's protests, I'm standing by my choice.

I have to. I still have no idea what happened to yank Massimo out of Brno like that. I called him this morning to make sure he got home okay, but he didn't answer. He said whatever this was, it wasn't Dario, but there was so much friction in his eyes last night, so much he wasn't telling me. And I'm not happy that he couldn't just tell me the truth instead of making a joke about beating me, but he showed up for me in Memphis when I needed him.

I can make this sacrifice for Massimo.

Take a deep breath, do a quick pit and breath check, unwrap my messy bun and finger comb my curls to one side, and then I knock.

Two seconds. Four seconds.

"Un momento," a female voice calls out. Before I can collapse in frustration and even further exhaustion at apparently being at the wrong address, again, the door swings open. "Lorelai!"

Oh no. *No. No. No.* Anyone but her.

She chuckles as she splays her hand on her chest. "I am so sorry. I am Chiara. Please, come in." She steps aside, tossing back slick brown hair that nearly meets her waist but is full of graceful, spunky layers that start above her chin and cascade all the way down. Her eyes are popping with the smoky eye she perfectly applied, lips pert with gloss, and I want to leave. I want to go find an overly expensive hotel with the world's most comfortable bed and an all-night menu, then sleep and cry and eat until I forget his name.

Not until I kick his ass first.

I keep my fake-as-polyester smile plastered on my face, and I step over the threshold, Chiara shutting the door behind me. Her high heels click on the wood floor, then muffle on one of the many areas rugs as she leads me into a small but open apartment.

"Massimo did not tell me you were coming." She takes a cell phone out of her clutch, set on a glass-top dinette, then starts tapping away on the screen. I can only guess she's texting him I'm here?

"I, um, I didn't tell him."

"No?" Her eyes lift from the screen of her phone, then she turns and puts it away. "I am sorry, Lorelai." She turns to face me, a model hostess. "Please, make yourself comfortable."

Setting down my bags, I turn to the right. It's not all that surprising, the décor and the space. Low wooden beams, ultramodern black leather sofa, abstract art with thick, black frames hung expertly on the walls. Not that far from what I'd have picked out, probably. Especially considering the light coming through the high arched windows, gleaming off the blue mosaic tile in the open kitchenette and the stainless steel appliances.

What's bothering me is the smell. Light and clean...and feminine. Just underneath is him: spicy and dark and unmistakably familiar. It's not the last of the contradictions either: vases of arranged flowers placed on side tables next to decorative candles, a creamy chenille throw blanket draped on a side chair, and a bright-pink espresso cup poised and ready to go under the espresso maker.

I was told this is his apartment. I'm hoping it's hers. But I'm starting to think there's a third option here I really don't want to face.

"So where does Massimo think you are?" Chiara asks.

Turning to her, I answer, "Austria. I, um, I wanted it to be a surprise."

She smiles, leaning over to whisper, "Then we should have some fun!"

Fantastic.

"Massimo!" Chiara calls out, and my stomach drops straight through the wood floor underneath my custom cowgirl boots. "C'è qualcuno qui che vuole vederti."

There's someone here to see you.

Quietly, she explains, "He is in the shower, but he should be done in a minute."

I nod, not trusting my voice. Please, Lord, don't let me start crying in front of her.

"Chi?" he calls back, and I barely resist cringing. "Marco? Digli fanculo."

"È una sorpresa," she responds.

It's a surprise.

I cross my arms, swallowing down the bile chewing its way through my esophagus.

"So," Chiara says cheerfully, crossing her own arms. It pushes her breasts up to the top of her dress's low neckline, and I take a slow, deep breath, trying to control my jealous temper. Easier said than done when I'm staring down the woman living with my boyfriend. The roommate he lied to me about the first night we slept together. "How long will you be in Ravenna?"

"I don't know," I answer, attempting to keep my voice as light as possible. At least it doesn't break. Not like my heart is doing right now. "It all kind of depends."

She nods. "It must be difficult for you, traveling all the time."

"Mm-hmm."

I should say something else. Compliment her dress. Her English. Something.

My mouth is sealed with liquid cement.

Apparently, Chiara feels the need to break the awkward silence. "Lorelai, I do want you to know you are always welcome here with us." My back stiffens. *Us.* "This can be, well, like a second home." She shrugs innocently, and I'm just opening my mouth to give her the verbal bitch slap I can hardly contain when Massimo appears from around the corner.

My jaw clamps shut, my heart thundering as he stops dead in his tracks. His eyes are huge when they land on me, shocked with surprise that quickly fades to cold, blanching fear. My gaze travels over his jeans and bare feet, his shirt not yet fully buttoned, and I'm officially breaking up with his lying, cheating ass in four, three, two—

"Isn't it fantastic?" Chiara squeals. "Lorelai is here!"

Both Massimo and I glance at her, and then he looks to me.

"Surprise," I drawl darkly. He swallows, the last bit of color fading from his face.

Chiara clears her throat, shifting her weight more in my direction. "We were about to go out for a drink and maybe some dancing, Lorelai, if you would like to come?"

"No, thank you," I tell her, still looking at him. I discreetly shake my head, then force a smile toward Chiara. "I'm really tired from traveling, so I'm probably going to go find a hotel and get some sleep."

"Oh." She pouts. "Maybe tomorrow, then?"

"Yes," I repeat, nodding. Then I look at Massimo. "Not today. Maybe domani. Maybe tomorrow."

His eyes close for just a second too long to be considered a blink, but Chiara doesn't seem to notice, busy walking over to the table to grab her purse. She strides toward the door, grinning and flicking her long hair over her shoulder. "Guess I will go have fun by myself!"

I'm already back to burying Massimo with nothing more than the ice in my eyes when instead of leaving, Chiara stops in her tracks. She pivots and double kisses my cheeks, then actually freaking hugs me, Massimo wincing behind her back.

"I am so glad I got to meet you," she whispers. "I hope we can talk again soon. When you have more time. There is something I'd like to give you."

I nod, biting my trembling lip.

She pulls back, her heels clicking on the floor until the door shuts behind her, and I can't even look at him.

Turning away, I breathe deeply in through my nose, doing everything I can to keep my eyes clear.

"Cara..."

The single word ignites a wave of fury through me. I whip around, pointing at him. "Don't call me that. I am not your darling. Not anymore." He shoves his hands in his pockets, and there's nothing to do but let my own hands fall to my sides as I shake my head. "So this is why. She's the roommate. You live with...her."

He takes a deep breath, his words slow and calm when he speaks. "Lorina, Chiara and I have been friends since we were very little, and she has lived with and been a part of my family for many years now. Her home is not good. Her papà, he drinks. Then he gets very angry. I had enough of this. She is my friend, and she needed somewhere safe to be. But her and my mamma"—he shakes his head—"they only argue, argue, argue. So we moved in here. Appartamento. That is why I stay here, in a different room, because it makes her feel better when I help pay the bills."

I drop my face into my hands, unsure whether I want to laugh or cry or both. I think I would've rather he just slept with her and that was it. What's even more screwed up is I'm not even surprised something like this has happened.

Massimo has spent countless moments over the last ten years building me up, making me think things I'm embarrassed even now to admit. And then with one snap of his fingers, he pulls the rug out from under me—this one in particular being a geometric five-by-seven with competing shades of gray.

"Lorina..." Massimo's voice is quiet and thin and more scared than I've ever heard from him. "Per favore, Lorina, say something. I do not know what you are thinking."

He doesn't know what I'm thinking? Where to freaking start?

I feel awful for Chiara, for the home she ran from.

My heart is asking me to let it melt over the fact that he took care of his friend, set her up with someplace safe to call home in the best way he could.

But my blood is running cold with the knowledge that their friendship has blurred into lovers more often than not and probably all over this damn apartment.

That she decorated. With his money. That he made by beating me.

God, I can't...

"I'm so tired," I breathe, chuckling dryly to cover the fact that I'm a second away from breaking down into really ugly sobs. "I can't deal with this right now."

He pulls my hands away from my face, cupping my jaw in his hands. There's so much tension in his eyes, it feels like we're back in my hospital room in Jerez—a massive unspoken truth between us, pressuring us apart. "What do you need?"

I need to know he didn't screw her the second he walked in the door. That's what I need.

Massimo drops his forehead to mine, engulfing me in clean soap and a fresh splash of the cologne my lungs have been aching for since he left me in Brno. "Ask me." There's no tremor in his voice anymore, his thumbs sweeping sweetly over my cheekbones. "I will not lie to you."

Fear chills me to the core, and I don't want to know anymore.

There won't be any way to take it back.

"I can't," I whisper, my voice cracking.

He presses a kiss to my forehead, then pulls me into him. He hugs me not like I'm the one who needs to be comforted but like he is: his arms wound tightly around me, his lips against my shoulder. My body jolts under a single, silent sob, my hands clinging to his shoulders like some sort of anchor against the waves of reality threatening to drown me.

"Even if you will not ask… I did not," he whispers. "I would not. I am with you, only you."

Tucking my face into his neck, I nod, breathing him in. I believe him, and I want to trust him, but he just…he makes it so *hard*.

I'm not quite ready when he pulls back to look at me. His mouth falls into a pout when he wipes off my cheeks, then sweeps a knuckle under my eye. "When was the last time you slept?"

"Last night. I just…" I exhale, then tell him, "Long day. Delayed flights and missed trains, and I really need to go find a hotel and deal with all this"—I gesture to the apartment—"tomorrow."

"No."

My head jerks back. "No?"

"Stay here, with me."

"Massimo," I say slowly. "I am not staying here."

He rolls his eyes, as though I'm not dead freaking serious. "Different rooms."

I shake my head. "Don't care."

His hands catch mine, then he ducks his head, his voice so private I barely hear him. "Never in my room. Never in my bed."

The words are a punch straight to the gut, and I look away, blinking rapidly. *What does that leave?*

He tugs on my hands, adding, "I promise, Lorina."

It's the last part that totally screws me over. In ten years, I can count the promises he's made to me on one hand. I've made so many, I can't even count them all: you'll never see me cry, never touch me, never, never, never. I've broken every single one, and yet he's held to all of his.

I take a deep breath. "Just tonight. And only because it's too late to figure out anything else."

The corner of his mouth turns up, and he nods, letting me go so he can pick up my bags. "You are doing me a big favor," he says, straightening. "I did not want to go out tonight anyway. I have been sad. Missed my girlfriend."

My temper can't resist popping off. "Kinda brought that on yourself by leaving, which you still have yet to explain."

His eyebrow arches.

I sigh, trying to calm down before I say something I'll regret. "Whatever. We'll fight about it tomorrow."

He holds his hand out to me, and I take it, my steps heavy as he starts walking toward what must be his bedroom, bringing me along with him.

I want to tell him I missed him too. That I wish this had all gone a different, better way.

It didn't, though, and I don't say anything.

—⁂—

I wake to deep warmth and slatted light from the shutters, my shoulder a little sore, though I only have myself to blame. Because even though I had sworn I wouldn't start a fight I was too tired to finish, I picked one anyway when I refused to sleep in his bed.

I wasn't going to just curl up next to him like he didn't purposefully omit that he lived with *Chiara* when he said he had a roommate. I opted for a pallet on the floor. Massimo responded by throwing a pillow at me. Spiraling us into the most immature thing I've ever done in an adult relationship, but he wanted a pillow fight? He got a goddamn war.

I still slept on the floor.

Which I'm no longer on, somehow back in the bed I said I wouldn't sleep in.

My hand extends out toward the other pillow, empty but still sunken in the middle. I shouldn't be surprised that sometime after I fell asleep, he moved me. And I don't know what took him from me so early, but I can guess.

I clutch the sheet a little closer to my chest, bare apart from my bra, and the foreign fabric names me as the intruder I feel like.

He didn't want me here.

I throw back the covers, searching for the jeans and shirt I was wearing yesterday, but I have no clothes. Did he wash them? And where the hell is my suitcase?

I head toward his wardrobe, the only other thing in his room apart from his bed and single nightstand. I open the sliding door, looking over the shirts hanging up, but something red at the bottom catches my attention. My brow furrows, and after I pull aside the lazily draped blanket, my eyes widen in shock as I gingerly pick up my missing helmet.

It's so much worse than I ever imagined.

The face shield is shattered like someone sledgehammered it. The

American flag is cracked, all the way across the top and even down to the chin. Goose bumps streak across my skin at the straps dangling but still buckled because they were cut.

My eyes close. Of course he had it. Hidden where I couldn't see just how close I had come to dying. Where he could control it like it didn't happen and it wasn't real.

Another secret.

I hug my broken helmet to my chest, trying to smother the sting of betrayal. From Massimo, from Frank. And it's not that I don't understand why they hid it—especially Frank, with how he is about that kind of stuff—but it wasn't their decision. I deserved the choice, the opportunity to confront my fears.

But they didn't think I could handle it. That I was strong enough.

A door bangs, and my eyes fly open. That was the fridge. I scramble to put my stolen helmet back in the closet and cover it up. I'm also still nearly naked, but I don't want him to know I was in here. We are absolutely going to have to talk about my helmet and when it came into his possession, but there are too many other things that have to be argued first. I don't have the energy to battle him on multiple fronts this morning when everything is already so shaky.

I shut the door and glance around once more. No laundry piled on furniture, no towels over a desk chair, because he doesn't have a desk or a chair, *nothing*. The closest thing I find to wearable is Massimo's shirt from last night. I slip my arms through the sleeves, but I'm too late.

The bedroom door opens. Closes. I snatch the cotton dress shirt closed over my chest.

Massimo's eyes lock with mine, but there's no trace of any tremble as he takes a sip from his coffee mug, then clears his throat. "Buongiorno, Lorina."

My brow furrows as he heads over to the nightstand and sets

down the mug. *Oh right.* I told him not to call me cara anymore. I swallow my guilt as he collapses onto the bed, crossing his ankles and lacing his hands behind his head, and I arch my eyebrow at his staunchly casual posture. "What are you doing?"

"I am waiting."

I glance down at my unbuttoned shirt. My lack of pants. I peek back up at him. "Waiting for what?"

He shrugs. "You are Tigrotta. I have always known that one day, you would get too angry, and you would go. So I am waiting."

It feels like I just got hit by my Dabria all over again—the dizzying knockback from out of nowhere, the pain bursting from my chest and rippling out atomically. Because this is that same "Don't get attached; be prepared to lose it all" dogma he's always spouting. Except now, he's waiting for me to walk out, and he's not even denying he deserves it.

"Is that what you want? For me to go?"

He reaches over to pick up his coffee mug. "No. But it does not matter what I think. You always do what you want, Lorina. So do what you want. I am not going to stop you."

He takes a drink of coffee, not even looking at me, and *there it was*. The tremble. Just a tiny one, in his pinkie, where his hand is too big for all his fingers to fit in the handle.

I swear, he is *such* a hypocrite.

"Massimo," I breathe, heading over to the bed and sitting on the edge, facing him. "Look, I know last night was a mess, and yeah, I am really, really mad that you didn't tell me you lived with Chiara. But I'm not...I'm not leaving you."

He sets down his mug. It takes him a long time before he looks at me. "No?"

I shake my head. "No."

He reaches over and takes my hand, squeezing it so tight, it actually hurts a little. But it's worth it when he nods, his jaw locked tight. "Okay."

Everything in me melts even more, and I curl up on his chest, relief flooding through my body when his arms gather me to him, his lips pressing a hard kiss to my hair.

It doesn't erase the anger still simmering in my stomach, and I know—*I know*—there's something else he's still not telling me. But for right now, I don't need to know what it was that pulled him from Brno.

I know Massimo. And he might do messed-up stuff sometimes, but he would never, ever do anything to hurt me. He always puts me first.

Chapter 19

Massimo Vitolo—August; Ravenna, Italy

SO MUCH FOR STUDYING AUSTRIA.

Lorina moans deeper as she kisses the hell out of me, straddling my lap on the sofa and speeding our make-out session into something that requires a little more privacy than my living room. At least Chiara's at work. And Lorina was supposed to be reading in bed while I was learning these turns, but she came out here and ripped the telemetry map from my hands, now full of her curves as she grinds against my erection, begging to burst from my jeans.

She nips at my lip, then moves to my jaw, kissing her way down my neck as I thread my hand through her hair, and I lean hard to the right in my mind—turn one: Nikki Lauda Kurve. Lorina shifts on top of me, and I tug her hips down and thrust up against her. Fourth gear. Fifth. She bites the spot on my neck that makes my cock swell into steel, and I keep on it: touch left for turn two, hard tight right for turn three, the Remus.

She sits back, pulling off her red T-shirt before she tears off my black one, and *God*, I love it when she wears navy-blue lingerie—it matches my moto perfectly. Lorina crashes her mouth back to mine, her hands desperate on my jaw before she reaches for the buckle on my belt, and I can't touch enough of her: smoothing my hands up her silky back, grasping at her shoulders, palming her breasts, and coming out of the turn in second gear, prepping for the sharp-as-hell Rauch to the right. Swing to the right for turn five, downshift for turn six, the Pirelli, and lean…right? No, left.

Damn it.

Lorina starts kissing her way down my chest, slipping down to the floor between my legs. My head falls back on the couch, my heart pounding as I weave my fist tight into her hair.

Back on the grid. Pole position. Red lights are out. Go.

Right for Lauda, touch left for two. Her teeth scrape my nipple, and I hiss, Lorina undoing the button on my jeans and lowering the zipper.

Right for Remus, right for Rauch. Her breath sweeps down my abs as her kisses dip lower, and I tighten my hand in her hair. Right for turn five, Pirelli left, Würth right—no. Würth is left.

Wait, was Pirelli left or right?

Fuck!

I grit out a sigh, laying my palm flat on the back of Lorina's neck, my erection already waning because I'm the weak piece of crap who can't get these turns down.

God, Angelo was right.

Lorina sits back on her heels, but her hands are sweet on my thighs, her voice infinitely patient. "You okay?"

I shake my head. "Cannot concentrate."

She pouts, but it's fake. Supposed to be cute. "Is it 'cause I interrupted your study session?" She pushes up on her knees, smoothing her hands up my legs and doing something with her shoulders so her breasts somehow look even more gorgeous than before. "Right-left-right, right-right-left, left-right-right, right."

My heart stutters, and I stare at her. Freaking show-off.

Lorina grins like she's waiting for me to thank her, or at the very least be impressed.

I stand instead, stepping around her and heading into the kitchen, refastening my jeans.

"Mas…" she says, but I don't stop.

I need to beat her in Austria. Especially after I screwed up into letting her win in Brno. It's practically a miracle that Angelo didn't fire me on the spot, and that cannot happen when I'm four, maybe three races away from paying off Gabriele. I just…

I don't know what happened out there.

I've always been able to cut around her, chase her down, and push her out, and I never blinked an eye, because that's what we *do*. But in Brno, all I could think about was where she was, what place she was in, who she had to overtake next so she'd keep her contract. Once we took out Santos, I was too overcome by the relief that Lorina was in fourth place to remember I had served myself up to my executioner. I didn't realize she had passed me until I read "Wreckless" on the back of her leathers, and *God, Angelo was right*.

I wanted her win more than I wanted it for myself, and I put her ahead of everything. Everyone. Which is exactly why instead of celebrating with her, I had Vinicio call four different airlines to get us immediately the hell home. She's too sweet. Too fun. Way too sexy, and too…*distracting*. And I'm not complaining about the sex, because the sex is fantastic, but this is exactly why I didn't want her to come to Ravenna in the first place.

I pull open the refrigerator and grab a bottle of water, except I'm holding it too hard when I twist off the top, water squirting out everywhere. I pretend that didn't just happen, taking a drink and punching the door shut.

Lorina sighs behind me. "Do you want to talk about it?"

Guilt scrapes over everywhere my frustration has left me raw, and I turn around, leaning against the counter. "No."

She put her shirt back on, now leaning against the back of the couch, and it's so unfair how naturally she fits in my apartment. How comfortable she seems here, despite everything.

It's almost impossible to get myself to leave the bed in the morning so I can work out under Vinicio's supervision. It's even harder when we're in my bedroom the rest of the time because I can't risk anyone seeing us and the truth getting back to Dabria.

If Angelo's coming after me for this, Dabria can go after her, and Ravenna is not the same as Memphis. People in Italy know who we are. Our names, our faces, how many pets we have, what I'm allergic to, and all it'll take is one photo in a café, at a club, and it won't just be her placements they're hitting her with. It'll be the conflict of interest too. And I already know what her answer will be.

For Lorina, racing comes before all else. Always has, always will, and it's the whole reason she took forever to admit she cares about me even *after* I followed her to Memphis. Where I wasn't supposed to be, stayed too long, and didn't look at a single map of the Automotodrom the entire time I was there.

God, how was that son-of-a-bitch *right*?

I chug the rest of my bottle of water, crushing the plastic harshly in my fist before I toss it into the sink.

Lorina clears her throat. "I, um, I always screw up turn eight in Malaysia." She shrugs like I don't already know that. "Don't know what it is. I just come out of seven and I can't—"

"Lorina."

She tosses up a hand. "Is it a problem with your Yaalon? Because you seemed like you were liking—"

"Do not ask about my moto," I snap, the hairs on the back of my neck standing on end like somehow, some way, Angelo can hear us. "I do not ask about your Dabria. Do not ask about my Yaalon."

Lorina stares at me, completely frozen. Except for her eyes: burning and hurt, confused and betrayed. And absolutely pissed the hell off.

She straightens. Hooks her thumbs in the back pockets of her jeans. Then she nods. "Yeah. Okay."

My blood is liquid ice from the coldness in her voice, and she turns and heads toward my bedroom. Her steps slow, controlled, silent the whole way there.

She slams the door behind her, and I curse, my head falling back on my neck.

Great. I'm probably sleeping on the couch tonight.

A gross voice in my head whispers that it's gonna make it easier to sneak out and drop off a payment to Gabriele, and I'll have more time to study when I get back. But it doesn't help the irritation churning my stomach that I can't just go after her and explain why I'm acting like this.

The texts I got from Gabriele while I was in Brno didn't exactly help:

Heard you got a new girlfriend and the sponsors aren't too happy.
I'd be careful about losing my job if I were you.
Keep her out of this.

Freaking nephew spy. I shouldn't be surprised he's feeding information back from the circuit, whether he's doing it purposefully or not. But Gabriele knowing I'm on thin ice with my sponsors is exactly the kind of extra stress I don't need.

I really didn't want him knowing about Lorina.

He already spooked and nearly put me in default when he found out about Chiara, and I know Lorina. If I tell her what's going on, she'll want to help. Telling her she can't get involved in something is exactly the kind of taunt she can't resist, and she doesn't understand that losing is sometimes the safest option. That bringing her family's money into this will only make it worse.

I am too close to the finish line to take those kinds of risks. It won't be easy, but I can hang on a little longer. I can make it through this—Angelo and Gabriele and anyone else who wants to come for me.

I won't choose between Lorina and my family. I won't choose between her and moto. I can't go into default, and I have to keep my contract. And I have to make sure the only thing in the way of hers is a few measly placements, and not me.

I have to make this worth it.

I stride out of Spielberg's victory lane and cut through the garages toward the paddock, ignoring the roar of the crowd and the calls of the press. My first place win is still screaming through my veins, but I keep my head down and keep moving toward my RV, my helmet trembling in my fist as my pulse throbs in my temples. Fifty meters. That's all. Fifty meters to my RV. Fifty meters to safety. Fifty meters before—

"Yeah, run away!" Lorina shouts behind me, and *fuck*. "Would hate for you to have to take responsibility for what you just did!"

"Whoa, Lori! Hold on!" Mason calls out.

I grind to a halt and face down the pair of Dabria leathers I just passed on the track, trying to ignore the crowd of people on the paddock who have all stopped to stare. "What did I do now, Lorina?"

She storms closer until she's nearly on my toes, that fire of hers blazing bright and hot under the Austrian sun. "You cut me off in the last turn, and you almost hit Mason!"

Mason starts shaking his head, one hand held out between us and the other on Lorina's arm like he's ready to hold her back from me. "Nah! Uh-uh! We're totally cool, man. I swear it. It's just racing. That's all."

She slaps his hand off her arm. "Bullshit we're cool."

"Mason," an older country accent yells, and great—Billy's joining the fray with long strides of his legs that have him here before he's done bossing around his brother. "Get back to the garages. This isn't your fight."

Angelo comes jogging out of the garages right behind his returning World Champion, Vinicio too, and panic locks me in place—they're all heading our way. Any second, a camera crew is bound to appear. For now, though, they're still locked behind the press fence.

"I'm not trying to fight with anyone," Mason snaps at Billy. "I'm trying to make sure Lori don't start one between me and Massimo."

I wave him off. "We are fine." Then I look back to Lorina. "You need to go back to your RV. I cannot do this with you now."

Lorina's harsh, cruel laugh echoes through the hills of Styria, and everybody goes still. "Excuse me while I write an editorial to the *Who Gives a Shit Daily News*!"

My brow furrows. "Cosa?"

"You have nowhere to go except an airport, and I have the tickets, so you're going to tell me right now whether you—"

"Yes, I cut you off," I grit out in Italian.

She's suddenly taller than she was a minute ago, and based on the fury in her eyes, I know she understood me. Everyone did.

I'd be careful about losing my job if I were you.

Billy reaches between us and fists a hand in Mason's leathers, tugging him back toward the garages. "Let's go."

"But Lori—"

"Can handle her own battles." He trades glances with Vinicio and Angelo as they come to a stop a few feet behind Lorina, but Lorina doesn't seem to notice. Too pissed off and too many other people still running around. They're just giving us a wide berth because to them, this is normal for us.

I just... I don't understand how I was always able to do it

before—love her and race her—and now, I *can't*. I can't find the balance we need, can't find the rhythm. But the worst part is I think maybe she was right and I was wrong: you can't compete against the person you care about. It does make a difference, and I should've known better than to think I could have it all, consequences be damned.

"*...we expect that same focus to be applied to seeing Yaalon Moto on the podium for World Champion. For that to be your only focus. Are we clear?*"

The words are so loud in my mind that when I look in her eyes, I don't let her see in mine how much, how long I've loved her. How I followed my father's voice telling me what to look for. How I would know when I found her. The things I dreamt about once I did.

Keep her out of this.

It was so much easier when she didn't know. When she only hated me and glared instead of smiled and kissed me. And I never should have put myself in a position where I would wonder if she might actually love me. Because the truth is, it doesn't matter.

There's only room for one of us at the top of the podium, and racing has to come first.

She always wanted it to come first.

I narrow my eyes, peering down at her. "I did nothing today other than what I have always done. What you have done to me. And I do not give a shit if you are angry! It is not my fault that you chose to take that turn in the wrong gear, so when you could not speed up fast enough, I took first. So go." I jerk my head toward her own RV. "Run away and cry to the world how Massimo is so mean to you, how I would not let you win."

She steps forward, poking her finger into my chest. "I don't expect you to let me win. And if I find out you've ever backed off a race, we're going to have a problem that can't be fixed. But I do expect for you to be a decent human being and not to be a raging asshole 150 percent of the time."

I flick away her finger like it was a bug. "What if this is what I am, Lorelai? One hundred fifty percent asshole, all the time?"

Her head jerks back, her eyes huge. But her voice is so quiet I can barely hear her over the roar of the fans in the grandstands. "Since when do you call me Lorelai?"

I don't.

I shift my helmet to my other hand, tucking it under my arm. Vinicio and Angelo are still watching, but they're also still not interfering, and I hate myself so much that I said it. For them.

After a minute that stretches out forever, Lorina turns on her heel, walking away while saying over her shoulder, "Congratulations, Massimo. You win."

I nearly pinch myself. She's admitting defeat? Really?

"I always do, Lorina!" I call after her.

She falls for the bait and turns around, flipping me off with both her fists. "Yeah? Well, here's your gold fucking star!"

"At least I understand that reference!"

Vinicio and Angelo start heading toward me as she tears open the door of her RV, my Yaalon rep looking disgustingly satisfied while my stepfather lays his hand on my shoulder, guiding me toward my own. I shake him off, storming ahead of him and Angelo and slamming the door of my RV so hard behind me, a tremor shakes the walls.

I hurl my helmet across the RV, something shattering that doesn't begin to compare to what's happening in my chest. Because if I keep cutting her off, keep diving for her, before long, it won't even matter what my contract says. She'll declare herself my enemy whether I want it to be that way or not. But I don't have a choice: I have to keep winning.

It's the only way to get Angelo to change his mind.

GRAND PRIX VON ÖSTERREICH
Spielberg, Sunday, August 11

Pos	Pts	Rider	Time	World Rank
1	25	Massimo VITOLO	39'40.688	164
2	20	Lorelai HARGROVE	+2.130	114
3	16	Billy KING	+4.656	216
4	13	Santos SAUCEDO	+9.434	189
5	11	Mason KING	+13.169	108
6	10	Galeno GIRÓN	+14.026	57
7	9	Gregorio PAREDES	+14.156	57
8	8	Gustavo LIMÓN	+16.644	25
9	7	Elliston LAMBIRTH	+20.760	47
10	6	Donato MALDONADO	+20.844	43
11	5	Deven HORSLEY	+21.114	72
12	4	Cristiano ARELLANO	+22.939	90
13	3	Fredek SULZBACH	+26.523	57
14	2	Rainier HERRE	+29.168	50
15	1	Aurelio LOGGIA	+30.072	57
16		Giovanni MARCHESA	+30.343	100
17		Harleigh ELIN	+31.775	41
18		Diarmaid DEAN	+34.375	16
19		Timo GONZALES	+40.171	17
Not Classified				
		Cesaro SOTO	18 Laps	20

Chapter 20

Lorelai Hargrove—August; Ravenna, Italy

THE GROUND RUSHES BY AS I STARE OUT THE WINDOW, THE TRAIN from Bologna to Ravenna rocking slightly from side to side as it clings to the rails. I've always loved trains, found the speed comforting. Now, it's just a box with people chatting quietly in the rows around me, a baby crying somewhere farther back. The aroma of stale espresso and hours-old mayo from forgotten packed lunches wafts through the circulated air, sinking into my clothes and skin. I blow out a nauseated breath, warring against my headache and adjusting my sunglasses.

I didn't sleep at all last night in my RV. It was hours of tossing and turning because I don't freaking get it: how Massimo can go from being so sweet, so romantic, to reverting back to his customary asshole self without even blinking. It's so...*disorienting.*

Shifting a little in my seat, my eyes dart to the right, where the jerk in question is sitting next to me with his earbuds plugged in, watching something on his phone. Like he's been doing the entire freaking flight from Spielberg to Bologna, and the whole train ride from Bologna to Ravenna.

I'd hoped that when we left Austria, we'd be able to start fresh and forget about our blowup in the paddock yesterday. That the prospect of spending ten days in Ravenna together would dissolve whatever stress is causing his jaw to be locked that tight. But crossing into Italy only seems to have made it worse.

The world outside the windows slows and comes into focus, and it's not much longer before we're pulling into the station. I sigh and tuck my book into my backpack. The one I barely made ten pages' progress through the entire trip here, because every time I went to turn a page, I realized I had no idea what I had just read. All I can hear in my head is Frank telling me not to get distracted. That I still have a long climb back to making the final podium for World Champion.

He's right; I do. And I plan on fighting like hell for it. But I've also been waking up to the idea that I don't actually have to put all my eggs in one Dabria-shaped basket. Because the truth is, Massimo was right, and I don't really care about the sponsors or the colors or the team names or rivalries or any of it. That's not what makes me *me*.

I just want to race, whatever that means, wherever it takes me.

People start standing and moving into the aisle, and I nudge Massimo, waiting until he takes out his earbuds. Well, one of them at least. "Line's clearing."

He checks, then looks to his phone, waving his hand dismissively and speaking in rapid-fire Italian. "Go ahead and get a taxi. I'd rather walk." He hooks his earbud in.

My eyes flare, but it's not just anger burning me up. It's the fact that those were the first words he's said to me in hours, and he's telling me to leave him. On a train. In the station. Because he's going to sit here and watch that abominable stand-up comedian, be the last person off the platform, then walk all the way to his apartment instead of sharing a cab with me. Like he's not still punishing me for whatever I did that he won't tell me.

My hands tighten into fists in my lap, and I'm sixteen years old again—trembling after a fight with him in the paddock, then retreating to my RV so I could cry in private, knowing it's my fault he hates me and not knowing exactly what I did to cause it or why it hurts so much.

Massimo's eyes flicker in my direction but don't stray near my face. He grabs his sunglasses and puts them on, and tears threaten my eyes. But I won't let him see me cry. Not after yesterday.

I stand. I grab my backpack. I cross over Massimo and reach up, getting my bag from the overhead compartment. I don't touch his.

"Lorina."

Hope sparks in my chest. Until I find that he's handing me a set of keys, still without bothering to look at me.

I take them. Turn. Walk away. Past the attendant who smiles at me. Past the couples strolling through the platform, hand in hand. Through the station, where people are hugging, smiling.

In the cab. Through the winding streets of Ravenna. Get out.

Climb the stairs, unlock the front door. Check for Chiara, find no one.

I should be relieved I'm alone. But my house is never empty when I get there. My mom and dad are always talking my ear off with stories of the horses and farmhands until I'm kicking them out of my room, annoyed.

I shake my head at myself, muttering to the empty apartment, "The hell am I even doing here?"

Nothingness answers me. Because both me and the apartment know exactly what I'm doing here. I just don't know if I'm making the right choice anymore.

I roll my suitcase across the wood floor and into his bedroom, dropping it under the window. Open the shutters to reveal the view into the Piazza del Popolo, and my phone vibrates in my back pocket. I pull it out to answer, my shoulders dropping at the wrong name.

"Hey," I answer, trying to put a smile in my voice because I don't want her to know. Taryn makes it all seem so easy: balancing racing and ranching and romance, even while she and Billy are constantly apart. But she's happy, *really* happy, and she's not afraid of the things I am.

Actually, I don't know if she's scared of anything anymore.

"How's the new sofa looking with the—"

Taryn gasps out a strangled breath on the phone, her voice heartbroken over the words, "Aston's pregnant."

My eyes pop in shock. Taryn was ridiculously protective of her horse's unblemished virtue. "How the hell did that even happen with Dax and Bryan there to—"

"Freaking fence-jumping Gidget!"

I slap my hand over my mouth to keep from laughing. It's not funny.

"Yes, I am mad at you because your horny-ass stallion knocked up my mare!" she yells into the background. "I don't care, Billy! You're the one who taught him to jump fences like that!"

Yeah, jumping the fence into your backyard while your parents were asleep.

"Fine," she says to Billy in a way that means anything but. Then her voice goes back to normal. "Honestly, that's not even why I'm calling you." Taryn lets out another sigh. "I just got off the phone with Mike and Werner, and the women's division is happening."

I freeze in place, then double-check to make sure Massimo or Chiara didn't come in. But nope, I'm still alone in their apartment. I quickly walk over and shut Massimo's bedroom door, just to be safe. "Where? Is it Moto or—"

"I don't know. No one does." Taryn drops her voice, a door closing in the background on her end. I'm guessing to put more space between her and Billy before she says this. "You sure you still want that meeting with Werner and MMW? I mean, I know I always joke about you 'crossing over to the dark side' to hang with Sophie and me in Superbike, even though you'd have to put up with Miette. But especially considering...ya know...I didn't think you'd actually—"

"I know what I want," I tell her, goose bumps streaking across my skin. "Just get me that meeting."

She blows out a heavy breath. "Okay... Give me ten minutes."

Taryn hangs up, and I thwack my phone against my palm, pacing past the end of Massimo's bed and wishing Frank was next to me for this. It's not out of the question or even frowned upon to do what I'm about to, especially toward the end of the circuit. All the teams are busy making adjustments for next year. And especially if women's is happening? Those manufacturers have spots to fill. A lot of them.

But if the women's division is in Superbike, it doesn't bring me any closer to staying with Massimo. We'll be living our dreams on opposite sides of the world.

My heart pounds faster as I press my phone desperately between my palms, holding it to my lips in prayer. I tell myself on repeat that I'm making the right choice. That I'm still going to fight with every-thing in me to make the World Champion podium and stay with Dabria. I've never backed down from anything, and I didn't come this far, work this hard to get back on my bike, just to give up now.

I'm not losing my ride—wherever, whomever it's with.

Yet with every minute that passes while I'm waiting for my phone to ring, all I can think is that the door to his bedroom never, ever opens.

The tears that were threatening to take me down in the train start to rise all over again, and even though I'm waiting on Taryn to call me back with her Superbike sponsor rep in tow, I dial Massimo's number.

My knee bounces, nervous, as it rings and rings. I don't even know what I'm going to say to him. I know what I want to say: Come back to the apartment. Come take a shower with me. Come lie down with me. Just come fucking be with me and look at me like you used to, and whatever is wrong, whatever is causing this, just tell me, and I'll find a way to fix it.

His voicemail clicks on. My eyes close, tears slipping down my cheeks at his voice on the recording. Saying he's sorry he wasn't available, but he'll get back to me as soon as he can.

I wish it were the truth. That he's sorry. That he's coming back.

But that recording isn't for me, and I don't leave a message. Taryn beeps in with Werner first.

I shift restlessly on the sofa, my mind numb to the book in front of my eyes. My head is too full of the conversation I had with Werner and relayed immediately to Frank, along with promising him that he didn't have to follow me to Superbike if I ended up leaving Moto. That I understood if he wanted to stay with Billy and Mason after everything. Frank's response was that we started all this together, and we stay together, whether I'm riding a bike or a six-legged duck. And as relieved as I am, I have no idea how the King brothers are going to take that if it comes down to it. Especially Mason, who probably needs Frank's guidance more than I do at this point.

But nothing is getting decided until after Valencia.

"Psst!"

My head pops up, and I lock my e-reader that's been on the same page forever, pulling out my earbuds.

"Want to sneak out?" Chiara whispers, her laptop open in front of her at the kitchen table.

I sit up a little more on the sofa. She's hardly here considering she's usually working, and when she is, we're...polite. She keeps mentioning going out for lunch, but I figured that was a courtesy invite and not a real one. But right now, her eyes are filled with mischief and aimed entirely in my direction. I glance toward the bathroom. Where Massimo just went to take a shower. After going running. By himself.

His bad mood is only getting worse the closer we get to Silverstone in Great Britain—quiet until he snaps at me—and at this point, I'm just praying things will get better once he's back on a bike, and that's all this is.

"He's going to be pissed," I whisper back.

Chiara snorts. "Like that's any different from how he is already? Let's go have some fun, and he can stay here and sulk."

I look toward the bathroom. I don't want to make things worse, but I'm sick to death of sitting on my ass just because he never wants to go anywhere unless it's to his mom's to see Dario. And while the junior of the Vitolo brothers is freaking awesome, their mom completely hates me. Maria's apparently convinced I'm going to make Massimo move to the United States and never let him come back to Italy. Right. He'd have to want to go *anywhere* with me first.

Screw it. I don't need his permission to do what I want.

I toss down my tablet. Chiara shoots up from the table, and in ten seconds, we've got shoes on, my wallet shoved in her purse, and we're out the door, running down the stairs and straight into the piazza, bustling with life.

The noise and air slam into me, and it's like I can finally breathe after being cooped up in the apartment rippling with tension.

Chiara nudges my elbow. "Where do you want to go first?"

I look up toward the building we just ran out of, then forward again, dropping down the sunglasses I stole from Massimo. "As far as we can, as fast as we can."

She hooks her arm through mine, and I startle a little.

Chiara grins. "I know exactly where to take you."

I tilt back my face and let the sun shine on me, full from lunch and a little drunk and having the best damn girl date with Chiara. Just like...ever.

She took me to Mirabilandia. A freaking *amusement park*, and it made everything so much easier, because we didn't have to talk about anything real. We just took turns deciding which roller coaster to ride next, and we rode them all. The iSpeed twice—it reaches the same speed as Formula 1 cars, which isn't quite as fast as my bike, but it's close, and I didn't realize how much I had been starving for adrenaline while stuck on Massimo's couch. Also because Chiara is a freaking nut.

She has more energy than Mason on three Red Bulls, a refined palate for Flamin' Hot Cheetos and red wine, and has perfected the art of answering catcalls by blowing kisses that end with burps. I've spent all day laughing. And eating. And drinking.

And I don't regret a thing.

"What do you think?" Chiara asks, sitting up in her chair to top off my wineglass before emptying the bottle into hers. We've been hogging the table at this outdoor café for more courses than I can count. All of them delicious. "One more bottle, or should we order two and another dessert?"

"One bottle, two desserts."

She snaps and points at me. "So much better. Ehi!" She signals for a waiter, and I chuckle into my glass as one zooms over, practically drooling as Chiara rattles off something that sounded like one bottle of wine and three desserts, not two. He's still staring at her when she's done, so she shoos at him, and he finally scampers away, nearly bumping into another table. Chiara looks at me, rolling her eyes. "I bet he brings the wrong wine, and only two of the things I ordered will be correct."

I laugh, raising my glass to her. "Gotta be tough, being so gorgeous."

She dramatically flips her hair over her shoulder. "Who am I kidding? I love it!"

I crack up, Chiara touching her glass to mine before I drink deeper than I should, but I don't care. I'm having fun, and it's so good to be out. Free. Happily basking in the salty-sweet Ravenna breeze and far, far away from the drama.

"I swear," Chiara says, setting down her glass, "men are only good for two things." She counts on her fingers. "Making love or moving furniture—and they are not even that good at the first one." I crack up harder, Chiara shaking her head at me with a grin. "Honestly, I don't know how you put up with them at the circuit."

I groan, setting down my glass. "Me either."

Her nose wrinkles. "Is it bad?"

I glance around, thankful none of the people at the nearby tables appear to be listening to our conversation. "They bet on me."

Chiara twitches. "What? Like...they really..."

I nod, my eyes drifting to double-check once more that no one is listening. But everyone is eating, laughing, enjoying the weather and the food and their company. "They have a running pool whether I'm gonna crash or finish. They've done it for years, and they think I don't know."

Chiara's face falls, her whole body sinking back into her chair. "Lorelai..."

I shrug it off, taking a sip of my wine with a smile. "It's okay. My teammate, Mason King, told me when he found out about it. Actually, he keeps trying to convince me to get in on it and clean them all out." I chuckle off the thought, shrugging again. "At least I get to ride."

Chiara sighs, shaking her head like she's disappointed in all of them. Then she looks at me. Really looks at me. "You know, Massimo would never do that."

My eyes widen a little. It's the first time his name has come up since we left the apartment, and I was kinda hoping to keep it that way.

"I am serious." She picks up her glass, winking at me. "He hates gambling."

My smile feels a little more real, and I swirl what's left in my glass before I throw it back. "How long have you known him?"

"Ugh," she groans. "I have been stuck with that boy since I was six."

"That long?"

"Mm-hmm." She takes another drink, finishing her glass. "I met him at church. He was a mean little choir boy," she says with a wrinkle of her nose. "Always making jokes. Always talking, talking, talking. He used to annoy his father so much, just following him around, never shutting up, and Cesare would say, 'Massimo! Close your mouth and see with your ears, listen with your eyes.'"

I snort. Then feel kind of bad about it.

The waiter appears with a new bottle of wine that Chiara approves, then he sets down a plate of chocolate crepes topped with strawberries and whipped cream, a large slice of tiramisu, and a stack of the most incredible-looking cannoli I have ever seen in my life.

My diet is gonna be so screwed, but it's so gonna be worth it.

Chiara shoos the waiter away again, scooping a huge bite of tiramisu onto her fork and holding it out to me. I lean forward and take the bite, a low moan crawling from my throat as Chiara nods at me. "The best, no?"

"So good." I refill our wineglasses as Chiara serves out a little bit of everything, kissing the chocolate off her fingers. "Massimo doesn't ever really talk about his dad."

Chiara smiles at me like she's got the keys to every car I've ever wanted to drive. "What do you want to know?"

For some reason, I feel myself blush. "I don't know."

She chuckles, happily cutting into her crepes. "He was a lot like Massimo. Impossible," she says, and I can't help but laugh as I dig into my cannoli. "He loved riddles and politics and Massimo's mother, Maria, more than he needed to eat. But...he liked to take risks. He liked to gamble. And his death..." She shakes her head. "It was very difficult for Massimo." She shoves a big bite of crepes in her mouth, whipped cream on her lip when she tilts her head, gesturing with her fork. "It was the only time I have ever seen him cry."

My stomach turns at the thought. Not just Massimo crying but the idea of standing over my parents' graves. Their funerals. I set down my fork, muttering, "I can't even imagine."

She nods, taking another bite. "After, he was very quiet. Still made jokes, but..."

"He listened with his eyes?"

"Yes," she says, nodding. "And the things he saw, as a thirteen-year-old boy with a very sick young brother, these were not things he wanted to see."

I can't bring myself to ask what they were. I'm not sure I even want to know. But Chiara takes a bite of cannoli, then fills in the blanks anyway.

"His father, he had a moto shop," she says, her voice a little more private as she sets down her fork. "But it was not very successful. He let his customers promise to pay him, but then he never collected on the money. Massimo says Cesare did not want to put other people in tough positions."

I pick up my wine, taking a sip, trying to figure out what to say to that. I know what my rancher mother would say to that. My CPA of a father too. "He sounds nice," I finally offer.

"Nice to them, yes," Chiara says. "But when he died, all the money he owed, all his debts, plus the unpaid taxes for the business and for their home, they all became due. Plus an estate tax, just to transfer it all to Maria." The words land hard on the table, and *please*, let her be joking. Except, she doesn't look like she's joking. She glances at the table next to us, then her eyes flick back to me. "Massimo ran his father's shop for a while so he could help," she says with a resigned shake of her head. "But even that was not enough, so he did...other things. Things I do not agree with," she says, her eyes flaring a little. "But he has always taken care of his family."

I make a mental note to ask Massimo about that later, carefully. "What about racing, though? At that age, he would have been training all the time, preparing for the Rookie Cups."

The corner of her mouth turns up. "He quit."

"He what?"

"For about a week," she says, taking a sip of her wine. "Then Vinicio took hold of him and said, 'Massimo, you want to help your family? Follow your dreams and be a big moto star, and then your family will be saved.' So he did."

Hope perks up in my chest. He signed with some official sponsors pretty fast, I remember. And all those win bonuses, even at that level, they would have made a huge difference. They must have. "Did he save the shop?"

A funny look flits across Chiara's face, a little surprised and a tad disappointed. But I'm not sure if that's in me or because of the story. "No. It was seized."

"Jesus." He's lost, just, everything. I take another deep pull on my wine, wishing I was drunker. "I never knew...any of this."

Chiara shrugs like she's not surprised and not sure why I am either. "Of course you would not. The man does not talk anymore except to say something probably rude because he thinks it is funny.

He only has one thing on his mind, and that is how to protect his family. The rest is all bullshit."

I try really hard to ignore the whisper in my heart that wonders if that was directed at me.

Chiara sits back in her chair, stretching like she's got all the time in the world before tossing her hair. "You like Batman?"

"What?"

"Batman," she repeats. "You know, Bruce Wayne: wears a mask and a utility belt, is a vigilante in Gotham City?"

"Okay," I say with a chuckle. "No more wine for you."

Chiara laughs, sitting forward again and propping her chin in her hand. "I love comic books." She bites her lip like comics are a delicious lover. "When Batman's parents died, he had so much pain and so much money, he did not know what to do with it all. So he gave his money to an orphanage, to help the little boys who were like him." Her smile grows wider, her voice a little softer. "Batman has a big heart, but he spends so much time fighting crime, being Batman, that people sometimes forget he is still little orphaned Bruce Wayne."

My brow furrows, trying to figure out what the hell she's talking about. Then my eyes widen. "No…"

She laughs. "Oh yes." Chiara leans closer, whispering over tiramisu and cannoli, "Listen with your eyes, Lorelai."

I sit back in my chair, the white linen tablecloth tickling my thighs as sunlight glints off crystal water glasses. All I can think about is his room.

It's basically just a bed. One table, one lamp. One clock, not even digital. No art, no TV. Just one small cluster of three-by-five-inch photos hung with thumbtacks.

He lives like a freaking monk.

It takes me a second before I'm able to speak. "What does he do with it? The money, from racing?"

She shrugs, digging back into chocolate crepes. "He takes care of his family. When the debt collector came for Maria's house—"

I hold up my hand to stop her for a second, because it's too much after them losing the shop. But Chiara keeps going.

"—Massimo made him a deal. If Gabriele would move the inheritance and all the debt from Maria's name to Massimo's, Massimo would pay him an additional interest on the whole sum. Cash, under the table."

"What?" I nearly shriek. "Why offer to pay him more?"

"So that whatever Maria earned would remain hers, and she could take care of Dario." Chiara levels a look at me, reality blaring from her eyes. "Lorelai, making sure Dario's future is secure, that there is no debt tied to Maria's name, this is very important. He cannot inherit the mess that Massimo did."

"This can't be real," I mutter. "All that money…"

She tilts her head, squinting. "Not all of his money. Just most. Vinicio takes his manager salary, and Massimo hides the rest in my name, because the official debts will not allow him to buy anything. Not a moto, not a car, not a house, not anything until he pays that off first. And if he doesn't meet his interest payment, his accountant will move the debt back to Maria's name, seize everything she's built for herself since, and take Dario's security with it."

I glance around at the rest of the piazza, moving right along like the center of the world didn't just shatter, a big gaping hole left down the middle. "That is…so messed up."

"Yes," she agrees. "But with every win, Massimo becomes closer to freedom. And after Austria, he is now very, very close. He should be happy. Celebrating. But for some reason, he's not."

I look back to Chiara, and I don't know why she expects him to be happy about any of this. I'm *pissed*. Furious for him, for his family. Everything he's fought for…every time he races, he puts his life on the line. And it's all going to some greedy accountant? "Does his mom even know? I mean, this is…"

Chiara nods slowly, now looking as mad about the whole thing as I am. There's no love lost between her and Maria either, though I'm not sure what the specific beef is. Just that it's old. "Yes. She knows. She was furious when he told her, but there was nothing she could do. And in a way, she has to know that she would have lost even more if he had not done what he did."

"Batman…" I breathe, Chiara nodding as she returns to shoveling whipped cream and strawberries into her mouth. "What about the rest of his family? Or the church? Can't they help?"

She shakes her head, wiping her mouth. "No. Cesare was the last of his brothers, and Maria's family does not have that kind of money. And Massimo will not ask for help from anyone else. He turned from the church many years ago." My brow furrows as she takes a deep drink of wine, then sets down her glass with a sigh. "It was my fault."

I wait for her to elaborate on that, but she doesn't.

I clear my throat. "He still wears his cross, though."

She shrugs. "It was his father's. He may not believe in becoming attached to any of his possessions, even though his obsession with his mother's house makes him a hypocrite—"

"Thank you!" Finally, someone agrees with me on that.

She laughs, nodding. "But if he has one thing he would never sell or give away, it is that cross. It is his Wayne Manor."

I look over our plates of half-eaten desserts. "Massimo as Batman."

"Yes," she repeats. "Only now, he wears his mask all the time, and very little is he Bruce Wayne. Except for this." Chiara digs in her purse until she takes out an envelope, but not a letter-sized one. This is larger and square, like for photographs. "I have wanted to give this to you for a while, but I did not want to do it with Massimo glaring over our shoulders. So...here," she says, handing it to me.

My nerves spike more than justifiably for an envelope, but I open the folded flap and slide out the picture. I instantly smile, looking at Massimo in racing leathers in front of a track. He's young, maybe sixteen, possibly seventeen.

"MotoB," I realize when I pay closer attention to the leathers he's wearing.

Chiara stands and brings her chair around to my side of the table, sitting next to me. "Now," she says, scooting closer, "look at his face, and tell me what you see."

"He's smiling," I answer, fighting the craziest urge to cry, because that's not quite the word for it. He's grinning like everything is perfect. Like he's alive with joy, and the thing is, it's just a profile. He's looking off to the side at something, but I don't know what.

"Yes, he is smiling." Chiara chuckles. "And this is why." She messes with the back of the picture, and I distinctly hear the sound of tape popping off. Two more inches are added to the side of the photo, Chiara straightening it from where it had been folded back.

The tears I was fighting come rushing in, because Massimo is smiling at *me*. Walking away, not looking at him but flipping him off over my shoulder.

"Lorelai," Chiara says, her voice low and more serious than it's been all day. "I know you love Bruce Wayne, and he loves you, more than you realize. But right now, I think that maybe Gotham City is under attack, and whether we like it or not, all we have left is—"

"Batman," I answer.

Chiara lays her hand on my arm. "Batman can be cruel, even to those he cares about. Batman can be cold and yell and hide away in his bat cave. But I beg you, Lorelai. Do not forget that underneath, he will always be Bruce Wayne. And one day, if we are lucky, he will remember too."

I swallow, looking at her. "And what am I supposed to do in the meantime? Just...deal with it?"

She smiles, wiping off my tears. "No. You will be Wolverine. And you cut that mask off if you have to, any way you can."

BRITISH GRAND PRIX
Silverstone, Sunday, August 25

Pos	Pts	Rider	Time	World Rank
1	25	Giovanni MARCHESA	46'15.617	125
2	20	Santos SAUCEDO	+3.010	209
3	16	Lorelai HARGROVE	+4.117	130
4	13	Massimo VITOLO	+10.726	177
5	11	Mason KING	+11.132	124
6	10	Billy KING	+25.467	226
7	9	Diarmaid DEAN	+26.717	25
8	8	Aurelio LOGGIA	+29.393	65
9	7	Harleigh ELIN	+38.815	48
10	6	Gregorio PAREDES	+41.712	63
11	5	Cesaro SOTO	+44.776	25
12	4	Rainier HERRE	+52.489	54
13	3	Gustavo LIMÓN	+1'11.211	28
14	2	Donato MALDONADO	+1'15.292	45
15	1	Deven HORSLEY	+1'17.863	73
16		Elliston LAMBIRTH	+1'19.310	47
17		Cristiano ARELLANO	+1'19.735	90
18		Timo GONZALES	+1'58.086	17
Not Classified				
		Galeno GIRÓN	1 Lap	57
		Fredek SULZBACH	6 Laps	57

GP OCTO DI SAN MARINO E DELLA RIVIERA DI RIMINI
Misano Adriatico, Sunday, September 15

Pos	Pts	Rider	Time	World Rank
1	25	Massimo VITOLO	44'06.586	202
2	20	Lorelai HARGROVE	+4.001	150
3	16	Santos SAUCEDO	+6.451	225
4	13	Billy KING	+9.078	239
5	11	Giovanni MARCHESA	+13.939	136
6	10	Cristiano ARELLANO	+19.615	100
7	9	Mason KING	+25.309	133
8	8	Timo GONZALES	+31.812	25
9	7	Diarmaid DEAN	+36.225	32
10	6	Cesaro SOTO	+42.701	31
11	5	Deven HORSLEY	+47.493	78
12	4	Rainier HERRE	+51.998	58
13	3	Aurelio LOGGIA	+54.048	68
14	2	Gregorio PAREDES	+1'02.396	65
15	1	Harleigh ELIN	+1'12.775	49
16		Fredek SULZBACH	+1'25.469	57
Not Classified				
		Elliston LAMBIRTH	20 Laps	47
		Donato MALDONADO	26 Laps	45
Not Finished 1st Lap				
		Galeno GIRÓN	0 Lap	57
		Gustavo LIMÓN	0 Lap	28

GRAN PREMIO DE ARAGÓN
Alcañiz, Sunday, September 22

Pos	Pts	Rider	Time	World Rank
1	25	Santos SAUCEDO	44'18.296	250
2	20	Billy KING	+3.741	259
3	16	Massimo VITOLO	+4.028	218
4	13	Lorelai HARGROVE	+6.935	163
5	11	Giovanni MARCHESA	+11.885	147
6	10	Mason KING	+15.465	143
7	9	Cesaro SOTO	+19.038	40
8	8	Harleigh ELIN	+29.797	57
9	7	Timo GONZALES	+36.521	32
10	6	Donato MALDONADO	+40.286	51
11	5	Galeno GIRÓN	+51.335	62
12	4	Gustavo LIMÓN	+53.761	32
13	3	Gregorio PAREDES	+57.602	68
14	2	Elliston LAMBIRTH	+1'05.189	49
15	1	Aurelio LOGGIA	+1'17.674	69
16		Rainier HERRE	+1'38.449	58
17		Diarmaid DEAN	+1'58.036	32
Not Classified				
		Fredek SULZBACH	1 Lap	57
		Deven HORSLEY	1 Lap	78
		Cristiano ARELLANO	1 Lap	100

Chapter 21

Massimo Vitolo—September; Ravenna, Italy

SILVERSTONE WAS A MESS. IT RAINED THE WHOLE WEEK, EVERYONE kept crashing during practice and qualifying, and it didn't matter how hard I pushed it during the race. Lorina pushed back harder, and she beat me. Beat me bad. But that was Britain. I smoked her in Rimini and Aragón, and I am *one more* race from paying off Gabriele. I am so damn close.

Was so close.

I pull up in front of my mother's house but park on the street instead of the driveway. We've been home for less than eighteen hours, and I'd planned on spending today sleeping, playing video games, and doing some laundry. Maybe grocery shopping, because there's nothing to eat in the apartment. But all that went out the window when Vinicio texted me ten minutes ago saying I need to come to the house—*alone*—for a "development."

I *knew* Lorina going for a run this morning was a bad idea, but I'm running out of excuses on how to keep us inside in Ravenna when the sky is blue and the weather is perfect. The worst part is, I thought it was working. Dabria still hasn't raised a conflict of interest warning, and Angelo was just starting to back off. I'm playing by his rules on the circuit, and my eyes feel like they've shifted to the back of my head so I can catch Lorina before she's anywhere near my garage. It's the same with my RV on the paddock, in which I spend as little time as possible so she doesn't come looking for me there.

She's always *looking* for me, but I don't know why. After she sits, she doesn't talk. I don't either. There's nothing to say when being together puts her at risk. Something I was expressly reminded of this morning.

Time to get fired.

I slam my palm against the steering wheel, then get out of Chiara's car and shove the keys into my pocket. Her transmission's getting harder and harder to shift, and I already replaced the clutch. The master cylinder is next. I can do it without bleeding the wheels if I can get it on a hoist, but that means talking my way into a shop. At least I'll have time now—considering it looks like I'm *not* going back to the circuit in a week.

The word *default* blares in my mind like the world's ugliest neon sign, and I try not to puke on my way up the driveway. I don't know how long I'm gonna make it, though.

"What's the emergency?" I ask Vinicio in Italian, currently waiting inside the open garage for me.

He crosses his arms from where he's leaning against the waist-high toolbox. It's taking everything I have not to let the acid gurgling in my stomach show on my face, but he...doesn't look nearly as pissed off as I expected. "Have you seen the breaker bar?"

I stop in place, gaping at him. "What?"

I was prepared for a lecture. Maybe a choked-up announcement that it's over: Lorina and I got busted, Angelo's had enough, and I'm getting replaced with a wild card rider.

"The breaker bar," Vinicio repeats. "I've got a bolt that won't come free. I need it."

All my breath comes rushing out of me, a bead of sweat sneaking down the back of my neck. He couldn't have just texted me that?

After I regain some kind of feeling in my legs, I walk the rest of the way into the garage and nudge him off the toolbox, checking two different drawers before I pull open the third and find the tool he needs. But that's not all I find.

Resting against the organized row of wrenches is a white letter envelope. Swollen thick.

"I knew where it was," he says quietly. "I needed to talk to you. Privately."

I look at Vinicio, my heart beating out of my chest again but for a brand-new reason. "No." I close the tool drawer, shoving the breaker bar flat against his chest.

"You're joking, right?"

I turn, walking back to the car.

"Damn it, Massimo!" he calls after me. "You are going to have to learn to listen to someone at some point. You cannot go through life thinking you know everything, that everything is your decision and your responsibility—"

I whip around, my temper raging in my chest. "This is my responsibility."

"It doesn't give you the right to refuse my help." He points the breaker bar at me. "The worst part is that despite having one hell of an attitude problem, you've actually become a good man who has taken damn good care of this family. And it's only made you more fucking arrogant." Metal clangs as he throws down the breaker bar onto the toolbox. "But I don't know why I'm surprised. You're too much like Cesare that way."

There's a sadness in his voice that cuts right through me, strangling all my words in my throat. Sometimes, I forget that long before everything, they were friends. Good friends.

"Enough is enough." He goes back into the third drawer in the toolbox, then walks toward me, placing the envelope in my hand.

It's heavy. Heavier than any I've ever filled.

"You're not the only one capable of making sacrifices for this family," he says, his voice low with frustration. But his palm lands on the back of my neck, and there's nothing frustrated about it. It feels like it did when I was little and he would crouch down next to me, teaching me piece by piece everything I know about racing. "And your mom and I...we want you to have your life back. You've done more than enough, more than we ever could, and it's time this was over. You deserve to have a clean shot at a future with Lorelai, if that's what you want. This was never supposed to be your burden."

I blink, unable to feel anything but the warmth of his palm on my neck, the weight of the envelope in my hand. How real it feels, how very close I am to freedom, and how much I absolutely hate the idea of giving it to Gabriele. "I, um..." I shake my head, trying to think of all the reasons I need to give it back to Vinicio. "I don't need it. After Thailand—"

"No," he cuts me off, voice stern. "You need to do this *now*, Massimo. Don't wait for another race, or two or three or however many it ends up taking. We may not have them."

There's no accusation in his voice, just a calm acceptance that Angelo could fire me at any time because I've refused to walk away from Lorina. It only makes me feel worse, because even with how much Vinicio's fate is tied to mine, he's never asked me to choose.

He's never even brought it up.

His hand on my neck gently pulls me closer, his voice dropping lower. "Go over there and pay off that asshole today, and decide whether to stay with Yaalon on *your* terms. I will find someone else to sign you—don't worry about that. But no one should have to live in fear, and I know *you* know that."

I lock my jaw and glance away, no idea what to do. He's been telling me that for as long as I can remember. And while everything in me is screaming to give the money back to him and my mom...I want to take it.

I want to be free from the debt pressing on me every day from the time I wake up until the moment I go to sleep. I want to buy an espresso and not feel guilty for not saving five bucks, forever caught between keeping up appearances and trying to survive. More than anything, I want my future back.

An actual, real future with Lorina where I can stand up to Angelo's threats because they don't threaten everyone else I love too.

"I will pay you back," I tell Vinicio, my voice cracking, because there's no way to stop it.

He shakes his head. "We won't accept it."

I don't know what else to do. I hug him, Vinicio coughing out a laugh before he hugs me back. For a second in the quiet sunlit garage, he feels more like a dad to me than he ever has. But that's probably my fault. I never really gave him a chance on that front. "Thank you."

"Of course." He claps my back, letting me go as I push back from him and stride back down the driveway, stuffing the envelope into my pocket and trying to wrap my head around what I'm about to do. All that it's going to mean.

But there's no way to do that when I'm finally going to get Gabriele out of my life.

—◊◊◊—

I spent almost all day waiting in the alley across the street to make sure there was no one else inside, going over in my mind all the dozens of ways I imagined doing this through the years. The shit I'd say, the things I'd break.

In the end, the broken look on Gabriele's face was more than enough.

He snatches up a piece of paper from the printer, then pushes back from his antique desk, going over to a file cabinet and searching through it. My phone vibrates in my pocket, and after I slip it out to check, I send Lorina straight to voicemail. I can't tap into that part of myself right now, the soft part, and she's fine—still back at the apartment with Chiara.

Gabriele pulls out a thick file, slides in the new paper, then hands it to me, sitting back down in his big leather chair. "Here."

I don't sit in mine. Way too wound up. "What's the matter, buddy?" I glance into the folder in my hands. I'm not surprised to see my name on top. Very surprised to see the final numbers at the bottom. Part of me never thought I would. "Seems like something's got you in a bad mood."

"Divorce has a way of doing that." My gaze lifts, and sure enough, that picture of him and his wife on a yacht is gone. "So what's next? You gonna fire my nephew too?"

I close the folder and lean against his big old desk that I hate, unable to resist a dark smirk. "Haven't decided."

Gabriele shakes his head. "He's a good kid. He doesn't know anything."

I suspected that might be the case. He didn't seem like the kind of guy to purposefully do that, and it will be taken into consideration. "Why do I get the feeling that your wife didn't know anything either?"

Gabriele clears his throat.

"But now she does," I fill in.

"I was trying to…prepare her. For things changing. When you kept winning."

I *tsk* and shake my head like I feel bad for him. "Gotta be tough, not being able to spend my money anymore."

He flips me off. "Go ahead. Gloat. I lost my wife, my daughter won't talk to me, I'll probably have to close my business to afford my divorce, and you have your whole life ahead of you."

Huh, I almost do feel bad for the guy.

"The fuck are you still doing here?" he asks.

I push off his desk and leave without another word, all the threats and warnings I'd planned on struck dead now that he has nothing left to lose. It's better this way, cleaner.

Once I'm past the receptionist, I fold the file and tuck it into the back of my jeans under my jacket. Stiff-arm the door outside into the street, the sun already moved from one side of the sky to well below the horizon, streetlights coming on and the sounds of the world getting more aggressive. I let it feed me and fill me, and I still can't believe I'm never going to walk into that office again. Never see that asshole again. Never watch my winnings disappear from my bank account before I could even count how much they were.

My heart stutters not two steps out of the building—*not yet*.

A Vespa cruises around me, but I barely hear it. I stride quickly across the street, ducking into the alley I've been hiding out in all day after I dropped off the car and walked here, getting up my nerve to confront him for the very last time.

I'm breathing hard out of my mouth as I dart past the yellow glow of the streetlight. Once I'm in the dark, I fall against the wall of the building, my chest ballooning in staggered bursts as goose bumps prickle my skin and water itches at my eyes. And I finally let it hit me.

I did it. A strangled laugh chokes my throat, because it's too much to hold in at once. Too much joy and anger and relief and rage after all the fear and the hate and the hate and the fear, and a roar tears from my lungs, echoing all around me—I'm fucking free.

His name is clear. *My* name is clear. I lost the shop, but I protected them in the end. Like I swore to him I would. They're safe now, no matter what.

It's finally *over*.

I gasp for breath in the pitch-black alley, my city's stars shining bright above me, and there's only one thing in the world that I can think of now:

I want to kiss Lorina.

Really kiss her, like I haven't kissed her in far too long. Where she's wrapped in my arms and I don't know where we are and I don't fucking care because I could get lost in her lips for years, but she hasn't let me touch her for weeks. And I know she's mad, and I know I deserve it. But she can't stay mad at me forever, and I need to kiss her. Right now.

I shove myself off the wall and start walking back to my apartment. Jogging. *Running* through the streets and cutting through every back alley I know, pushing harder with everything in me the closer I get because I can't wait to do everything with her I've been waiting my whole life to do. Starting with buying us that perfect three-bedroom villa and getting out of that crowded-as-hell apartment.

"Lorina!" I yell when I blow through the front door, flying so high, my boots barely touch the floor on my way to my room. I don't even bother with English. "Lorina, get dressed. We're going—"

I stop when I throw open the door, finding the room empty.

Bed made. Tigrotta's not by the pillows. No hair ties on my nightstand, sitting on a stack of romance novels. No suitcase under the window. *No...*

Something moves behind me, and I spin to find Chiara leaning against the door to her room. Her arms are hugged over her faded "Vulcan in the streets, Klingon in the sheets" T-shirt, and wearing a pissed-off scowl that's quickly downgrading to pity. "Where have you been all day?" she asks in Italian.

"Paying off Gabriele," I growl at her. "Where is she?"

Chiara flinches, suddenly looking a lot more like my oldest friend rather than another roadblock. She blinks, a lifetime's worth of hope in her voice. "You paid off Gabriele? Completely?"

"Where is she, Chiara?"

Her expression falls. Hardens. "She left."

I nearly drop to my knees.

Chiara swallows, her voice losing all the accusation in it from a second ago. "She said she'd be back for the gala in Rimini…"

I shake my head, turning and striding back into my room. Grab my bag, start packing. Shirts, pants, wallet. I don't need much.

"Massimo, where are you going?"

"After her."

"You can't. She didn't go to Memphis." Chiara sighs behind me. "Her manager called her, something about testing in Germany…"

I punch my bag off my bed. If she's testing, I absolutely can't be there.

I round on Chiara, all the pressure in my chest booming out through my voice because I can't believe this is happening *tonight* of all fucking nights. "How could you let her leave?"

Chiara stares at me, her chest rising quickly, but she never raises her voice. "She promised me she was coming back," she repeats. "And how about instead of blaming me, you try answering your phone once in a while. She waited for you as long as she could, Massimo. Don't think she didn't. You were just too busy to notice."

I gesture absently in Chiara's direction, then sink down to the mattress, my head falling into my hands.

She's coming back, I tell myself. *It's going to be okay.*

But who is she testing for? *Please*, don't be anyone Superbike.

"Are you ready to talk about whatever the hell is going on with you?" Chiara asks. "Because this isn't the first time you've dodged her calls, and I don't get it, Massimo. You waited ten years for this moment, it's finally here, and you're *blowing* it. So what was the point of *everything* if this is what you were going to do?"

My knees bounce as my stomach flips, totally screwed because she's right. I am blowing it. "It's not that simple, Chiara."

"Then explain to me what's making this so freaking complicated."

I look up at her, leaning against the doorway and staring me down. She'll stand there all night if I don't come clean, and I really do suck at keeping secrets from her. So with my eyes trained on the floor and my hands laced together, I tell her. Just the bare minimum at first. Except it's *Chiara*, and once I start talking, it all comes out: Angelo watching my every move, him threatening to rewrite my contract if he doesn't end it first, hiding my relationship with Lorina so Dabria can't use that against her too.

Everything.

I feel scraped raw from the inside when I'm done, flattened from the impossible pull between trying to provide for my family, to protect the woman I love, and realizing there's no way to be what everyone needs, everywhere they need me to be, every time they need me to be there, without also hurting everyone along the way.

"Wow." Chiara lets out a deep sigh, nods slowly, then half shrugs. "So...that's it?"

I flip her off. So much for best friends. "Screw you."

Chiara rolls her eyes, shoving off the doorframe. She comes over and sits next to me, bumping her shoulder against mine. "Fine. You're right. Everything is terrible, and I think you should definitely keep ignoring her calls, because this is clearly her fault. Super smart play."

I stare at my best friend. "What do you think I should do?"

"Turn your freaking phone back on," she says. "Call Lorelai and tell her what's been going on, get your tux cleaned, and YouTube some videos on how to waltz, because you need to dance with her at the gala."

I'm already shaking my head. "If I do that, Angelo is going to cut me."

"Why? He already knows about you. How is dancing with her gonna hurt? Besides, everyone else already suspects you're together, and Dabria doesn't really seem to care."

"I can't take that—"

"You're *not* though," Chiara says, exasperated. "You're giving her the choice of whether *she* wants to risk it. And it is her choice." Chiara arches an eyebrow at me. "You know, you said that she always puts racing first, but I've spent time with her too, and that's not what it looks like from here. She might just surprise you." Chiara pats my knee and pushes up to standing. "And you need to surprise her with how well you can waltz at that gala. So get practicing."

She leaves me with that as she heads out of my room, shutting the door behind her. I pull my phone out of my pocket, calling Lorina. It rings twice before her voicemail clicks on, and my eyes pinch shut.

Fair is fair, but it doesn't hurt any less that she just rolled me.

"Hi. I, um…" I can't do this over voicemail. "I'm sorry I missed you. Call me back when you get a chance."

I hang up. Lie back on my bed and wait, tapping my phone against my chest. Get up with a sigh and put away my bag and clothes, my eyes continually glancing toward the dark screen. But the more minutes pass without my phone ringing, the more I know that Chiara's right. I thought I had this under control. But I don't. I so fucking *don't* because I've been so pissed off at the injustice of everything I thought I was going to lose, I threw it all away before they ever actually took it from me, and—

God, what the hell have I been doing?

———

My tie is already bugging the shit out of me as I head outside and down the lit path into the sponsor gala, humidity settling thick through the courtyard of the hotel, right on the beach in Rimini. Angelo laughs loudly from the far corner of the tent, and it isn't hard to spot Lorina in the crowd: talking with Frank and some sponsor rep I think works for Blue Gator.

She gracefully laughs at whatever they said, her watercolor gray chiffon gown drifting in the breeze and her earrings sparkling against the white canopy, her curled hair draping over her very bare shoulder.

She's *stunning*.

Which is exactly what I was going to tell her earlier, but she wouldn't look at me when she came out of the bathroom—she strode straight out the door. She barely took my calls the whole time she was gone; it was always too early or too late, her voice drained like she'd left it all on the track, and I couldn't bring myself to dump the truth of all my problems on her over the phone. But she hasn't said a word since she got to the hotel with less than an hour to spare before the gala, her bags tagged from Munich.

"Is that supposed to be convincing?" Santos sneers next to me.

I glance at him. I didn't even hear the asshole walk over.

"Lorelai comes down, then you show up ten minutes later, and you think the sponsors won't know you are staying in the same room?"

I arch my eyebrow like that's news to me. "You think we are staying together?"

"Yep." He grins, taking a smug sip from his glass.

I nod, clapping him hard enough on the back that he chokes on his whiskey. "You are right. We are."

Shock ripples across his face, but Santos is the least of my concerns tonight. I look toward Lorina, and it's not far, but my pulse rises with every step across the room. She immediately freezes when she sees me walking toward her, but I don't care who she's talking to or what they're talking about. I don't care who's watching or what it's gonna cost me—my contract included.

I can't wait another two hours to talk to her. I can't wait two minutes.

I grab her hand and pull her away, Lorina stuttering to her manager, "Sorry, uh, excuse me." I lead her to an open spot on the semi-crowded dance floor and pull her into me, ignoring Angelo scowling at me from the corner.

Her body clicks into mine with an ease that's been there since those country bars in Memphis. Thank Christ, at least this still works.

"I can't believe you just did that," Lorina whispers harshly, though she still has a sweetly fake smile on her lips. "Not only was I in the middle of a very important conversation, but now, everyone is staring at us."

I check around, and she's right: Santos and Giovanni are whispering, others nodding our way and a couple of cell phones making appearances. "Sorry."

"That's a first."

God, I'm too late. I spin her out, then back in, Lorina following my lead but giving me a look like it's not gonna work this time. I settle my palm on her lower back, just dancing with her for a minute and trying to calm myself under the scent of her perfume. It's never changed.

"What is going on with you?" she hisses.

I bring her closer, telling myself to go slow. To take my time and memorize everything about the way she feels in my hands. "You have been gone, cara," I whisper. "And I have missed you."

"Oh, I'm cara now, huh?" She rolls her eyes. "That's convenient."

I keep my palm light on her waist as I cradle her other hand in mine, but everything in me is screaming. How did I let it get this bad? "If you are angry with me, then let us go upstairs and talk about it. I do not want to fight with you at a place like this."

"I'm not leaving when we just got here, and I'm not angry," she whispers. "Just tired of the emotional whiplash."

Emotional what? "What does that mean?"

"It means you can't just call me 'cara' when this is the most you've said to me in weeks."

I look at her, but she won't meet my eyes, and even though there's a room full of people watching us, I can't see a single one of them. "I talk to you. All the time."

Her hand rises from my shoulder for a moment like she waved at someone, then she lowers her voice. "You ask what time zone we're in or if I'm hungry, sure, but you don't tell me how Dario is doing in school. You don't ask what I think about Taryn possibly coming to MotoPro if MMW expands beyond Superbike or what it'll mean for us if the rumors are true about the women's division. You don't ask about my family or the ranch. Hell, you never even sent my dad those pictures of your father racing in the fifties you promised you'd show him."

"I did send them," I tell her. "Copies of every single photo I have. If he did not tell you, this is not my fault."

"Yeah? Well, it's not like you told me either. Or considered I may want to see them."

She's right. I didn't.

"It's fine," she mutters, shifting her hand on my shoulder, but the weight is wrong, like she's not really touching me. She's just acting like it. "They're just pictures. But when I have to find out the truth about your family—about Gabriele—from your best friend instead of you…"

My eyes fly to hers. *She knows?*

"Yeah," she says. "But that was after I found my helmet hidden in your room."

I barely contain my wince. Of course she found it.

"And when you won't even go for a run with me, much less out to a movie or to dinner, it's pretty obvious that you're just…you're not in love with me anymore."

The words are so wrong, it takes everything I have not to stop dead still.

"And I get it. I really do," she says. "People grow apart; it happens. But you used to be honest with me, Massimo. You used to tell me the truth, and I—" She blinks a little too rapidly, shaking her hair back from her face. "I asked you not to break my heart, but I should've known you'd do it anyway. So you may as well just get it over with."

She looks away, and my hands are shaking, my heart pounding, but there's nothing to say once she's finished. No way to tell her that her pain is wrong or that I didn't cause it when I did.

This is my fault.

I've hurt her so much more than I ever knew I was capable of, because she trusts me to tell her the truth, and I haven't been honest with her. Worse, I don't have anyone else to blame. Angelo might've made his threats, but I made all the decisions without ever bothering to ask what she thinks, and I can't take the secrets and the lies anymore.

I drop her hand, tightening my other arm around her waist and leading her off the dance floor.

"Where are we going?" Lorina asks, her voice rushed as she checks over her shoulder, then looks to me. "We can't just leave. People expect us to be here."

"They will get over it."

"Mas—"

"I need to tell you something," I say, ducking us out of the side of the tent. "But not here."

Chapter 22

Lorelai Hargrove—September; Rimini, Italy

I DON'T KNOW HOW TONIGHT CAN GET ANY WORSE. TEARS BITE AT my eyes as I let him lead me out of the canopy, hopefully before we make more of a scene. I glance toward the tent, but none of the other gala guests are watching us, still chatting in the hotel courtyard. Thank God the paparazzi were banned from entering so they're none the wiser of the headline they're on the verge of writing.

I can see it now: "Still No Mercy for Wreckless."

Massimo's quiet on the short walk toward the beach, the long stretch of sand thankfully deserted, apart from the umbrellas and chairs permanently set up. A wave crashes ahead of us, and my breath catches in my throat at the moon reflecting on the water. It's so torturously beautiful, everything else infinitely more terrible by comparison.

Chiara was right about him, but she was wrong about me. No matter what I do, I can't break through that wall, that mask. I'm not Wolverine. I'm not even Tigrotta anymore.

But she was right about something else too: I'm in love with him.

Despite the fights, the anger, the coldness between us, I'm listening with my eyes and seeing with my ears, and I'm totally in love with the jerk who hasn't once asked me to sacrifice anything for him. Who, some days, I want to sacrifice everything for. It only makes everything that went down in Germany a million times more complicated, but I can't think about that now.

He turns us off the lit path and toward the rest of the beach, pausing to take off his shoes.

"It's too late to go swimming, and I'm wearing a dress." I pray he doesn't hear it when my voice cracks. If he does, he doesn't mention it. He only crouches down and takes my ankle in his hand. I nearly fall, having to scrabble for a grip on his shoulder, the rich fabric of his death-black suit more than a little slick. "Massimo—"

"When my papà was sick," he interrupts, his voice quiet in the darkness as his hands slip my high heels from my feet with expert care, "he told me that one day, I would meet a woman so beautiful, I would forget to breathe."

I swallow thickly in the sticky, salty air, Massimo rising with an easy smile. It calms my nerves a little when he takes my hand again, walking us toward the surf that's coming in with the tide, close enough to our path that the sand is soft and cool, but water doesn't touch the hem of my dress.

"He told me that I would know this is the woman I was going to love because not only would she be beautiful, but she would be difficult."

Something warm seeps through me, healing little scrapes and cuts, soothing almost everything. It's a wondrous kind of comfort, hearing him say that again when there's been so much silence between us lately.

"She would ask me questions I would not want to answer," he continues. "She would make me angry, and she would make me afraid. I thought *no*, this will never happen to me. But my papà, he told me that when I found this woman, and when I was sure I loved her, I must do this one thing…" Massimo looks at me, his steps slow and calm through the surf, but the intensity of his gaze sends a shiver down my spine. "I must be the worst of my heart."

I flinch. "What?"

Massimo's eyebrow arches, but there's also a smirk in the edge of his lips. "He said I was good, yes, but there was also bad in me. Monsters, demons in my soul that will try to win: pride, vanity, greed. It is these demons that make me Centauro, same as it was for him. And so, when I found this woman, I was to show her my demons. He told me: if she was the right woman, she would love me anyway."

I can't do more than blink at him, my heart broken for the little boy who heard this. To tell your son he's so evil, no woman would accept him unless he did that... I don't know if I've ever heard anything more screwed up.

"My papà died when I was thirteen," Massimo says, "and for many months, I thought about what he said. After some time, I decided that he was old, sick, and it was not possible that there was any truth in this. I chose to forget it."

"Okay..." I drawl, not quite sure where he's going with this. I don't really care—he's talking to me. In full sentences. He could be reciting the latest soccer stats for the Roma team he loves and I can't seem to muster any affection for, and I still wouldn't care, as long as he just keeps talking.

"When I was fifteen..." He pauses to shift us farther into the beach when a wave crashes a little too close for comfort. "I had my first real moto race. I went to Blue Gator. I thought *yes*," he says, animated, "I will win this race, and everyone will see how fast I am."

A smile pulls at the corner of my lips, starting to see the connection he's drawing.

"I go and begin to race," he says, "and there is a problem. On the track, I find I am racing against an asshole."

I bite my lip, a blush rising in my cheeks.

"He pushes me hard in the turns, flies past me on the straight, forgets to see the braking markers and goes too fast to be safe. This asshole wins this race, and I was so angry. Everyone saw me lose the first time they saw me."

I shift my grip on his hand so our fingers lace together, my other palm curling around the smooth bump of his bicep under the soft fabric of his jacket. I play along, doing my best to sound sincere. "That's awful."

He nods, pouting dramatically, and he's so cute that I almost feel bad for him—*almost*. "We crossed the finish line, and the asshole takes off his helmet." My pulse speeds up as Massimo peeks at me, his eyes growing scandalized. "It is a girl."

"You don't say…"

He winks, continuing our walk along the beach as the moonlight rains down, and I've *missed* this version of him. The hopeless romantic he hid behind deathly tattoos.

"Long brown hair, twisted into a braid over her shoulder," he says, his voice low and reverently nostalgic. "Smooth skin, eyes gold like fire. She is the most beautiful girl I have ever seen, and she races moto. *Moto*," he says as though he can't believe it. "And she beat me. I had no words for this."

Everything in me is so entranced watching him talk about us meeting, I don't even care when a wave surges up, water tickling my feet and ankles. Screw the dress and the gala and everyone and everything except this moment, sponsors and contracts and all.

"So this girl," he says, quiet yet starting to smile, "she looks at me, and she wrinkles her nose like I am a bug. She flips her braid over her shoulder, then walks away with her helmet under her arm, an American flag painted on top." Heat flames my skin when he leans closer, whispering, "This was the first time ever that I forgot to breathe." He pulls back, grinning brighter than I've seen from him since Memphis. "I am in love."

I melt fully and completely, letting his arm go to hug him around his middle. His arm comes around me, squeezing my shoulder as he drops a kiss to my hair.

So much for Germany, a voice in my mind whispers, and I bat it away. Not now. Not yet.

Tonight, Massimo comes first.

"Now, I remember the words of my papà," he says, somehow continuing to walk even as I refuse to let go of him. "If this is the woman, she will make me angry, and she will make me afraid. So I wait and see."

"Oh God…" I chuckle, knowing I did exactly that.

Massimo chuckles too, but his is nearly silent. "Many years, this girl and I, we race together. Over time, I find that my papà was right. This woman is strong, but she is also dangerous, reckless, and she scares me with how little she values her safety. It scares me how much I am worried for her. And now," he says, softer, "I am supposed to show her the worst of me." He slowly shakes his head, and my heart sinks for him. "I did not want to do this. We had already argued many times, this girl and I, and I worried that if I was to do more, she would never love me."

My temple falls against his shoulder, and I have no idea how a guy who seems to see straight through me can't see it: how much I love him, have loved him, for longer than even I wanted to admit it.

"But I did not have a choice," he says. "I had faith in my papà, in his wisdom, so I did as he said. I showed her my pride, my anger, and I told her awful things. They were the truth, but they were not sweet."

Right now, I can't seem to remember a single harsh word he's ever said to me. Even if I could, it wouldn't sound the same. Everything now has to be refiltered from the truth that he was given the absolute worst advice ever from the person he trusted most.

"It is easy to love a man who is all nice words and soft kisses," he whispers. "I have those things in me, but this woman, she would need to know what I am capable of if she is to love me. So for many years, I was the worst of me. And always, I waited. I waited for this woman to see me, to know what I have done and why. But this woman, she did not understand. And she did not love me."

I tighten my jaw to keep it from quivering, because I know what's coming, and I don't want to hear it. I want to go back and rewrite history where I wasn't stubborn, he wasn't on a mission to make me see his worst, and everything would've been different from the beginning.

"She hated me."

The words drop from his lips like a detonation.

My feet slow to a stop, the regret so heavy, I can't even move. Massimo stops and looks at me, his brow furrowed in concern at the goose bumps on my skin that have nothing do with my bare shoulders and everything to do with all the ways I've hurt him.

He quickly shrugs off his jacket and drapes it around my shoulders, the leftover heat from his body soothing into mine. I'd rather have him, but maybe there's hope. That tonight, he won't stay away on the far side of the mattress, endless space between us. That maybe, *maybe*, he'll be with me. Hold me and let me hold him, and we can try again.

He lifts my hair from the jacket collar, letting it rest gently against my shoulder. "I worried that maybe this would never change," he says quietly. "Maybe my papà was wrong, and I was ruined to love her forever."

He sweeps his thumb across my bottom lip, and the words are right behind it—I should've told him already. But when it comes to telling him how I feel, the things I want, and the future I see for us, I've been the worst kind of coward.

It felt like more power for him to wield over me. One more way for him to crush me. But now, it sounds like freedom. And no one deserves to be free more than Massimo.

As soon as he's done telling me his secrets, I'm telling him mine.

"Then, something happened," he says. "This woman, she crashed her moto. She has crashed before, but this..." He shakes his head. "This was different."

My heart races, terrified to hear the answer only he can give. "Why?"

He tilts his head like he's considering that, then he retakes my hand, this time covering it with his other so mine is cradled between his palms. Like he knows how hard it is, even now, for me to talk about the wreck. How scared I still get sometimes, and how the nightmares have never really stopped. What I never expected was that he has them too.

Dreams that cause him to wake up in a breathless rush, sitting up straight and staring into the darkness for a long, long time before he finally lies down, clutching me to him. He won't tell me what happens in them, but I know. I've always known.

He starts walking again, my hand cradled in his and the surf rising higher with each new wave. "Her moto came after her in the crash, and it hit her in her helmet." He clears his throat, looking down and his voice unsteady. "For a long time, she lay very still in the dirt, and I thought her neck was broken. I thought she was dead."

God, there it is. Just like I worried it would be, and I can't imagine how paralyzing that would be: to see him crash the way I did.

Massimo's jaw pops and flexes as his eyes lift and skitter over the ocean.

"Hey," I breathe. He tries to smile at me, but it's filled with the pain of the memory. "She's okay now."

He nods. "They, um, they took her to hospital." He clears his throat again, his voice strengthening. "I followed. I decided that if she was alive, then I must tell her the truth. I must tell her what she is to me." His right hand replaces his left, his fingers lacing through mine as his other arm winds around my waist, holding me closer to him. "I will tell her how she is in all my dreams," he whispers. "I will tell her how beautiful I think she is, and that I see she is like me: she has pride, and she has anger, and I love her for this. She is my Tigrotta."

I can't resist smiling at the nickname I've missed most over the past weeks.

"I also see that she is sweet, and she is soft, and I love this too. I waited for her to wake up."

The reality of the memory crashes hard into the fantasy he's weaving. Because when I woke up, I accused him of being there only to gloat over my crash.

I didn't see. I didn't want to, and he was trying so hard, and I was such an ass.

"But when her eyes opened, she was afraid," he says. "She was sad and crying, and I decided that I could not tell her this now. She needed me to be strong for her, not to change the rules when she was lost." He takes a deep breath, squeezing my waist. "She asked me the question, and I did not tell her the answer. I left."

I look away from him, ashamed. All he wanted was to tell me he loved me, and I ruined it, for both of us. Everything could've been different from that one moment if I'd just listened. But I never listen. I always do what I want and never consider the consequences until it's too late. Like how many times I've broken Massimo's heart out of nothing more than the fear he'd break mine first.

Massimo slides me in front of him so his chest aligns with my back, his arms coming around me. I grip his hands desperately, locking them against my chest, terrified of all the decisions I've yet to make. All the ones that might break him too.

I'm so tired of hurting him. I can't stand it, not after all he's been through. And for the first time, I understand *exactly* why Taryn dropped two and a half million dollars to shovel horse stalls with Billy instead of living rent-free in a high-rise condo in Munich alone.

I just have no idea if I'm going to have the guts to make the same call when it comes down to it, after Valencia.

"After her crash, she was different," Massimo tells me, his voice brushing over the collar of his jacket and tingling down my neck. "She was in pain and had anger and fear in her heart like a sickness. She crashed again and again, and this sickness, it grew." He hugs me tighter, his lips settling on the back of my shoulder. "I tried to be both: be strong, be the worst. But sometimes, I could not do this, and I failed."

I peek over my shoulder at his last word, Massimo gently turning me around the rest of the way to face him.

His eyes search my own, his fingertips tender on my jaw as the surf rushes over our bare feet. "I had shown this woman who I am, what I am capable of. She knows me. What she did not know is how I feel. So…" He takes a deep breath like he's gathering the courage all over again. A flash of him appears in my memory, timidly walking around the corner from his hotel bathroom, very purposefully not wearing a shirt and simply watching me, waiting for my reaction. "I told her. For the first time in ten years, she knows."

There's no way to resist kissing him. Just once, softly, because I can't imagine how scary that must've been for him: to reveal his true feelings after all that time. After all the pains he'd taken to hide them.

When I pull back, he rolls in his bottom lip like he's savoring the taste of me. Then his voice drops. "This knowing, this was difficult for her, because I am not what she wanted."

I suck in a breath. "Massimo, no! I was surprised, that's all. I never really considered—"

"I am not a hero." He shakes his head, his nose wrinkled like I'm the one who's cracked. "I am not the prince in a fairy tale. I have monsters in my soul, demons on my skin." His face falls further, guilt plaguing his features as the words descend like a confession. "I have yelled at her, been cruel to her. I have watched her crash and not stopped to help her."

I swallow, looking down. He could've skipped that part.

"But this woman I love," he continues, "she is brave. And despite all these things, she gave me a chance. She did not know if she loved me, if she could love me. That was okay."

I glance up, surprised to find the start of a smile on his lips.

"I asked her to let me love her, and she said yes." His face breaks into a wide grin, and I'd almost forgotten how mesmerizingly beautiful he is when he's this happy; it's been so long since I've seen it. "Now, I love her more than ever. Now, I can tell her. I can show her."

I can't help but smile, a blush dusting my cheeks. "You've shown me quite a bit."

"Maybe one day," he says, pulling me close enough to drop his forehead to mine, "she will love me too. Maybe not."

My heart sinks. "Massimo—"

"Remember," he cuts me off, "I love this woman for her fire." He pulls away, taking my hands and walking backward, leading us back toward where we started. "And for the good parts of me, I deserve her. I think I can be what she deserves," he says, turning to walk beside me. "I can be good to her. I can be strong for her. There are bad parts of her also." He squeezes my hand with a wink. "And I deserve that too. But I can walk through her fire and still live. I think this could work, for always."

Warmth melts through me, and I glance up at him. "Really?"

He nods. "For many years, I loved this woman before I told her. I will love her all the years after. But there is a problem."

No, no problems. I'm sick of problems. Back to loving me forever. The end.

"Because of her crash," he says, "when I thought she was dead, there is now a chance she will no longer race moto."

I wince, looking down at the footprints in the sand we made only a few minutes ago, not yet washed away. I don't want to think about that right now. I can't.

"She will leave and go home to America forever."

"Please stop," I whisper.

"Or maybe she will still race moto," he continues, "only now she will ride for Superbike, and when I am in one place, she will be in another. I do not know."

I try not to flinch, no idea how much he's put together surrounding my last-minute trip to test in Germany. Chiara said he was visibly upset when he found out I'd left. That he had wanted to come after me until she stopped him, like I asked her to do. She also said he'd apparently paid off Gabriele that night, which is where he'd been all day.

I'm not mad about it anymore, but I only got to the hotel barely an hour before tonight's gala, and we haven't had a chance to talk about any of it. Not that I'm sure I know what I'd say. I don't have any answers for him, only more possibilities that don't even guarantee we'd be able to stay together if the worst happens with Dabria.

Massimo doesn't ask if his suspicions are correct. He only takes a heavy breath, then says, "What she does not know is that now there is a chance that even if she keeps her moto and stays in MotoPro, I may lose my contract, and then, we will still be apart."

My heart crashes from my chest into the beach, and I whirl toward him. "What?"

There's no way I heard him right.

He's not in danger. I am.

And then, it just *clicks*.

"Yaalon." He swallows, the words thick like he's struggling to get them out. "They are angry with me for loving her, because to them, we are supposed to be enemies. Angelo thinks—he knows—I have wanted this woman to win more than I have wanted it for myself. And so he said to me: I am not to tell her anything about my moto. I am not to let her into places where our team names are different. He tells me I have to choose."

My head is reeling, and I just...I don't know why I didn't realize it sooner. Why he always catches me before I go into his garage, leading me the other way. Why he keeps cutting me off during races like he doesn't care who finishes before him, as long as it's not me.

Chiara was right. And I didn't listen.

My hands come up to cradle his jaw, my voice broken with fear for him. "Why didn't you tell me?" I whisper.

He scoffs like the suggestion is utterly ridiculous. "She had enough fear in her heart. She did not need to worry for me. And I know that if Yaalon could say these things to me, if they could make these threats, Dabria could make them to her. But I cannot be in the middle of this choice for this woman. I cannot be another threat. She *loves* moto, more than anything, and I have to make sure she has her dreams. I have to make sure that if she loses them, it is not because of me."

I have no air in my lungs. He...he pushed me away because he was trying to protect me? That's why he's been the way he's been? Avoiding me, abandoning me...

He's been making it look like we're not together. Not just for him but for me too.

As I search his eyes, I can't wrap my head around the mess of it all, all the wrong things he's done for all the right reasons. The decisions he made and the burden he put on himself without ever asking if it was necessary. If it was the choice I would've wanted him to make.

But he never asks. He just decides.

"So after years of battling," he continues, "making this woman angry and trying to prove who I am and finally telling her I love her, she is going to be taken away from me. And there is nothing I can do."

I pull my hands from him, because now, I get it. He's been pulling away from me because he made his decision. He chose racing over me. And the fact that he thinks I would've chosen the same for us... *God*, it hurts.

I turn and lengthen my strides away from him, ready to run anywhere this conversation, this reality, isn't happening. The things this means, what I'm going to have to do, and the places I'll have to go just to have a chance of one day getting over him.

I'll never be able to come back to Italy.

He's instantly behind me, grabbing the crook of my elbow and spinning me toward him. "My papà, he told me I would love this woman," he says, his grip desperate as his hands move to my shoulders. "He did not say she would love me back, and he did not say I would get to keep her. Just that I would love her."

I've got about three seconds to get out of here before I start bawling. I won't let him see me cry. Not tonight. Not ever again.

He ducks his head, catching my eyes in the darkness of moonlight as his hands slide up to cradle my jaw. "So I must be ready for when she leaves. I must decide what she will leave with knowing. And so to this woman, this woman I love more than anyone, I say this: If you love me, do not tell me. Not until the end."

The little bit of air I'd managed to hold onto bursts from me in a strangled sob, my emotions such a mess that I can't decide whether to be more shocked or heartbroken. "What?"

"Make my last day with you my best, and that way, I will have some small peace when you go."

My hands cover his wrists, but where mine are shaking, his are steady. More than a few tears slip down my cheeks when he kisses me: infinitely soft and full of longing for a future that we can't be sure will happen. Not with everyone trying to tear us apart.

Massimo pulls back slowly and leans his forehead to mine, and I have no idea what he's going to say next, but whatever it is, I can't take it. "I have not done as I should," he whispers. "I have been angry at others, angry at myself for what I have allowed to come between us, and because of this, she thinks I am going to leave her. It is not the truth."

I nearly break, hearing him say it when I've been so convinced that I'd lost him. I bite my lip to keep from dissolving even more, but my voice is still small when I ask, "No? Because if they're going to cut your contract because we're—"

"No." He shakes his head. "I will find a way to fix the contract. I do not know how, not yet, but I am going to keep looking. Leaving her? I will *never* do."

Everything in me melts and plummets, relief twisted with guilt, and I can't get a handle on it. How much I've missed him. How much he's willing to risk, possibly sacrifice for me. How much I want to tell him not to—not because the magnitude of it doesn't mean everything to me but because it's not what I want from him. What I want *for* him.

Wondering if because he's willing to do it, I'm supposed to be able to too.

"So to make sure she remembers how much I love her, even when I am my worst," he says, "to her, I give this."

My brow furrows, but then he lets me go and reaches up, unclasping the chain from around his neck. "Massimo, no..." But he doesn't listen. He takes off the necklace, then drapes it around my own neck, clasping it shut as my sight blurs with tears.

"This cross was given from my mamma to my papà on the day they were married. He told me, I was to give it to this woman when I found her."

I am locked completely in awe, filled with infinite pride as he adjusts the cross so it settles perfectly against my skin. When he's finished, he rests his hands on my hips, pulling me closer into him, and I don't care what it takes—I will find us a way through this.

"We may not always be together, Lorina," he says, "but if you have this, then I will know the truth. You are the woman I love, and this belongs to you."

I can't hug my arms around his neck tight enough. His own arms come around me, pressing so tight into my ribs that they ache where he watched them be broken. But his other hand is tender in my hair, massaging it gently as I tuck my face into his neck, breathing him in and succumbing to all the different flavors of him, soothing all the rough edges of me.

"For all the ways," he breathes, "all the times I have hurt you, I am sorry."

I choke back a sob, nodding because I'm sorry too. For just... everything.

"I only did what I thought was right, even as it was wrong, because I wanted for you to see me. I wanted you to feel safe when I told you—that you will know the man who loves you. Maybe not all of me that is good, Lorina, but all of me that is bad."

I pull back, cupping his face in my palms. "I see you," I promise. "All the good and all the bad, and knowing you are that man..." I suck in a steadying breath, unable to resist smiling from the unbridled truth flowing through me. "Nothing has ever made me feel safer than that. Than knowing you are him."

"I have missed you, cara." Then, more softly, as if it's a secret we're only allowed to share among the beach, the stars, and the moon, he breathes, "Ti amo."

THAILAND GRAND PRIX
Buriram, Sunday, October 06

Pos	Pts	Rider	Time	World Rank
1	25	Lorelai HARGROVE	39'55.722	188
2	20	Santos SAUCEDO	+0.115	270
3	16	Cristiano ARELLANO	+0.270	116
4	13	Billy KING	+1.564	272
5	11	Giovanni MARCHESA	+2.747	158
6	10	Gregorio PAREDES	+3.023	78
7	9	Rainier HERRE	+6.520	67
8	8	Mason KING	+6.691	151
9	7	Elliston LAMBIRTH	+9.944	56
10	6	Deven HORSLEY	+11.077	84
11	5	Donato MALDONADO	+15.488	56
12	4	Diarmaid DEAN	+17.691	36
13	3	Galeno GIRÓN	+21.413	65
14	2	Cesaro SOTO	+22.802	42
15	1	Harleigh ELIN	+23.628	58
16		Aurelio LOGGIA	+23.804	69
17		Fredek SULZBACH	+32.507	57
18		Timo GONZALES	+37.216	32
Not Classified				
		Gustavo LIMÓN	5 Laps	32
		Massimo VITOLO	10 Laps	218

GRAND PRIX OF JAPAN
Motegi, Sunday, October 20

Pos	Pts	Rider	Time	World Rank
1	25	Lorelai HARGROVE	42'20.989	213
2	20	Santos SAUCEDO	+5.862	290
3	16	Billy KING	+8.987	288
4	13	Giovanni MARCHESA	+9.796	171
5	11	Massimo VITOLO	+11.048	229
6	10	Aurelio LOGGIA	+14.534	79
7	9	Mason KING	+17.202	160
8	8	Timo GONZALES	+22.273	40
9	7	Cesaro SOTO	+27.641	49
10	6	Donato MALDONADO	+31.998	62
11	5	Elliston LAMBIRTH	+38.572	61
12	4	Deven HORSLEY	+49.603	88
13	3	Cristiano ARELLANO	+57.128	119
14	2	Fredek SULZBACH	+1'06.673	59
15	1	Galeno GIRÓN	+1'27.081	66
16		Gregorio PAREDES	+1'45.854	78
17		Harleigh ELIN	+1'54.159	58
Not Classified				
		Rainier HERRE	1 Lap	67
		Gustavo LIMÓN	1 Lap	32
		Diarmaid DEAN	22 Laps	36

AUSTRALIAN MOTORCYCLE GRAND PRIX
Phillip Island, Sunday, October 27

Pos	Pts	Rider	Time	World Rank
1	25	Billy KING	40'44.798	313
2	20	Lorelai HARGROVE	+2.194	233
3	16	Santos SAUCEDO	+3.601	306
4	13	Massimo VITOLO	+7.645	242
5	11	Giovanni MARCHESA	+11.009	182
6	10	Mason KING	+15.732	170
7	9	Cristiano ARELLANO	+19.571	128
8	8	Deven HORSLEY	+24.285	96
9	7	Cesaro SOTO	+30.668	56
10	6	Galeno GIRÓN	+36.910	72
11	5	Diarmaid DEAN	+43.476	41
12	4	Harleigh ELIN	+49.351	62
13	3	Gustavo LIMÓN	+57.299	35
14	2	Timo GONZALES	+1'06.752	42
15	1	Donato MALDONADO	+1'12.833	63
Not Classified				
		Rainier HERRE	3 Laps	67
		Elliston LAMBIRTH	9 Laps	61
		Fredek SULZBACH	12 Laps	59
		Gregorio PAREDES	15 Laps	78
		Aurelio LOGGIA	22 Laps	79

MALAYSIA MOTORCYCLE GRAND PRIX
Sepang, Sunday, November 03

Pos	Pts	Rider	Time	World Rank
1	25	Lorelai HARGROVE	40'39.984	258
2	20	Billy KING	+1.502	333
3	16	Massimo VITOLO	+4.104	258
4	13	Giovanni MARCHESA	+8.263	195
5	11	Santos SAUCEDO	+13.979	317
6	10	Rainier HERRE	+21.041	77
7	9	Elliston LAMBIRTH	+24.822	70
8	8	Donato MALDONADO	+28.431	71
9	7	Galeno GIRÓN	+39.616	79
10	6	Cesaro SOTO	+44.094	62
11	5	Deven HORSLEY	+52.713	101
12	4	Cristiano ARELLANO	+1'09.446	132
13	3	Mason KING	+1'27.897	173
14	2	Fredek SULZBACH	+1'46.521	61
15	1	Harleigh ELIN	+1'53.729	63
Not Classified				
		Gregorio PAREDES	3 Laps	78
		Gustavo LIMÓN	7 Laps	35
		Aurelio LOGGIA	15 Laps	79
		Timo GONZALES	16 Laps	42
Not Finished First Lap				
		Diarmaid DEAN	0 Lap	41

Chapter 23

Massimo Vitolo—November; Valencia, Spain

LORINA YAWNS ON MY SHOULDER FOR THE THIRD TIME AS I TOY with the room key in my hand, watching the numbers go by too slowly as the lift climbs. Asia was brutally exhausting—bouncing from Thailand to Japan to Australia and back to Malaysia before we booked it to Memphis for an early Thanksgiving with her parents. Which went very, *very* well, as far as I'm concerned.

I have officially been green-lit.

I cross one ankle over the other, dropping a kiss to her hair. "So you think Frank and Vinicio are going to go to dinner?" I ask just to keep her awake. I'm too tired to carry her plus our bags to the room; she's gonna have to walk tonight. Lorina shrugs. "What do you think they talk about when they are alone, hmm?"

She groans and rolls off my shoulder, propping one foot on the wall behind her. "Probably scheduling. Or food. Maybe comparing our financial value as racers."

"Interessante," I drawl as the lift comes to a stop, waiting for Lorina to head out into the corridor before me. "How much do you think I can trade Dabria to keep you? I think maybe four goats is sufficiente."

She narrows her eyes my direction. "Four? Four goats?"

"Sì, quattro," I tell her. "You cannot be very smart."

"Excuse me?"

"You misspell your own nickname. Reckless is supposed to be with an *R*, not a *W*."

Lorina rolls her eyes, yawning again as she says into her palm, "It's a pun, genius."

I stop in front of the room, attempting to unlock the door. "Bene. But we were not even together, and you let me cut your hair in a bathroom."

She sighs, stealing the room card from me and swiping it when I can't get it to make the green light. "That was stupid." She gets it open on her second try.

"Maybe I think you are worth five goats," I say, Lorina ducking under my arm as I hold open the door. "You are the fastest woman alive on a moto."

"Fastest woman, yes." She heads straight for the bathroom, flipping on the light. She's already got the sink running to wash her hands by the time I'm unzipping her backpack and taking out Tigrotta, tossing her up by the pillows on the bed. "As for the fastest racer, I'm still tied for third place."

I nod to myself as I pull out clean clothes for her to sleep in, then unfold my hanging bag, putting away my dress shirts, emergency tux, and Lorina's sundresses that she's taken to packing in my bag instead of folding in her duffel.

She's tied for third place behind Billy King. And so am I. Meaning if she's going to make the podium for World Champion and keep her contract with Dabria, she has to beat me at Valencia. And with Angelo more pissed off than ever that I'm still refusing to break up with Lorina, I can't afford to lose.

I absolutely won't lose her, and I'm prepared to do whatever's necessary to make sure we survive. I always will, and I'm ready. I think she is too. Her mom says she is.

We'll see.

"Third?" I repeat, pretending to be shocked as I unpack the last of our stuff. We'll be in this hotel for a week before we transition to the paddock, and I refuse to live in wrinkled clothes I'm digging out of bags. "You are tied for third place behind the leader?"

"Mm-hmm." The sink shuts off. "But that's gotta be worth something, right?"

I grab our bags of toiletries, then head into the bathroom, stopping behind her. "In that case," I drawl, setting the bags on the counter, "maybe I will pay to keep you: three goats."

Lorina gives me a look in the mirror that might have worked if I hadn't been raised Catholic. Instead, I shrug off the guilt trip with a smile, hugging my arm over her chest and dropping my chin to her shoulder.

"So angry," I tease in Italian. "What are you going to do, Tigrotta? Make me sleep on the floor?"

She grabs her toiletry bag and digs through it, but she has a hard time hiding the smile in her voice as she responds in country-twanged Italian. "That was once, and I...um"—she wrinkles her nose as she concentrates, conjugating under her breath before she says—"I slept on the floor, not you."

"Nope. I slept on the floor *with* you."

Lorina pauses, her head turning toward me. "Really?" she says in English.

"For a little bit. Then I realized it was ridiculous, and I took you back to bed."

Lorina laughs as I drop a kiss on her neck, then let her go so I can turn on the shower.

"That reminds me..." She massages into her hands something that smells a little bit like lemon and a lot like home. "Chiara called while you were asleep in wherever we were when we missed our connection. She says hi, everything is good with her new waitressing job, but the pipes in the bathroom are making that chewing, gurgling sound again."

"Bene," I say, but it's more of a sigh than anything else. "Tell her I will call someone domani." I ditch my shirt on the floor, debating. I hate paying people to fix stuff I can do myself. "Actually, she can live with it for another week. Tell her I will take care of it when we go home to Ravenna."

"Like hell she has to live with that." Lorina tucks her bottle of lotion into her bag. "I'll call the plumber."

I wrinkle my nose mockingly, then start unbuckling my belt. Lorina doesn't know it yet, but I'm taking her to see the house next week. I've got an appointment with the real estate agent to meet us out there. I'm gonna take her for a ride, and we're going. My mother is so thrilled at the prospect that she's turned no less than six corners overnight, and she's already asked Lorina to have lunch with her when we get back to Ravenna. Lorina thinks she's planning a hit on her.

But we need a place that's just for us when we come home, and she deserves a space that's hers. Totally and completely hers. It's time—way past time—and her parents agreed with me from top to bottom about the whole thing, so that's that.

The only problem I foresee with any of this, besides Lorina being difficult for the sake of being difficult, is whatever happened in Germany. We've talked about everything else since then—Gabriele, my past with Chiara, my subsequent arrest record, hiding her helmet and swearing I'll never make decisions like that again—*everything*. But when I asked why she went to Munich, all she said was that it was a test. That when she knew something, I'd know something.

She's testing me all right.

Lorina clears her throat. "I also gave Mason's phone number to Chiara."

I lose my balance while stepping out of my jeans, having to catch myself on the wall.

Lorina stares at me. "Wow. Overprotective much?"

I fling my traitorous jeans out of the bathroom. "Do not start. You know I do not care who she dates. But Mason King is an ass."

"Thank you for proving my point. And no, he's not." Lorina leans against the counter, crossing her arms. "He's usually really nice, and kinda goofy. Besides, he likes her, and she likes him, and they like all the same stuff…"

I wave my hand, at a loss for words. "Disgusting."

I really don't care who Chiara is with, as long as it's someone not just after her ass and who will actually support her so she can do all the weird stuff she wants to do. She's been through enough crap for more than one lifetime, and just as Lorina deserves to have her moto career without being threatened every five seconds, Chiara should get what she wants—the one thing I could never give her.

But *not* with Mason King.

"I don't know why you have to be so against this," Lorina says. "Chiara really likes him."

I chuckle off the rest of the argument I already know I'm not gonna win, testing the temperature of the water in the shower. "Bene. When am I supposed to start sleeping on the floor, cara?"

"We…" She pulls her phone out of her pocket, sighing. "Can't go to sleep for at least two hours or we're gonna be screwed by jet lag." She tosses her phone on the counter. "Wanna raid the minibar and play Never Have I Ever until one of us passes out?" She flashes me a tight smirk before she starts to stomp out of the bathroom, but I catch her quick.

"No," I drawl, hugging my arms around her. "You are going to take a shower with me."

She lets me turn her back into the bathroom but still grumbles under her breath, "Why? So you can steal all the hot water and make me stand in the back where it's cold?"

"Not tonight," I promise. "Tonight, you can have as much hot water as you like."

Lorina stops, turning to face me. "You're officially starting to worry me. What did you do?"

I sneak my fingertips under the hem of her shirt, skimming her stomach. "Niente." Once her shirt falls to the floor, I shift my weight, my mouth twisting with guilt as I start to undo the button on her jeans. "But maybe I got Tigrotta's tail stuck in the zip when I closed your backpack this morning."

"Oh," she drawls, but there's a hint of a chuckle in there. "So that's what's going on."

"Mm-hmm." I smooth the denim over her hips, snagging the cotton of her panties on my way past and bringing them along for the ride down her thighs.

After she steps out of her jeans, I leave a kiss on her bare stomach, hugging my arms around her waist for a moment, because it still hits me sometimes: how dangerously close I came to losing her. How lucky I am that she forgave me and let us try again.

Lorina draws her nails through my hair, and I squeeze her once more before I rise, tickling my fingertips over her waist and around to her back, undoing the clasp on her bra. I only let myself kiss her twice before I take her hand and escort her into the shower, letting her have the first of the hot water—as I promised—while I get rid of my boxer briefs as fast as humanly freaking possible.

When I join her a second later, all I want to know is the glint of sparkle from my father's chain around her neck, to revel in the sweet slip of her skin against mine. But when I sweep her hair to the side, kissing each little space between her neck and shoulders, all I feel is tension in her muscles.

I don't know if there's a way to calm her down about the coming race, but I'm gonna give it my best shot. She needs to sleep tonight, and she said we have to wait two hours...

"So much stress, Tigrotta," I whisper as I squeeze the tops of her arms, her body melting against mine. She hums something I can't make out as I massage my way down to her wrists, then gather enough soap that my palms glide easily over the planes of her stomach, across the curves of her hips, and up to the gentle weight of her breasts. She's so goddamn sexy, and my fingertips happily follow the trail of soapy water dripping down to the top of her thigh, then daring farther inside where she's soft and smooth and deliciously silky.

Lorina giggles as I tickle a little closer to my goal, but it melts into a moan when I get my first taste of her heat on my fingers, my lips trailing across her shoulder and unable to resist kissing every delicious inch of her.

Her arm comes back, her nails combing through my hair, and with only a warning nip to her shoulder, I sink a long finger into her. Once, then twice, Lorina moaning deeply and hugging my knuckles below, and *Christ*, she feels so good.

Fuck it—I need her.

I nip at her shoulder again, then bite her hard enough that I owe her a kiss for it. But she's soft and compliant as I turn us around, my hand cupping her thigh and guiding her legs apart so she rests her foot on the edge of the tub. My lovely Lorina simply smiles over her shoulder and stretches her arms up the back wall of the shower, arching a little more for me.

God, I love this woman.

I take a minute just to enjoy the view of her wet and dripping with water, running my palms down her sides, her back, over the curves of her ass and up to her breasts. But Lorina is impatient and tilts her ass back against me, the head of my cock slipping to where she's silky and ready, and it knows exactly how to find the sweetest part of her.

I hug my arm around her chest, nuzzling a kiss onto her neck. "Ti amo," I whisper.

She covers my arm with hers.

I drive into her fast, slamming into her hard and harder as she gasps in pleasure, her hands failing to find purchase on the wet shower wall, but I've got her.

I fist my hand in her hair and tug her head back, biting kisses onto her neck as she claims me even tighter inside, and I tweak her nipple and push my palm down her stomach, below her hips and between her legs, cupping her clit and my fingers ready to claim their finish.

It doesn't take me long to craft her orgasm, her body trembling more with every tighter circle I draw around her clit, fucking her rougher as her moans and gasps swirl around me until I've got her there and she breaks—wave after wave, pulse after pulse, tighter and stronger as I push her to ride it longer, fearlessly. Recklessly.

It's over too soon. She's up and down, already waving me off and leaning against the wall for support. I pull out and turn her toward me, kissing the hell out of her with everything I've got, with everything I feel. I don't stop until she's breathing hard but is soft in my arms, her leg drawing easily over my hip so I can rest her foot on the edge of the tub once again.

I've got other tricks up my sleeve.

"Massimo?"

I pause instantly at the worry in her voice, at the fear in my Tigrotta who claims to be fearless, and I hold her body a little more securely in my hands as I look at her. I already know: whatever this is, it has nothing to do with me and everything to do with what's being done to us.

She strokes her thumb over my cheek, her palm shivering against my jaw as she tightens her other arm around my neck, hugging herself tighter to me. "Tell me it's going to be okay."

Her voice is the kind of private she rarely uses even when we're this alone, and my forehead falls against hers, the water of the shower raining brutally down.

The words are right there. The promise that I'll do everything I can to make sure all her decisions in life will be simple and that she has everything she's ever dreamed of having. But this isn't the moment, and even though I wish I could, I can't promise her those things.

I can't promise that after Valencia, she's going to keep her contract or that I'm going to keep mine. All I know is that I love her. I've always loved *her*, and so I do the only thing I can. I kiss her and hope that when I try to fix it, she's finally going to let me.

Eleven times I've asked her, and she's never said yes.

Chapter 24

Lorelai Hargrove—November; Valencia, Spain

My legs tingle with the climb up the empty Valencia stadium, the sun setting at my back and the note he left for me to meet him folded safely in my pocket. I don't know what this is about when our schedule has been packed with prerace prep every minute of every day, and it's all coming down to tomorrow. The final race that determines everything about where we're going to spend the next years of our lives.

But there Massimo is: sitting on the very top row of the grandstands, eating ice cream out of a cup like he's got all the time in the world.

"Been waiting long?" I ask once I stop beside him. He shrugs. I step onto the bench in front of him, hopping down on the opposite side of his legs before I sit. He doesn't say anything, just continuing to rest his elbows on his knees and swirling the ice cream with the tip of his spoon.

Blowing out a breath, I look forward, pressing my hands between my knees. The wind lazily ruffles the long strands of my hair, cool against my freshly shaved undercut. I have to admit, there's so much peace to be found in the silence of a place that's normally a sea of colors and overlapping chants, typically more explosive than a rock concert.

"It's nice up here," I tell him, bumping his shoulder with mine. "The track all quiet and deserted."

He takes another bite, not looking at me.

"So…" I drawl, searching for an icebreaker. I glance over at his ice cream, and I smile to myself. Vanilla. He prefers chocolate. I do too—too much. "You really went all the way to Ravenna and back for some authentic gelato? That's a pretty fast trip, even for you."

"I went to pick up my suit and your dress from the tailor."

Endless affection warms me. I forgot we were supposed to do that today.

After we got to Spain and caught up on some z's, we had a shopping trip to make. The end of season award ceremony is always held Sunday night after the final race, where medals and trophies galore are handed out for everything from most poles won to crowning the official World Champions. I usually pick up a dress somewhere in the last few stops before getting to Valencia, but I'd been so distracted with the points and placements and enjoying the hell out of Massimo, I forgot. He didn't, and so to Carrer de la Pau we went—the upscale boutique strip in downtown Valencia.

We had way too much fun bickering at Hugo Boss and Michael Kors, embarrassing sales people while we battled over blue suits versus black, dresses that were (in my opinion) too sexy and, according to him, not sexy enough. But we came away with a suit that would crush James Bond's ego if he laid eyes on Massimo and a creamy Chantilly lace cocktail dress that I want to be buried in. Even if Massimo had a heart attack when he peeked at my credit card receipt, I don't care. It could be my last awards ceremony with Moto Grand Prix, and I wanted to feel good.

"Thanks for doing that," I tell him, and he nods.

"Dress looks good. Cannot tell they changed it."

I smile to myself as he takes another bite of his ice cream, not even sure he'd know what to look for but loving that he checked.

"You know you have to wear your Tissot watch from winning the first pole," he says.

"Yeah." Standard procedure.

"Also, the top of your dress is too high for a necklace, so I got you some earrings."

God, could he be any sweeter? "You didn't have to do that."

He shrugs, then pulls a small box from his pocket and hands it to me. More than a little curious about the design and style he chose—the man has exquisite taste—I open the box. All the air in the universe rushes into my lungs, and I immediately snap it shut, frozen as blood drains from my face.

Massimo glances at the box, then at my eyes before looking forward once more. He sets the ice cream cup on the bench, his hands lacing together. "Stay with me," he says. "Even if you do not race moto, even if I do not, we would still be together. It will…" His jaw locks, barely getting out the words, "I will make this okay."

Tears blur my vision, but it's not enough to erase the sight of him blinking more than normal as his gaze drops to the bench in front of us. I clench the box in my hand, everything in me breaking when he tries to cover a sniffle by clearing his throat.

Never once has he been anything but calm about the possibility of me losing my contract. Never once has he let it slip that it's worrying him or that he's upset about it. But this box, his silent tears he won't let fall, they say everything.

How scared he is.

How hard he'll fight.

How much pain he's been keeping from me.

"Massimo…" I breathe, but it's so choked, I don't know if he even hears me.

"I love you," he says fiercely, his eyes snapping to mine. "And if Angelo allows me to stay, I will not let him tell us we cannot be together. He cannot keep us apart if we are married, Lorina, and I could quit moto to follow you home, yes, but I cannot do that. I have to race. It is everything that makes me the man you are with, but if I stay... I do not want to do this with you gone. I do not know how to win when you are not here, making me crazy. I just—" He blows out a breath. "I want you to have what you want, but you are what I want. So stay, Lorina. Stay with me."

I cup his cheek with my free hand, trying to get him to calm down. "Listen to me." My voice is slow as I bring him forward until I can lean my forehead to his. "You are going to be fine. You're the best racer I've ever seen, and I'm so proud of you." I pause to pull in a shaky breath, but my voice is still raw. "And even if Angelo changes or backs out of your contract, someone else is always going to sign you. The things you can do? It's only right that the whole world knows your name."

Massimo's hand covers mine. "What good is the world knowing my name when you are not here to say it?"

More tears stream down my cheeks. Especially when I make myself place the box back in his palm, then cover it with mine, our fingers lacing together around it. "I don't want to lose you," I promise. "It hurts so much, I can't even describe it. And I know you're hurting too, but this...this isn't the answer. As much as I wish it could be, it just isn't."

He exhales, his voice unsteady when he asks, "No?"

"No."

He grits out a curse, looking away.

I bring him right back to me, my thumb sweeping over his cheek and catching a trail of moisture that absolutely wrecks me. "Hey." My voice is broken—so, so broken. "Only because there are things that have to be fixed, things we need to talk about first. Things you need to let me say."

Like how I can't dare tell him that I know what he's really doing. Because I have no doubt that in his mind, not only would this keep us together if we both stay on the circuit—no way will Angelo be able to stipulate Massimo stay away from his wife—but it's also a safety net for me in case I lose my contract with Dabria. Something to make me happy enough to forget all I've lost.

But I didn't start dating him as an escape to my problems on the track, and I won't marry him as a way to avoid the conditions in his contract, as a consolation prize to losing my ride. The future of our relationship should have nothing to do with racing, and this is exactly why I haven't told him about Germany. Right now, it's too tied up to say yes.

And yet there is already a part of me secretly praying that one day soon, he'll ask again. I have to say no to him today—I *have* to until he's asking for the right reasons and not out of fear—but it doesn't change the fact that the idea of spending my life with him is so *right*, I'm barely resisting giving him the answer that's always lived in my heart.

Massimo sighs, then tries to smile, but it's all wrecked and wrong. "Why do you always have to be so difficult?"

Shaking my head, I force my own smile through my tears. "I don't know," I breathe. "But I blame your dad."

He lifts the softest kiss from my lips I've ever felt. It doesn't help the pain, the thousand apologies I wish I could tell him for failing to see him sooner. But it helps, just a little, that it's not over yet. That *we're* not over yet, even after this.

He turns forward, scrubbing a hand over his face and putting the box in his pocket. Then he picks up the ice cream cup.

I hug his arm, leaning my head against his shoulder as he takes a bite. Swiping my fingertips under my eyes, I listen to the silence of the track.

It's too quiet.

I bump against him a little. "You could at least offer me some." He holds out the spoon to me, and it's cool and soothing, the vanilla rich on my tongue. "Holy crap, that's good."

"Mm-hmm."

He takes another bite, and I snuggle a little closer. The sun is dropping lower and lower, turning the sky the sweetest mix of orange and purple. "Massimo?"

"Hmm?"

"Did you really just propose to me, and I said no?"

He takes another bite of ice cream. "Sì."

I bite my bottom lip, then I peek at him. "Can I see the ring again?"

He reaches into his pocket. Low in front of us, he pops the box open with one hand. I sigh longingly at the sleek platinum band and the pear-shaped diamond, the widest part of the stone racing away from the pointed end.

Massimo snaps the box shut, putting it back in his pocket.

"Hey!"

He offers me another bite of ice cream. "You said no."

I sputter, my mouth full. "It was the right thing to do!" His eyes dart to mine. "Well, what are you going to do with it?"

He scoffs. "I am going to take it back. You know how many euro I paid for this? Too much." My nose wrinkles as Massimo holds the spoon out to me once more, a grin growing in the corner of his mouth. I'm just wrapping my lips around the spoon when he adds, "Too bad I have to take it back. It would have gone perfect with your dress."

"Ugh," I groan, my head falling against his shoulder. He's

absolutely right—with the creamy lace and my Jimmy Choos? "I'm
so freaking stupid."

   "I told you," he says, "three goats."

Chapter 25

Massimo Vitolo—November; Valencia, Spain

THE SKY IS GRAY, LIKE THE WEATHER IS SICK TO ITS STOMACH WITH nerves, just like the rest of us. My eyes travel over the commotion down pit lane, people scurrying around in preparation, but I don't see Lorina anywhere. *Damn it.*

This could be it. The last race I ever ride, the last race she ever rides, and I don't want to go out there without seeing her first. I just don't.

Still can't believe she said no.

I head into my garage, grabbing my gloves and yanking them on, then picking up arguably the most important part of my gear. A smile pulls at the corner of my lips as I tug on my helmet and clasp the buckle, my crew rolling out my moto for me.

Swinging my leg over, I let the vibration touch every part of me when it starts. It growls and rumbles, eager to take the win, and both my stomach and my height drop as Lucio pulls out my tire stand, Vinicio nodding at me.

As calm as possible, I pull out and cruise down pit lane behind Lorina. The crowd explodes when sunlight settles on my shoulders; thousands of people are on their feet, screaming and jumping up and down. She flips up the face shield on her new helmet and smiles back at me. Instead of her standard American flag on top, there are four wide, diagonal claw marks, her country's flag waving out from behind them.

The design I whispered to her constructor came out nothing short of badass, and I wonder what she thought when she saw it. She looks forward and tests a controlled lean to the left, then to the right, and I do the same: my moto obeying my every command like it was its idea first.

We come to a stop on the white lines, and Lorina doesn't have pole position, because I do. I glance at her, and she gives me a thumbs-up. I don't look any farther behind us, where Billy is in third, Santos is in fourth, and Mason is starting in fifth. We're about to see them in every turn, every push for more speed in the straightaways over the next forty-seven minutes, broken down into twenty-seven laps that blur by in just over a minute and a half.

It's going to be the longest, fastest race of my life.

Vinicio and my crew jog to my side, propping up my back tire and doing one final check over my moto while some girl in a Motul outfit appears with an umbrella. I peer past swarms of people in different colored sponsor T-shirts, and I finally see Lorina's manager holding up her mobile phone and her earbuds. She waves him off. I don't know how she'd hear music right now anyway, not with 150,000 fanatical Spaniards in the stands chanting "Wreckless."

"You need earplugs," Vinicio tells me in Italian.

I roll my eyes at myself. I've got to get my head in the damn game. I unsnap my helmet and lift it off, leaning past Lucio to take the small foam earplugs from Vinicio's hand. A drop of water hits my cheek. I straighten and wave off the Motul girl, looking to the sky. The clouds are churning, their color darkening.

Oh shit.

"It's going to rain," I tell Vinicio. "I need to be on wets. Now."

If I start on wet tires, I'll be fine through the rain and I won't have to pit to change motos. My slicks don't have enough traction for the water, the rain cooling the rubber so they're not as sticky. But if I go on wets and it stays dry, I'm screwed. I won't be able to get enough speed to win. And I have to win, according to my last conversation with Angelo.

Vinicio shakes his head. "The storm won't break until an hour after you're done. You're fine."

My crew chief appears beside him, nodding. "We're going on slicks. It's still declared a dry race."

I glance around, and he's right: everyone else is still on slicks. No one is changing—not Santos, not Giovanni, not even Billy. Lorina definitely isn't switching, but I'm not surprised after how many times she's won off the gamble of using slick tires in the rain. I blow out a breath, left with no choice but to put in my earplugs and slide on my helmet.

My ass drops as someone pulls out my stand, the rest of my crew and Vinicio all clapping my shoulder before they exit the track with everyone else. My eyes search the sky, and I lift up my face shield to see if I feel any more drops. Nothing but wind.

I flip it down, cameras on cranes rising from where they were swooping low over the track in front of us. I check on Lorina, and she's smoothing her hands over her fairings, probably praying, like she always does.

I check forward in time to see the green flag being walked off the track, the lights on the clock tower counting down to the practice lap. Then the green lights are out. Go.

My toes push off the ground as I shift from first gear up to sixth, the transmission growling hungrily with every drop of my heel. I cruise smoothly with no one in front of me, feeling the flex in the fairings and the torque in the throttle, and it's all perfect.

Ducking low, I test the traction in the small straight between turns six and seven, and I can feel every bump and ripple in the track. The brakes bite in the sharp swings between eight, nine, ten, and eleven, and the moto is flawless. Like an extension of my body. And my body feels *fast*.

Tight corner of turn twelve, long half-circle of thirteen.

It's there that I hear the crack of thunder.

It snaps loud and close, and after the hard left of turn fourteen, my eyes dart up to the sky. It's not going to hold. I glance around for an exit, but I'm too far past the pit lane entrance, and I've got nineteen riders behind me, all slowing but still going too fast for me to turn around.

"Fuck!" I yell in my helmet, stopping on the white line.

I lift up my face shield, and yep, I definitely just felt water. I slam it down. We need to switch. It's too dangerous to stay on slicks, no matter what Lorina thinks. I may have sworn after Rimini that I'd stop trying to protect her from herself, but she made promises too: that she'd try to be more careful about what risks she took and when she took them. And while I'm perfectly okay with the fact that my girlfriend races at deathly speeds, I'm not going to applaud her if she decides to race without her helmet or if she doesn't use the right tires.

"Lorina!" I shout with everything in me. Her helmet turns my direction. "It is going to rain!"

"Massimo, what are you doing, man?" Billy yells behind me. "Whose team are you on?"

I don't respond. Let him tell Angelo about what I just did. Her safety is more important than any contract.

Lorina looks up, flips up her face shield. But she doesn't flinch, doesn't jolt. She doesn't feel it. *Christ*, please let her believe me. For all I know, she could think I'm lying to her and it's a ploy to slow her down so I can assure my own win.

It would be a brilliant play, and yeah, I want the win, but not at the expense of making her crash. I'm still holding out hope that there can be some kind of life for us together after the crowd forgets our names and our motos are given to those who are younger, faster. But we can't have that life if we die.

"Frank!" she screams toward the fence line. A relief I've never felt takes my veins, and I sink back a little on my seat, finally able to start breathing again—*she believes me.* But I have no idea if her manager can hear her over the roar of the idling engines on the track. Not to mention the league of raging fans still chanting her name. "Frank!"

He finally straightens, cupping his hand behind his ear.

"Get the wets ready!" she shouts, but he shakes her off like he can't hear her. "Get the wets!"

"Shut up, Lorelai!" someone behind us yells. I think it was Santos.

"Get the wets!" she screams again, and I check the clock tower. The red lights are still lit. My pulse is hammering like it can feel the call to fly, and I look to Lorina. She's leaning forward and patting her tires, then pointing to the sky. Frank's head jerks upward, then he gives her a thumbs-up before slapping his palm on his wrist—needing to know when she's going to pit. She shoves her fist into the air, lassos once, then punches again.

One lap.

I see him curse, then slash through the air before hitting his wrist. No time.

"Stop arguing with me and get her ready!" she screams. He takes off toward her garage, and I look to the clock tower.

The red lights disappear, and I charge off the white line, opening my throttle and shifting up as fast as possible. Lorina somehow cuts in front of me, taking the hole-shot—first place in the first turn.

"Damn it!" I curse, trying to find a way to pass her, but she's as ruthless as ever.

Engines growl behind us, pushing us, and I don't look back. I need to find a way around her. I need to make this lap the fastest I've ever run, because if no one else pits and I do, I'll lose so much time that winning is straight out the window.

I take my engine to the limit in the sharp switchback of turn two, pushing hard and then harder through three, four, five, and six. I'm so low over the handlebars in the straight from six to seven, the vibration into my chest makes my teeth chatter, and the whole time, I'm praying.

Praying my crew gets the wets out of the warmers and onto my second moto in time for us to switch. Praying it'll be out of the garage when we pull in. Praying I didn't just make a huge mistake that is going to cost me everything.

I lean hard to the left in turn eight, another slight left to nine and a nudge to the right for ten. Lorina doesn't give me an inch, still dead ahead. She doesn't look back at me, though, and I swing through eleven and barrel toward twelve, glancing up at the sky in the straightaway. It's not raining. My face shield is clear, the track dry, and I don't know what to—

Hard right in twelve. Long swing left of thirteen. By the time I downshift for fourteen, I still don't know what to do. I can bypass the pit and keep going on slicks, but I don't know if Lorina is going to pit. She's stubborn and dangerous, and it could be she only called out to Frank because she was banking on the fact that acting like she was going to switch would send me into the garages after her. But then she won't at the last minute, and I'll be screwed.

It's a strategy right up her alley—to send me back in the lineup and assure she's got a clear hold on first place. We can't trust each other when we're racing, because we both live to win and...*fuck*.

I pull out of turn fourteen, Lorina's second moto set out in front of her garage, but mine isn't. Because I didn't tell Vinicio to get mine out—I only told Lorina.

Son of a bitch. I didn't stay focused on winning; I was only focused on her.

I don't have a choice. I stay on the track as Lorina pulls off into pit lane, people jumping out of the way to clear a path as she flies down it.

Fifth gear. Sixth. My heartbeat rises to meet my redline—I'm in first.

I look for her. She waits until the last possible moment, then slams the brakes so hard, her back tire lifts up as her front tire locks to a halt.

Check my speedometer. Downshift. Throw a look at the garages. People are screaming at her as she hops from one moto to the other. It's still not raining, and with every second, people are passing by where she's stuck, absolutely still.

Turn one. Hard lean to the left, fourth gear, fifth, six. Transmissions growl behind me, but they can't catch me. My moto is perfect, and I own Valencia. I always do.

Wait until the last moment, then drop all the way into first gear, nearly flat on my side through the left turn. Gravel wants me, pavement reaching up to grab me, but it will never taste my skin. I will take the podium here, then a second tonight, my name on a list that declares me a World Champion.

I punch it when I come out, everyone else already falling behind, and Lorina swerves back onto the track. Pull to the right in turn three, and she leans hard to the left in turn one—all the way back in twentieth place.

It's done.

I'm going to win, but there's more than a good chance Lorina is going to lose her contract. It's going to hurt like hell, but I don't care who she ends up racing for, whether it's MotoPro or Superbike. If Billy and Taryn can figure this out, then so can we, and I'm not going to stop trying to convince her that just because we're not racing together anymore, it doesn't mean we can't take the next steps forward.

Some things just are, and Lorina and I…

Third gear. I don't know how to stop fighting.

Fourth. Not with her.

Fifth. Definitely not for her, over what I'm allowed to call her.

Sixth gear. She has always been my win, and I'm not fucking losing.

Chapter 26

Lorelai Hargrove—November; Valencia, Spain

MY BREATH ECHOES IN MY EARS AS I LEAN THROUGH TURN SEVEN, the fans in the stands hopping to their feet as I fly past. They're decked out in ponchos and doing their best to shield themselves with umbrellas, but it doesn't stop them from cheering when we come around.

I narrow my eyes in my helmet, squinting through the rain splattered across my face shield. The sky didn't fully open up until lap eighteen, and everyone headed for the pits to switch to wets. Everyone except me and Massimo, who pitted in lap two. Until he did, I was horrified that maybe he had done it on purpose. Scared me into changing bikes to secure his win and keep his contract. But I saw him make the change the second his bike had been rolled out, and I'm trying to let it go.

He loves me. He wouldn't do that.

At least I had managed to make up some ground before the rest of the riders ducked off, managing twelfth place. The belated blessing of their pit stops wasn't enough to put me into first or even second place, though. The pack came back onto the track, and I slipped into ninth.

Twenty-four laps down, three to go, and I'm *tired*. Water is soaked into my leathers, shivers chattering my teeth, and it's nearly impossible to see with the spray from tires hitting my face shield.

Leaning hard to the left through turn eight, I'm once again staring at the blue fairings of Gregorio Paredes from Spain. He straightens and wobbles, and panic strikes me in my chest. If he falls, I'm too close to dodge him.

I downshift to steal RPMs, opening the throttle to blur past Gregorio before dropping to the left for turn nine. The speed is too much with the water on the track. My back tire skids. I suck in a breath and shift up a gear to level out, pulling it vertical to control the wobble before leaning into the right of ten.

Jesus, that was close.

My heart is pounding in my chest, but I check to make sure Gregorio is okay. He's fine. Looking forward, I focus on the curves ahead, blinking rapidly.

"You're okay," I tell myself. "You're okay. Just breathe…"

Flying down the straightaway, I check the tower. Two laps. I can do this.

I open the throttle, my speedometer topping at 211 while Massimo, Mason, then Cristiano bank into turn one in front of me, Billy and Santos already into turn four. I downshift just as the three guys in front of me are coming out of it, and I can't be more than three seconds behind them. Probably closer to two.

Giving it everything I've got, I wait to brake until the last possible second through turns two, three, and four. My front tire is inches behind Cristiano's as we head into turn five. Ducking into his slipstream, I wait for my moment.

One heartbeat, two, then I charge. Pop from third gear to second without backing off the throttle, RPMs screaming as I careen around him on the right, then shift into third and lie deep for turn six, my knee scraping the track. An inner roar cheers me on at passing him, not at all dampened by the rain still kicking up into my face shield from Mason's back tire.

I inch as close as I can, trying to gain on my Dabria teammate through the straight before turn seven.

I can't get there. He's slipstreaming Massimo, and he's blocking me.

Seven through fourteen, he never gives an inch. Every time I shift left, he does the same. I feign right, and he doesn't fall for it. The finish line holds no escape as we fly past, counting one lap to go.

Turn one, no hole to move. Turn two, nothing.

"Damn it!" I yell, losing my mind that I can't beat this guy.

That's when it hits me. Fear is death. Speed is savior.

Massimo and Mason downshift for turn three, but it's barely a turn, and this is so freaking dangerous, but it could be my last race ever, and screw it!

I back off the throttle but don't downshift, and when Mason leans to the left, I don't.

Soaring past him, I dip at the last possible minute to account for the curve. My back tire skids on the water but holds on the curbstone, and I rip her vertical, popping the clutch to get back into sixth gear.

The people in the stands scream to their feet, feeding the explosion in my chest. I look over my shoulder to see Mason failing to accelerate like he's a little shaken. I can't blame him; that scared the shit out of me too. But for all the crap we give him, no one can deny he's got serious guts. Probably how he didn't crash.

Looking forward, I focus on Massimo.

God, here we go.

Royal-blue fairings lean to the right through turns four and five, and I gain as much as I can, but he doesn't give me an inch in turn six. I'm right on his exhaust pipe in the stretch to turn seven, but in eight, nine, ten, and eleven, I can't find a way to pass him. There's nowhere to go, and this is it. Billy and Santos are already across the finish line, and after two more turns, for me and Massimo, it's over.

Fifth gear.

Fourth.

Third, and lean.

My knee scrapes the track as my braid hangs over my right shoulder, flirting with the wet pavement inches away. I pull vertical and shift up to fourth, starting through the long left curve of thirteen. Fifth gear. Sixth. Sodden green grass flashes on my left, gray pavement and bailout gravel rushing by my right.

Just like I did to him in Qatar, Massimo fades left, forcing me farther inside than I want to be. He's pushed me out of the apex for turn fourteen, and when we bank hard and harder to the left, I'm going to run wide into the right side of the track. All he'll have to do is cut around behind me, and then he'll fly past on the inside, taking third place for the podium and securing himself as a World Champion.

I can't let him.

My body lies flat, bike flexing under ruthless speed and gravity pulling it further down. His transmission winds down as he makes the same mistake I did: letting off the accelerator so he can duck around behind me.

Taking a page from his playbook, I slow down with him. Massimo speeds up, and I do the same, then slowly start to drift outside and directly into his left knee and elbow.

It's a risky move, and I'm still out of the apex, but he is now too. What I don't know is how he held the turn once I hit the bailout in Qatar.

God, why didn't I ask him how he did that?

Think, Lorelai, think.

But I can't. All I know is that every time I've come up against the choice of choosing to win instead of live, I've lost. So against every instinct in my body, I tap the brakes, gritting my teeth through the hard pull to the left.

"Oh fuck!" I yell, my bike flexing and begging me to let her fall. It takes every ounce of strength in my exhausted body to tilt her vertical, and I shift up to sixth as quickly as I can, letting the torque do the work for me.

Holy crap. I'm in the straightaway.

I can barely feel my body to breathe, but I peek over my shoulder. Massimo isn't behind me, grappling for control as he wobbles in the gravel. He's *beside me*, somehow pulling off what I couldn't at the beginning of the year. A flicker of jealousy stirs in my stomach, but whatever. I'll deal with that later.

My face shield clears with no one in front of me, and I bend low over my handlebars. My bike screams as I push it for every ounce of power it has, racing toward the finish line with Massimo creeping up beside me, the difference between us too close to determine who is in front.

Faster, faster, faster, I push my bike until the checkered flag waves, the finish line flying under us.

The stands explode, and I let off the throttle, bursting with pride and relief and excitement and fear and a thousand other things at knowing that was it. It's done.

I sit back and look toward Massimo. No matter what happens now, we're free. But he's not looking at me. He's checking the clock tower. Then he curses loudly in Italian.

His gaze meets mine, his voice full of guilt as he calls out, "It was all I could do, Lorina! I did not have a choice."

Didn't have a choice to do what? Race me for the win? And why the hell would that make him feel guilty? It's not like he...

I look over my shoulder at the clock tower, my eyes popping.

No, please say he didn't. Anything but that.

But this is *Massimo.*

Who pushed me away to protect me. Who makes terrible decisions for all the right reasons and thinks my dreams are worth sacrificing his for.

Who doesn't know how to lose me.

I don't know whether I'm right—if he pulled the throttle and let me finish first—but it doesn't erase the fury stinging my veins as I look forward, my heel dropping and wrist twitching to pass him before I lean into turn one for the cooldown lap.

Because first place went to Billy. Second to Santos Saucedo. But the spots on the leaderboard for places three and four are blank.

Chapter 27

Massimo Vitolo—November; Valencia, Spain

I PULL INTO VICTORY LANE BEHIND LORINA, BUT IT FEELS CLOSER TO cruising down death row. My crew and Vinicio rush toward me, everyone screaming and jumping and hugging one another as I tear off my helmet. But I have no idea how they're celebrating when the apocalypse just happened.

The crowd is in a frenzy that blasts into full surround sound when I take out my earplugs, and my eyes go back to the clock tower and the leaderboard. Two names still missing in the places for third and fourth. What the hell is taking them so long?

My eyes snap forward to my executioner, Lorina taking off her own helmet, shrugging off her manager and crew. Then she turns in my direction.

Yep. I know that look, and I'm a dead man.

"What did you do?" She rushes toward me, and I swallow, swinging my leg off my moto. My heart is still pounding, adrenaline tearing through me, and I catch sight of Angelo jogging down pit lane in our direction. This just went from bad to worse.

Lorina's hands collide with my chest with enough force to send me stumbling back.

"Hey!" Vinicio shouts.

"Lorelai!" Frank echoes, running over to us.

The flash of the press cameras ignite into a steady glaring light, all aimed in our direction, and this is so not good. "Lorelai! Massimo! What's going on?" a photographer shouts. "Does Lorelai abuse you when you're alone?"

"Someone get her away from him!" Angelo yells, running into the garage.

Lorina's crew crowds in front of her, glaring at me as they corral her away.

"Screw you," Lorina shouts at Angelo, her whole body vibrating as she points over the arms of the men holding her back. "You don't own my life, and I don't care what you threaten me with, you're not going to keep me from yelling at him right now!"

"What is this I did?" I yell at her. "I did not tell you it was going to rain to trick you. I tried to save your life because you make bad decisions that are fucking dangerous!"

"It's not about the goddamn rain," she blasts out, Angelo's eyes going wide as he comes to a stop next to us. "It's about keeping your promise to stop trying to control everything, about you sacrificing yourself because you think you know better!" She sobs out a disappointed breath, then says the worst thing she's ever said to me. "It's about whether or not you backed off the throttle at the last moment."

"You did what?" Angelo yells in Italian, his gaze narrowing in my direction.

"Massimo! Massimo!" the photographers shout. "When did you decide to throw the race?"

My pulse explodes as lights flash and stun me, my chest and airways constricting, and I think I'm having a heart attack.

Lorina shoves past her crew and Angelo, her hands fisting in the front of my leathers. "Answer me!" she yells in English. "Did you back off the fucking throttle?"

"No, I did not!" I shout back. "I raced you with everything in me, and I do not care what contract you are going to lose or if it means you never race again. I will never let you win on purpose!"

Lorina's hands fly to her mouth, her eyes watering and her fire raging in a way I've never seen. I swallow, unable to feel any part of my body. All I know is that Lorina is crying, and it's my fault.

"Lorelai, are you definitely going to lose your contract with Dabria?" the press shouts. "How does it feel that Massimo doesn't care if you win or lose?"

"All right, that's enough," Frank says.

"Give them some space," Vinicio chimes in.

Both our managers and the combined force of our crews push the press back into pit lane, creating a barricade between us and the rest of the gawkers, standing shoulder to shoulder along the edge of the garage.

Angelo claps me on the shoulder, and bile rises in my throat. I don't look at him when he speaks, just keeping my eyes locked with Lorina's, who is shedding more and more tears as the seconds pass.

"Massimo," he says in Italian, "I have to go congratulate Billy, but you made the right decision today. We'll look forward to seeing you in February for testing next year."

He walks away as more tears slip down Lorina's cheeks, and all I can think is that I should have backed off the throttle. I should have made sure she won.

Holy fuck. What did I just do?

Chapter 28

Lorelai Hargrove—November; Valencia, Spain

THE CROWD RAGES OUTSIDE, FRANK AND VINICIO ARGUING FROM where they're guarding us at the edge of the garage, and my eyes frantically search Massimo's for some sign he's lying. A twitch, a flicker, anything. But there's nothing there but the truth: he didn't back off the throttle at the last minute. He raced me with everything he had, and I just…

I leap onto him, Massimo stumbling back from the assault.

"Thank you," I gasp out, my voice broken from crying. Massimo is apparently in too much shock to hold me back, but I don't care, only clawing at his leathers to hold him closer as I press a kiss to his neck, his cheek, the brutal shortness of the sides of his hair. "Thank you, for always believing in me."

A love with some kind of name I don't even know floods my limbs, and it's a snap of a movement between the air rushing from his lungs and his arms coming around me, clutching me against him. And I know, as well as I know how to open my eyes when I wake up in the morning, I'm right.

He'll never let me win, because he doesn't have to hold back for me. He doesn't ask me to give up my dreams for him, and he won't do it for me either. He truly believes I'm strong enough to stand toe-to-toe with him, and yes, he bitches about me being dangerous, but only because he loves me, wants a future with me. But even that doesn't stop him from chasing me down and cutting me off. From fighting for what he wants, because on the track, he may be my biggest rival, but when we're away from it, he's also the absolute love of my life.

And God help the guy, because he's shaking all over, but I don't think it's from the cold or the rain soaked into his leathers. Although I'm not sure why he was so scared I'd be mad that he didn't pull the throttle. A part of him must've known that if he did, I'd never forgive him. But believing something and doing it, then having a swarm of photographers shout in your face your worst fear as though it's already fact...

I hold him closer, regret sinking deep in my stomach. "I'm so sorry," I tell him. "I never should've—"

"I am sorry," he breathes, his face tucked into my neck as he shakes his head. "I do not want you to lose, Lorina. I do not want you to go. But I do not know how to lose either when I am racing and I—"

"It's okay," I tell him as I pull back, cupping his face in my hands as I smile. "I'd rather lose today and know it happened because you were faster than win the other way. I just..." I sniffle, blinking a few times to clear my eyes. "The only thing that matters is that I got to race my last race with you. That's all I care about."

His hand comes up to wipe away my tears, his brow furrowed. "You are not going to care if you lose?"

Never in ten years has he heard me say that. Before today, I haven't been okay with anything close to the notion. But it's not that simple anymore. I don't know if it ever was.

A broken chuckle bursts out of me. "Of course I care," I tell him, swiping at my eyes before I grab his hands, my fingers lacing between his. "I still want to win. I will always want to win when I race. I can't change that, and I won't apologize for it, because that's just how I'm built. It's how we both are. But I care more that you're still *you* with me."

It takes him a moment, but when Massimo nods, it's tight, shaky, his jaw locked taut probably to hide the fact that it's quivering. I settle my palms on his chest, aching for the color of his skin and for the embrace of the monsters that cradle me in my sleep. And I wish I had prepared for this, that we had some semblance of privacy before I say what I'm about to. But I can't change the past, and I don't want to change how we live. All I can do is ask for more time—even with the fans still screaming outside, the rain pouring like a hundred-year flood, our crews and managers no more than a few feet away.

"Ti amo," I tell him.

His eyes pop. "What the hell, Lorina! You are going to leave me now after you just said—"

"No, no…" I rush out. "It's okay. I'm not going anywhere, ever, so there's no reason why I can't tell you that. You don't have to wait until our last days to know how I feel about you, so…get over it."

He grunts, irritated, and it takes him a second to catch his breath after I probably just scared the crap out of him. But he gets there, the corner of his mouth turning up. "Ti amo, cara."

I tilt my head, smiling as I ask in Italian, "Do you love me? Really?"

Massimo sighs, a teasing tone to his voice. "What do you want now, Lorina?"

"I, um…" I have to pause when my voice gets stuck in my throat. God, my hands are shaking. "I want you to marry me."

Massimo's eyes widen, but even over the crowd and the rain, I know he heard me. Yet he doesn't say a word. And as much as his silence is paralyzing me, I'm not taking it back.

I want him to say yes. I want him to marry me. And not because I'm scared I'm going to lose him if I don't. Not because it's a safety net for whatever is going to try to wreck us next. But because I *love* him.

The fastest, biggest jerk on the planet, who lets me boss him around in the gym before he asks me to cut his hair and then complains the whole time about the way I do it. Who doesn't care I have some kind of kink about tying him up in bed and who writes dirty jokes inside romantic greeting cards, tucked into a bouquet of tulips. Who will never ask me to walk away from my dreams, trusts me to keep them with my own strength, and who is still freaking staring at me.

My knee bounces in bashful nerves. "Look, I know this is probably bad timing and not really romantic or anything… And yes, I'm fully aware we haven't talked about where we would live or about having kids or any of that stuff, and it's soon too. Like, really, really soon."

He looks away, muttering something I can't make out. *God*, why is he being like this when I'm trying to propose?

"You asked me first!" I hear myself snap. "And I know I said no at the time but…" I take a deep breath, trying to calm down. "I would really like you to marry me. As soon as possible. Please."

Massimo shifts his weight, making me wait the longest ten seconds *ever*, then he leans closer, his voice harsher than I expected. "You do not get to make the rules about when we will be married, Lorina. The priest decides, and most of the time, they make you wait at least six months. And before you start to cry about it, yes, it has to be in the Catholic church, or my mamma will die."

I blink at him. Over the chatter of our crews and the roar of the fans, the thunder and the rain. It takes me a second to translate what he said, even though it was in English. Then I get it.

My hands fly to my mouth, my eyes blurred with tears.

He said yes. I asked Massimo to marry me, and he said yes.

I don't even care about the people around us; that the press are capturing the most important moment of my life and are probably going to sell it to the tabloids with some ridiculous headline. None of it matters when Massimo winks, just like that, and then something in him shifts. His shoulders relax as though he can finally breathe, all while wearing a smile I've never seen before but know I'll always remember.

He pulls me into him—thank God—because I can't even think to move right now. But it's everything I want and need when his hand cradles the back of my neck as I tuck my face into his chest, his other arm wrapped snugly around me.

I don't even know if he did that because he hates to see me cry—whether they're good tears or bad—or he just needed to feel me. But I think I figure it out when he takes a deep, shaky breath, then whispers, "You could have just said yes the first time, cara, but that would probably mean you would have to stop being difficult."

A smile breaks across my lips, and I sniffle, my words mumbled against his leathers and over his heart. "I wouldn't count on that happening anytime soon."

Massimo chuckles, pressing a kiss to my temple. Then he leans back, the pad of his fingertip tilting up my chin and his face entirely stoic. "Good thing I love you anyway."

Tears streak into my eyes, my heart so full that I have no idea how I'm going to survive a lifetime of him making me this happy, and then I'm his. His kiss is slow and deep, my tears caught between our lips as tingles surge all the way through me. And as I rise up on my toes to hug my arms around his neck, it breaks my heart for every person who doesn't know this feeling and worries they never will. I want them to be filled with this sense of awe when they realize: I found him. My one. And he was there, right where he was supposed to be.

My manager pointedly clears his throat.

I rip my mouth from Massimo's, biting off over my shoulder, "Get over it, Frank!"

Before he ever responds—if he responded—I have some kind of freaking aneurysm. The entire Grand Prix Commission is taking turns shaking Frank's hand. Along with Taryn's rep for Munich Motor Works.

"Lorina," Massimo breathes, "you see who is over there?"

I flash him a smile, then grab his hand, bringing him over with me. "I've got a surprise for you."

His brow furrows as we stop next to the team of suits, Werner extending his hand to me. "Congratulations, Lorelai."

"Thank you."

"Well…" He glances toward the leaderboard, then back at me. "I know we said MMW would be prepared to offer you a spot on our women's MotoPro team—"

"Women's what?" Massimo asks, and I dart him a look that is every translation of *shut the hell up.*

Werner chuckles. "That we'd be prepared to offer you a spot based on your final time today. But even though Tissot has still not released your placements, I see no reason to keep you in suspense."

I swallow, slipping my fingers through Massimo's.

Werner leans forward, a massive grin on his face. "Ready to ride for MMW and get us on the podium in women's MotoPro?"

"Absolutely," I promise, my heart thundering in my chest as Massimo clamps the ever-living hell out of my hand. "Whatever it takes, I'll get you there."

Werner nods once, satisfied, extending his hand once more. "I'll make sure to get the contract to you right away, and we look forward to your first practice. We have a lot of work to do."

"Yes, we do." Because the bike I tested for him in Germany had never been ridden at the speeds I pushed it, and it doesn't have the years of development behind it the rest of them have. But it's no fun if it's not a challenge, and when we're done crafting their untested prototype into a titan of the tracks, we'll not only have changed the face of racing a dozen times over. We'll have made a bike that is 100 percent me.

Werner dips his head. "Congratulations to you both."

My grin is ear to ear as he leaves, waiting for the rest of the racing commission to head out into pit lane. As soon as they're gone, I collapse against Massimo, hiding my face in the front of his leathers as it hits me, all at once.

I did it. I found a way to keep winning. And yeah, I cut a backroom deal that sliced Dabria out of my life before they could pen their Dear John letter, but so what? Everyone talks to everyone about moving to new teams, and they do it all the time. But the second I saw that picture of Miette in Dabria leathers next to the MotoPro prototype, I knew it was proof Dabria wasn't interested in finding a place for me on their team next year. Talking? Sure. Pictures? Whole other ball game. So I hit a grounder toward MMW.

If Taryn was right and they were coming to Moto Grand Prix, they had spots to fill. Quietly. Quickly. Not that it stopped me from calling every other manufacturer on the circuit and letting them know I was separating, and it was their call over who was going to get me. No matter what, I wasn't going home empty-handed.

Massimo's hand runs down my hair. "Women's MotoPro, hmm?"

I nod. "Yep. For MMW."

"Hmm. I think I can live with that." I chuckle against his chest, loving every bit of pressure when he drops a kiss to my hair. "Però you, cara, still have a lot of explaining to do. Most importante, why you did not tell me when we agreed: no more secrets."

I raise my head, because he's right: we did promise each other in Rimini that no matter how bad or complicated or difficult it was to explain, we wouldn't hide the truth from each other ever again. But I didn't want to get his hopes up until I knew for sure that MMW was going to offer. Scarier, if they offered, I was going to get one of two options: women's Moto Grand Prix or women's Superbike. But I didn't *know* anything.

Massimo tilts his head, waiting, and I start to tell him everything: about testing in Germany and how absolutely terrified I was when we crossed the finish line—that he may have forfeited his career to save mine, but only because I hadn't told him I might have already saved myself. "So basically—"

"Lorelai!" Frank calls out.

I groan, waving him off. "Yeah, yeah, yeah, we'll celebrate later."

"No. Listen."

I look to Massimo to see if he knows what's going on, and that's when I realize that all I hear is silence. In a crowd of 150,000 fans, hundreds of reporters, dozens of racers, and each with their own crews. It should not be this quiet.

A clap of thunder rings out, followed by the crowd in the stands exploding into cheers so loud, it's actually a little scary. Massimo smiles, then lifts a kiss from my lips.

"We are not finished talking about MMW." His palms slide smoothly down my arms. "But for now, cara, it is time to know who was faster. And not domani. Not tomorrow. Today."

I bite my lip, and Massimo wrinkles his nose, growling at me. I can't help but chuckle, but I know he's right. It's time to know whether he beat me or I beat him, and I need to be brave enough to look. I *am* brave enough to look. I'm Wreckless, damn it. More than that, I am Tigrotta—the Centauro racer who rocks an undercut and can stare down two names on a leaderboard without shaking in her racing boots.

Still, because I'm also Lorelai, *darling* only and ever to Massimo,

I squeeze my eyes shut before I turn around. Strong and familiar arms lock around my chest, monsters hidden under leathers protecting the heart that beats beneath mine, my fingers grasping the cross dangling from my neck. And with only a single deep breath between the rest of mine and Massimo's racing careers—but not the rest of our lives—my eyes lift to the clock tower.

Enjoy this sneak peek at what's coming next
for the stars of the MotoGP...
RELENTLESS

Chapter 1

Mason King—November

WHAT THE HELL WAS I THINKING LAST NIGHT?

My hungover head throbs with a vengeance as I glance toward the bright-as-hell light coming in through the windows. Turns out, I'm a dumbass and forgot to pull the curtains closed before I passed out. Wonder how many people saw the X-rated show that went down in here? My hotel room is on a higher floor, but that doesn't mean anything with the almighty power of today's camera phones. At least it can't be on YouTube yet, because Billy would be beating on my door to ream me out for risking my sponsorships. Or he'd send Frank, our manager, to do it.

I scrub a hand through my hair, blowing out a stream of air for like the millionth time in my disastrous life. Who am I kidding? No one gives a shit what I do.

Except for maybe this girl—the naked woman on the pillow next to me moans and stretches luxuriously my way, her eyelashes fluttering open and a smile teasing her lips. Fuzzy memories of last night flash through my mind: the end of season award ceremony, the bikes and the medals, the music and fountains of champagne between whiskey shots sipped from my secret flask. Stumbling past the press corps back to the hotel and up to the room, where I unzipped her green sequin dress and she shredded my tux and rode me like I was a Moto Grand Prix World Champion, even though I'm not.

A guilty grin dares to stretch across my mouth—talk about getting lucky. She's freaking *gorgeous*: the kind of woman I always swore I got, but my redneck ass only ever really dreamed of. All smooth skin and long eyelashes, brown hair that's long in the front and short in the back, and with the sweetest curves. And she definitely knows how to use them.

Her freezing-cold hands start exploring the finer aspects of my chest, and *Christ, what's her name?* Stella? Sabrina? Definitely started with an S.

"Buenos dias," she purrs in Spanish, and that makes a lot of sense considering we're in Valencia, but I just...I remember her being German for some reason. "¿Descansaste bien?"

I don't know what that last part means, but I smile real pretty and run a tentative knuckle down her prettier cheek, soaking up the way she leans into my touch. Even better, she's not really waiting for an answer as she starts kissing her way up my outstretched arm and across my good shoulder, and I'm certainly not about to stop her to ask for a translation. I haven't been laid in *weeks* before last night.

Too much time traveling between motorcycle races—bouncing between so many countries, I'm gonna have to get another passport soon. And too many rodeos when I'm home in Memphis. Too many bulls to remember all their names, too much drinking to cover the pain of getting bucked, and too many managers trying to help me make better decisions.

As far as I can see, I'm doing just fine on my own. Especially when one of those icicle hands of hers drops way below the sheet-line. I cough out a grin, nearly lurching into the ceiling in the best way—*buenos dias* indeed.

"You are so big, Billy," she growls, and I lurch again. But for a brand new, super-sucky reason.

I tug her hand away from my already-wilting cock, scooting back on the bed and my throat starting to itch like my digestive system just shifted into reverse. Because why wouldn't my hangover decide to kick my ass even worse when I'm already down?

"Billy? I'm not Billy."

Sexy-Sa-Something's staring at me like I'm the one who's done something wrong, even though she's in my hotel room calling me the wrong damn name.

Christ, I hope I wasn't aware of this mix-up last night.

She scrambles for the bedsheet, clutching it to her bare chest until she's covered. Apart from one gloriously-dusty nipple. "Then who are you?"

"I'm Mason." No spark of recognition, no nothing as she blinks those thick black eyelashes at me. "Billy King's little brother."

Her hand flies to her mouth, a whole bunch of horrified Spanish being muttered behind it.

"And what did you think I was Billy for anyhow? He's blond," I snap, "and...tall."

Her eyes dart to my dark hair, then over my shorter, brawny body she spent all night kissing and touching, and she's getting it. But she isn't happy about it.

She shoves at my chest, cursing me out in Spanish before she switches to English. "¡Dios Mío! Is that why you were at the award party? For your brother?"

"Are you—Why were you there?" I burst out. "Party crasher?"

She looks just as offended as I feel. Especially considering the amount of orgasms I recall her having. And that's not even counting all the ones I was too drunk to remember.

"I'm a model. For Blue Gator." She smooths her hair until it's all sleek and sharp, and okay, now that she said it, I'm pretty sure I've seen her on the paddock holding an umbrella in one of those little outfits before. "Do you even race moto?"

"Do I even—*oh*, I see how it is." I scoff as I get out of the bed, my dick totally depressed and all but useless. "For your information, I do race. MotoPro, baby. And I'm the best damn bull rider in the state of Tennessee."

As long as we're not counting the Cornucopia Exhibition. And everyone just *loves* to talk about last year's Cornucopia Exhibition. The one where "I" got eight seconds on Smashbox.

Worst day of my whole fucking life.

"Where?"

Awesome. As soon as I find my feet, I nearly lose my lunch from the world swirling and tilting in circles. I place a steadying hand on the nightstand littered with condom wrappers—thank God—and empty little liquor bottles. *Oh no.* That's gonna be on the bill.

It takes me a good thirty seconds before I can straighten myself and start looking for my clothes. Not that I can seem to find them: the room's a freaking wreck. I don't even want to know what that lamp's gonna cost. But I'm definitely sure to hear about it.

I swear, this is what I get for trying to be a good brother. I should've known better than to spend all night celebrating Billy being crowned Moto Grand Prix World Champion. *Again.*

I came in sixth. And sixth isn't nothing when you're racing motorcycles against the fastest people on the planet, on the toughest race tracks they can throw at us. But no one ever seems to care about where I finished. Should be used to it by now—that's what happens when you're born to be second best.

"Well…" Sexy-Sa-Something now sounds more curious than regretful, and is still sitting wrapped like a present on the mattress hanging crooked off the box spring. Guess that explains why my lower back is killing me. "Who do you race for?"

I set right an upturned desk chair and find my hat, setting it on my head and starting to feel a little more human. I always think better under my black Stetson. "Dabria. I ride for Dabria Corse." Where the hell are my pants? My red duffel bag is empty and my stuff's scattered, but there's gotta be some underwear somewhere. *Shit*, not that I remembered to wash any.

Commando it is. Once I find my Wranglers.

"Dabria? Are you Lorelai Hargrove's teammate?" Of course, that name she knows. Then, in an announcer voice, she adds, "The First Woman of Moto."

I swallow a burp that tastes like tequila and something a little dirtier, and I should probably wash my hands. Soon. "Yeah. I'm her teammate. Or was. She's moving to Women's Moto. For MMW."

Sexy snuggles her bedsheet as I pick through the tangled bedspread on the floor, pure gossipy joy on her face. "Are she and Massimo Vitolo really together now? After all those years of fighting? I knew their rivalry was all a publicity scam."

"Yeah, they're together now, but it wasn't a scam," I answer automatically, and I need to shut up. My mouth's been known to be a little big sometimes, and it's safer to stay quiet. Not that I've quite learned how to do that. "And Billy's probably about to be married, so pass that through the...grapevine." I barely edit out the word groupie in time.

She gasps, looking oddly offended. "He cheats on his girlfriend?"

"No!"

God, if that gets back to Taryn...

I stop my clothes search and wrench myself vertical, and *God*, my lower back is really killing me. I hope I didn't hurt myself; it's gonna make my bull ride on Saturday even more risky.

I turn toward Sexy, my hands desperately indicating to myself. "You slept with me, Mason. Not Billy. Remember?"

She slumps on the bed we all but broke, suddenly disappointed again. "Oh, right."

Geez. And so much for finding my pants. Actually, you know what—

I let out a sharp whistle that catches her off guard, Sexy popping up straight on the bed as her eyes go big and her hands go slack. I smile innocently. Then I grab the sheet she's clutching and rip it away from her, sending her tumbling back into the pillows with a squeal and a giggle. *God, what an ass she's got.* Still, I wrap the sheet around my waist, like a good boy.

This was a mistake. I think? Rules seem kinda fuzzy on mistaken identity.

The muffled theme from *Star Trek* starts interspersing the steady sound of giggles and not getting dressed, and I follow the sound of Captain Kirk's voice encouraging me to go where no man has gone before. Even though the nightstand says I was all up in that last night.

A pile of pillows turns out to be the culprit hiding a green sequined dress and a mound of my wrinkled black tux, and I dig out my cell phone. When I check the screen, a wide smile cracks across my face: the most gorgeous woman I've ever seen in any hemisphere (apart from the one in my bed) is smiling at me in an expert selfie, a little camera icon asking if I want to accept the video call.

Um, *fuck yeah* I want to accept this call. Guess my good behavior is finally paying off.

"I uh, I gotta take this. It's my…manager."

Sexy-Sa-Something waves a sleek tan limb at me, can't really tell whether it's an arm or leg. Don't stay to find out. I dart past the crooked mattress and leap over the shattered lamp, the bedsheet clutched in my fist around my hips and trailing behind me as I hit the hallway. The door barely swings shut behind me before I swipe my thumb across the phone screen, and I didn't miss her, did I?

My pulse jumps triple the speed as the screen pixelates and then catches up, my eyes gorging on the blue sky and *Chiara Freaking Martes* beaming at me in a purple knit scarf with her layers of brown hair cascading around her face like she's in an Italian shampoo commercial.

Goddamn, she's so pretty. How did Massimo ever leave her for Lorelai?

"Well hi," I drawl as smoothly as I can, country boy charm turned all the way up high. But my voice doesn't work right and it comes out sounding a lot more like I'm speaking Klingon instead of English.

"Congratulations!" Chiara cheers. "Sixth place, Mason. That is fantastic!"

Did she just—?

I fall back against my hotel room door, naked under a see-through bedsheet and still half-hard from another woman's hand. But I'm so touched that for a second, I think I might cry.

Chiara called me to say congratulations? She knows what place I finished?

No one ever cares where I place—if they even remember that I race at all.

Then the wind blows where Chiara's at, catching a lock of hair across her nude lipstick, and there's no half about my hardness anymore. This bedsheet was a bad idea.

I know it for sure when a door opens across the hall, an older couple coming out of their room and stopping dead in their tracks at the sight of me. The husband flares red the more he absorbs my bare body and black Stetson and white bedsheet, and I scramble to bunch the sheet better over my erection while still holding the phone, but it's too late. He huffs out something in a different language that doesn't exactly sound approving, ushering his wife back into the hotel room and slamming the door. *Whoops.*

I look back to my phone screen to find Chiara quietly laughing like she must've heard that. "Yeah... I'm sorry to ask this, but can you hold on?" I wait until she nods, then I stick my phone between my teeth and address my situation.

This is so embarrassing. I've spent *years* drooling over Chiara Martes from afar in the Moto Grand Prix paddock, but she was always off limits. Massimo "No Mercy" Vitolo has warned me to stay away from her before. Except I don't see why he gets a say— Chiara's best friend or not—so I don't really care to ask for his permission, or for his blessing.

I'm not my righteous big brother, and I've never been known for making the best decisions. I'm known for making the *wrong* ones.

I finally get myself situated enough to look back at my phone, and nearly get in trouble all over again. Chiara reaches up to tuck her chestnut hair behind her ear, another naughty lock daring to caress her cheek, and I love the wind, just, *so much.*

"Did I call at a bad time?" Chiara asks in her fancy Italian accent, and she sounds so sincere that it melts me on the spot.

I swallow thickly to make sure my voice works right this time. "Nah, not at all. I'm real glad you called." At least now if I die on my Saturday bull ride, I'll get to take this with me to the grave. But I'm not planning on dying; I'm planning on *winning.*

All that grace of hers slips into a mischievous smirk, and when she looks pointedly toward my bare chest, a blush darkens her high cheekbones that could satisfy my ego for the rest of my days. "Good. You raced so wonderful yesterday. So fast, and so fearless. I thought Lorelai was going to hit you in that turn, or push you out, but nope!" Chiara's whole gorgeous face lights up, the sharp angles of her jaw tilting up with triumph. "You were never afraid."

"I uh…" I was scared shitless, truthfully. "Thank you, for saying that."

"Of course."

Chiara takes a sexy sip from her espresso cup, tilting her head at me when she's done and waiting since it's my turn to say something. Except I still can't believe she's on my phone right now! Luckily, she takes care of moving along our stalled conversation.

"I would like to see you."

Yeah, she really takes care of it, all right. Blood pumps heavily from my chest to my lap, growing thicker as she bites her bottom lip.

"Before you leave Europe to go home to America," she adds.

Italy isn't exactly on my way home to Memphis from racing in Spain—not that I really care. "That right?"

"Yes," she says, no bashfulness or beating around the bush about it. "Lorelai says you are nice, and you are a very successful racer, so someone at Dabria must think you are trustworthy. And you asked for me to call you, so here I am." She shrugs with a bright smile, and I'm *sunk*.

She's hot as fuck, and I seriously did not expect her to be this sweet. Especially to me. She doesn't even know me, and I didn't know a woman as pretty as her could *be* this sweet. I mean, the country girls I grew up around are almost always pretty, but they're also usually kinda mean. I think it's because all their fathers are assholes.

"I think we should have a date," she says. "I will cook. You can come to my apartment in Ravenna. Unless that is a problem?"

"No problem." I mean it too. Come hell or high water, I'll be there.

"Perfect. I will text you the address." She blows me a kiss through the screen that's terribly cruel, and I'm absolutely gonna have to do something about this situation she's got me in before Frank or anyone finds me. "Congratulations again, Mason. Ciao!"

I smile like a lovesick dope. "Bye."

I wait until she disconnects the video call, struggling to keep my feet on this earth as I weigh out my options:

Be a good boy and go home to Memphis, win the rodeo like my father wants. *Or...*

Sneak off to Italy and go see Chiara.

Yeah, it isn't really a choice.

I turn toward my room, trying to keep my feet on the ground, but my palm hasn't even hit the handle yet when the door next to me opens, my brother coming out into the hallway.

Damn it.

He's just gonna *love* this.

I tighten my jaw, holding onto the last of my dignity. And my bedsheet.

"Oh-ho-ho-ho." Billy lets out a low chuckle, coming fully out into the hallway. All tall and perfect, perpetually sober, and freshly showered. There isn't a single wrinkle in his pearl-snap shirt or his pressed Wranglers, and I wonder if he was ironing them in his black Stetson, Ariat boots, and his underwear no more than two minutes ago.

"You sound like the Santa Claus from hell." My head starts to pound all over again under his abuse of Old Spice cologne.

He gleefully eyes my bare chest and bed-sheet sarong with the blue eyes we share from our jerk father. Right before he takes a long-armed swipe at my hat.

I reach up out of instinct and almost drop my bedsheet in the process, my big brother cracking up laughing as I scramble to hang onto the last bits covering me. "Stop, dick! We're not twelve no more."

I barely get myself decent again before Taryn comes out of their room looking like an advertisement for How Ex-Beauty Queens Should Travel: a layered cardigan over a flowy tank top, yoga pants, and her long blond hair tied up in a shiny ponytail. No one ever expects her to be such a damn shark on the Superbike circuit, too. But Taryn is not to be trifled with.

Billy instantly takes the duffel bag hooked on her shoulder, threading it over his.

"Okay, we have to be at the—oh good Lord, Mason." Taryn waves her airplane tickets and passport at me like my nudity is contagious. "Really?"

"Hey, I did y'all a favor." I hook my thumb toward my hotel room door. "This girl was trying to sleep with Billy, and I ran interference."

My brother's pale face loses what's left of its color. He whips toward Taryn. "Honey, I was with you the whole night—"

"Shut up, I know you were." Then she zeroes in on me. All her country girl meanness out in force. "You"—and it's a sharp as fuck you—"have got to stop doing that. We all know this isn't the first time this has happened, and I expect better of you, Mason."

Boom.

The shame sours my already flipping stomach, and I open my mouth to say something back to her. But I only catch my brother's palm across the back of my head. "Shut up. Don't talk to Taryn that way."

"I didn't say nothing!"

"Yeah, but I know how you think."

I take a step toward the finger he's pointing in my face, and get a blast of cool air across my nether regions. "Shit!" I whirl to look at what happened, and the end of the damn sheet is caught in the door. The rest is all over the hallway floor, now lying around my ankles.

"Mason!" Taryn hisses, my brother groaning as I scramble to pick up the bedsheet and re-tie it around my waist.

"What?" I can't help it. I smirk at her and throw in a wink for good measure. "I told you when we all met that I was bigger."

Taryn puts a stilling hand on Billy's growling chest as our manager, Frank, comes half-jogging down the hall, checking his watch. "Oh good, y'all are—Mason, what the hell?"

"Oh don't worry, Frank," Taryn offers with a spiteful snort. "He's been busy saving mine and Billy's relationship."

Frank looks more confused than usual. Probably because Billy and Taryn have been obsessed with each other since the first time he saw her barrel race, and she told his bull-riding ass to get lost. That was almost two years ago, now—longest relationship I've ever had was three weeks in high school that turned out to be two-and-a-half weeks too many.

"Well, save it for the plane," Frank says. "We gotta go."

"Aren't we waiting for Lorelai?" Taryn asks.

He shakes his head. "She and Massimo are staying in Valencia for a few days before going back to Italy. It's just us."

Well, isn't that going to be helpful? "I'm, um, I'm gonna catch the next flight." I try my best not to notice the reaction on Billy's face. Not that it's easy to ignore when someone's eyebrows shoot that high.

It's Taryn who says all patronizing, "Mason, it's real nice that you met someone, but you can get laid at home. Now let's go."

"Goddammit, that isn't what's going on." Even though I'm kinda hoping it is. "I just...there's something I gotta go do, and I'll be home in a couple of days."

Because Chiara Martes called me. And off to Italy I will gladly go.

I dare anyone try and stop me.

ACKNOWLEDGMENTS

The first time I attended a MotoGP race was in April 2014. My husband came by tickets through his work, and I had no idea just how much my life would change after that day. I've always been a car girl. I swoon for loud engines, I've been known to drive a little too fast, and I frequently joke that I met my husband through his Mustang. He rode a motorcycle before we were together, and I think he knew introducing motorcycle racing into our lives was going to be a *thing*. Whether he knew how much of a thing, I have no idea.

When we left the racetrack that hot April day, we were sunburned and exhilarated, our camera full of pictures of the world's best racers, endless photos of our son pretending to rev a parked Ducati, and on the verge of a brand-new book idea. "What if you wrote a romance with a motorcycle racer heroine?" my husband said.

Through our early brainstorm sessions, he named her Lorelai—a nod to one of our favorite TV characters. His mechanical and technical knowledge of all things bikes and racing was invaluable through drafting and research. But it was everything else he did for this book and series that makes it *his*. All the contests he watched me enter and how many times he picked me up when I fell short. The queries I read to him before I pressed Send. The encouragement he gave when I had none and all the dinners he cooked and laundry he washed while I was busy writing and rewriting again and again. How amazing a father he is every day and all the sacrifices he has made to ensure I follow my dreams.

Thank you, darling, for always believing in me. I couldn't do any of this without you. And I wouldn't want to.

All my thanks to my amazing agent, Kelly Peterson, for loving Massimo as much as I do and helping find a place for him in the world.

I am continually grateful to Mary Altman and the entire team at Sourcebooks for giving this story a chance and bringing my dreams to life in the coolest way possible. Additional thanks to Christa Soulé Désir for having some of my favorite feedback reactions of all time.

Michelle Hazen...you've stuck by me and this book for half a decade. Thank you so much for reading it a million times. I'm sorry about all the emails.

All the awards (and tacos) should be given to Sandra Lombardo, Hoku Clements, Maxym Martineau, Lindsay Hess, Shanna Alderliesten, and Andrea Contos, who also provided their invaluable feedback on early drafts of this book. (And boy, were there a lot of drafts.)

Grazie mille to Marisa Escolar for translating all the Italian and making sure my coffee details were correct, along with everything else Italian related. You are a life saver.

Everyone else who had a hand in this through years of querying and writing contests and teaching me pretty much everything I know (though they may not know it): Shira Hoffman, Shannon Powers, Kat Kerr, Lisa Rodgers, Michelle Hauck, Amy Trueblood, Sun vs Snow, Query Kombat, Brenda Drake, Pitch Wars and PitMad, and the Fellowship. Y'all really know your stuff. (And I probably forgot a lot of people. I'm sorry! I love you!)

I am incredibly lucky to have the support of an adoring father and doting stepmother. Thank you for making books such a big part of our lives. And for not freaking out when I called and said I was going to be a romance author.

To my mother in heaven: Massimo is not Billy, Mom. You may wanna go back to Billy.

Morgan Lancaster, you are the kind of best friend people write books about. I'm so glad you shared your bus seat with me.

My wonderful son: you are the joy in my heart and the reason for everything I do. Thank you for every hug, and I'm so proud of the young man you're growing into.

And finally, to my darling husband: I still need five more minutes. Though I doubt forever will be enough time with you.

ABOUT THE AUTHOR

Katie Golding is a sports fan with a writing problem. Based in Austin, Texas, she publishes contemporary romance novels with the support of her loving husband and son. She is currently at work on her next romance novel, unless she's tweeting about it. Visit her website at katiegoldingbooks.com.